Also by Jonathan Kellerman
Available from Random House Large Print

THE
MURDERER'S
DAUGHTER

THE
MURDERER'S
DAUGHTER

—A Novel—

JONATHAN
KELLERMAN

RANDOM HOUSE
LARGE PRINT

Copyright © 2015 by Jonathan Kellerman

All rights reserved.
Published in the United States of America by Random House Large Print in association with Ballantine Books, an imprint of Random House, a division of Penguin Random House LLC, New York.

Cover design by Scott Biel
Cover photograph (desert road): © Elisabeth Ansley/ Trevillion Images
Title page image: copyright © iStock.com/© tropicalpixsingapore

ISBN: 978-1-62953-574-6

Printed in the United States of America

This Large Print edition published in accord with the standards of the N.A.V.H.

To Judah

THE
MURDERER'S
DAUGHTER

1

Five-year-old Grace lived with two strangers on the fringes of a desert. Biology and the law labeled them her parents but Grace had never found them other than alien. As best she could tell, they felt the same way.

Ardis Normand Blades was twenty-eight years old, tall, reedy, long-haired, and patchily blond-bearded, with a sliver of morose face dramatized by jug ears. Those bat-like appendages notwithstanding, he was semi–decent-looking in a greasy, vaguely dangerous way. Only semi because some of his God-given looks were long eroded by dope and alcohol and a near-perfect record of bad decisions.

Ardis's childhood had been a swamp of neglect and apathy. Troublesome at school, he'd been tested numerous times by counselors of uneven qualifications. Each of them had been surprised to find Ardis's IQ significantly higher than his dull mien and chronically maladaptive behavior suggested. He'd made it through ninth grade grudgingly, could read at the fourth-grade level, had abandoned arithmetic before mastering long division.

All that limited Ardis's occupational goals and when he wasn't maxing out his welfare and his unemployment benefits, his jobs ranged from dishwasher to janitor to fry cook. The exception was a brief, unfortunate tenure as a carpenter's assistant that left him minus a pinkie and phobic of heavy machinery.

Women of a certain type were drawn to Ardis's easy smile and good bone structure. Dodie Funderburk was one of those. Her academic achievements rivaled Ardis's and helped cement a shallow rapport.

Dodie and Ardis met when they both worked at Flapper-

Jack's Pancake Palace, a struggling highway stop on the out-skirts of the Antelope Valley. Ardis was charged with scraping the grill and mopping the floors after closing. Dodie bussed tables during the night shift then lingered so she could earn some extra money draining the grease traps and sweeping the dining room. The side benefit of her working late was hanging with Ardis, just the two of them smoking and trudging in the shabby eatery.

They began flirting the first night they met, were doing it by the second, Dodie perched spread-legged on the kitchen counter, Ardis just tall enough to get to the goal without a footstool. He was barely shy of twenty-two and already a serious alcoholic and dabbler in meth. Dodie, three years younger, had never enjoyed regular periods and she'd always been a little curvy so it took four months for her to realize she and Ardis had created an embryo.

One night at Flapper she figured she should say some-thing because her belly was getting swelled up. Walking over to Ardis, who was smoking a blunt and mopping, she lifted up her T-shirt.

"Yeah," he said. "That's what happens."

Dodie said, "Sure does."

Ardis puffed and shrugged. "Got no money to get rid of it."

"Okay," said Dodie. "Maybe I'll keep it."

He walked away from her.

"You love me, Ardie?"

"Sure."

"Okay, I'll keep it."

"You think?"

"Maybe."

"Whatever."

Marriage had never been considered. Ardis had no desire for it and while Dodie might not have minded, the way she figured they were already living together in her single-wide in a nice slot at Desert Dreams Park because it was bigger than Ardis's horse trailer at the rear of the long-dead palm tree farm where he'd been squatting for two years. On top of that, filing paper was a hassle and cost money and no one Dodie knew, including her own parents, ever bothered. Dodie's father had booked before she was born and she figured Ardis might do the same thing. She could handle living alone, her mother had lived alone just fine and anything that retarded bitch could do, Dodie could do better.

She didn't show a real big bump for a while and went back to pretending it wasn't happening. That got harder and harder and sometimes, when she was by herself, her thoughts tried to get happy with the situation. Other times she got low and had feelings deep inside that rose up like heartburn and made her cry. Maybe a baby would be fun, dressing it up, buying toys you could also play with. Having someone think she was smart.

Pushing out the baby was eighteen hours of torture and Ardis wouldn't stick around in the delivery room for more than a few minutes, getting grossed out or bored with Dodie's screaming and cussing. Mostly, he just craved a smoke. Each time he returned, Dodie screamed at him worse, yelling filthy things that made the nurses flinch. Then she got too exhausted to even do that and became a crawled-up little worm, suffering by herself, oh God how long could she **last** this way?

When Dodie cried out in agony she mostly got ignored unless a nurse felt like being nice and shot stuff into her I.V. that didn't work so good, anyway. What Dodie really could've used she couldn't have because it was illegal.

After all that hell, the baby wasn't laying right, had to be turned like a hot dog on a grill, and guess who that made feel like she was being all torn up? Finally, Dodie felt the slimy thing shoot out of her and the glimpse she caught was gray and not moving.

The doctor, a black guy who'd just showed up, said, "That's a serious cord, wrapped around . . . three places."

Then the room got all quiet and Dodie figured she'd pushed out something dead and at that moment, no big deal, main thing is she wasn't hurting no more and her and Ardis could go back to the way it was before.

A slapping noise then a humongous **Waaaaah!**

"There we go," said the doctor. "Nice and pink, Apgar two elevated to eight."

After that, there was all sorts of murmuring and clicking and buzzing. Dodie lay there feeling she'd been hollowed out like a melon, just wanting to sleep forever.

One of the nurses, the short one with the cheeks like tomatoes, said, "Here's your new daughter, dear. Fresh out of the oven, loud and healthy, good set of lungs on her."

Which was stupid, bread and cake didn't make noise and they didn't chew up your insides like a chain saw. But Dodie, too spent to argue, closed her eyes and felt the weight of the baby settle on her chest.

The apple-cheeked nurse said, "Hold her, dear. With your arms, she needs your comfort." Folding Dodie's limbs over the blanket-wrapped bundle and pressing down so they'd stay there.

Dodie wanted to smack the bitch. She kept her hands in place so the cow would finally let go.

The nurse said, "There you go, dear, that's right—oh, she's a cute one. After all your hard work, a fine bit of grace, no?"

Dodie thought: **At least I got a name for it.**

That night, they brought the baby to her to feed, even though she said all she wanted was to sleep.

"Oh, sweetie," said another nurse, "you can forget about sleep for a while."

Two days later, Dodie and Ardis took the baby home.

Bitch was right.

.   .   .

Five-year-old Grace had no idea how she'd survived from infancy. She'd seen other families with babies in the trailer park, had a notion of what it took to raise an infant. Had the strangers actually done all that when she was tiny and helpless? Hard to believe, they sure didn't feed her much now.

It wasn't a matter of no food, there were always leftovers from the McDonald's, where Ardis now worked along with junk pilfered from the Dairy Queen, where Dodie swept up nightly. Plus stuff each of them shoplifted. They just never had real meals where everyone sat down together. The few times it happened, Grace would cram as much as she could into her mouth, chew fast, swallow hard, and go for more. When Ardis was feeling mellow he'd slip her candy. But there was rarely an offer to prepare a meal and mostly Grace went to sleep with a gnawing in her tummy.

Sometimes, when the strangers were asleep, she'd sneak into the kitchenette and stuff her face with whatever was there. Careful to clean up. Though she was the only one who really did any cleaning of the trailer.

By five, Grace had learned how to take care of herself.

Sometimes when she left the single-wide hungry, a neighbor would notice and give her something. Mrs. Reilly was the best. She actually cooked and baked and when she wasn't wild-eyed and dehydrated from vodka and ranting about niggers and greasers, she'd be generous with Grace and the other kids in the trailer park. Even the Mexican kids.

During the day, Mrs. Reilly cleaned model homes in sprawling developments that remained mostly unsold. The Antelope Valley, with its punishing heat and bitter night winds, was up and down economically, usually more down than up.

The bulk of the residents at Desert Dreams worked low-paying jobs. Some were disabled, mentally or physically or both, and sat around wondering how long they'd live. A few able-bodied idlers did nothing but drink and toke and loaf.

Everyone at the trailer park was knowledgeable about the alphabet soup of government programs a person could score when functioning at or near the poverty line.

One of those funds was for day care, which at Desert Dreams meant that the state and the county paid Mrs. Rodriguez to watch a dozen children at her Peach State double-wide with the pots of cactus ringing the trailer. With that many kids, no one got much attention, but with the TV always on to cartoons, and boxes of books and toys left over from Mrs. Rodriguez's now-adult children, plus castoffs and dumpster-dive prizes, plus plenty of space in the dirt to crawl around, just be careful of the needly plants, the day care was okay with Grace.

She wasn't much for playing with other children, liked watching **Sesame Street** and **Electric Company,** and by four she'd learned from the shows how to put letters together into rudimentary words. Years later, she realized she'd been blessed with an inherent grasp of the architecture of language. At the day care, she just looked at it as word-fun, another way of figuring things out because that was her thing: figuring the strangers out, figuring out how to eat, how to stay clean, what people meant when they did and said things.

Grace at five could read at an advanced first-grade level but she never told anyone, why would she?

For sure the strangers wouldn't care; by now Ardis was mostly drunk when he bothered to show up at all and Dodie had taken to mumbling about getting the hell out of there and going somewhere she could be free.

When drunk and mumbling collided, the result could be scary. Ardis never hit Dodie with a closed fist but there was plenty of faking blows like he was going to and a whole lot of open-hand slaps that connected with flesh haphazardly. Sometimes Ardis barely touched Dodie. Sometimes his hand on her flesh made loud, snappy noises.

Sometimes Dodie had marks on her and had to use extra makeup. Lots of women at Desert Dreams were patching up the same way.

Some of the men were hiding injuries, too. Like Mr. Rodriguez, who didn't usually live with Mrs. Rodriguez—one day Grace saw him bleeding from his nose and running away from the double-wide, Mrs. Rodriguez stepping out and picking up a cactus pot like she was going to throw it at him.

She didn't. He was gone too fast and Mrs. Rodriguez loved her plants.

With Ardis and Dodie, the damage could go both ways, Dodie butting into Ardis's chair on purpose when he slumped in the kitchenette, snoring. That made him wake with a start and drool and start choking on his drool, then he'd nod off again and Dodie would point at him and make stupid faces and laugh.

Sometimes she flipped him off behind his back or called him dirty names, not caring that Grace could see and hear.

Sometimes, when Ardis was deeply asleep, really stoned, Dodie would sneak up behind him and use her nails to flick the back of his head hard and if that didn't do the trick, she'd give his hair a yank and wait to see what happened.

When Ardis's droopy eyes opened, confused, Dodie would be standing behind him pointing and laughing silently.

Grace pretended not to notice any of that. Mostly she crawled into the corner of the trailer's front room that served as her sleeping space. The single fetid bedroom at the back of the trailer was reserved for Dodie and when Ardis showed up, both of them. Often at night, instead of sleeping Grace would turn on the TV and watch without sound, laughing to herself at how crazy people could look moving their lips. Or, she'd read one of the books she stole from Mrs. Rodriguez and, later, from the preschool.

She had her collection of words, new ones arriving all the

time, and she could also add up numbers and make sense of how numbers worked and how to figure things out without asking anyone.

One day, she figured, she'd be by herself and that stuff could probably help.

2

Dr. Grace Blades cradled the woman in her arms.

Many therapists shied away from physical contact. Grace shied away from nothing.

The Haunted needed more than kind words, soft looks, and **uh-huhs.** They **deserved** more than the pathetic lie known as empathy.

Grace had no respect for the concept of empathy. She'd lived in the red room.

The woman continued to cry on Grace's shoulder. Her hands, nestled in Grace's cool, firm grip, were small and moist and limp. Watching the way she melted into Grace's comfort, an observer might guess this was an early phase of treatment.

The woman was a therapeutic success who returned yearly for what Grace thought of as "show-off" sessions.

Look how well I'm doing, Doctor.

Yes, you are.

This year, as always, she'd requested an appointment on that worst of days, the anniversary, and Grace knew much of the forty-five minutes would be spent in tears.

The woman's name was Helen. She'd begun treatment three years ago, seeing Grace as often as she needed, until moving from L.A. to Montana. Grace had offered to find her a local referral but Helen refused, as Grace figured she would.

Four years ago, to the day, Helen's nineteen-year-old daughter had been raped, strangled, and mutilated. Identifying the monster who'd accomplished all that hadn't taken much in the way of detection. He lived with his parents across an alley from the girl's studio apartment in Culver City, with a rear window affording him a full view of the girl's bedroom. Despite an extensive record of peeping that had escalated to sexual battery, he'd been coddled by the courts and allowed to live his life at will. Stupid and impulsive, he hadn't bothered to dispose of his bloody clothing or the bent, crimson-stained knife he'd lifted from his victim's kitchen.

A trial would've been torture but useful for Helen. She'd been cheated again by the monster, as he'd charged a phalanx of arresting officers with a screwdriver and ended up sieved by LAPD bullets.

Case closed for everyone but Helen. She kept calling the district attorney's office, only to break into sobs and apologetic confession that there was no reason for her to be phoning. Once or twice she forgot who she'd dialed. Eventually, the deputy D.A. in charge of the case stopped taking her calls. His secretary, far more insightful and caring, had suggested that Helen see Grace.

A psychologist? I am not crazy!

Of course not, ma'am. Dr. Blades is different.

What do you mean?

She really gets it.

As was true of every patient she saw, Grace made Helen feel as if she were Grace's sole focus. The key was always about finding the kernel of individuality within each human being, but the truth was, a commonality existed among the Haunted and over the years Grace had distilled her treatment paradigm: Do what it takes to establish rapport because without rapport, there's no therapy. Be available 24/7 and when the time is right—and here the art of therapy took over—begin the process of rebuilding. With all that, it was important to set realistic goals: Pre-monster happiness was out of the question.

Which wasn't to say success was flimsy. Nearly everyone could be guided toward accepting pleasure, and pleasure was the nutrient of healing.

The final principle applied to Grace: Take frequent vacations.

The process could take months, years, decades. Forever. Grace had patients who visited her on tenth and twentieth anniversaries. Reliving horror that had occurred when Grace was in grade school.

Helen, now crumpled in Grace's arms, might turn out to be one of those, no way to know. No way to know about people, period, which was what made Grace's job so interesting.

She felt Helen tighten up. Out came a hoarse, terrible growl of a sob.

Grace held Helen tighter. Began rocking her like a baby. Helen whimpered, turned quiet, fell into a trance-like state that brought a serene smile to her lips. Grace had expected that, she was generally excellent at guessing her patients' inner worlds. Despite that, she worked at staying humble, because the job had nothing to do with cure, one didn't talk about cure.

Still, nearly everyone got somewhat better, and how many endeavors could provide that level of satisfaction?

This month, Grace had reached one of those nice lulls where the patient load had thinned and allowed her to schedule another vacation. Tomorrow would be her last day before she checked out for two weeks.

Vacation was a loose concept. Sometimes she flew to faraway places and stayed at luxurious hotels and had adventures. Sometimes, she remained home and vegged out.

The nice thing was, it was all up to her and as yet she had no specific plans for next week, could entertain possibilities from Malibu to Mongolia.

When she worked, her appointment book was solid ink for months in advance, with spots opening up only when patients flew from the nest. She'd never engaged in any sort of self-promotion but word got around and judges and lawyers—more important, their perceptive assistants and secretaries—came to appreciate her work. But most of her business came from patients talking her up.

Her fee was slightly above average and everyone paid by check or cash upon entering the treatment room, no sliding scale, no insurance forms, no billing. Making money wasn't the point—she could have lived quite well without her practice. Being businesslike and ethical was, and that included avoiding patients building up mountains of debt.

Treatment needed to be a partnership valued by both sides, meaning hard work for all concerned. Grace had never shirked anything in her life and by the time the Haunted came to her, they were ready to do whatever it took.

God bless them.

Helen continued to cling to Grace. She was fifteen years older than Grace but today, in this quiet, pretty room, Grace was the mother and she was the child.

Grace was younger than most of her patients but felt centuries older. She suspected none of them thought much about her age. Considered anything about her, other than her ability to help them. The way it should be.

She'd turned thirty-four a month and a half ago, but could pass for early twenties when the situation called for it. A prodigy throughout her formal schooling, she'd earned a Ph.D. in clinical psychology at an unreasonably young age, compressing a six-year program to four, the second of only two doctoral candidates at USC to pull that off.

The first was a man from whom Grace took the required seminar in child clinical. Not her cup of tea, working with the little ones, but Alex Delaware had made it sound as interesting as anyone could. He was obviously brilliant, quite likely compulsive, driven, and perfectionistic, not the easiest man to live with. But Grace appreciated his no-bullshit attitude, and his success at pushing his way through the academic bureaucracy spurred her to try it herself.

Now, at an age when adulthood-deferring wimps were still "trying to figure it out," Grace relished being a grown-up.

She was comfortable with everything about maturity—her place in life, the luxuries she afforded herself, her rhythms and routines. Even her looks, without that translating to self-centered delusion.

She'd been called beautiful by men but blew that off as post-orgasmic Y-chromosome myopia. She was, at best, **attractive**, occupying a body assembled of flat planes rather than curves. Too broad at the shoulders, too narrow at the hips, both of which served to de-emphasize her small waist, she was light-years from centerfold territory.

Speaking of which, her breasts.

At fourteen, she'd flattered herself by rating them perky, figuring at some point they'd blossom into lush. At more than double that age, she'd come to celebrate perky.

Her eyes were wide-set but plain-wrap brown. She was especially amused when more than one man claimed to discover tiny flecks of gold floating near her pupils. Try as she might, she never found them.

One tiresome would-be poet tagged her eyes "twin lodes of precious ore." Fool's gold was more like it and the face they occupied was too long for the perfect oval, though sheathed with smooth ivory skin stretched tight over fine bones. Sprinkles of butterscotch freckles sprouted in interesting spots all over her body. One man had designated the pointillist patches "dessert" and set about licking every one of them. Grace let him do his thing until she started to feel like a dog's water bowl.

Her hair was a plus, a bounty of chestnut silk that looked good no matter how it was cut. A few months ago, she'd allowed a Beverly Hills stylist to run riot, ending up with a loosely layered mop that terminated just above her shoulder blades and shook out easily.

But the winner was . . . her chin, a firm, pointy thing, crisp and defined and strong.

Not a hint of indecision.

Therapeutic chin.

Helen drew away from the embrace and offered a face full of confidence. Accepting the scented tissue Grace offered, she sat back down in the patient chair. The session had run over significantly, something Grace tried to avoid. But you needed to be flexible and Helen was her final patient of the day and Grace had plenty of energy for what lay ahead tonight.

She did, however, shift her head to the side so Helen had a clear view of the bronze art nouveau clock atop her mantel.

Helen's mouth formed an O. "I'm so sorry, Doctor—here, let me pay you extra."

"Not a chance, Helen."

"But Dr. Blades—"

"It's been wonderful seeing you, Helen. I'm proud of you."

"Really? Even though I freaked out?"

The same question she asked on each anniversary.

"Helen, what I saw tonight wasn't freaking out, it was honesty."

Helen attempted a smile. "The best policy?"

"Not always, Helen, but in this case, yes. You're an impressive person."

"Pardon?"

Grace repeated the compliment. Helen blushed and looked down at her brand-new cowgirl boots, at odds with her dress, but pretty, nonetheless.

She now lived on ranch land outside Bozeman with her new dream man, a large, concrete-thinking block of oak who liked to hunt and fish and opined that he'd have loved to get his hands on the bastard who'd . . .

"Sometimes, Dr. Blades, I think honesty can be the worst thing."

"It can be, but look at it this way, Helen: Honesty is like

one of Roy's guns. Only someone with training can be trusted to use it properly."

Helen pondered that. "Oh . . . yes, I see . . ."

"To my mind, Helen, you're well on your way to becoming a crack shot."

"Oh . . . thank you, Dr. Blades . . . well, I'm catching an early flight tomorrow, better be shoving off."

"Have a great trip."

Another stifled smile. "I think I can, Dr. Blades. Like you always say, at some point we need to decide to be good to ourselves."

Grace stood and squeezed both of Helen's hands, dropped the left gently after a second but held on to the right as she steered Helen out of the therapy room. Doing it smoothly, adroit as a tango champion, so that Helen felt guided, not dismissed. They walked silently through the bare, dim hallway that led to the waiting room, made it to the front door before Helen paused.

"Doctor, may I . . . you know?"

Another habitual question.

Grace smiled. "Of course, e or snail. Or Pony Express, if that works for you."

The same answer Grace always provided. Both women laughed.

"And, Helen, should you find yourself in L.A., don't be a stranger. Even if it's just to say hi."

Now Helen's smile was warm and full, untrammeled by conflict. When they smiled like that, Grace knew she was in the right profession.

"Never a stranger, Dr. Blades. Never."

3

Grace's therapy room had once been the master bedroom of the country-English cottage that served as her professional headquarters. A cute little twenties thing, the house occupied a quiet corner on an obscure side street in West Hollywood, like many of its neighbors hidden behind tall hedges.

The location was walkable from the flats of Beverly Hills but set well away from B.H. glitz and the frenetic activity of WeHo's Boystown. The corner location was no accident: Grace had insisted on it, so patients could enter on one street and exit on another.

On the surface, the people who came to her for help had much in common but they would never meet one another. A different therapist might question that, reasoning that post-traumatic patients could benefit from sharing common experiences.

Maybe so, but in Grace's mind that was outweighed by the need for depth probing, the magic of one-on-one. Sometimes she thought of herself as a one-woman emotional vaccine.

She'd done the place up with soft seating, flattering lighting, inoffensive hues, the only feature hinting at herself, an array of framed diplomas, licenses, and honors, displayed behind her desk.

The house had come with wainscoting, Greek-key moldings, decorative alcoves, a tile fireplace, and diamond-pane windows. The day Grace took ownership, she began painting and scrubbing, ended up polishing the oak floors on hands and knees. After teaching herself the rudiments of commercial sewing—plenty of trial, even more error—she created ecru silk drapes from remnants scored in a thrift shop, hung the finished product from antique brass rods she nabbed online.

Proud of me, Malcolm?

The result: a work environment that felt **right.**

Now, with her workday over, she poured herself a glass of water and glided into the living room/waiting room. Parting two of the curtain panels, she gazed out on blackness.

Starless: her favorite flavor of night.

Double-bolting the front door and switching off the lights, she returned to the therapy room and unlocked the closet, a walk-in intended for a wardrobe that now held far less. Retrieving a small leather box, she plucked out a pair of nonprescription color contact lenses from a collection she'd assembled.

Tonight: light blue, allowing some of her natural brown to peek through and create an intriguing sea green.

Stepping out of oxblood flats, she unbuttoned her work blouse—one of the dozen white silk button-downs she'd had custom-tailored by a Hong Kong tailor who visited L.A. twice a year for trunk shows—and shed man-tailored black slacks, also purchased from Mr. Lam in a lot of twelve. Off came her bra and panties and on went tonight's dress.

She'd selected it yesterday, a long-sleeved, gray, cowl-necked cashmere sheath she'd christened One Piece Wonder. Silk lining eliminated the need for underwear. The gray was a medium shade that adored her chestnut hair, the hem ended an inch below her knees, promising an interesting journey, and the sleeves flattered her arms.

No buttons, no zippers, no froufrou of any sort. Over the head, in with the arms, slithering down her body, liquid as a coat of lotion.

Tonight's shoes were maroon suede pumps handmade by a Barcelona cobbler who specialized in flamenco shoes.

Add to that the chocolate-brown single-clasp briefcase and matching drawstring bag already hosting money, keys, lipstick, and a gray-matte .22 Beretta, and she was ready.

Playtime.

It had been a while—months—since Grace had surrendered to The Leap. Abstention had nothing to do with self-doubt or restraint, it was simply a matter of professional responsibility: Busy time in her practice, her priority was the mental health of her flock.

Which wasn't to say she hadn't taken a few small jumps.

Driving home late at night on Pacific Coast Highway, making sure the road was clear then bearing down delicately on the Aston Martin's accelerator.

Pushing the car to seventy, eighty, ninety, a hundred and twenty.

Holding that speed while clamping her eyes shut, hurtling forward, blind.

The joy of weightlessness.

A couple of Sundays ago, she'd woken at sunrise and hiked up a canyon on the land side of PCH, finding herself the sole explorer of a series of well-marked trails that snaked up into the Santa Monica Mountains. After two miles of following the rules, she'd stripped herself naked, balled her clothes and tucked them into her backpack, and veered off the trail, stepping randomly into brush.

It didn't take long for the foliage to turn dense, obscuring landmarks.

Soon, Grace was giddy with disorientation.

Losing herself.

Nearing a grunt. Spying a flash of beige.

Letting in the fear. Reprocessing it as arousal.

Reaching deep into her core and reminding herself of all that she'd been through, everything she'd accomplished.

The key was to survive. She walked on.

It took a while, but eventually she found her way back

to the Aston, scratched and bruised and dirty, a mountain lion's warning reverberating in her head.

Abrasions were easily touched up with cosmetics. The beast's bravado remained a barb in her brain and that night she went to sleep imagining its rage and its bloodlust and slept wonderfully.

Oh, you gorgeous killer.

Maybe one day she'd return and look for the cat. Toting a slab of raw steak in her backpack.

Naked Woman with Meat. Great title for a painting.

4

Grace's exit took her through the kitchen, out the rear patient door, and onto the impatiens-ringed, jacaranda-shaded lawn that served as the cottage's backyard.

A narrow door cut into the facing wall of the garage. Though tiny, the house had been built for L.A. and even in the twenties that meant **Worship the Automobile** and space for two vehicles.

Waiting for her, side by side, were her twin chariots, both black, both spotless, both, in Grace's mind, female.

The Toyota Matrix S station wagon was logic and function, as obtrusive as a tree in a forest.

The Aston Martin DB7 screamed irrationality.

Tonight, the choice was obvious.

Sliding into the low-slung beauty, she home-linked the garage door open, inserted the ignition key, pushed the red starter button, and brought four hundred fifteen snorting broncos roaring to life. Switching on her iPod, she called up Bach's Sixth Brandenburg Concerto and backed the Aston out just past the garage door. Looking up and down the street, she idled, giving the car time for its rarefied organ system to reach optimal body temperature.

Automotive foreplay; rush a girl and she could grow balky and cranky.

When the Aston's noises signaled readiness, Grace looked around again and pressed a maroon toe down on the gas.

The car shot forward like the land-rocket it was. Grace raced a block or two before slowing to a cruise as she manipulated a maze of narrow streets and exited east onto Sunset.

Heading in the opposite direction of her destination because she needed time to wind down, she turned up the volume on Bach and drove until her body grew cool and loose and itchy in that wonderful pre-Leap way. Hanging a left turn, she roared up several blocks of inky residential hillside, drove past a **Dead End** sign, and zipped around the curve of a cul-de-sac. Reversing direction in a quick swoop, she returned to Sunset, slid into light traffic, and floated west over the Beverly Hills border.

As if she'd entered a new country, the scenery shifted from clubs and cafés and show-business office buildings to gated mansions graced with chlorophyll. Another half a mile of relative quiet passed before she headed south on broad, flat avenues, continued past both big and little Santa Monica boulevards, and entered the B.H. business district.

At this hour, not much business going on; all but a few shops were dark. Rich folk had pools, tennis courts, home theaters, home spas, home everything. Why venture out to mingle with the yokels?

Precious few yokels, as well, just a scatter of tourists and window-shoppers. Easing the Aston toward Wilshire, Grace caught an eyeful of her goal but stopped half a block shy.

The Beverly Opus was a ziggurat of pink limestone and smoked glass, introduced by a valet parking area paved in slate and centered by a palm-fringed fountain. High-end chrome was routinely displayed as proof of the hotel's elite clientele but valets in top hats and tails were more than happy to park any decent vehicle out front for a twenty-dollar tip.

It wasn't thrift that led Grace to enter a public lot charging a flat fee of three bucks after eight p.m., providing you had a credit card to feed the robotic entry machine.

Preparation was all.

Driving straight up to the top level, she searched for the darkest, most remote corner she could find, one blocked from easy view by a pillar.

She nailed it easily, tucked in the southeast corner, a grease-spotted slot flanked by **two** pillars.

The kind of space self-defense manuals warned women to avoid.

Perfect.

The Beverly Opus was three years old and rumors of its closure had circulated since its opening. Maybe that would finally come true—there were, she noticed, fewer glitz-mobiles than the last time she'd been here, half a year ago.

No paparazzi glomming from the sidewalk, another bad sign.

There was never a shortage of camera-demons at the nail salon on Camden Drive where Grace got her weekly mani-pedi, but the Opus had been abandoned.

Tsk.

She continued past the valets and the doormen. Six months ago she'd arrived with a different hairstyle, different dress, different makeup, different stride. But even if she hadn't varied her appearance for tonight, no one would notice another slim youngish woman toting a briefcase.

Business traveler, synonym for invisible.

Sure enough, the three clerks at the reception desk didn't look up as she passed.

She strode across the marble lobby, past an oversized **pietra dura** center table graced with a flower arrangement that could've supplied a month of funerals. Continuing up a long hall lined with still-open but customer-less gift shops peddling cashmere and silk and velour leisure wear, she found her way to the lounge, a cavernous place made larger by a thirty-foot coffered ceiling, and set up with nebulous seating areas, potted orchids, and a burnt-orange grand piano currently unoccupied.

The room was two-thirds empty, every drinker scoring plenty of personal space. Taped smooth jazz competed with the clink of glasses and the draggy murmur of obligatory chitchat.

Selecting a two-person loveseat that faced the piano but

was well distant from it and from the bar beyond, Grace settled, placed the snakeskin briefcase next to her, the bag on the sofa. Crossing her legs, she dangled a shoe, appeared to grow contemplative. Then, as if coming to a conclusion, she unclasped the case and drew out a packet of investment mailers from a cold-call fool angling for her business— boring crap she stockpiled for nights like this one. Pulling out a jargon-ridden pamphlet on emerging markets, she pretended to be fascinated by charts and graphs and dishonest attempts to prognosticate.

It didn't take long for a Spanish-accented voice to say, "Can I help you, ma'am?"

Looking up, Grace smiled at a small, thick waiter in his fifties. **Miguel** engraved on a little brass badge.

"Negroni on the rocks, please. Hendrick's Gin, if you have it."

"Sure we have, ma'am."

"Great. Thanks."

"Something to eat, ma'am?"

"Hmm . . . do you still have cheese toast?"

"We do, sure."

"Cheese toast with the Negroni, then." Favoring Miguel with another smile, she returned to her financial miseducation. A few minutes later, the drink and the snack were placed near her right hand and she nodded and thanked Miguel without laying it on too thick.

Sip, nibble, sip some more.

The bitterness of Campari was perfect, cutting through all the financial pie-in-the-sky, and the cucumber nuance of the Scottish gin was an additional pleasure. Last year, Grace had gifted herself with a week in Florence, staying in a far-too-large suite at the Four Seasons. The bar had served up something called a Valentino, riffing on the classic Negroni with more cucumber and other stuff Grace couldn't identify. She'd promised herself to learn the recipe, hadn't so far.

Such a busy girl.

Continuing to fake-read the financial b.s., she thought about Florence, mind flashing like a fast-shutter camera.

The Leap she'd taken there.

Just after midnight, the hotel's perfect Tuscan gardens.

A lovely man in his late forties named Anthony, British, a banker, reserved and polite, not at all handsome. Beautifully surprised when she responded to him in the bar with a cool upturn of lip and flash of black-brown eyes.

Then the rest of it, the poor fool crying out that he loved her as he came.

Figuring he'd try to find her the following morning, she'd checked out early, drove to the Tuscan outlets, and scored some budget Prada. Then on to Rome, where she ate salt cod and fettuccine with dried beef in the old Jewish ghetto and girded herself for the eleven-hour flight back to home sweet home.

The Haunted needed her. Anthony would cope.

Drinking and nibbling and reading in the Opus lounge for precisely five minutes, Grace looked up, pretended to stifle a yawn, kept her head and eyes as immobile as possible, and scoped out the room.

Near the piano were four useless multiples: three triads of business-types and a quartet of nerdy-looking weeds who were probably computer wizards and a whole lot richer than their inept fashion suggested.

To her right sat two solo females: a sixtyish but still foxy blonde, maybe even an experienced hooker with way-off-the-charts boobs, a pre-melanoma tan, and a platinum dye-job that seemed to provide its own illumination. All that came packaged in a minimal sleeveless black thing that showed off slim but age-hardened legs and overbaked, sun-puckered cleavage.

The woman's demeanor shouted **Someone fuck me, already!** and Grace figured she'd eventually get her way.

The second woman was plain, dressed in a brown suit that

wasn't her friend. Like Grace she was reading what appeared to be business papers. Unlike Grace, she was probably serious about it.

Last but not least, to Grace's left, two possible targets.

Solo males.

The first was an extremely tall black guy with stilt-legs who might be a retired athlete, drinking Diet Coke. His eyes met Grace's with momentary interest, then shifted abruptly to the right as he got up to greet the gorgeous wife and ten-year-old daughter who'd suddenly materialized. Final swig of soda and Happy Family was off.

The second solo Y-chromo was at least eighty. Grace had no bias against well-mellowed types—years ago, at a convention in New York, she'd captured a French surgeon twice her age, found him gentle, considerate, much smarter than any young man she'd met. But patience and tenderness and little blue pills weren't what she craved tonight.

Assuming a target showed up.

Over the next twenty-two minutes, none did, and as Grace nursed her drink and moved on to a second brochure, she began to wonder if she'd have to shift locales. Maybe back to WeHo, one of the obnoxiously hip hotels that lined Sunset. If that didn't work, she might have to settle for a painfully retro cocktail lounge catering to trust-fund slackers.

Or be content with nothing.

A bit more time passed and she was resigning herself to nothing when she looked up and there he was.

5

He drifted into the lounge looking a bit disoriented, took a while to select his place, finally opted for an armchair diagonal to Grace's stakeout position.

Grace's age or slightly older, he was of medium height, pleasant looking, with a thatch of black hair worn at a length that suggested neglect of barbering rather than design. His clothes were consistent with that: tweed sport coat far too heavy for L.A., pale-blue button-down shirt, rumpled khakis, brown loafers.

The coat was boxy. The khakis sagged over the shoes. But none of that calculated rumpled preppy thing you saw in pretenders. This was not someone who spent time in front of the mirror.

Things were looking up.

Grace continued to read, sneaking peeks above her brochure, watched him accept a bar menu from a server—Miguel had gone off shift, replaced by a mini-skirted chicklet whose body posture said she was an ace at flirting for tips.

Wasted effort with this guy; he didn't bother to look up.

Nothing like a challenge.

Scanning the menu, he put it aside, slouched lower in the chair, squinted at nothing in particular, closed his eyes and appeared to be initiating a nap.

Chicklet returned with a beer, still working her bod. This time, he made eye contact and smiled briefly and paid up front—letting her know he wouldn't be ordering more, didn't want to be pestered?

Maybe because after one sip, his eyes closed again.

A few moments later, he took another sip as Grace watched

from behind her brochure. When his eyes remained open and he seemed to grow restless, she lowered the pages, sipped her Negroni, recrossed her legs, exposing a foot of ivory calf and an inch of thigh.

The maroon pump dangled and swung, a suede pendulum.

Grace widened the arc, allowed the gray dress to ride up just a bit. The movement caught Tweed's eye. He watched briefly, turned away. Returned to eyeing Grace who pretended to be back in the world of derivatives.

He'd been nursing his beer, now he took a generous swig. Wiped foam from his lips with a finger. Stared at the finger and dried it on a paper cocktail napkin.

Grace flipped a page, fake-sipped her Negroni, and turned her head, catching him looking away hurriedly. The next time, her eyes nabbed him before he could escape. She held his gaze then pretended she hadn't been and proceeded to ignore him. Recrossing her legs.

Sitting up straighter and arching her back just a tad, cashmere stretching tautly over her body.

He drank away and now his beer glass was empty. Pushing hair off his forehead, he repeated the gesture when the mop fell back into place.

Grace read while dangling her other shoe. Rotated her head gently so that her hair cascaded. Smoothing the chestnut tsunami, she swiveled away from the target.

Then toward him.

Their eyes met again.

This time she held the stare without breaking, lips positioned neutrally. He looked appalled at being caught.

Grace smiled.

Grateful, he smiled back. Picked up his glass. Realized it was empty and looked at Grace again and shrugged.

She laughed.

She couldn't carry a tune but she did have a lovely speaking voice, half a tone into alto, smooth as flan. That same appeal extended to her Leap-laugh, a throaty burst of amusement men found beguiling.

She made sure her laughter floated above the conversational buzz, drained her own glass and lofted it and grinned warmly.

We're in this together, friend.

His turn to laugh. Too softly to be audible but it spread his mouth in a nice way.

Well-formed mouth. Grace bet his lips were soft.

And now that she could take a better look at him, she realized this one was actually handsome. Not that it mattered. Anthony in Florence had a face like a toad but he'd made Grace's body scream.

The target turned shy suddenly and looked away.

Endearing.

Definitely a looker. Not in that craggy, hyper-Y, heavy-jaw, brow-ridge way. More like . . . nothing remarkable about any single feature but taken as a whole, a fine composition. Symmetrical. And at the core, attractiveness boiled down to symmetry.

Boyish, she supposed some women would label him. Some women went for boyish.

For the next four minutes, she alternated between jots of eye contact, some followed by warm smiles, others by neutral looks.

The target's hand began drumming a lamp table and he started rocking his head ever so slightly.

The dance had begun.

Then, darn her, Chicklet was back, asking if he wanted a refill. He began to shake his head no, then looked past the waitress at Grace.

Grace lofted her glass, pointed at his, rotated her free hand palms up.

What the heck, let's both go for it.

He said something to Chicklet, paid for both drinks, and

pointed. Chicklet turned around, saw Grace, frowned and left.

Now he was clearly fixed on Grace, not even pretending to be cool. Grace summoned him over with a curled index finger.

He pointed to his chest.

Who, me?

By the time he arrived, he was breathing fast.

She patted the cushion next to her.

He sat down and said, "Thank you."

Nice voice, mellow, soft. A bit shaky—no big stud accustomed to this.

Grace couldn't have custom-ordered it better.

6

Grace's lies were perfectly prepared.

Her name was Helen, she worked "in finance," was in L.A. for a conference. When he asked about the topic, she grinned and said, "Trust me, you don't want to know. Unless it's instant sleep you're after."

He laughed. "Guess I'd rather be awake."

She tossed her hair. "Okay, your turn."

He said, "Talk about boring."

Grace's smile was blinding. "I'll be the judge of that."

His name was Roger, he was a civil engineer in L.A. for meetings concerning "a corporate project—trust me, **you** don't want to know."

Aiming for easygoing rapport but he'd turned grave.

Grace said, "Tough project?"

His face tightened up and the smile he struggled to keep in place was uneasy. "No, it's fine, the usual."

Grace waited.

He drank beer. "Guess I'm a little off—jet lag. Sorry."

"Long flight?"

"Aren't they all, nowadays?"

"Don't like plastic food and being treated like a criminal, huh? Picky, picky." Grace pointed a finger-gun at him. Then, dropping her arm, she allowed her fingertips to graze his khakis, touching the outer curve of his kneecap. Less than a second of contact but he felt it and his eyes shot downward.

Grace picked up her drink. The look on her face was pure innocence. His shoulders had bunched and his lips had dried.

He downed more beer. Let his eyes flit to her legs then forced himself away from the view. Grace slipped the financial nonsense back in her briefcase, pretended to discover how much bare skin she'd been exposing and, again, tugged the dress down. Her breasts mounded through the soft fabric of the dress. Her nipples were fully inflated and couldn't be missed.

Roger the Engineer's Adam's apple rose and fell twice. His blue eyes made it easy to nail the nonverbal message: wildly dilated pupils. Serious interest.

Mission accomplished.

He cleared his throat. "So . . . thanks for the company, Helen."

"Ditto, Roger."

"This is a bit . . ." He shook his head.

"What, Roger?"

He shrugged. "This is nice."

"It is nice but that wasn't what you were going to say."

He looked away.

Grace touched his shoulder briefly. "What is it?"

"Nothing. Really. Refill?"

Grace hadn't touched her second Negroni. She pointed to her glass and smiled.

Roger blushed. "Mr. Observant . . . what I was about to say—this feels—okay, I guess I'm feeling a bit out of my league."

"That's sweet."

"No, I mean it."

"What league do you play in, Roger?"

"Frankly, none," he said. He shook his head. "I'm not making sense, am I?" He put his glass down. "This is going to sound inane but I don't do this as a matter of course."

Strange, almost archaic phrasing. This time Grace's smile was unplanned amusement. "You don't do what?"

"Talk to strange women—oh, crap, sorry, that came out

wrong—talk to . . . unfamiliar . . ." His fingers fluttered, almost effeminately. "I'm not good at this."

Grace lowered her hand over his, let it rest lightly. Her touch made him jump. She said, "There's nothing to be good at, we're just talking."

He bit his lip and Grace thought he'd draw away. She'd overvamped and blown it?

But he relaxed. Retrieved his glass and raised it. "Cheers, Helen."

Grace freed his hand from hers. He drank; she pretended to. They sat there, side by side, not listening to the piped-in music, unaware of anyone else in the room. Finally, Grace ingested a few drops of Negroni.

Thinking of that Valentino in Florence. Thinking of all of them. Lovely.

Roger drained his glass. Suppressed a burp. Grimaced and murmured, "Smooth. Geez, this is . . ."

"I abhor smooth, Roger."

"You do?" Bit of slur in his speech, now. "Why's that?"

"Because smooth is just another form of phony, Roger. Like charisma. And what's worse than charisma?"

He flinched. Looked upward. "Agreed, charisma sucks." His voice had deepened. As if Grace's comments had supercharged him.

"It does, indeed, Roger. Are you a political person?"

"God forbid," he said, with sudden vehemence. "I try to avoid politics."

"Unaffiliated?"

"Pardon?"

"No major commitments?"

"Nothing. Political or personal."

"Same here, Roger." Showing him her hands, free of rings. "That way I'm assured of pleasant company after a tedious workday."

He laughed. "Hope I haven't disrupted that."

Grace let a moment pass before answering. "You apologize a lot, Roger."

"I do? Sor—" He gaped. Cracked up.

Grace brushed his knee with her nails again, moved her hand atop his, squeezed his fingers gently. His tongue glided over his lower lip. A pulse had begun to pound in his carotid, let's hear it for that paragon of honesty: the autonomic nervous system.

Grace let some silence sink in before half whispering, "Roger?"

He leaned forward. No aftershave, just a nice soap-and-water lightness. "Yes?"

"Would you be so kind as to walk me to my car?"

"Pardon—"

Grace squeezed again. "It's been a long day. Would you walk me?"

She stood, took hold of her purse and her briefcase. Roger remained on the love seat, staring up at her, his face a pitiable mask of disappointment.

Crushed and adolescently charming. Grace almost felt sorry for him.

"If it's too much of a hassle, Roger—"

"No, no, sure, no problem." But he continued to sit there.

"I'm not talking a hike, Roger. Just half a block, a girl can't be too careful."

He shot to his feet. Teetered for an instant, threw back his shoulders and drew himself up. "Absolutely. My pleasure. Let's do it."

Grace took his arm. A shiver ran up his biceps. Nice muscles, stronger than he looked.

They left the lounge together.

No one noticed.

The brief stroll was spent without talking. Roger was baffled, worked at hiding it, sneaking quick looks at Grace, trying to understand her behavior. But he took care to match Grace's stride. She tested that, slowing down, speeding up, slowing again.

He might hesitate for a sec but he always got back on track. A good one.

Roger, if you don't know how to dance you can be taught quickly.

As they approached the city lot, Grace firmed up her grip on his arm. He flinched, stumbled half a step, recovered fairly gracefully but his balance remained a mite off as they entered the structure.

A quick downward glance and an even quicker upturn of his eyes suggested the reason.

Khakis, as it turned out, were an inadequate shield for that lovely bulge. Grace slowed down further, savoring.

Once inside the lot, she continued toward the elevator. "I'm at the top. Would you mind walking me up, Roger?"

"Sure, no problem."

Bypassing the elevator, she led him to the stairwell, clung to his arm as they climbed. "Here's my stop." One level short of where the Aston waited.

Guiding him across the tier to the farthest, darkest unoccupied corner, she pulled him into the empty space, pressed her back against the wall, shook her hair so that it fanned beautifully across her face before parting to reveal the heat in her eyes.

She knew the parking lot well. Every space came equipped with a cement stop. Perfect perch for her right foot. She hoisted it, bending her leg nearly perpendicular to its mate.

Geometrical Woman. On the face of it, a strange stance.

Roger's nice blue eyes darted around. Absolutely addled.

Grace said, "Thank you so much for being a gentleman."

"There's no car here—"

Taking his face in both of her hands she kissed him softly, then harder. He resisted for an instant, then surrendered.

Insinuating her tongue between his lips, she worked her way in easily.

He yielded like meringue. Placed a tentative hand on her shoulder then moved it to her breast. She pressed down gently, letting him know he was on the right track.

He kneaded gently.

Nice subtle touch, Roger. You really are turning out to be a winner.

Unzipping his fly, she freed his cock, stroked slowly. His breath caught. His eyes clamped shut as he groped for the front of the gray dress. But she'd gotten there before him, hiking cashmere above her hips, keeping the right leg bent and the left leg straight and thrusting her pelvis forward as his fingers made contact.

She offered herself to his touch, guided him into her. His eyes shot open, rounded and bright as those of a frightened child.

True blue; no lenses for Roger.

Grace set the rhythm, starting slowly, quickening gradually, one hand around his neck.

He said, "Oh, God," and shut his eyes. Grace held him fast and sped up.

"Oh . . . God." Weak, panting voice, baffled, frightened, ecstatic.

He seemed to teeter again.

She braced him with a hand on his ass.

"Go for it, Roger," she whispered into his ear.

He obeyed. They always did.

Lovely Leap into molten gold as he trembled and let out a sound that was part gratitude, part triumphant war whoop, and Grace kissed him hungrily, maintained capture with both sets of lips and gave him time to finish completely.

Basic etiquette. She had no further need for him, had finished earlier, within seconds.

7

When Roger's breathing eased and Grace felt him grow soft, she moved away from their embrace, kissed his cheek, and zipped him up. His eyes remained shut. Tugging the gray dress back into place, she took his hand and held it until his pulse had slowed sufficiently.

"Roger?"

His eyes fluttered, struggled to stay open. A faint, loopy smile took hold of his mouth. He exhaled and Grace smelled herself streaming out of him.

"Thank you, Roger. Now I really do need to go."

"Your car—"

A finger on his lips silenced him. Kissing the tip of his nose lightly, she took hold of his shoulders and pointed him toward the stairwell, a window dresser positioning a mannequin.

He said, "Helen?" Hoarse voice. Plaintive.

"It was really nice meeting you, Roger. Good luck with your project."

He flinched again. Dreading whatever business had brought him to L.A.? Nudging him forward gently, she watched as he took a few rocky steps.

He stopped. Looked back at Grace.

"Good night, Roger."

Salvaging pride, he strode across the parking tier, taking extra-long strides, flung the stairwell door open and was gone.

Concealed in the shadows, Grace waited a few moments before making her way up the ramp to the Aston. As she got into the car, her head filled with power and joy, the most delicious variety of déjà vu: triumph revisited.

Her days were spent nurturing others, she **deserved** to feel this good. To feel **herself**—a discrete person, separated from the universe by her skin, her mental boundaries, delectable spikes of sensation and pleasure.

Random Leaps into bottomless pits of possibility.

She drove out of the lot, listening to Bach and smiling.

Chalk another one up to intuition. In all the time she'd been Leaping she'd only felt threatened twice.

The first time, the target had turned out to be a heavy-handed oaf, a banker in a three-thousand-dollar suit who'd played football in college and believed he was still an irresistible wall of meat. He started off easygoing but got overly enthusiastic, eyes turning piggy, thick hands approaching Grace's neck.

The bigger they are, the harder . . .

Grace had left him writhing on the ground.

The second one, the really bad one that had shaken her confidence, was a Hungarian diplomatic attaché, a slender, long-haired, bruised-poet type she'd met at the Warwick Hotel in New York who'd managed to eye-signal an unseen pal without Grace noticing. When said friend had materialized in the back alley and tried to turn the one-on-one into a team effort and wouldn't take no for an answer, Grace found herself uncharacteristically frightened.

A not totally unpleasant sensation. But . . .

Close call, that one, but it had worked out okay and Grace integrated the experience as a learning opportunity. Neither of the Hungarians would walk normally for a while and she relished the damage she'd wrought.

She found another target soon after. Get right back on the horse.

So only two negatives among all those pluses and when you got down to it uncertainty was the thing that fueled her excitement. Psychosexual question marks squelched by the afterglow of certainty, a state not unlike nirvana that left Grace feeling controlled and controlling.

As she watched men leave, she felt smug as a religious fanatic, secure in her faith that the earth rotated and revolved and swiveled precisely the way she desired.

Now, cruising west on Wilshire, she appeared to be just another pretty, spoiled young woman, glimpsed briefly through the tinted window of an impractical, frightfully expensive black car.

Heading to a house on the sand and the most wonderful night of sleep anyone could imagine.

Twenty-eight minutes after passing through Beverly Hills, the Aston was gliding along Pacific Coast Highway, the ocean to the west a series of gray-cresting waves on black satin, the mountains to the east an endless chocolate bar.

Grace kept her eyes open, and didn't push much above the speed limit. At this hour, the highway was thinly traveled and the DB7 had no problem drawing a straight line to Grace's wood-and-glass box on La Costa Beach.

For all its good-life notoriety, Malibu was a hick town that retired early and the only vehicles Grace encountered were the occasional semi hauling produce down from Oxnard, a car here and there, a highway patrol hotshot who tailgated Grace for half a mile before swerving in front of her and speeding away.

Fool in a uniform showing off. Once he was out of sight, Grace maroon-pumped more speed, letting the car do its natural thing. Her iPod had been running on shuffle since she'd eased out of the parking lot and she continued to be entertained by a random mix of sound: Stevie Ray Vaughan's "Crossroads" followed by Debussy's "Clair de Lune" followed by the Staple Singers' "I'll Take You There." As she neared home, a blast from the fifties came on, the Diamonds riffing on "Little Darlin'."

One of Malcolm's favorites. Like Grace, his musical tastes had been eclectic.

Malcolm . . . her eyes grew tight as her house came into

view and she hooked across PCH, remote-clicked her garage door open, and headed in.

Switching off the Aston's engine, she shut the door and sat out the rest of the ditty.

Half-century-old doo-wop spoof by a bunch of clean-cut Canadians that had turned into their only monster hit. Way before her time, she knew all that because Malcolm had told her. A lesson, Grace realized, years later.

Life could only be predicted to a point.

"Plus," he'd told her, "when the basso does that talking bit, it's funny as hell."

The song ended with cha-cha-cha finality and Grace got out of the car humming off-key. Even to her own ears her singing was annoying!

Chuckling, she retrieved her bag and her briefcase from the trunk, exited the garage dancing along the five feet of walkway that led to her front door.

Key-turn, disable the alarm, home sweet home.

As always, she'd left the house dark except for the single weak bulb that yellowed the deck girding the house's ocean side. Sagging planks of redwood hovered ten feet above sand, supported by creosote-swabbed pilings. The feeble glow highlighted the water beyond, showcasing the wondrous fact that Grace was living at the edge of a continent. Just enough light for her to wind her way toward the space she'd designated as her sleeping area.

Along the way, she disrobed, reached her bed naked, chilled, cheered by a day lived to the fullest.

Instant sleep would've been easy but she followed routine and called her service for messages. They always mattered.

Nothing. Terrific. She reminded the operator that next week, the office would be closed.

"Got that right here, Dr. Blades. You have a nice time."

"You, as well."

"Thanks for saying that, Dr. Blades," said the operator. "You're always thoughtful."

. . .

Slipping on her yellow silk kimono, Grace managed something approaching a short ponytail from her new hairdo, stretched for a few minutes, and did forty girl push-ups. Brushing her teeth she made a circuit of her house. Quick trip, the place was a six-hundred-twenty-square-foot box on a thirty-foot lot, dwarfed by every other home on La Costa. But Grace was one of the few full-time residents; for the most part the trophies all around her remained empty.

In a past life, the house had served as servants' quarters for a vast estate. A minimal assemblage of wood and glass, it sat on now-precious Malibu silica, arbitrarily divided into sitting area, kitchenette, a slot for her narrow bed. Only one walled-off area: a fiberglass booth that contained Grace's bathroom, barely large enough for the clawfoot-tub/hand-shower combo she'd installed soon after taking ownership.

Beyond that, she'd done little to the place, opting for white on white on white because choosing a color scheme was a needless hassle and any other hues seemed intrusive when a blue ocean filled your windows. Even the floor was white, covered with remnant carpeting she'd installed herself, way too plush to be fashionable but she liked the way it kissed her ankles.

Not much detail to the structure but an asymmetrical beamed ceiling, twelve feet at its apex, tossed in a little visual interest and created the illusion of more space. Even without that, Grace wouldn't have minded the meager area; she was comfortable doing the mouse-hole thing.

Nurtured by memories of hiding in plain sight.

The house's current market value neared three million bucks but that was a useless statistic; Grace had no intention of ever leaving. Nor did she intend to entertain visitors. Another reason not to waste time and money on interior decoration.

During the four years Grace had lived here, no one had intruded save for the occasional plumber, electrician, or cable installer. After initial friendliness, Grace avoided them by retreating to the deck and reading.

That hadn't stopped one of the cable dudes who'd showed up last year—a surfer-type with a nasal voice—from flirting with her with what he thought was smoothness. She'd handed him a beer then propelled him straight out.

Tough luck, Hotdog.

Home was where the heart was and Grace's heart was a hunk of muscle that worked just fine on its own.

Running a bath, she soaked in the clawfoot for a count of one thousand, toweled off, retrieved her briefcase, and checked her appointment book for tomorrow's schedule.

Light day prior to vacation: six patients, three before noon, three after, all but one of them a follow-up. One newcomer who'd been apprised by her service that she was leaving soon but had made the appointment anyway. So maybe one of those ambivalent "consultations."

Lying in bed, she planned tomorrow: Her morning would begin by peering into the soft eyes of a twenty-eight-year-old woman named Bev whose husband had died of a rare connective tissue cancer, the illness occupying most of their time together. He'd finally given up fourteen months after their honeymoon. Now newly engaged, her second wedding approaching, she'd be flying in from Oregon.

More than matrimonial jitters. Grace was ready for whatever came up. Check.

Patient number two was a sixty-four-year-old man named Roosevelt whose wife had been murdered by an armed robber while tending the couple's South L.A. liquor store. Guilt was a big issue there, because the night shift had always been Roosevelt's domain and Lucretia had taken over so he could attend a reunion with his high school football buddies.

The unfortunate woman had been shot in the head within

minutes of arriving at the store. Six years ago. Roosevelt's therapy had lasted three years. Grace knew the date of the murder by heart. Another anniversary.

Lovely man, Roosevelt, quiet, genteel, hardworking, Grace liked him. Not that liking mattered. She could comfort a wolverine if that's what the job called for.

Session number three was for a married couple, Stan and Barb, whose only son had fatally slashed his own wrists. No tentative cry-for-help by Ian; this was a deep, artery-demolishing excursion that led him to bleed out quickly. Toward the end of the process, he'd staggered into the bedroom where his parents slept, managed to switch on the light, and gurgled himself to nothingness in front of the people who'd given him life.

Grace had obtained the poor kid's psych records, found clear evidence of blossoming schizophrenia. So no clinical surprise, but that didn't squelch the horror for Stan and Barb. Memories of what Stan called "sadistic etching." That always made Barb wince and grow nauseous. Several times she'd rushed to the patient bathroom and vomited.

Of course there was nothing much Stan and Barb could've done to help the boy, his brain was deteriorating. But that didn't stop them from tormenting themselves. It took just over two years for Grace to guide them past that and their sessions had thinned to twice a month. So far so good.

Patient four was Dexter, a young man who'd lost both parents in a plane crash. The usual small-craft disaster, amateur-pilot Dad at the helm of a single-engine, probable heart attack. Lots of anger to work through, there.

Five was a woman whose in-vitro-conceived only child had perished from a rare liver disorder in infancy. Grace didn't want to think much about that one because kids got to her and she needed to preserve herself so she could be useful. If she felt she lacked expertise, she could call Delaware.

Last, and possibly least, was the new one, a man named Andrew Toner from San Antonio, Texas, who'd waited seven weeks for a slot to open up. Now that Grace thought about it, that was at odds with ambivalence, but who knew, she'd learn the details tomorrow.

What she did know was that it was a self-referral spurred, according to the info recorded by her service, by Mr. Toner's coming across some research she'd published. Not the typical treatises on stress and coping Malcolm and she had churned out for years.

The piece Malcolm insisted Grace write alone.

Grace regarded that article—all of her publications—as ancient history, but a patient citing it told her something about Mr. Toner: good chance he came from a frighteningly rotten family.

Maybe all he needed was permission to cut off some toxic relatives. If so, not nearly as complex an issue as Bev's or Helen's or the arm gouger's poor parents.

Grace could say that with authority.

Placing the appointment book back in her bag and still warmed by her bath, she shrugged out of the kimono and walked to the French doors opening to the deck. Turning off the weak bulb, she stepped out on weathered wood, stood bare and vulnerable as a newborn.

Taking in the murmured comfort of the tides as they rolled in, the swoosh of farewell as they embarked on the return trip to Asia.

A gust kicked up from the water. Sudden burst of energy from—Hawaii? Japan?

Grace remained on the deck as something other than time passed. Finally, she felt herself growing drowsy and made her way back into the house. She should've been hungry but wasn't. Going to bed on an empty stomach was fine. She'd had plenty of practice.

Now, of course, an empty gut could be filled by a humongous breakfast. The following morning, how wonderful life was when you ran your own show.

Relatching the French doors, she got into bed, crawled

under the covers, drew them over her head. Taking a moment, as she always did, to reach under the box spring and pat the reassuring hunk of dense black plastic resting on the carpet beneath the bed.

Her house gun, a 9mm Glock, just like the cops used. Unregistered and perfectly maintained, same as the .22. Most likely, she'd never need either weapon. Same for the twin S&W .38 revolvers she'd bought at a gun show in Nevada last year and secreted in the file cabinet at her office.

Nighty-night, beloved instruments of destruction.

Curling fetally, Grace slipped her thumb between her lips. Sucked greedily.

8

She rose at dawn, famished, watched through the French doors as a gray pelican dove for breakfast. Shorebirds skittered along the tide line. An intermittent dot caught Grace's attention and she got up and wrapped herself in the yellow kimono and went outside.

Focusing her eye where the dot had last been, she waited. There it was again, a few yards north. California sea lion, drifting and submerging. Keeping a slow pace, lovely, entitled predator that it was.

Grace watched for a while, made coffee and drank the first of three cups while scrambling four eggs tossed with cheese, Genoa salami, rehydrated porcinis, and garlic chives. Buttering two rolls, she downed every greasy crumb. By seven thirty she was back on PCH, letting the Aston do its thing as she warmed herself with thoughts of the care she'd be giving all day.

Bev, soon to be married, was better dressed and coiffed and conspicuously more put together than the red-eyed young widow who'd first showed up at Grace's office shaking uncontrollably and barely able to speak. This morning, those eyes were clear, alternating between the warmth of pleasant expectation and flashes of furtive heat that Grace knew meant guilt.

No big puzzle: At a moment when the poor thing felt husband-to-be should take precedence, all she could think about was husband-who-was.

A thirty-year-old Portland firefighter when Bev met him, Greg had the equilibrium and easy confidence of a man whose body worked perfectly. Till it didn't.

The cancer that had ended his life was so rare there was no treatment protocol. Bev had watched him waste away.

Who could blame her for abandoning hope? It had taken Grace a long time to get the sweet, warmhearted young woman to see that the concept of **future** could still be relevant. Now Bev was about to embark on a second attempt at faith, good for her!

"I'm not terrified, Dr. Blades. I guess I'm just . . . anxious. Okay, honest? I'm scared as heck."

Grace said, "Then you're ahead of the game."

"Pardon?"

"If you were totally terrified, it would be understandable, Bev. Anything less than terror is heroism."

Bev stared. "You're serious."

"I am."

Bev looked doubtful.

Grace said, "When did you start feeling anxious?" Deliberately downgrading from "scared." It was her job to recontextualize.

Bev said, "I guess . . . a few weeks ago."

"As the wedding date grew near."

Nod.

"Until then, for the most part, would you say you were pretty happy?"

"Yes. Of course."

"Of course . . ."

"I'm marrying Brian. He's wonderful."

"But . . ."

"No buts," said Bev. She burst into tears. "I feel disloyal! Like I'm cheating on Greg!"

"You loved Greg. It's only natural you'd feel obligated to him."

Bev sniffed.

Grace said, "To everyone else, Greg is a memory. To you he's the other man."

That unleashed another torrent of sobs.

Grace let Bev cry for a while, then leaned in close and dried Bev's eyes and squeezed her hand. When Bev took a deep breath, Grace settled her back in her chair in a posture of forced relaxation.

In matters of healing, the body initiates and the mind follows. Malcolm had told her that. Only once, but it stuck.

And it worked: Bev's facial muscles slackened. The tears stopped.

Grace gave her the softest smile she could muster. Bev smiled back.

A casual glance could register them as two pretty young women hanging out in a pleasant, well-lit room.

When the time was right, Grace said, "Because Greg loved you so much, we know one thing for sure."

Bev looked at her through tear-smudged eyes. "What?"

"He'd absolutely want you to be happy."

Silence.

Finally, Bev said, "Yes, I know." That sounded like a confession.

Grace said, "Still, that bothers you."

No answer.

Grace tried another tack. "Maybe instead of looking at Greg as laying siege to your emotions you could start thinking of him as a partner."

"A partner in what?"

"The life that awaits you," said Grace.

"Life," said Bev. As if the idea was distasteful.

Grace said, "Let's be clear: What you and Greg had together was profound. And profound things just don't vanish because social niceties say they should. That doesn't make you unfaithful to Greg. Or to Brian."

"But still," said Bev. "I do feel unfaithful. Yes, you're right, to both of them."

"To Greg for letting joy into your life. To Brian because you think about Greg."

"Yes."

"That makes total sense, honey. But think of it this way: The three of you—Brian and you **and** Greg—could tackle the agenda as a team."

"I . . . what agenda?"

"The agenda of what lies in store for Bev. The agenda of Bev deserves to be happy," said Grace. "Approved by unanimous voice vote." She smiled. "For what it's worth, I second the motion."

Bev shifted in her chair. Her lips set grimly. "I guess."

Grace knew she'd come on too strong. She let Bev sit there and ponder for a while and when Bev hadn't shifted out of the relaxed position and her facial muscles had loosened again, she took **another** tack.

"Officially, your wedding's a celebration. But there's no need for you to snap into joy instantaneously just because you've printed invitations and people will be sitting in church. An emotionally shallow person could pull that off. But you remember what I told you last year: You're emotionally substantial."

Silence.

"You feel deeply, Bev. You always have. Those stories you told me about taking care of wounded animals."

Makes two of us, girlfriend.

Nothing from Bev. Then, finally, a slow nod.

"Feeling deeply is a virtue, Bev. It allows life to take on meaning and at some point your joy will be even greater than if you'd simply drifted with the currents."

Long silence. "I sure hope so."

Grace placed a hand on Bev's shoulder. "Of course you can't see that, right now. How could you? But it'll happen, there'll be joy in your future but flavored with even greater depth than if you didn't go through this, right now. That will be sweet."

Bev stared at her. Muttered, "Thank you."

Grace kept her hand on Bev's shoulder. Exerting just

enough pressure to let Bev know she was cared for. Cared about.

"Take your time. Feel whatever you need to feel. Eventually, you'll sense that Greg's on board. That he approves and wants you to be happy because that's what people who love unconditionally do."

The outer edges of Beverly's lips tugged wider, as if manipulated by a puppeteer. "You're scary, Dr. Blades."

Grace had heard that so many times. "Me?" she said, innocently.

"Scary-smart is what I mean. It's like you have a direct view into here." Patting her breast.

"Thanks for the compliment, Bev, but smart has nothing to do with it. Whatever I know comes from working at understanding people." Grace leaned forward. "Because once we get past the nonsense, we're all the same. Yet unique at the same time. No one has lived your life or thought your thoughts or felt your feelings. Even so, if I was in your situation, I'm pretty sure I'd feel exactly the same way."

"You would?" Amazed.

The honest answer: **Who knows?**

Grace said, "Of course."

"So what would you do about it?"

Grace smiled. "I'd go talk to someone scary-smart. Because we all need help from time to time."

Flashing to Malcolm. Sophie. The new experience of sleeping in a clean, sweet-smelling bed. Breakfast. Dinner. Tentative attempts to hug, however briefly.

Human touch Grace had to train herself to tolerate. Thinking about all that brought a smile to her lips, which was perfect, the moment called for a smile, let Bev think it was all about her.

Sighing, Bev hugged herself. "I appreciate what you're saying, Dr. Blades, but once I get back home . . . it might be difficult."

"It might be. But you'll handle it. You always do."

Bev pinged her lower lip with a finger. The finger that bore her diamond-chip ring. Brian, a plumber's assistant, splurging at Zales. "You're saying sometimes life needs to be difficult to be meaningful."

"I'm saying when we're well put together emotionally, Bev—as you are—we learn to trust ourselves."

Oh, do we . . .

Bev took a long time before she spoke next. "I guess I need to just roll with it."

Grace said nothing.

Bev said, "Okay, I need to roll with it even if that means thinking about Greg."

"Don't fight thinking about Greg. Greg was precious to you," said Grace. "Why would you exile him from your consciousness?"

Bev thought some more, face tightening as if struggling with a weighty puzzle. "On the flight from Portland, Dr. Blades, I spent most of the time remembering. One memory really stuck with me. Like it was glued to my brain. There was a lake. We used to take a canoe and Greg would row me. He was so strong. Muscles on muscles. Each time he moved the oar, they rippled. The sun made them glisten. Sometimes we'd start out on a sunny day and it would rain and he'd be dripping with sweat and rain and just **shine.**"

She inhaled. "I'd sit in the canoe and watch him and . . . I'd **want** him. Right then and there. In the boat." She blushed. "We never did anything like that. I never told him."

Grace smiled. "You didn't want to rock the boat. Literally and figuratively. Balance is important to you and right now you're feeling off balance because life has taken a new turn."

Bev gawked. Smiled. "You're more than scary, Dr. Blades. I bless the God that brought me to you."

The rest of the day rolled on with reassuring predictability. Grace knew that objectively she was young but sometimes felt as if she'd seen everything. That didn't sour her on her job, nor did it bore her. On the contrary, she found it reassuring and invigorating.

This is what I've been created for.

Nevertheless, she needed to make sure confidence never slid into smugness. Nor would she ever allow the Haunted to enter a millimeter of her private world.

Friendly, yes. Friend, never.

Because friendship was a limited concept: Pals and chums and confidantes—what the textbooks sanitized as a **social support system**—were fine when you stubbed your emotional toe. With deep wounds, you needed a surgeon, not a barber.

To Grace, the concept of therapy as paid friendship was a horrid cliché. The **last** thing patients needed was some sloppy, mawkish do-gooder brimming with sickly-sweet smiles, contrived pauses, the phony gravity of by-the-book sympathy, the smarmy rote of catchphrases.

What I hear you saying . . .

Cram a patient's throat with sugar and they'll choke.

Phonies who practiced that way either were money-hungry quacks or just wanted to feel good about themselves. Which was why you saw so many fucked-up people seeking second careers as **ahem** counselors.

Some of the Haunted came to Grace **seeking** the eye-locking, intensely theatrical **concern** they'd seen on talk shows and movies of the week.

I'm not a shrink but I play one on TV.

When the expectation was for Dr. Soft Voice, Grace dispelled it gently by supplying constructive reality. For four hundred fifty bucks an hour you deserved more than an emotional adult diaper.

You deserved an actual **adult.**

Checking her desk clock, she brewed herself a strong shot of espresso, downed it just in time for the red light on the wall above her desk to illuminate.

Time for Roosevelt. Thoughtful, gracious, polite. Old enough to be her father.

If she'd had a real father . . .

Grace felt her breath catch. Her heart skipped a beat, obviously too much caffeine, she'd cut back.

Rising, she smoothed her hair, straightened her posture. Onward.

As the end of the day approached, Grace felt uncharacteristically tired. Things had gone a little tougher than anticipated with Stan and Barb, the couple entering the therapy room outwardly hostile to each other in a way Grace had never seen.

No need to probe, they told her straight out: Both had a history of affairs and they were finally divorcing. The dual infidelity had been kept from Grace. They figured it didn't matter, had begun years before Ian's suicide.

A pair of fools truly believing Ian had never known, after all he was crazy, everyone told them so.

Now the marriage was coming apart and despite the mutual decision, Stan and Barb were angry.

At themselves for failing.

At embarking on an unsuitable marriage in the first place.

Then the inevitable segue: anger at Ian for walking into their bedroom and waking them up as he collapsed onto their duvet, spurting and leaking and seeping and dying.

Grace hadn't spent much time wondering what had led a nineteen-year-old to nuclear self-destruction. Ian was gone, life was for the living, if she'd felt otherwise she'd have gone to mortician school.

But now, she wondered what else she'd missed.

Stan was saying, "So that's it, we're dividing everything in half and it's done, we're being mature and logical." Grinding his jaws.

Barb snapped, "Over and done, put a fork in it." Stan shot her a hard look.

Grace knew the answer to her next question but she asked it anyway.

"So you're both in the same place with it?"

"Yes."

"Yes."

Lousy liars. So why the hell are you here?

Grace asked them.

Barb said, "We decided we needed it for closure. Your being such a big part of our family over the last few years and now there'll be no family."

Divorcing Grace first. She smiled internally.

Stan said, "We didn't want you to think you failed us, this had nothing to do with Ian."

"Definitely nothing," said Barb.

"The two of us are still friends," lied Stan. "Which I think is an accomplishment in itself."

To prove it, he reached for Barb's hand. She frowned but squeezed his fingers, let go quickly and positioned herself out of reach.

Grace said, "You're moving on and were kind enough to think of me."

"Yes, we are!" said Barb. "Perfect way to put it. Moving on."

"You bet," said Stan, with perhaps a bit less confidence.

Grace said, "Well, I appreciate the thought you've put into this and I wish you the best. I also want you to know that I'm always here for you."

Trust me, guys, I'll see both of you eventually. Separate sessions.

Papers would be filed, property divided, but these two would never lead totally separate lives.

Ian had seen to that.

By the time Grace had completed her sketchy case notes and the light went on announcing the last patient of the day, she was already planning her evening.

Quick stop at the casual fish place near Dog Beach for halibut and chips and a Sidecar, enjoyed in a vinyl booth well away from the bar. Concentrating on her food and flashing stay-away signals at any man who had designs.

Oh, yeah, a salad to start. And maybe not halibut, possibly Dover sole if they had it fresh. Or that scallops/softshell crab combo. Then zip home, change into shorts and a tee, take a run on the dark beach. After that, a long shower, masturbating under the spray. Followed by a quick review of the pile of psych journals that had climbed way too high and when her eyelids lost the battle with gravity, a nightcap of junk TV.

Maybe she'd think of the red room, maybe not.

Yawning, she checked the mirror in the closet, touched up her makeup, tugged her white blouse tight into black slacks, and reminded herself she was an authority figure and ready for Mr. Andrew Toner from San Antonio, who'd found her through an esoteric article in an obscure journal.

Written without Malcolm but aping Malcolm's style because Grace, though adroit at psych-prose, hated it and refused to develop a style of her own. In the beginning, she'd looked forward to seeing her name in print, read every pub word for word, only to find them arid.

Malcolm, for all his virtues, was the typical professorial scribe, unable to scare excitement out of an asteroid strike.

For a layman to find Grace's solo venture, he had to be motivated.

Of course Andrew Toner was, he'd come to see her all the way from the Great State of Texas.

When patients from out of town sought her help—not as rare as you might think—they were often perfectionistic, compulsive types. The kind of folk who'd google **psychological treatment aftermath violence** or something similar and scroll for hours.

Let's see if she was right about Mr. Andrew Toner.

She walked down the bare hall that served as a decompression tunnel for her patients, smiled, and opened the door to the waiting room.

Found herself staring at the face of Roger, the man she'd fucked mindlessly last night and dismissed the moment it was over.

No way to dismiss him, now. Ever.

He laid eyes on her and seemed to shrink. Then he loomed in Grace's visual field.

Him. Oh God. Neurons popped as Grace's brain worked to make sense of what was happening. All that mental activity produced . . . nothing.

Roger/Andrew was doing no better. Still seated, a magazine in his lap, his jaw had dropped and he'd turned ghostly pallid and Grace felt her own mandible sag uncontrollably.

Aping a patient? She'd never been suggestible. What was **happening**?

The authoritative smile she'd entered with lingered, unwanted, idiotic. Grace forced her lips shut, wasn't sure what expression was squatting on her face.

She felt stiff, inanimate, a waxwork dummy. Had no idea what to say. Even if she'd managed to come up with words, they'd have remained trapped by her strangulated larynx.

Roger/Andrew kept staring at her, finally moved **his** lips. Out came a mouse-squeak of humiliation.

Grace turned hot. Cold. Frozen.

Andrew and Grace.

Roger and Helen.

He'd lied about his name, too.

No comfort, there. Grace's limbs were permafrost.

Sound filtered through a window. A car with a faulty muffler rumbling by.

Thankful for the distraction, Grace prayed for more noise. None followed. She remained rooted. Paralyzed.

This was new, different, this was **dreadfully** different.

Sweat pooled in Grace's armpits. Trickled down her rib cage. Pores opened, she felt herself bathed in perspiration.

She **never** sweated.

And now her chest was tight and breathing had become a challenge. As if a huge animal had settled on her diaphragm.

Andrew Toner stared. Grace stared. Two helpless . . . offenders?

No, no, no, she was stronger than that, there was always a solution.

None came to her.

Stupid girl.

redredredredred.

Grace remained standing in the doorway. Andrew Toner remained seated.

Both of them encased in an aspic of shame.

Again, he was the first to find his voice. Dry-croaking: "My God."

Grace thought: **If there is a God, He's laughing His deified head off.**

Her brilliant response: "Well . . ."

Why had she **said** that?

What **could** she say?

Stupid girl. **No no no I'm smart.**

And I haven't done anything **willfully** wrong.

Miles from actually believing that, she dredged up enough rationalization to look straight in the pretty blue eyes of Andrew from San Antonio, Texas. A man who'd traveled to see her because she had something valuable to say about . . . wearing the same tweed sport coat and rumpled khakis as last night.

Different shirt.

So his hygiene is decent. Who gives a fuck!

Grace forced air into cement lungs. Thought about how to phrase her apology.

Yet **again,** he beat her to it. "I'm so sorry."

What did **he** have to apologize for?

Grace said, "You'd better come in."

He didn't budge.

"Really," said Grace. "This isn't the end of the world. We need to work it out."

With nothing more than hope and bluster to propel her, she headed back toward the therapy room.

Hearing footsteps behind her.

There he was. Following instructions.

Just as he had last night.

9

Five-and-a-half-year-old Grace was an expert at hiding.

With no alcoves or nooks in the single-wide and only one door in and out, the key was to stay close to walls. As far as she could from the strangers.

Out of arm's reach, when possible.

She didn't have a word for the concept but had learned about arm's reach by accumulating bruises and sore spots, a couple of bloody noses, the loss of one tooth. A baby tooth, but when Ardis's hand shot out to slap Dodie's face and the combination of weed, whiskey, and anger shoved him off course and his knuckles collided with Grace's mouth, it hurt a lot.

She didn't cry. Crying didn't come naturally to her and besides, she didn't want to be noticed. She'd been eating a Fudgsicle and dropped it and stooped to pick it up.

The blow hurt Ardis, too. He kept shaking his hand and screaming in pain.

Dodie laughed and that made Ardis even more mad and the second time he went for her, he punched her in the forehead and it was her turn to scream, calling him filthy names.

That made him laugh and he lunged for her again. She feinted out of the way and tried to outlaugh him, which enraged him further and he wound up to deliver one of his roundhouses, the blows that left Dodie's face swollen and, the next day, all black-and-blue.

But Ardis's rhythm was off and he ended up on the floor and Dodie got off with a fingernail graze.

Grace thought: **Now he's using his fist all the time. They're both so stupid.**

Throughout the melee, neither of them noticed her,

backed into the farthest spot she could find, blood mixing with chocolate from the Fudgsicle, creating a sweet, repellent mud that streamed down her face.

Her mouth hurt really bad but, of course, she kept quiet about her pain because when you complained it got worse; they—especially Dodie—could get mad at you.

Instead, she thought of nice things, anything that wasn't pain.

Sometimes that meant shows she'd seen on TV or books she'd read at preschool. Sometimes it meant imagining the strangers gone. Like tonight.

She tried to eat more Fudgsicle. That's when her tooth crunched and bent and she reached inside her mouth and it came right out and she could feel air whistling through the space.

More blood than chocolate now and the Fudgsicle was tasting like liver and she didn't want it anymore.

It had been her entire dinner but she wasn't hungry.

Across the cramped trailer, Ardis was sitting on his butt, dazed, and Dodie was laughing at him. And then both of them were laughing and Dodie was pulling him up and he was touching her booby and she was touching his zipper.

The two of them drunk-waltzed toward their sleeping space, Dodie yanking at the curtain as she giggled and got dragged along by Ardis. The curtain only closed part of the way and if Grace had wanted to, she could've seen everything.

Wiping her face with a piece from one of the toilet paper rolls Ardis stole from the McDonald's, she left the single-wide and walked into the night.

Not even having to do it quietly; no one was interested in her.

She covered a few feet, found a spot in the dry dirt where she could sit, and swabbed away blood with paper napkins until all that was left was a copper-penny taste in her mouth.

The air was cold. Sounds came from other trailers, most of them electronic. Grace shivered. Opened her mouth and created her own little breeze whistling through the new space in her mouth.

After that fight, Ardis wasn't around much and sometimes Dodie muttered complaints about him to Grace, because no one else was around to listen. "Good riddance to bad rubbish. Know what that means?"

"Uh-huh."

"What?" Dodie demanded. She'd just fooled with the trailer's chemical toilet and everything smelled bad and Dodie had got stuff on her hands and cussed like crazy. All that made her super grumpy and when she got like that she always demanded Grace say what she wanted her to say.

"What?" she repeated. "You tell me right now what that means."

"You're happy he's not here."

"Yeah," Dodie conceded. "But it's more than that, you're a kid, you don't get it."

"Get what?" said a voice from the door and there was Ardis, carrying a bucket of fried chicken. He shot a quick glance at Grace and raised his eyebrows, as if surprised she was still around. Then he gave Dodie a long look and did that wiggly thing with his hips and swung the bucket.

Dodie clamped her hands on **her** hips and didn't move them at all. The more Ardis wiggled, the stiffer she got. Sniffing her fingers, she cursed and frowned and washed some more. "Well, look what the wind blew in. Figures."

"Hey, dinner." Ardis wrinkled his nose. "Stinks like shit in here."

"Yeah, well, that's what it's like in a luxury condo." Dodie eyed the bucket. "You're at KFC, now? They kick your ass out of Mickey D?"

"Nah, still Mickey D, but I got connections."

"Connections for some fuckin' chicken." Dodie curled a finger. "Whoopy doo."

"Breasts and thighs." Ardis winked. Checked to see if

Grace had noticed. She had but she'd turned around to pretend she hadn't.

"Breasts and thighs, thighs and breasts," said Dodie, with lightness in her voice.

"Uh-huh."

The two of them shuffled off to the sleeping space, Ardis taking time to put the bucket on the kitchenette counter.

Grace went outside. When she passed Mrs. Washington's trailer, Mrs. Washington was having a sober evening and called out, "Child? C'mere," and gave Grace a rib from a batch she'd cooked yesterday on her outdoor grill made out of an oil can.

"Thank you."

"Least I can do, you living with those . . . never mind, go on and find yourself a place to eat."

Grace didn't settle, she just walked around the trailer park, eating the rib. Gnawing on the bone well after she'd stripped it of meat. Her tooth still hadn't come in totally and the hot sauce made the hole Ardis's fist had created weeks ago tingle and hurt.

When she returned to the single-wide, Ardis was inside sitting on a lawn chair with a bottle of whiskey and Dodie was cutting up chicken in the kitchenette.

He looked mean and Grace stayed out of arm's reach.

Dodie said, "Fuckin' KFC, what's with all the bones."

Ardis said, "Chicken has bones, stupid. If it didn't, it would be . . . boneless chicken." Throwing his head back, he laughed and took a swallow from the bottle.

Dodie stopped cutting. "You just call me stupid?"

No answer from Ardis.

"I asked you a question. You call me stupid?"

"Whatever."

"Whatever?"

"Hey," said Ardis, taking another drink. "Stupid is like stupid does."

"Fuck that," said Dodie. "Fuck **you**—I gotta take **that** from a **retard**?"

"Who you callin' a retard?"

No answer from Dodie.

Ardis repeated the question.

Dodie snickered. "If the retard shoe fits."

Both of them talking in that loose, hard-to-understand way they always did when they drank too much or smoked too much weed or took pills. Which was almost always when they emerged from the sleeping space.

Ardis said, "What fits is my dick up your fat ass."

Silence.

Dodie said, "What'd you just shit outta your pie-hole? Re-tard."

Ardis repeated the insult. Stood up and advanced toward the kitchenette.

Dodie said, "You know, you just need to just leave. And never come back. Retard."

"Fuck that. This is my home."

"Like hell it is," said Dodie and now she was screaming. "I pay, you don't do shit. Your home is someplace they stick useless retards!"

"You **pay**?" Ardis bellowed. "Your **welfare** pays, bitch. You're useless, sitting around, that ass a' yours getting bigger and bigger, soon you're not gonna fit through the fuckin' door."

Dodie turned from the chicken and faced him.

Ardis said, "What?"

"You ain't worth the time—you just go."

"I go when I say I go, I stay when I say I stay." Ardis gave a crooked smile. "My dick goes up your ass when I say it's the time for fun."

He laughed.

Dodie had turned red as ketchup.

"Look at you." Ardis laughed. "You like a . . . tomato. You

all ugly, you been whupped with the biggest fuckin' ugly stick in the biggest fuckin' planet."

"The planet is earth!" screamed Dodie. "We can't live on another one 'cause there's no air. Retard. You don't know shit about science or anything because you're stupid, know what they call you, even people you think like you? Dead Brain! Dead Brain Retard!"

"Bullshit!"

"Bull-**no** shit!"

Quick as a snakebite, Ardis lunged toward Dodie, shooting out a shaky hand that still managed to connect with her nose. Blood spurted. Dodie's nose looked different than ever before. Flat. Crushed.

Breathing must've hurt because she began crying, tried to stanch the blood with KFC napkins, white turning to red real fast.

Ardis laughed and hit her again, this time with the usual open hand, like he didn't even care. But hard, slapping the side of her head so hard that it flipped to the side and sprayed blood from her ruined nose.

This is different, thought Grace.

Then something really different happened. Dodie turned and put her weight into it and hit Ardis back. A real fast upward swoop.

Tracing the space beneath his chin.

Weird place to hit someone. Then Grace saw it.

A thin red line forming, Ardis's eyes opening in wonder as the line started seeping and Ardis stumbled back causing the line to widen into a gaping slash.

A second mouth, grinning across his neck.

Now Ardis's blood was coming out a lot faster than the blood from Dodie's nose.

He staggered, tried to talk. Nothing came out. One hand flew toward his throat but dropped before arriving. Weakly, he waved a fist at Dodie.

Then he collapsed. Blood pooled beneath him.

Dodie stared at him. Shifted her eyes to the knife in her hand. Little tan specks and bits—breading from the chicken pieces—clung to the blade, turning into red lumps as they mixed with blood.

Dodie looked down at Ardis. Screamed his name and went over to him and shook him.

He didn't move. Flat on his back, eyes sightless, mouth gaping. The blood kept spurting out of his neck.

Dodie's attention now shifted to Grace, hugging herself with crossed arms. Pressed to the wall, wishing she could push herself **through** the wall.

"You saw that," said Dodie. "I **had** to."

Grace said nothing.

"What? You think I **started** it?"

Grace tried to shrivel to nothingness.

"What?" screamed Dodie, advancing on her. "You're saying it was my fault? That what you're saying?"

Grace remained silent.

Dodie said, "You keep looking at me with that **look.** Like I'm—fine, have it your way, remember this."

Giving a weird, drunken smile, Dodie clutched the knife with both hands and raised it high. Letting out a laugh that sounded like a screaming coyote, she stiffened her arms and plunged the blade into her own belly.

Laughter turned to an agonized shriek as the pain hit her and she looked down and saw what she'd done. Shaking hands fumbled to dislodge the blade, buried in her abdomen to the hilt. Each attempt twisted the knife, doing more damage.

Dodie fell to her knees. Inches from Ardis.

Her hands faltered and dropped. The knife remained deeply embedded but turned to one side.

"Hep me," she croaked to Grace. "Puh it ou." Eyes dropping to the knife.

She moaned in pain.

Grace stood there.

Dodie's eyes fluttered. Slammed shut. The trailer was quiet but for the **drip-drop** of blood on the linoleum floor.

Grace watched as the room turned red.

10

By the time Grace was sitting behind the precious barrier provided by her desk, Andrew Toner was perched rigidly on the edge of the patient chair, shoulders tight as bridge struts, looking everywhere but at Grace.

She had yet to completely collect her thoughts but began a cardboard speech that was better than nothing.

"Obviously," she began, "this is awkward for both of us. Let me begin by saying I'm sorry."

"No need, you didn't know," he said. "How could you?"

"I couldn't," she said. "Still. You traveled a long distance for my help."

He brushed a wing of hair from his unlined brow and sat for a long time before mustering the faintest of smiles.

"Guess there are all kinds of therapy."

Being a cheeky bastard? Would he be bragging to his friends in Texas the moment he left the office? Facebook, Twitter, some other hideous communication?

Guys, you'll never believe what happened, I shit you not, this was straight out of bad porn. I fly to L.A. to meet this shrink, go for a drink the night before and . . .

But then he said, "Sorry, that was glib. I guess I just—I've never been that great at making conversation."

Not a lout. Too bad. Seeing his faults would've been a pathetic way for her to feel less stupid . . .

She cleared her throat. He looked up. His mouth was set tight. Nothing more to say.

"I'm terribly sorry, Andrew. But what happened, happened, no sense dwelling. On the contrary, I'm thinking we could try to use this time constructively."

His eyebrows arced.

Oh, no, not that, not that at all.

Grace leaned forward, faking calm and authoritative . . . **professional.**

"What I mean," she said, "is that you traveled a distance because of questions you have. If you can put aside the distraction, I'd be happy to hear what they are. Obviously I can't treat you long-term, but I can do my best to direct you to the best local referral possible."

She had no dependable referrals in Texas but damn, she'd find one.

Andrew Toner didn't respond.

"On the other hand," she said, "if you find that too difficult, I understand."

"I . . . maybe . . ." Pinching khaki, he began to cross a leg. Changed his mind and replanted both feet flat on the carpet. "Do you have any idea what I'm after?"

"If the article you mentioned to my answering service is relevant, I might."

"Yes!" A single whispered word, emphatic. He sat up straighter. "When I came across it, I said **this** is the person I need to talk to." He turned to the side. "It took me a while to find it. It's not a topic psychologists seem to pay much attention to." A beat. "Why is that?"

"Hard to know for sure," said Grace, grateful to be discussing anything but last night. "I suspect some of it has to do with what we call small sample size. There aren't enough people to do the kind of studies that get grant money."

"Really?" said Andrew. "With all that goes on, you'd think there would be."

"I imagine most people in that situation wouldn't be interested in being studied."

"Hmm. Yes, I can see that."

Oh, you have no idea, Andrew.

Or maybe you do . . . you're here.

"Anyway," he said. "That's how I found you. Researching."

Grace pictured him clicking away at his computer, patient, methodical, like an engineer should be. If he **was** an engineer . . . whatever, he'd investigated because of his own situation, finally come across **that** article.

The piece was six years old, tucked at the rear of an arcane British criminology journal now out of circulation. Because Malcolm had guessed, probably correctly, that psych journals might not go for it.

An outlier, Grace's only solo effort. Malcolm had been suggesting it for a while, finally she'd relented.

He'd so enjoyed seeing it in print.

Living with Evil: Emotional Aspects of Kinship with a Murderer

What the journal referees hadn't known—what no one but Grace and Malcolm and Sophie knew—was that Grace had done double duty.

Author **and** subject.

Referring to herself as Jane X and altering details so no one would ever detect autobiography masquerading as clinical case history.

She'd placed the "precipitating event" in another state, transformed the father into the initial killer and suicide, the mother into a hapless victim—in addition to camouflaging the facts, that would play well with the feminist editor of the journal. And, let's face it, Ardis **had** been a star player in the tawdry melodrama that ended with his neck slit open. All that stupid testosterone unleashed by booze and dope. All those backhand slaps.

The stink of tension and fear when he entered the trailer.

Across from her, Andrew sat there and Grace realized she'd drifted off. She wheeled back her desk chair, pressed her back into leather, wishing she could melt into oblivion.

Was she showing discomfort? Andrew's blue eyes were ripe with concern.

Oh, just dandy. Not only had she failed him, she was **burdening** him with her personal shit.

Wheeling forward, she recited the title of the article. Hoping the incantation would free her of subjectivity.

Andrew nodded. Suddenly, Grace felt as if she was about to choke. Covering with a cough, she muttered, "'Scuse me," placed her hand over her mouth and inhaled long and slow, exchanging air through her nose in order to conceal her craving for oxygen.

A victim. No way, nono way—

Andrew Toner continued to regard her with . . . tenderness?

I'm okay, you softhearted bastard.

Grace knew she had to regain control or . . . what?

Distraction is the enemy. Stay focused.

"So," she said, in her best therapist voice, "what villain has been occupying your thoughts and dreams?"

"I'm not sure I'm ready to talk about it."

"I understand."

"That's part of what you wrote about, right? That woman—Jane—was never sure she was ready to deal with it. Had no way of knowing because who could provide a map?"

Grace nodded. Going through the motions felt good. Shrinkyshrinkshrink.

Andrew went on, "That I can absolutely relate to. Sometimes I wake up in the middle of the night thinking, This is the moment I need to . . . confront reality. Then the impulse passes and I convince myself I'm able to just forget about it."

Grace said, "Of course." The warmth in her voice surprised her. Not having to think it out. Just **being.**

Maybe Andrew picked up on her newfound confidence because his body relaxed a bit.

But his eyes had grown moist.

Grace guessed why: sudden onrush of memories.

When he spoke next, she learned she was wrong.

"It's not about me. There's a . . . moral parameter."

Grace waited.

Andrew shook his head. "Not important."

"Important enough for you to come from San Antonio."

His eyes raced to the left. The Texas bit, a lie? What else wasn't he telling her?

Everything. Of course.

She said, "Without getting into details, can you tell me about the villain?"

He thought about that. "It's not that simple."

"It never is."

"I know, I know—listen, I'm sorry." His laugh was harsh. "Another obnoxious apology, I do it too much, it's my problem." Another laugh—an angry bark, really. "One of my problems . . . anyway I'm glad I made the trip because it gave me time to think but it's just not going to work."

His hand sliced air horizontally. "Nothing to do with you, please believe that, no . . . regrets. I just . . . can't. Still not ready, I guess." He smiled. "No doubt you hear that all the time."

Trying to normalize the situation. For Grace as much as for himself. Someone who cares about others. That made it worse.

He got to his feet, face flushed. Remembering her? Tongue, legs, everything?

Grace said, "We've got time. You can **take** your time."

He shook his head violently. "Can't, sorry—there I go again. Apologizing to the damn world, like I feel I'm . . ."

"Different."

"No, no," he said, with surprising ire. "That's . . ." Impatient wave. "Everyone's different, different is meaningless, what I feel is . . . polluted."

"Makes sense," said Grace.

"Does it? Did Jane X feel polluted? Because that doesn't come out in your article, you just talk about her having to construct her own system of morality. All those steps she took to cope."

Grace said, "An article has limitations, Andrew. Why don't you sit back down, give yourself some time?"

Andrew's eyes scanned the therapy room. "You mean well. I know that. Maybe you're right and I should. But I can't. Thanks for your time. I mean that."

He strode to the door. Wrong door, the one that led back into the front waiting room, rather than toward the side-street exit.

No one around, no need to stand on ceremony. Grace got up.

He said, "I can see myself out. Please."

She held back, watched him open the door gingerly, take two steps into the waiting room before half turning and offering a slice of his pleasant, handsome, tortured face.

"Andrew?"

"I'm—would it be possible—just say no if it's not—would it be possible if tomorrow I felt that I **could** handle returning—would you be able to find some time? I understand that you're probably extremely busy, so if it doesn't work out—"

First day of her intended vacation. She said, "Of course, I'll make time for you, Andrew. As much time as you need."

"Thank you," he said. "You're . . . quite . . . I think you might be able to help me."

Blushing deeply, he escaped.

Relieved that he'd made no attempt to pay her, Grace returned to the therapy room and stood there for a long time. Hoping she'd finally return to normal but she didn't and left, trudging out to the garage.

Wondering if he **would** call.

Aware of the multiple meanings that question could evoke.

She hoped she'd see him again. Hoped she was being honest about why.

As she backed the Aston into the street, a car, a squarish sedan parked several houses up, switched on its headlights and rolled toward her.

Unusual on this quiet block, but it happened.

Still, ever watchful, the way a single woman needed to be, Grace made sure the DB7's doors were locked as she eased out and headed east.

The car remained behind her and she prepared to jackrabbit away if necessary. But then the sedan stopped for a moment, swung a three-point turn in a neighboring driveway, and reversed direction.

Grace watched its taillights diminish then vanish. Maybe she'd just seen a cop's allegedly undercover wheels, some sort of burglary stakeout, WeHo had its share of break-ins.

Or just a car with a perfectly logical reason for being there and she was letting her thoughts ooze into irrational anxiety because today had been . . . different.

New day, new dawn.

Would he call?

11

Grace's eighth birthday went unnoticed. Since the red room, she'd lived in seven foster homes. All were business ventures operated by unremarkable people lured by government money and, occasionally, the chance to feel noble.

She'd heard stories from other foster kids about disgusting men creeping into bedrooms in the middle of the night, disgusting women pretending to be unaware. One of her many roommates, an eleven-year-old girl named Brittany, lifted her blouse soon after showing up and showed Grace a lump of scar tissue she said was the result of being scalded on purpose by a foster mom.

Grace had no trouble believing that; from what she'd seen, people were capable of anything. But Brittany liked to lie, including about stupid stuff, like what she'd had for snack at school, and she also stole Grace's underwear, so Grace didn't pay much attention to her.

In three years, Grace had never been physically or sexually abused. Mostly, she was ignored and left to do what she wanted if she didn't bother anyone, because having a foster meant serious income for foster-folk and they tried to crowd as many kids as they could into their homes for as long as possible.

That didn't explain why the caseworkers kept moving Grace from house to house, but she didn't ask because she didn't care. One place was the same as another, long as they gave her time to be by herself and read.

One day a caseworker named Wayne Knutsen who'd moved her from House Six to Seven showed up and smiled uneasily.

"Guess what? Yup, sorry, kiddo."

A ponytailed, potbellied man, Wayne was always accompanied by the smell of spearmint and, sometimes, stale body odor. He wore thick glasses that made his eyes look huge and fishy. Even when he smiled, he looked nervous, and today was no exception.

Grace got ready to pack up her stuff but Wayne said, "Sit down for a sec," and when she did, he offered her a Tootsie Roll.

Grace pocketed the candy.

"Saving up for your retirement, huh?"

Grace had learned that some questions weren't meant to be answered so she just kept her mouth shut. Wayne sighed and looked sad.

"Those big old kid-eyes of yours, Ms. Grace Blades. It's like you're saying it's my fault . . . I know it's only been four months with this one—you been okay?"

Grace nodded.

"Damn. I have to tell you, moving you again, I'm feeling like a week-old pile of dog-do."

Grace didn't answer. It wasn't her job to make anyone feel better.

"Anyway, I checked your records, this'll be eight damn times. Man."

Grace sat there.

"Anyway," Wayne said again. "Well, I figure you're old enough, you might as well know how the system works. How it sucks. Are you? Old enough?"

Grace nodded.

"God, you're a quiet one . . . okay, here's how it is, kiddo: The geniuses in the state legislature—that's a place where stupid people meet and pass stupid laws because special interests pay them to do that."

Grace said, "Politicians."

Wayne said, "Yeah, you're a sharp one. So you know what I'm talking about?"

"Rich people pay other people to listen to them."

"Hey!" Wayne slapped Grace's back a bit too hard. "You really are a genius. Yeah, that's right, kiddo. So anyway, one of the laws the idiots passed gives more money to people who take in special-needs children. Know what that is?"

"Sick kids?"

"Sometimes but not necessarily. Could be sick, could be anything . . . different. I mean it makes sense on a certain level, kids can need extra help. But special needs is a tricky deal, Ms. Grace Blades. It could be something really bad—a one-legged kid, a one-eyed kid, you can see how that would be justified, they'd need special help. But the way the law's written, it gets corrupted—gets used the wrong way. Know the right doctor and you can get a kid certified as SN for anything—clumsy, just plain stupid, you name it. The point is, there's bigger bucks to be made with special needs than with regular kids and unfortunately for you, you're a regular kid."

He winked at her. "Or so I've been told. That true? You regular?"

Grace nodded.

"Quiet," he said. "Still waters . . . anyway, that's the situation, Ms. G. Blades. You're being displaced because Mr. and Mrs. Samah can up their income significantly by taking in a new available kid with a seizure disorder—know what this is? Nah, forget it, you don't need to know all this crap."

"Okay," said Grace.

"Okay?"

"I'm leaving. It's okay." She didn't like the Samahs anyway. Two boring people who kept a pair of nervous, smelly dogs, bland food and not that much of it, a bed as hard as wood. Sometimes Mrs. Samah took the time to smile but it was hard to figure out what she was smiling about.

"Indeed," said Wayne. "So let's pack up and move on."

"Where am I going?"

"Well," said Wayne, "maybe this will work out, I'm sure

aiming at that—something long term. 'Cause I've had my eye on you since I had to move you from the Kennedys after they scored a special-needs baby. A Level Five baby, which is the highest, meaning the most dough. Kid had some sort of birth defect, the Kennedys get paid to use oxygen tanks and all sorts of drugs. I mean that's okay, a baby who can't breathe needs extra attention. But I still think it sucks, why should you be penalized for being normal? And hell, even being smart doesn't help, if it did, I'd file papers for you, myself. Special needs because you're a sharp one, right?"

Grace nodded.

"But no go, that's what's crazy, kid. If you were retarded, you'd be in good shape, but there's no law benefiting smart kids, doesn't that suck? Isn't the world a suck place? Which is why you're my last case, after I move you out of here, I'm quitting and going to law school. Know why?"

Grace shook her head.

"'Course not, how could you?" Wayne winked again. Gave her another Tootsie Roll that she stashed with the first one, you never knew when you were going to be hungry.

Wayne Knutsen said, "That candy's what we call a guilt offering, kid. Anyway, I'd like to tell you I'm going to be a lawyer so I can change the system and turn water into grape juice, but I'm no better than the rest, I intend to make some serious money suing rich people and try not to think about the time I spent in the system. It was supposed to be a temporary job, anyway."

"Okay," said Grace.

"You keep saying that."

"I feel okay."

"The system's okay by you?"

"It's like animals," said Grace. "The jungle. Everyone takes care of themselves."

Wayne stared at her, emitted a low whistle. "You know there're some Level One things I was thinking of tagging you with—mostly psych stuff—emotional—whatever. Excessive dependence. But that's not you. I could've also tried excessively irritable, but that's not you, either. Then I figured why saddle you with stuff on your record, you've done this well so far, you've got a decent chance. 'Mi right?"

Grace, not sure what he was talking about, nodded, yet again.

"Good self-esteem," said Wayne. "Thought so. Anyway, even if I Level One'd you, it wouldn't have helped because this new kid, the seizures, is a Five, no way you could compete. Anyway, let's go pack your stuff. This time maybe I got a good place for you. I think. If not, sorry, I tried."

12

Andrew Toner didn't call and by nightfall, back at home, Grace felt like jumping out of her skin. Mindless TV didn't help. Neither did music, exercise, wine, or the stack of journals. Finally, she slipped under the covers shortly after one a.m., stretching her body and relaxing her limbs, hoping her brain waves would conform to her posture.

She awoke at 2:15, 3:19, 4:37, 6:09 a.m.

Interrupted sleep wasn't foreign to Grace. Because of the way she'd grown up—a variety of rooms, beds, and room-mates, including a fair share of kids who screamed in terror—her adult slumber often broke into two patterns. Most of the time, she'd sack out for eight refreshing hours, but every so often she was in and out, like a newborn. She'd come to terms with her episodic nights, as they didn't seem to con-nect to daytime events, nor did they pose a problem. She'd always found it easy to slip back into the void.

But the night after meeting Andrew Toner—the second time—was a sheet-twisting, pillow-contorting ordeal filled with taunts of drowsiness followed by stretches of wide-eyed arousal. No bad dreams, no residue of foul images. Just **up**.

By the time the sun rose, she'd long given up on REM.

Welcome to the first day of vacation.

Or maybe not, there was still time for Andrew to ask for a retry, maybe he just needed time.

To deal with **moral parameters**. Whatever that meant.

Unable to hold down much breakfast, Grace phoned her service at nine a.m. Not a single message. She was astonished at her disappointment.

Feeling as if she'd been stood up.

Dressing in sweats, she went out on the deck and checked out the beach. Plenty of dry sand, so she took an hour run up and down the entire stretch of La Costa. Returning no more settled, she made coffee, tried the service again.

Nothing, Dr. Blades.

You don't write, you don't call.

She resolved to forget the whole unfortunate episode because guilt wasn't a big part of her makeup.

So. What, now?

A stab at breakfast? Maybe just getting away would tweak her appetite. The Beach Cafe in Paradise Cove? Or Neptune's Net, at the northwestern tip of Malibu?

Both sounded fine in the abstract but she just didn't feel like it.

Suppressing the urge to try her service a third time, she stripped to panties and bra and practiced some self-defense moves, imagining terrible men coming at her, the vicious things she'd do to their eyes and their genitals and the vulnerable spot beneath their noses.

Going through the motions but unable to put any passion into it.

If some psychopath broke in now, she'd be toast.

A long shower filled a pitiable amount of time. Faced with two weeks of nothing, she still hadn't decided between hanging out at home or booking a random ticket to some pocket of luxury.

When she traveled, she nearly always found a man for a Leap.

Her stomach lurched.

No appetite for that, either.

She sat on the floor and tried to figure out what she actually **felt** like doing, ended up blank, small, hunched, a real nothing.

Not shattered; a piece of lint broken apart gradually and carried away by cruel, persistent wind.

Bad thinking, Grace. Erase erase erase, then replace.

What had she told so many patients? The key was to do **something**.

She could drive out to the range in Sylmar and practice her shooting. Not that she needed the drill, her most recent session had been three weeks ago Sunday and she'd turned the target's bland, politically correct, Caucasian head into a sieve. Her marksmanship had elicited stunned silence followed by a "Whoa" from the guy in the adjoining stall, a shaved-head, tatted-out gangbanger-type who was trying to look tough with a .357 Magnum.

Grace ignored him and demolished a second target the same way and Gangbang muttered **"Mama loca"** with a combination of loathing and admiration, then proceeded to mess up his shooting in all kinds of humiliating ways.

When she packed up her guns and left the range, he was starting to do better.

Pretending he'd never met her.

Grace had taken up shooting and serious self-defense training shortly after buying the house and the office. Finding herself alone and figuring that might be her status forever, she had no idea where to begin and had turned to Alex Delaware because she'd heard he was some sort of karate honcho, occasionally worked with the police.

She'd spotted him on campus, leaving Seeley Mudd, the psych building, in the company of two female grad students.

The three of them chatted and then the women left and Delaware kept walking, using a slow but long stride. Not an especially tall man but he moved like one. Dressed in a black turtleneck and jeans, wearing a backpack.

Grace moved into his line of vision and waved. He waved back, waited for her to reach him.

"Hi, Grace."

"Have a second?"

"Sure. What's up?"

"I'm thinking of getting into martial arts, wondered if you had any advice."

Delaware's eyes were a gray-blue that should've been cold but weren't. His pupils had dilated quickly. Serious interest but Grace didn't detect anything sexual, more like he was really thinking about the request.

He smiled. "Someone told you I'm a sensei?"

"Something like that."

"Sorry to disappoint you, I just dabble, haven't done much in a while."

"Whatever you know, I don't."

"Fair enough," he said. "Are you looking for a good workout or an actual means of defending yourself?"

"Possibly both."

A couple of undergrad girls in short-shorts passed, giggling. Both gave Delaware the once-over but he didn't notice. Guiding Grace to a shady bench across from Seeley, he said, "I don't want to pry, but I can't give you the best answer without knowing if you're concerned about a specific threat."

"I'm not," she said. "I'm living alone now and this is L.A."

Everyone knew the reason Grace was alone. Grace was sick of hearing about it and hoped Delaware wouldn't get into it and, bless him, he stayed on point: "Here's the thing about karate or any other martial arts system: It's great for exercise and personal discipline but outside of movie fight scenes, it's pretty much useless against an armed thug. So if that's your primary goal, I'd suggest you get some training in deadly assault—similar to what the Israelis do with krav maga but even rougher."

"Go-for-the-jugular stuff," said Grace.

Delaware smiled again. "The carotid's an easier target. One of many."

She said, "Sounds good. Got a referral?"

"One more thing: If you want to take it a step further, buy a gun and learn how to use it."

"Do you own a firearm?"

"I don't. But not because I used to do karate."

"You lost interest in it?"

"My teacher got old and died, I kept telling myself I'd find another dojo, finally realized I wouldn't. It's a fantastic workout, especially for balance, so one day I may get back to it. But up against a knife or a gun?" He shook his head.

"Where would I go for serious assault training?"

Removing his backpack, he took out a pad and pen, wrote down a name.

Shoshana Yaroslav.

"She's my teacher's daughter. Back when I was in training, she was just a kid. But she's grown up."

"Does she know about guns?"

"Among other things."

"Thanks, Alex."

"Anything else?"

"No, that's it."

"Hope you find what you're after," he said. "Hope you never need it."

13

By noon the serene beauty of the beach had frayed Grace's patience. An hour later, her composure was shredded, every roll of tide clenching her jaws, the tweets and snorts of shorebirds curling her hands into claws.

Locking up the house with no food in her belly and no desire to put any in there, she got in the Aston and drove north aimlessly. Speeding past Neptune's Net, she continued through the swath of state parkland dynamited decades ago to continue the highway—talk about forced entry.

As she passed the Thornhill Broome dune, an Everest of loose sand used by physical fitness types to test their endurance, she recalled something she'd seen last year: A baby seal had meandered onto the asphalt and been run over.

Maybe vacation was a bad idea; at this moment, she'd pay dearly to rescue anything.

She'd tackled the dune exactly once, avoiding small talk from the only other climber, a steroidal type who showed off by running up the near-vertical grade. Later, having completed the circuit and walking back to her car on PCH, Grace watched him slink behind his Jeep, doubled in agony as he retched and fought for breath.

The climb had winded her, too, but she had nothing to prove and that made for a nice, unruffled life.

In the end, no one cared about you.

Fifteen miles later, the coast highway split: to the west, Rice Avenue and Oxnard's strawberry fields, storage depots, and gas stations; to the east, Las Posas Road, where Camarillo's agricultural table presaged that clean, bright town. Choosing the latter, she pumped the Aston to seventy, zipped past artichokes, peppers, and tomatoes. As she neared the Camarillo business district, she slowed because this was a spot cops used to fill their quotas.

Sure enough, just past a wooden shack was a cruiser.

Grace decelerated to five miles under the limit, passed a couple of intersections before coming upon the on-ramps to the 101.

Another choice: northbound or southbound. Randomly, she chose the latter.

Big lie, the decision had been anything but random. But it took her twenty miles to realize it.

An hour after leaving her home, she was back in her office.

In the absence of human interaction, the entire cottage felt sterile and cold and that began to settle Grace down.

A safe place. Here, she determined the rules.

Here she could phone her service, yet again, and not be judged as neurotic because she was simply a responsible practitioner doing her job.

She waited an itchy five minutes before doing so, figuring she needed to test herself, the past day and a half had been . . . different.

Different required adaptation.

No message from Andrew Toner, nor from any other patient. But a Detective Henke had left a 213 number for call-back.

"Did he say what it was about?" Grace asked the operator.

"No, Doctor. And he's a she."

She Googled Henke, found no Facebook, just a single citation in a three-year-old **Daily News** piece on a North Hollywood Division gang bust. Detective Elaine Henke termed the arrests "the culmination of extended teamwork on the parts of LAPD, the district attorney, and the county sheriffs."

Henke had probably been chosen to talk to the press because she was dependable, media-friendly, knew how to speak bureaucratese.

Three years ago, she'd worked North Hollywood. Today, she'd left a downtown number.

Probably a referral. The only people Grace knew downtown were the occasional prosecutor or D.A.'s secretary who asked her to see patients.

Sorry, Detective, I'm on vacation.

Or not. Let's hear what Elaine has to say.

She called the number. A girlish pleasant voice said, "Detective Henke."

"This is Dr. Grace Blades returning your call."

"Doctor, thanks for getting back to me." Suddenly serious.

"If this is a referral, I was planning to be out of the office for two weeks. But if it's an emergency—"

"Actually," said Henke, "I called about a homicide that I picked up last night downtown—early morning, actually. The victim's a white male, early to midthirties with no identification, which is the worst thing for us. That's where I'm hoping you can help us, Doctor. When they got him to the morgue and undressed him they found one of your business cards in his left shoe."

"His shoe," said Grace, fighting to keep her voice even.

"Odd, no? Does that physical description mean anything to you?"

The queasy, vertiginous waves that had gnawed Grace since last night were replaced with new discomfort: a sudden, piercing stab of . . . despair?

Reality catching up with the signals her body had been giving her.

Fighting to sound unruffled, she said, "Can you tell me more than that?"

"Hmm, okay," said Henke. "Hold on . . . brown hair, blue

eyes, wearing a Harris Tweed sport coat and khaki pants . . .
brown shoes. Kind of generic, Doctor, but I'm afraid that's
it. If only everyone had tattoos."

Grace said, "I can't be sure." **Oh, yes, I can!** "He might be
a patient I saw yesterday evening."

"Name?"

"If it's not him, I'm bound by confidentiality."

"Hmm," said Henke. "I could email you a photo right
now. I promise to pick one of the . . . easier ones. You can
stay on the line. Up for that, Doctor?"

"Sure." Grace gave her the address.

Moments later, the terrible truth flashed on her screen.
Close-up of Andrew's handsome face, slackened and grayed
by death. No blood, no obvious wounds, maybe the bad
stuff was beneath his neckline.

She said, "The name he gave me was Andrew Toner. He
said he was from San Antonio, Texas."

"He said? You have reason to doubt him?"

**Well, his real name could be Roger. Or Beano. Or
Rumpelstiltskin.** "No . . . I'm just . . . thrown by this. I
saw him last night at six p.m. He left around fifteen minutes later."

"That's kind of a short session, no?" said Henke. "For
a psychologist, I mean. Unless it was just to dole out
medication—but no, you don't do that, that's for psychia-
trists, right?"

"Mr. Toner left the session early."

"May I ask why?"

"It was a first session, that kind of thing happens."

"Did he make a second appointment?"

All business, Elaine. "No."

"From Texas," said Henke. "That's pretty far to come for
therapy."

"It is."

"What else can you tell me about Mr. Toner?"

"Unfortunately, that's it."

"He's dead, Doctor, you don't need to worry about confidentiality."

"It's not that," said Grace. "As I said, I only met him once and not for very long."

Twice, really, but no sense getting into that, Elaine.

Though cradled by her desk chair, Grace felt her balance give way. Her head wobbled, unmoored, like overripe fruit swaying on a flimsy stalk. She clamped one hand on her desktop to steady herself.

"Well," said Henke, "at this point you're all I've got so would you mind if we chatted a bit further? I'm in the neighborhood."

The murder had taken place downtown. Why would Henke be in West Hollywood? Unless she considered Grace—what did the police call it—a person of interest?

Last person to see Andrew alive. Of course she did.

Or was it something Grace had said? Hadn't said. Had her voice, despite her best efforts, betrayed the turmoil coursing through her?

Or maybe Henke was just thorough.

Grace said, "Sure, I could see you right now."

"Um," said Henke. "How about in an hour, Doctor?"

In the neighborhood, indeed.

As soon as Henke hung up, Grace phoned the Beverly Opus and put on her own version of a chirpy Cal-Gal voice.

"Andrew Toner, please."

The desk clerk clicked an unseen mouse. "Sorry, no one by that name is registered."

"Are you sure?"

"I am, miss."

"Oh, geez, how can that be? He said he'd be there—the Beverly Opus."

"I don't know what to tell you, miss—"

"Wow," she said. "Oh, yeah, sometimes Andy uses his nickname. Roger."

"I searched using the surname, miss," said the clerk. "It wouldn't make a difference."

"This is weird. Did he maybe check in a few days ago and leave early for some reason? Why didn't he tell me? I'm supposed to pick him up for the reunion."

"Hold on." Click click. Muffled voices. "No one by that name has been here, miss."

"Okay . . . there are other hotels near where you are, right?"

"This is Beverly Hills," said the clerk and he hung up.

Andrew Roger Roger Andrew.

Grace had assumed he was staying at the Opus but obviously he'd just dropped in to . . . have a drink? A confidence-building snort before tomorrow's therapy when he'd be dealing with **moral parameters**?

He'd ended up with much more than booze.

Roger, the engineer. If the name was false, the same could apply to the occupation. Ditto a flight from Texas.

Was anything he told her true? Who'd been played?

But she remembered his shock at seeing her in her office, no one could act that well. So the part about having a problem was likely valid. And the fact that he'd been spurred by the Jane X article clarified the problem: a criminally dangerous murderous relative.

Moral parameters . . . not a blast from the past, something ongoing. A tortured, internal debate about whether or not to go public.

And now he was dead.

Just to make sure he hadn't learned about her some other way, Grace did something she found abhorrent: Googled herself. All that came up were academic citations, not a single image, lending credence to at least part of Andrew's story.

She thought about the geography of his last living day.

Drinks in B.H., therapy in West Hollywood.

Death downtown. For as long as Grace could recall, the district underwent development that seemed to end up overly optimistic. Despite Staples Center, converted lofts, yuppie condos, and bars, huge swaths of downtown L.A. remained bleak and dangerous as soon as rush hour ended and the streets were commandeered by armies of homeless schizophrenics, criminal illegals, addicts, dealers, and the like.

Had Andrew, new to the city, simply wandered into the wrong area and come up against a psychotic obeying a command hallucination?

Pitiful, dingy way to die.

Or did his murder indeed relate to his moral quest, best intentions and all?

An eddy of curiosity whipped up in Grace's gut, displacing some of her anxiety.

If Henke made good on that one-hour prediction, fifty-one minutes remained before Grace met her first homicide detective.

Meanwhile . . . a bracing walk around the neighborhood would kill some time but she felt oddly disinclined to move. She tried catching up on journal articles but couldn't focus.

Andrew Toner.

Something about the name bothered her but she couldn't figure out what until her eyes drifted to her date book. The notation she'd made regarding his appointment, followed by the phone number he'd given her exchange.

A. Toner. Viewed as a collection of letters, the answer was obvious.

Atoner.

A man seeking expiation.

What Detective Elaine Henke would consider a clue.

Grace decided not to mention it to Henke. She'd come across weirdly over-involved, turn herself into a person of greater interest.

Atoner.

What was your sin, Andrew? Or have you taken on someone else's iniquity?

Given what we did in the parking lot, do I really want to
know?

Ignorance could truly be bliss. But she called the number
he'd left, anyway.

Not in service.

14

By the time Grace's meager belongings were packed in Wayne the caseworker's car, the sun was sinking and graying the Valley, making everything look heavy, almost liquid.

He started up the engine and looked back at her. "You okay?"

Grace nodded.

"Can't hear you, kid."

"M'okay."

When Grace got moved from foster to foster, the trip was usually short—bounces from one small nondescript house to another. This time Wayne got on the freeway and drove for a long time.

Grace hoped that didn't mean a big change, some sort of special place. All she wanted was people feeding her and leaving her alone so she could think and read and imagine.

She was still hoping for all that when Wayne got off the freeway and she read the exit sign and a pain started high up in her belly. It had been a long time but the sign shone through the enveloping darkness and she remembered: The few times Dodie or Ardis had taken her out of the single-wide, this was the way they'd come back home.

She cracked her window, let in dust and heat and diesel fuel. The sun was gone now but you could still see things and they pricked her memory, too: The fringy tops of those wrinkled plants with their gray leaves. Discarded oil drums and other metal stuff heaped in piles off the side of the road.

Desert, miles of it.

And now Wayne had turned off onto a road that made

Grace's heart pound. A sign pointed the way to **Desert Dreams**. If he wasn't going so fast, she would've tried to jump out of the car.

Even though she couldn't escape, she imagined it. Balling her hands into fists so she could punch Wayne on the back of his fat neck, make him stop.

The desert. How long could she survive by herself?

Not long, no place to hide. Unless she could make it all the way to the mountains. But maybe it was worse up there, she had no idea, she'd never been.

All she had on was a Disneyland T-shirt, shorts, sneakers. Up in the mountains it could probably get real cold, even in the summer.

She knew that because sometimes when Dodie used to complain about living in a damn oven, Grace could see snow atop the mountains.

It was too dark to tell if there was snow, all Grace could see were the outlines of the mountains, big and sharp.

Like knives.

Wayne said, "Almost there. How ya doin'?"

Terrible, you stupid caseworker.

Grace said, "Okay."

"A little nervous, huh? That's natural, new surroundings. Tell the truth, kid, I don't know how any of you do it, the constant shuffling—being moved around." He chuckled. "Shuffled like cards in a deck. Come to think about it, it is kind of like a game of chance."

Grace stared at the back of his neck. Spotted a pimple to the side of his ponytail. If she used her nail to flick it, the pain might be enough to . . .

Then she realized he hadn't turned toward Desert Dreams, this was a road she'd never seen. Skinnier, real dark, and Wayne was muttering something about "out in the boonies" and making his headlights brighter, turning the area in front of the car into a cold, white tube.

Dust flew up from the tires, like upside-down rain. The sand stretched forever.

Why was he **taking** her here?

Now a different kind of fear crawled into her belly and kept going, lodging in her throat.

Was he one of **those**?

She searched for some detail to remember. It took a long time before anything rose above the desert. But then: A big yard of metal garbage. Broken-up trucks. Part of an old bus, too. Heaps of wheels and metal grilles and things that looked like metal branches.

As soon as the junkyard was gone, a fenced area that said **Water Station: No Admittance.**

Grace put one hand on her seat belt clasp so she could undo it fast if she needed to.

Wayne was fat, Grace figured she could outrun him.

He began to hum off-key.

All of a sudden more buildings appeared outside Grace's window. A trailer park just like Desert Dreams, this one was called Antelope Palms but with no palms or any other kind of plant around. To her surprise, she was happy seeing the mobiles.

Wayne kept driving and humming louder. More open space followed by another mobile park. And another. Brightly lit signs chewing their way through the darkness.

Sunrise Motor Estates.

Morningview Motorhaven.

Okay, so she'd end up somewhere like Desert Dreams, but without the memories . . . okay, that would be okay.

Despite telling herself that, she shuddered. Hugged herself tight and tried not to be sick.

Time for good thoughts, she'd been practicing that in order to drive out bad ones, it was hard but she was getting better at it.

Okay. Breathe. Think good . . . maybe her new fosters

would live in a double-wide with a real bed for her . . . maybe there'd be a big enough refrigerator so she wouldn't have to wait for scraps. Maybe—Wayne made a sudden turn and got on **another** road, this one really, really bumpy.

They were getting closer to the mountains.

Nothing out here but more of those fringy trees—Grace suddenly remembered what they were called. Joshuas, they were passing through kind of a forest of Joshuas—another turn, then another, and bigger trees appeared—now there **were** palms and some roundish ones with clusters of small leaves.

The road had turned straight and less bumpy and Wayne had stopped humming.

A gate appeared up ahead. He braked smoothly, slid to a stop. The gate was connected to metal fencing, like for a horse corral, but there were no horses Grace could see.

Maybe they were in a barn or something, asleep.

Above the gate was a spotlight that shone on a wooden plaque. Burned in the wood was cursive lettering.

Stagecoach Ranch

This caseworker was taking her to be a cowgirl?

He idled the car, got out, swung the gate open, returned to the driver's seat. "Pretty cool, no? I figure everything you been through, you deserve something better, kiddo. Guess what this place was used for back in the day?"

Grace said, "Animals?"

"Good answer but even better, Ms. Grace Blades. This was a film ranch, they used it to shoot movies." He laughed. "Who knows, you might even come across some memorabilia— that means old interesting stuff."

He drove through the gateway. Up ahead was a house, bigger than Grace had ever seen except in books. Two stories high, wide as two normal houses, with white wooden boards running along the front and up three steps, a front porch that tilted to one side.

Wayne whistled through his teeth. "Home sweet home, kiddo."

He gave a short honk. A woman came out of the house drying a dish with a towel. Old and small, she had white hair that hung below her waist, a sharp nose that reminded Grace of a bird, and skinny arms that moved fast as she kept up the drying.

Wayne got out and held out his hand for a shake. The woman barely touched his fingers and resumed her towel work. "You're a bit late, amigo."

"Yeah, sorry."

"Heck," said the woman, "it's not as if I'm booked with appointments." She approached the car, moving nimbly despite her age. Stooping, but not too much because she was short, didn't have to lower herself a lot to gaze through the window.

Peering at Grace, she made a rotary motion that Grace figured meant, "Roll it down."

She obeyed and the old woman studied her. "You're a pretty thing, aren't you? Nice to have both—brains and looks. I'm telling you that from personal experience." She laughed like a younger woman. "So what do you like to be called?"

"Grace."

"Simple enough. I'm Ramona Stage and for the most part you can stick with Ramona. When I get grumpy—it does happen, I'm human—you might try Mrs. Stage. But mostly Ramona'll be fine. Okay?"

"Okay."

"Get your stuff, I'll show you your room."

The house was even bigger inside, with heavy, dark furniture everywhere and wood-plank walls covered with paintings of flowers and photos of a man—the same man, over and over—in a fancy black shirt and white cowboy hat. Grace didn't have a chance to notice more; she was hurrying up the stairs after Ramona Stage, who'd grabbed Grace's bags and was moving like she was weightless.

At the top was a wide, brown-carpeted landing with six doors. The air smelled of tomato soup and maybe some kind of laundry detergent.

"That," said Ramona, pointing to the nearest door, "is my bedroom. Door's open, you can knock. If I say 'okay' or 'enter' or 'come in' or something along those lines, you can come in. You find the door closed, don't even try. That room at the far end is a linen closet. The one next to it is the bathroom. I've got my own so it's just for the kids. That leaves three bedrooms for the kids and right now I got two little ones in the left-hand room, one by himself over there, he's got special circumstances. All boys, but that could change. Meanwhile, you, being the only female, get your own space, which is something I can't always promise. Obviously it's going to be the smallest room. That seem unfair to you?"

Grace shook her head.

Ramona said, "You don't like to talk? Fine, a shake or a nod works just as well. Long as we have an understanding: No matter how you feel, I always try to be fair. Not just with kids, I treat everyone the same, big shots, kids, plain old working folk."

She waited.

Grace said nothing.

"Catch my drift, Grace? Whether it's Gary Cooper or the guy who comes to do my roof, they're the same. Get it?"

"Yes, ma'am."

Ramona Stage laughed and slapped her knee. "Look at that, a voice issues forth. I actually knew Gary Cooper and he never expected special treatment. Know what I'm talking about?"

"He's a movie star but okay."

Ramona's head cocked backward. "You have no idea who Gary Cooper was, do you? Someone your age never seen his movies."

Grace shook her head. "I just figured."

"Ah, good thinking," said Ramona, looking Grace up and down. "Makes sense, given what I've been told about you."

Heavy footsteps sounded. Wayne's meaty face appeared at the top of the stairs, then the rest of him.

"We're doing great," said Ramona.

"Terrific, Mrs. S. If I could have a word with Gracie."

No one called her Gracie. He hadn't until now.

No sense arguing.

Ramona said, "I'll take her stuff to her room and you can say your au revoirs." Opening the door to the smallest room, she stepped in.

Wayne said, "Like it?"

"Yes."

He drummed his fingers on his thigh. Like he was waiting for more.

Grace said, "Thanks."

"You're welcome, Gracie. And listen, you got a real good chance of sticking around here because she doesn't do it for the money, I'm not really sure why she does it, she's well-heeled—that means she has her own dough. Okay?"

"Okay," said Grace, not sure what she was agreeing to.

"Only problem is, if it **doesn't** work out, and I can't see any reason it wouldn't, but if it doesn't, you can't call me because as I told you, I'm leaving the department."

"I know."

"Good . . . anyway, I wanted to end on a positive note," said Wayne. "Doing something for you that can't always be done. You're really smart, kid. Given some breaks, you could make something of yourself."

"You, too," said Grace.

"Me?"

"Being a lawyer. You'll make more money."

Wayne gaped. "You really listen, don't you?"

Not the last time Grace would hear that.

Ramona Stage and Grace watched Wayne drive away. "That one's a total bleeding heart, but at least he tries. Okay, to your quarters, young lady, it's past bedtime."

The room was narrow, like a closet you could walk into. A single dormer window draped with white muslin let in nothing of the night. The roof sloped sharply and Mrs. Stage pointed that out and said, "Your size, you'll be okay unless you sit up too sharp in bed, but in general be careful not to bean your noggin, your noggin's the most important thing God gave you."

Grace's eyes were already fixed on the bed. Bigger than any she'd ever slept in, with a brass headboard that had turned greenish brown. Two big pillows in pink flowery cases were plumped against the board, each dimpled in the middle. The bedspread was pink with white stripes and looked new. A metal rack near the window served as hanging space. A two-drawer oak dresser sufficed for what Mrs. Stage called "foldables."

She and Grace put away Grace's things and a few times Mrs. Stage refolded something Grace had thought she'd done a good job with.

That done, she walked Grace out to the shared bathroom and sniffed. "Those boys, for the life of them they can't aim."

Grace smelled nothing but she kept that to herself. Ramona Stage said, "Brush your teeth good," and waited as Grace complied.

"Thorough brushing, excellent. Always take care of the body you've been gifted with. Now to bed."

But before they reached the smallest room, Ramona stopped Grace with a finger and cracked the door of the room where the one boy slept and stuck her head in.

Grace heard a faint hissing noise, like a tire losing air.

Ramona closed the door softly. "Okay. Want me to tuck you in?"

"I'm okay."

"I'll do it, anyway."

Tucking in consisted of ordering Grace to get under the covers and "arrange your pillows the way you like, then make sure to think pleasant thoughts because, trust me, life's too short for disconsolate thoughts."

The linens smelled sweet, like Grace was lying in a flower bed. Ramona Stage turned off the light and Grace drew the covers up to her chin. Now, with the room all dark, something **did** filter through the muslin curtains.

Moonglow, satiny silver, lighting on Ramona Stage's face as she stood in the doorway. It gave her a softness, as if she'd turned younger.

She returned to the bed. "You can do what you want but I suggest this for ultimate comfort," she said, and folded the covers down, creating a neat flap that bisected Grace's chest. Positioning Grace's hands atop her tummy, with the fingertips barely touching, she said, "You're making a letter V, see? As in you've got value. Something to think about, Grace. Now you go ahead and sleep perfectly."

To Grace's surprise, she did.

Despite the place's history as a ranch, Ramona kept no animals. "First the horses went, then the goats, then the geese. Finally, the chickens, because I got the cholesterol and went off eggs. The dogs I kept until they passed naturally."

It was six o'clock on Grace's first morning at Stagecoach Ranch. When she peeked out her bedroom door, Ramona was out on the landing, dressed in a plaid shirt, jeans, and flat shoes, her long white hair braided and coiled atop her head. One hand held a coffee cup, as if she'd been waiting for Grace to make an appearance. The two of them went downstairs to the kitchen, where Ramona drank the coffee and Grace had orange juice and some toast.

"You're sure no eggs or meats?"

"No, thank you."

"Not a big breakfast gal, huh? Suit yourself but you may change your mind."

The kitchen was huge, with a view of the mountains. The appliances were white and looked old. Over a mail table hung another photo of that same man in the fancy shirt and the cowboy hat, older than Grace remembered from last night, with a fuller face.

Ramona Stage said, "So no more dogs. You like dogs?"

"Never had one."

"I've had tons of them, they're as individual as people." She got up, pulled something out of a drawer, showed it to Grace. Faded photo of two big, sorry-looking mutts stretched on the house's front porch. "That one's Hercules, didn't live up to his name, the other's Jody, got him from a film crew, sometimes he ate his own poop, you could never predict when, which only made matters worse. After they both went off to doggie heaven, I figured I'd get at least one more because this is a big place to have with nothing else around that's breathing. But then I got to liking not having to deal with issues so the only zoology you're going to see here now are unwanted pests like mice and rats, possum and ground squirrels and skunks. For which I got a man named Ed Gonzales to spray regularly. I'm telling you this so should you come across a skinny Mexican man with strange equipment and he seems to be lurking around, you won't be scared."

"Okay."

Ramona studied her. "Toast too well done?"

The toast tasted like cardboard. Grace said, "It's good," and ate some as proof.

"I'll bet not much scares you, am I right?"

"I guess." Grace's eyes drifted to the man in the cowboy hat.

"Who do you think that is?"

"Your husband?"

Ramona's eyes danced. Grace noticed their color for the first time. Brown so dark it verged on black. "You are a smart one. Though I guess it's the logical assumption seeing as I've got him all over the place and I'm too old for a teenage crush."

More young-woman laughter. Then Ramona's lower lip quivered and she blinked. She flashed white teeth, as if to prove she was happy.

Grace said, "He was a cowboy?"

"He sure liked to think he was. He also fancied himself an actor and he did do a few B oaters—that means not-so-famous western movies, back when westerns were the thing. You ever see a western?"

Grace shook her head.

"He made fourteen," said Ramona, glancing at the photo. "But he was no Gary Cooper, so finally he got smart and bought this place and started renting it out to big-shot directors and we made a fine living. His movie name was Steve Stage. Think that was his real name?"

Grace shook her head.

"Correct," said Ramona. "But he made it his real name, legally and all, by the time I met him he was Steve Stage so I was Mrs. Stage. In fact, he didn't tell me different until we were driving to Las Vegas, that's where we got married, it was kind of a quick thing."

She smiled. "Fifty miles before we get to Vegas, he's already given me the ring and I say sure, so he probably figured he could risk telling me."

She showed Grace her hand. A shiny chip glinted in a white metal setting, bright and smooth against dry, weathered skin.

"Pretty," said Grace.

"Pawnshop find," said Ramona. "Place near the studio—Paramount, that's in Hollywood. Anyway, fifty miles away, he decides to tell me. Not just his name, his whole family, where he's from, the works. Guess where he was from."

"Texas."

"Good guess, dear. And totally wrong. New York City. Turns out the hunk of desperado I knew as Steve Stage was really Sidney Bluestone. What do you think of that?"

Grace shrugged.

Ramona said, "He figured—rightly so—that Sidney Bluestone wouldn't find much employment in oaters, so off to court he went and voilà, Steve Stage. When I wanted to kid him, I'd call him Sid from Brooklyn. He was good-natured about it but it wasn't his favorite thing. Remembering can be hard."

She looked at Grace.

Grace didn't feel like smiling but she did.

"Anyway, let's talk about your schooling," said Ramona. "Wayne Knutsen told me your history, moving around but mostly going to the same school because all those other people lived close to each other. Unfortunately, we got a problem: You're too far from that school now. From any school, period, because the city bus won't come out here and the county's not ponying up for private transportation. I'd drive and pick you up but it's just me and Maria-Luz, that's the woman who cleans, and we both need to be here. Top of that, she doesn't drive, her husband drops her off and picks her up. If you were a little younger, we'd be okay. There's a preschool over in Desert Dreams, a trailer park, which is where the two boys go, but it's basically some woman, nothing educational. So we have a problem. You like school?"

When no one bothers me and I can learn.

Not wanting Ramona Stage to feel bad, Grace said, "It's okay."

"So no big deal. Your IQ, you're most likely way ahead of grade anyway, most of what you learned you probably taught yourself. Am I right?"

Now Grace's smile was real. "Yes, ma'am."

"So what I'm thinking is we go for homeschooling. I already applied and it was no big deal. Basically we get books and lesson plans and do it ourselves. I went to college, got a degree from Cal State, so I figure I can handle fourth-, fifth-grade material, even math, though I kind of taper off at algebra. What do you think?"

Books and being alone; it sounded like heaven. Unable to believe it, Grace said, "I just read?"

"A lot of it will be reading but you'll also have to do exercises and take tests just like if you were in a real school and I have to grade everything. I'm not going to cheat, you get what you earn. You up for that?"

"Yes, ma'am."

"I figure it'll be easy once I know your level. To do that, I'm bringing in an expert to test you. A kind of doctor, but not the kind who gives shots or touches your body or anything like that, he'll just ask you questions."

"A psychologist."

Ramona's white eyebrows rose, clouds lofted by a breeze. "You know about psychologists?"

Grace nodded.

"Might I ask how?"

"Sometimes kids would have problems—in the other fosters—and they'd get sent to the psychologist."

"You're making it sound like punishment."

The kids who'd talked about it made it sound that way.

Grace was silent.

Ramona said, "Other kids."

Grace knew what she was getting at. "I never got sent."

"You have any other notions about psychologists?"

"No."

"Well this one, he's not going to be like punishment. I'm not talking through my hat, I know him as a person, not just a doctor. He's my husband's baby brother but that's not why

I picked him. He's a professor, Grace. That means he teaches people to be psychologists, so we're talking a top-of-the-line expert."

Ramona waited.

Grace nodded.

"His name is Dr. Malcolm Bluestone, Ph.D., and let me tell you, he's smart."

Ramona flashed another easy smile. "Maybe even as smart as you, young lady."

Soon after she'd finished her toast, Grace met the two boys who shared one room. Both were black and she knew they were five years old because Ramona had told her.

"They look alike but they're cousins, not brothers, have had hard lives, you don't want to know, I'm hoping their adoption goes through."

Grace couldn't see any resemblance between the boys. Rollo was much taller than DeShawn and his skin was lighter. Both entered the kitchen appearing sleepy. Rollo held on to a ragged blue blanket. DeShawn looked as if he would've liked something to hold.

"Rise and shine, troopers," said Ramona. She made the introductions. The cousins nodded absently at Grace and took chairs at the table. DeShawn managed a shy smile and Grace pretended she hadn't seen it.

The boys spread napkins on their laps and waited as Ramona set out scrambled eggs, sausage patties and links. They ate silently, began to wake up.

Ramona said, "You three are okay down here, right? Time to see how Bobby's doing."

The mention of Bobby's name caused Rollo and DeShawn to exchange a quick, nervous look. Ramona left and the kitchen turned silent. Grace had nothing to do so she just sat there. The boys ignored her and continued to eat, slowly but without pause, like robots. The eggs looked stiff and rubbery and Grace already knew what Ramona's toast tasted like. None of that gave the cousins pause and Grace wondered if they'd never gotten over feeling hungry.

It had been a while since she'd been hungry but you didn't forget that kind of thing.

She turned away from the cousins and looked up through the kitchen window over the sink. One of those roundish trees with the small leaves stood a few feet away from the glass.

Grace got up to have a closer look.

To her back, Ramona's voice, "California oak, water them too much, they die."

She hadn't heard the old woman enter, felt as if she'd been caught doing something wrong.

Turning, she saw Ramona holding the hand of a different-looking boy.

Small—no taller than DeShawn—he had the face of an older child, maybe even a teenager, with pimples and a large jaw and a shelf-like forehead that shadowed squinty eyes set crookedly, one a good quarter inch higher than the other. Curly red hair was thin in spots, like that of an old man. His mouth hung open in some kind of smile but Grace wasn't sure that meant he was happy. Widely spaced yellow teeth were separated by an oversized tongue. His body—sunken and bowed—swayed, as if he needed to move to stop from falling. Even though Ramona held his hand tightly.

Grace realized she was staring. Realized the cousins weren't.

She looked away, too.

The new boy—Bobby—gave a raspy laugh. Once again, it was hard to call that happy.

Ramona Stage said, "Bobby, this is Grace, she's eight and a half, so you're still the oldest." She patted Bobby's head. He smiled again, swayed more violently, let out a single loud cough, then bent double as a coughing fit overtook him.

Rollo and DeShawn stared down at their plates.

Ramona said, "Poor Bobby had a rough night, even with the oxygen."

Rollo said something.

"What's that, dear?"

"I'm sorry."

"For . . ."

"Him being sick."

"Well, that's kind of you, darling. And gentlemanly, Rollo, I'm extremely proud of you."

Rollo bobbed his head.

Grace thought of the hiss when Ramona had peeked in on Bobby. Oxygen. So he had some kind of breathing problem, but he looked like that wasn't all of his problems.

She studied Bobby's eyes. His irises were a strange yellow-brown and they seemed coated with something waxy.

She smiled.

He smiled back. This time, he seemed kind of happy.

15

Seventy-three minutes after her phone call from Detective Elaine Henke, the green light in the therapy room lit up.

Grace waited a couple of minutes before cracking the waiting room door. She kept an assortment of periodicals in a wall rack, covering topics from fashion to home renovation and she found it interesting, sometimes instructive, to note what patients chose to read.

The woman in the corner armchair had opted for **Car and Driver.** The new Corvettes.

"Doctor? Eileen Henke." She got up and placed the magazine in the rack. Firm dry handshake.

Forty-five or so, the detective was short and wide, packed tight like a gymnast easing into middle age. Her complexion was clear, a rosy backdrop for unremarkable features. An ash-blond bob did a decent job of firming her jawbone, lending a roundish face some definition. Her pantsuit was beige, her shoes were black, her purse a patchwork of both those colors.

A gold badge was clipped to the breast pocket of her jacket. The garment had been tailored loosely, probably to hide the bulge of the gun holstered near her left breast. Nice try but not quite. Or maybe cops liked reminding you they were armed.

Too-curious almost-hazel brown eyes pretended not to surveil; Grace knew when she was being x-rayed.

"Please come in, Detective."

"Elaine's really okay."

Only if we're buddies. I don't have buddies.

. . .

Henke said, "Never been in a psychologist's office before."

She'd settled in the chair facing Grace's desk, was taking in Grace's degrees and certificates.

"Always a first time, Detective."

Henke chuckled. "Thanks for meeting with me on such short notice."

"Of course. This is a terrible thing. Do you have any idea who killed Mr. Toner?"

"Unfortunately no, Doctor. And Andrew Toner may not be his real name."

That was quick. "Really?"

"Well," said Henke, "he told you he was from San Antonio but we haven't been able to find anyone by that name in San Antonio. We did find some Andrew Toners in other Texan cities but they have no connection to him."

Grace said, "I don't know why he'd give me a false name."

"You're sure about San Antonio."

"He contacted me through my service and they're generally accurate. More than that, he gave this number for callback." She handed Henke the ten digits she'd punched three-quarters of an hour ago.

"Two-ten area code," said Henke.

"It's San Antonio, all right," said Grace. "Unfortunately, it's out of service."

"You tried it?"

"I was curious."

Henke's eyes washed over Grace's impassive face. Producing a cellphone, she tried the number, frowned, clicked off. "Well, thanks anyway, Doctor. I might be able to trace it back to something useful."

She slipped the paper into a jacket pocket. "Okay, back to what I asked you before: traveling a distance for therapy, you didn't find that strange?"

"Not typical but not strange. In my practice it occurs more than you might think."

"Why is that, Doctor?"

"I treat victims of trauma and their loved ones. That can draw people from a wide area."

Henke smiled. "Because you're the best?"

"I'd love to see it that way, but it's probably because I specialize. And many of my cases are short-term, so travel becomes less of an issue."

"You get them over the rough spots quickly."

"I do my best."

"Trauma," said Henke. "Are we talking like PTSD?"

"That can be part of it, Detective."

"What's the rest of it?"

"Obviously I can't get into specific patients, but often they're crime victims or relatives of victims, people who've been in devastating accidents, lost loved ones to diseases."

"Sounds pretty intense," said Henke.

"I'm sure that also applies to your job, Detective."

"True. So, Mr. Toner—let's call him that until we know different—went through something really hairy or knew someone who did and maybe flew all the way from Texas to get therapy. Be nice to know what his trauma was."

Grace said, "I might be able to help you a bit with that. Years ago I published a paper on the psychological effects of being related to a murderer. Based on a patient I knew. Andrew Toner cited that article when he showed up. Unfortunately, when I probed for specifics, he aborted the session."

"Aborted?"

"He grew anxious and left."

"Anxious about what, Doctor?"

"I wish I could tell you."

Henke ticked her fingers. "Flew in, freaked out, flew the coop."

" 'Freaked out' is too strong," said Grace. "He grew uncomfortable."

"That happen a lot with your patients? People change their minds?"

"In my business, anything can happen."

Henke digested that. "How long was he actually here?"

"Just a few minutes—I'd estimate ten, fifteen."

"Long enough for you to remember what he was wearing."

"I try to be observant."

"Well, that's good. So what else did you observe about him?"

"He seemed like a nice man with something on his mind."

Henke slid a bit lower in her chair. Making herself comfortable, as if settling down for the long haul. "Any idea why he'd keep your business card in his shoe?"

"None. Sounds like he was hiding the fact that he was seeking therapy."

"Like from someone he was traveling with? He mention traveling with anyone?"

Grace shook her head.

Henke said, "And you have no idea what specifically made him anxious?"

When he recognized me as the chick he'd . . .

"No, I'm sorry."

"He got defensive and flew the coop," said Henke.

Persistent woman. Good trait for a detective. Unpleasant when you were the object of her snooping.

Grace said, "I wish I could tell you more."

Henke reached into her patchwork bag and pulled out a notepad. Flipping a page, then another, she said, "Don't want to take up too much of your time but it's the details you miss that end up coming back to bite you."

"I understand."

Henke read some more, closed the pad. "I keep coming back to that card in the shoe. Never seen that before, I mean that's pretty cloak and dagger, no?"

"It is."

"And now you're telling me this guy might be a relative of some murderer—do you have that paper you wrote, by the way? Sounds interesting."

"Not at hand, but here's the reference." Grace recited and Henke copied.

Grace said, "May I ask a question about the murder?"

Henke looked up. "If it's something I can answer, I will."

"On the photo you showed me, there were no wounds."

"How did he die? Multiple stabbing to the body. That's one reason what you told me sounds interesting—some low-life relative. Because this was what we call overkill. More wounds than necessary to effect death."

"Something personal," said Grace.

"Exactly, Doctor." But Henke's eyes had hardened and Grace figured she might've overstepped. "If Mr. Toner really was related to a serious bad guy, overkill could make sense. Especially if Mr. Toner was considering ratting him out."

Trying to put distance between himself and the object of his dread. Good reason to fly in from another city.

Grace said, "Poor man."

Henke shifted her pad from hand to hand, scanned several more pages. "Or I'm barking up the wrong tree and poor Mr. Andrew Toner was in the wrong place at the wrong time . . . you mentioned being gone for a couple of weeks."

"Vacation."

"Planned a while ago?"

"No specific plans, I just try to take off in order to recharge the batteries."

"Where you planning to recharge?"

Grace smiled. "I'm open to suggestions."

"Hmm," said Henke. "I like Hawaii."

"I'll consider it."

"So no plans yet, but the office will be closed."

"It will."

"Mr. Toner knew that but still made an appointment."

"He was informed but still wanted to come in."

"That says to me he might've intended it to be a one-shot deal."

"Good point."

"Is there anything else you can recall about him, Doctor? The slightest detail."

Grace pretended to ponder. Shook her head. "I'm sorry."

"Nasty business," said Henke. "The homeless guy who found him was pretty freaked out—oh, did you happen to see what Mr. Toner was driving?"

"I didn't walk him out to the street."

"Why would you?" Henke returned the pad to her bag and stood. "I'm just grasping, Doctor. Thanks again for your time. If you think of anything, even if it seems minor, please call me."

I've thought of plenty. "Atoner," for starts. Would Henke figure it out? Grace imagined the detective's reaction if Grace revealed the discovery.

Really, Doctor. You figured that out. Impressive.

A woman paid to see the worst in everyone would view any gift with suspicion.

Grace walked Henke to the mouth of the waiting room, hung back and let her reach the door by herself.

"Good luck, Detective—Elaine."

Henke said, "Doctor, I'm gonna need it."

16

Parting the drapes an inch, Grace watched Henke drive away in a white Taurus, then returned to the therapy room. The space felt different, no longer trustworthy, as if a security code had been breached.

In a sense, it had: This was the first time she'd sat behind her desk, backed by her diplomas and certificates, and been treated as anything other than an expert.

More than that: She had no idea if the meeting with Henke had freed her of this . . . this . . . mess. Did the detective still consider her "of interest"?

Had she made matters worse? Planned vacation but no plans? Objectively, it sounded odd. How could anyone, let alone a cop, understand the way she lived?

The big risk was Henke somehow finding out that a dark-haired man wearing tweed and khakis had left the Opus lounge arm in arm with a slim, chestnut-haired woman.

Remote probability, but not zero. Because lacking a real lead, someone like Henke—probably competent but not brilliant, choosing police work in the first place because she liked structure—could be counted on to develop tunnel vision and keep poking at what she had.

One positive: The details of what had taken place in the parking lot would never come to light.

Unless Andrew had told someone . . .

No reason to think he had, but if Henke somehow managed to connect him to the hotel—face flashed on the news, a newspaper article with accompanying photo—Grace had to face the possibility that someone—Chicklet, another drinker—could cause problems.

The mere fact that Grace had failed to mention the previous meeting would be damning.

Worst-case scenario: a Kafkaesque nightmare.

Best case: career damage.

Had she been overly confident?

Grace felt her gut begin to knot up again. Early-warning sign, like a prodrome before a seizure. She deep-breathed, ran through two circuits of muscle relaxation exercises, achieved mild parasympathetic stimulation, at best.

Forget all that mind-body crap. Keep the brain busy.

Focus.

Two cups of strong tea and the activity it took to brew them helped. So did imagining herself restored to expert status. Sitting in this chair behind this desk in this room.

Her room.

Her world: helping others.

One stupid mistake shouldn't disrupt that.

So **think.** How to minimize risk?

She washed her teacup, returned to her desk, closed her eyes, and created a mental list of strategies.

Dismissing all but one. The only plan that made sense was steering Henke away from the Opus with an alternative: Andrew's actual lodgings.

And for that, microanalyzing Andrew's behavior might be the key.

He hadn't stayed at the Opus but he had chosen it for bar snacks and a cocktail. Because his accommodations lacked atmosphere? Perks?

Was his own place limited to cheap booze from a coin-op mini-bar?

Or maybe he was staying somewhere perfectly nice and just felt like a change of scenery.

Either way, the weather had been mild and a young, healthy male from out of town, possibly just off the plane, might crave a pleasant walk.

Then again, he'd been knifed to death downtown. Did that mean his hotel room was in that area?

A cross-city slog didn't make sense if you were trying to mellow out. So maybe the poor guy had been driven there and dispatched precisely to hinder identification.

His murderer not counting on a card in a shoe.

Why had Andrew done that?

Seeking out Grace's help but knowing it was dangerous?

She cast that aside and concentrated on the immediate task: find out where and start by keeping it local.

Using the Opus as a hub, she fanned outward and searched for other seats of hospitality. The Internet yielded a list of candidates within four miles of the hotel. The yellow pages filled in missing establishments and soon Grace had compiled a handwritten alphabetic list, pushing aside a flood of intrusive what-ifs.

What if there was no hotel and he'd bunked down with a friend or relative?

What if the pleasant-stroll hypothesis was bunk and he wasn't weary from air travel because he lived right here in L.A.?

Atoner.

Roger. To Grace's Helen.

She'd called herself that because a patient by that name was the last person she'd spoken to before embarking. At the time, a cute little in-joke. Now it seemed tawdry. What if Andrew had employed a similar ruse? Something that might help identify him.

Could he have been that devious? Grace's bullshit detector was exquisitely tuned but he hadn't set it off. Was she slipping? Or would Andrew turn out to simply be a decent man seeking help?

Murderer's son/brother/cousin inspired by the tale of a murderer's daughter.

No sense wondering. She had a job to do.

. . .

Using the same airhead persona she'd presented to the Opus clerk, she began calling.

The Alastair, a "six-star guesthouse" on Burton Way, was fronted by a warm-voiced man. Regretfully, that establishment hadn't accommodated Andrew Toner nor anyone named Roger.

Same for the Beverly Carlton, the Beverly Carlyle, the Beverly Dumont, and fourteen other establishments.

But eighty minutes later, a man with a middle European accent at the St. Germain on the 400 block of North Maple Drive laughed unpleasantly.

"Funny you should ask, miss. Your Mr. Toner paid for two days then asked for a third day. When the maid went to clean his room this morning, he was gone, along with his belongings. We accepted cash as a courtesy. Where might we find him, miss?"

"I was hoping you could tell me."

"Hmph. Well, if you see him, let him know this is wrong."

Leaving the Aston in the garage and opting for the Toyota because conspicuous was the last thing she wanted to be, she drove south on Doheny Drive.

Maple between Civic Center and Alden was inaccessible from the north due to a long-dormant fenced-off area deeded to the Southern Pacific Railroad. Entry from Third Street to the south led Grace to a dark, quiet neighborhood zoned residential on the west side but hosting massive office buildings across the street.

Not where you'd expect a hotel and nothing looked like a hotel but the rationale hit her: close to her office. An easy walk if you knew how to sidle along the railyard and emerge at the psychotic interchange linking Melrose Avenue and Santa Monica Boulevard.

GPS could turn anyone into a navigator.

Grace cruised up the block, found the address painted on the curb, double-checked her notes to confirm. Driving on, she U-turned and came back, positioning herself across the street and up a bit.

The building was a Georgian Revival from the twenties, just another two-story apartment structure on a block filled with similar, nothing identifying a commercial enterprise. Whiskey-colored glow from a ground-floor window clarified when Grace parked and had a look from the sidewalk: light leaking through the slightly askew slats of old-fashioned Venetian blinds.

One way in: a dark-painted door, but there had to be a rear exit that led to a garden. An escutcheon-like plaque staked midway along a curving cement walkway was barely decipherable.

The St. Germain

Hanging below that, a smaller sign.

Vacancy

Grace hazarded a couple of steps closer. Over the door:

Reception. Ring In.

Not exactly warm and welcoming, but perfect if you wanted to remain obscure.

The Internet ratings she'd read were mixed: decent, clean lodgings but no restaurant, no lounge, no room service.

Just as she'd hypothesized: A guy could get thirsty, hungry, lonely. Go out exploring.

She got back in the station wagon and drove away thinking about Andrew's likely trajectory that first night. Heading north would earn him a chain-link barrier but south—

southwest—would lead him smack into the Beverly Hills business district and, once there, the Opus would be a conspicuous beacon of promise.

You go in, settle in a comfortable chair, order a drink.

You see a woman.

She sees you back.

Everything changes.

17

Nothing like success to settle one's stomach. Finally hungry, Grace drove to an Indian place in WeHo that she knew to be busy at lunch but thinly patronized for dinner.

Tonight, the clientele consisted of three tattooed hipsters eating sullenly and an older, well-dressed couple holding hands. The turbaned Sikh owner smiled gently and guided Grace to a quiet corner where she waved off a menu and ordered the shrimp special and chai. Nibbling **namak pare** crackers, she pondered when to favor Henke with her discovery.

Double gift: Not only had she learned where Andrew had stayed, the fact that he'd checked in three days ago could help the detective if she wanted to search travel schedules.

The owner brought her the milky tea along with assurance that her food would follow shortly, everything was prepared fresh.

Should she tell the detective about the hotel? If so, not tonight, maybe tomorrow morning. Late morning because that would imply curiosity but not an obsessive all-nighter quest.

She worked on her story: About to embark on a vacation, she'd been distracted by the horror of Andrew's death, had taken the time to investigate so she could feel she was doing **something.**

Too mushy? Should she frame it as intellectual curiosity, softened by empathy? She'd figure it out.

Be grateful, Detective Henke. Show your thanks by forgetting about me.

Then she thought of a possible hitch: Henke was sure to visit the St. Germain, where the grumpy night man would likely tell her about Grace's worried-cousin ruse. Would that retweak the detective's suspicions?

So be up front about it, maybe get Henke to laugh it off as an eccentric therapist playing girl detective—weren't shrinks all a bit off?

Partial honesty's the best policy . . . Grace's food arrived. Delicious. She seemed to be digesting well. Things were looking up.

She drove back to her office to pick up the Aston, and as long as she was at it, checked her service because that's what a responsible healer did.

The operator said, "Just one, Dr. Blades. An Elaine Henke. She said phone anytime, she'll be up late."

Ten thirty-three p.m. and the woman was still at her desk. "Have you thought of anything else, Dr. Blades?"

"Actually," said Grace. "I just did something a little different. But it might help you."

Henke listened, said, "Wow. That's impressive, Doctor. I like the cousin thing, sounds like something I might be able to use one day."

Grace laughed. "Have a nice night."

"The St. Germain," said Henke. "Never heard of it."

"Same here."

"Fake name, paying cash, maybe he was shady—you pick that up?"

Grace, feeling oddly defensive about Andrew, said, "Not at all."

"Guess not after such a brief—oh, I forgot to tell you, Doctor. I came up with something, myself. I was staring at the name, because something about it bothered me, I couldn't figure it out. Then I did. Because luckily I'd written his initial—A—instead of his name. A. Toner. Get it?"

Grace said, "Not really."

"A. Toner. **Atoner,** Doctor. If that's it, no surprise he doesn't show up under that name."

"But you said other people in Texas do."

"True," said Henke, sounding disappointed. "Maybe you're right . . . Still, they haven't shown up murdered and he has. Plus you told me about that article he mentioned, maybe having a criminal family. And that out-of-service number looks like it traces to a throwaway—a disposable cell, drug dealers love them. So all in all I'm getting a shady feeling."

"Sounds like it."

"It's usually that way, Doctor. People making mistakes, paying for them. Anyway, thanks for finding the hotel, it gives me something to work with."

"My pleasure."

"You said he got jumpy and left," said Henke. "Drugs can make you jumpy. Cocaine, amphetamines. Did you happen to notice his pupils?"

The night before, I sure did, Elaine. Dilated to the max, ripe with interest.

"I didn't," said Grace, "but there were no obvious indications of intoxication."

"And you'd know," said Henke. "Okay, thanks again, I'll check out that hotel first thing. You earned your vacation, enjoy—decided where to go, yet?"

The lie was easy. "Maybe it will be Hawaii."

"Back when I was married, my husband and I used to go regularly."

What was this, girlish chitchat?

Grace said, "Any recommendations?"

"I like the Big Island—oh yeah, one more thing. Did you happen to notice that Mr. Atoner colored his hair?"

"No," Grace said, with genuine surprise.

"The coroner noticed light roots, confirmed it. His natural color appears to be sandy brown. What do you think of that?"

"Men do it, now."

"If he was an old guy, covering gray, I'd say sure, vanity. But just darkening the brown, what's the point unless you're trying to disguise yourself? I'm definitely getting a feeling for this guy. Meanwhile, aloha."

18

Grace lingered at her desk, thinking about the behaviors that led Henke to see Andrew as suspicious. All of it, she knew, could be taken a whole other way: He'd embarked on a dangerous journey—a quest for atonement—and was trying to protect himself.

In the case of Grace's business card in his shoe, protecting her, as well?

No other reason she could think of.

My hero?

Her eyes began aching, every joint in her body had tightened up. Suddenly, she craved escape—from the office, the city. Her thoughts. Everything.

Maybe she **would** try the Big Island, again. Or Costa Rica, the rain forests sounded interesting.

Locking up, she hurried to the garage and got in the DB7. She'd take Sunset to Malibu, extending the journey a bit, she could use the decompression.

The car treated her like the smooth lover it was, working curves at far too high a speed. Maintaining control as she kept pushing the limits of her skill was first-rate distraction and by the time Grace reached the coast, she'd begun to feel just fine.

It took a while—passing through Las Tunas Beach—before she realized she was being followed.

Grace made a point of being watchful when driving alone. Tonight she hadn't.

Big-time screwup?

Or was she imagining the intrusion? A pair of bouncing

headlights—a vehicle with spongy suspension—for the last few miles?

She worked the rearview mirror. The lights were still there, shimmery amber moons.

Then they diminished as another vehicle slipped between them. And another.

Nothing to that? Or had she just seen what Shoshana Yaroslav had taught her: evasive driving? If the goal was to avoid detection, it accomplished the opposite; now Grace couldn't stop checking.

She sped up; the car with the bouncing lights moved up. Receded. Second time that had happened in five miles. Far too much movement given the sparse nighttime traffic on PCH.

She recalled the boxy sedan she'd spotted the night of Andrew's appointment. Rolling toward her from up the street and setting off her internal alarm, only to reverse direction and slip away. If someone really was following her, had the hunt commenced as she'd left West Hollywood?

Could this be the same car? The span between the headlights fit but that's all she could make out.

She switched to the slow lane.

Ninety seconds later, the bouncing car did the same and now it was unshielded.

Definitely not a compact or a truck, so maybe . . . Grace lowered her speed abruptly, caught the car unawares, and earned a closer look.

Sedan. Boxy? Probably.

The first time she'd seen it, it had been parked near her office well after Andrew's departure. Sometime that night, Andrew had been stalked, ending up human trash, dumped in a cold, dark place.

The timing didn't work. So maybe she was letting her mind run away with—unless there were two people involved.

One for Andrew, one to clean up Andrew's mess.

If he'd been tracked to her office, finding out why wouldn't be a challenge, her nameplate—small, bronze, discreet—graced the front door.

Talking to a shrink, the ultimate sin? First Andrew had been punished and now Grace needed to be taken care of? The sedan crept up on her, she put on speed, the sedan hung back, too dark to ascertain the make and model . . . now it had allowed a smaller car to get in front of it.

Grace shifted lanes again.

This time the sedan took its time getting directly behind her, but there it was, following closer than ever. Grace slowed down, forcing it to brake. The sedan recovered, slowing itself, allowing a pickup to cut in front.

For all Grace knew the truck was part of a team.

But she couldn't afford to let fear take hold, so she worked hard at building up anger. The nerve of these bastards . . . La Costa Beach was approaching, time to think clearly.

Going home was obviously out of the question. Once she entered her front door she'd be as vulnerable as a shooting range target. But the only escapes along PCH were dark, twisting roads snaking to canyons and dead ends.

So only one choice: keep going. But that provided no long-term solution because once she was past the Colony and the rolling hills fronting Pepperdine University, the traffic would thin further and the highway would darken and she'd be vulnerable to a bump or a swipe that ran her off the road.

A weapon aimed out of a window.

Unless she was wrong. She hoped she was but when the sedan moved up on her again and she had to push the Aston way past the speed limit, that hope died.

She knew.

Why had she let her guard down? The reason to consider that question wasn't to beat herself up, it was to prevent recurrence of stupidity.

The obvious answer: what the Brits called brain fag. The motor neurons in her brain had been preoccupied with Andrew. Then thinking about anything **but** Andrew.

All that mental energy had overloaded her circuits and caused her to neglect Shoshana Yaroslav's First Commandment: **I don't care how tough and liberated you think you are, you're a woman, always vulnerable. So pay attention to your surroundings.**

Commandment Two was: **Do whatever it takes. Unless you believe in reincarnation and enjoy the thought of coming back as a bug.**

No need for eight more.

Shifting slightly to the right so she could catch a better glimpse of the slow lane, Grace found it empty. Suddenly, she pushed the Aston's throttle to the floor, reaching eighty ninety a hundred in seconds. Leaving the pickup and the dancing car and everyone else far behind.

Even at that speed, the DB7 was barely working up RPMs. Power poles zipped by like stripes on a curtain. Twelve cylinders whined in appreciation—**finally you give me some exercise!**—and Grace smiled. This level of speed felt like a natural state and besides, she'd flown this road before with her eyes literally closed, knew the bumps and turns and quirks, and if some highway patrol cruiser blue-lighted her, all the better, she'd be nothing but cooperative, pretend to pay attention to the officer's tight-ass lecture, meanwhile she'd be watching from the shoulder as the bouncing car zipped by.

But as she reached La Costa, the nanosecond blur that was her house, and continued to the Malibu Pier and Surfrider, there wasn't a trace of law enforcement to be found.

And now, by terrible attrition, only one set of headlights was behind her, maybe ten car lengths back. No longer moons, Grace saw them as eyes, now. Twin amber beacons of scrutiny.

. . .

She decelerated to seventy and the sudden bounce of the dancing car's headlights told her it had braked precipitously, again. Pushing the Aston back up to eighty, she used its race-born agility to advantage, calling into service the performance-driving techniques Shoshana had showed her during an exhausting day at the Laguna Seca track in Salinas. Explaining to her that cars don't go out of control, drivers do.

So avoid braking except when necessary because braking and accelerating rocks a car like a cradle and at high speeds that risks serious loss of traction and if you absolutely must brake, do it briefly, at the apex of the curve, then accelerate.

Fun stuff, then. Useful, now. Grace sped through Malibu's western beaches, still hoping for a cop, but pleased as the bouncing headlights vanished.

Then she hit a straightaway near the fenced sprawl of the public beach at Zuma and all of a sudden they were back.

Gaining on her, coming right **at** her.

She veered sharply onto the shoulder, not liking the grinding, gnashing noise that ensued, and praying the Aston's low-slung underbelly hadn't been damaged.

Idling, she switched off her headlights, lifted her foot from the brake pedal to disengage the rear lights, and relied upon the emergency brake to keep the snorting beast at bay. Dark night, black car, she was sure of invisibility.

The Aston continued to fight being caged but remained in place and now she'd be ready when the sedan sped by.

But it didn't. Had it caught on, somehow—picking up a glint of starlit glossy paint or chrome wheels or shining window?

What had given Grace away didn't matter, only the result: Her pursuer was speeding directly at her again.

Releasing the emergency brake, she watched in her rear-view, waited, and when the time was right, she turned the wheel sharply and hung a radical U that made the Aston fishtail on squealing tires.

But it righted itself quickly and Grace had barely made it

across the center of the highway and into the southbound lanes when a massive shape came barreling down from the north.

During the seconds it took for Grace to speed out of its way, the semi she'd narrowly avoided sounded its Klaxons and roared by, enraged.

Eighteen-wheeler, according to the cheerful sign on its flank, a company hauling restaurant produce. Less than an instant to read all that but somehow she had.

She'd also absorbed details of the dancing car: dark, probably gray, blocky sedan as she'd theorized, maybe a Chrysler 300.

Spinning its wheels in the dirt of the shoulder as it tried to back its nose out of an embankment. Too dark to make out the plate.

Dark windows.

Stock wheels.

The sedan wouldn't budge. The tires stopped spinning. A man got out, bulky, broad.

Clutching something at his side.

Grace raced away.

She adhered to the speed limit, reached Kanan Dume Road quickly enough, and turned off. That took her over the mountains and into the Valley, where she hooked up with the 101 East. Even at this hour, the freeway provided a fine social circle—a thin but steady stream of fellow motorists and, yes, there it was, law enforcement in the person of a CHP black-and-white in the center lane, trawling for taxpayer money, where the hell were they when you needed them?

A few miles later, she spotted another patrol car lolling in a dark spot on the north shoulder.

Try hassling me now, Sedan Boy.

She continued completely through the Valley, stuck with the 101 as it transitioned to the 134. Crossing into Burbank, she kept going, exiting at Central Avenue in Glendale because she had no connection to that bedroom community. Within moments she spotted a tall stucco-and-green glass building that proclaimed itself to be a new Embassy Suites. Parking in the sub-lot, she took stairs up to the hotel lobby and booked a room with a businesslike desk-woman.

Two rooms; the place was true to its name, with square footage larger than Grace's beach house. Nice sterile hideaway, the welcome smell of chemically cleansed air, an amenities card boasting of high-speed Internet access, a flat-screen LCD TV, and a "cooked to order breakfast in our lush open-air atrium."

Grace charged up her laptop, stripped down, and got under the covers.

She slept deeply.

Up at six a.m., alert but not hungry, she used the high-speed Internet access to locate a twenty-four-hour pharmacy 1.2 miles away on Glendale Avenue. A quiet walk was welcome for all sorts of reasons and she kept up a brisk pace, aware of her surroundings despite feeling no threat. Purchasing what she needed, she took a different route back to her hotel suite, did what she needed to do.

At nine a.m., a thin, pretty, deeply tan woman with boyishly short dark-brown hair wearing a bit too much makeup entered the lush, open-air atrium and asked for a corner table that would afford her a wide view of the dining room.

Once settled, she read two newspapers and enjoyed a hearty breakfast.

The only distraction during her DIY hairstyle/dye job had been thoughts of Andrew coloring his thick locks.

Once again they seemed to be linked.

And something else: picturing him with lighter hair tweaked something in her memory. As if she'd seen him before. But of course she hadn't.

The whole point for him—the mess that had started it all—had been about finding a nonjudgmental stranger.

19

At ten a.m. Grace got back on the freeway and left Glendale, this time heading west. Linking to the 405 South, she drove toward LAX, located an off-site, indoor, long-term parking structure. Nosing the Aston into a corner slot, she looked around to check for security cameras or someone else's eyes before removing the box of .22 bullets she kept in a compartment concealed by the trunk deck—what had once housed a CD player. Into her purse went the ammunition, nestled alongside the little gun, along with her garage door openers, a Maglite, an old AAA map she hadn't consulted in years, Ray-Ban sunglasses, and a black baseball cap with no insignia that she kept for top-down beach drives.

After taking a tram to the car rental lots, she walked to the Enterprise lot and selected a black Jeep Grand Cherokee with a thousand miles on the odometer.

Her next stop was Macy's in Culver City where she bought running shoes, rubber-soled flats, underwear, black cargo pants and stretch jeans in that same color, same for T-shirts, cotton crewnecks, and mock turtles. A thin nylon jacket a size too large came outfitted with four generous pockets. Finally, a cheap but sturdy brown suitcase to house all that.

A stop at a discount food store on Sepulveda netted her all the trail mix on the shelves, caffeine-laced caramel chews, a case of bottled water, and two cheap disposable cellphones. She bought a third phone at a discount electronics shop run by a Persian guy, then beef and turkey jerky, corn chips, and dry salami at a deli near Washington Boulevard.

Now she was ready for fight or flight.

. . .

At ten p.m., she was back in WeHo. Darkness worked to her advantage as she rolled along the streets near her office. After an hour of surveillance she was satisfied the boxy sedan was nowhere in sight. She'd already convinced herself two enemies was a likely scenario, so a second car was a possibility. Another half hour of meandering and circling revealed none—and no one—out of place.

Her pursuer—Mr. Beefy—probably assumed this was the last place she'd return, especially after dark. That might make it the safest place in the city.

She parked a block away from the cottage, slipped on the lightweight jacket and the baseball hat, and dropped the Beretta into the lower right-hand pocket.

Taking a circuitous route, she arrived at her garden exit door, looked around before easing in, waited until the gate clicked behind her.

The alarm was still set. No sign of disturbance.

Keeping the house lights off, she used the Maglite to create a focused beam of guidance, proceeded to her office, and unlocked the massive five-drawer file cabinet she kept in the therapy room closet.

In the bottom drawer at the back, hidden behind personal papers, was a strongbox from which she took the Glock and a box of 9mm bullets, plus all the cash she'd stored there, which came to just over thirty-eight hundred dollars. After a bathroom break, she exited through the front of the cottage, took a different route back to the Jeep, drove for a quarter hour, returned, and parked with a view of both doors to the cottage.

Now she waited.

Nothing happened and she left before daybreak. Sitting there watching, eating jerky and caffeine candy and sipping water, had given her ample time to order her thoughts.

She had no doubt that Andrew's visit, brief as it was,

had put her in the crosshairs of people with a secret serious enough to kill for.

Atoner. Something terrible in his past. Violent. Males created nine-tenths of the bloodshed so probably a brother nephew cousin. Even a dad.

So what to do?

A vacation—any type of flight—wouldn't solve anything. On the contrary, it would cut her off and leave her ill prepared and vulnerable when she returned.

Her pursuer knew where she worked. Maybe where she lived, as well, because let's face it, a fifth grader with computer skills could find anyone's legal address.

Nasty situation.

She searched for something positive, finally came up with one: the message her service would deliver to all callers: Dr. Blades is out of the office for two weeks.

Granting Grace fourteen days to get something done.

Another person would probably contact the police—in Grace's case, a brand-new cop contact.

Detective, this is Grace Blades. Someone followed me last night.

Really, Doctor? Who?

Someone in what I think was a Chrysler 300, I didn't get a good look.

Did you get the license plate?

No.

Where did this happen?

Pacific Coast Highway, Malibu.

That's sheriff turf. May I ask what were you doing there, Doctor?

Driving home. I'm concerned they know where I live.

They. We're talking more than one person?

They, he, I really don't know.

Did you call the sheriffs'?

No . . .

Every word Grace uttered would convince Henke of either duplicitousness or poor judgment. Or worse, mental instability, you know those shrinks.

Recontacting Henke, period, could reverse any progress Grace had made at no longer being a person of interest.

In the best of circumstances, the detective would believe Grace but have nothing to offer other than a mini-course on basic personal safety.

Do you have an alarm, Doctor? How about a dog?

So where to turn? Shoshana Yaroslav might conceivably be a source of wisdom, but two years ago she'd married an Israeli high-tech whiz and moved to Tel Aviv.

Delaware could hook her up with his police contact but the guy worked West L.A. homicide and would regard her tale as an out-of-jurisdiction annoyance.

The big question: What could anyone do for her?

The answer: What it had always been.

She was on her own. The way she liked it.

The way it had been before Malcolm came into her life.

The so-called formative years.

20

Two months into Grace's stay at Stagecoach Ranch, Ramona said, "He's coming today."

"Who?"

"Professor Bluestone."

They'd just sat down for breakfast, which was usually just Grace and Ramona because they got up earlier than everyone else.

Rollo and DeShawn were leaving in a few days, some aunt had agreed to adopt them, and a new ward, a five-year-old girl named Amber, had moved in but she cried at everything and didn't like to get out of bed. Bobby needed Ramona's help to get downstairs and sometimes he needed to stay on his oxygen all day, so Grace rarely saw him at all.

As she spread strawberry preserves on a piece of flat-tasting toast, Ramona repeated, "Professor Bluestone." As if Grace had been expected to react.

Grace ate.

"You don't remember? That psychologist I told you about? I know it's been a while since I mentioned it, he's been off in Europe delivering lectures. Teaching other professors."

Grace reached for the jam jar, found a whole strawberry, soggy and sure to be juicy-sweet, and impaled it on her knife.

Ramona said, "Anyway, he's coming today. Hopefully that'll enrich your education."

During the two months, Grace had sped through the public school curriculum materials Ramona provided in weekly packets, finding everything super easy and pretty much boring but liking the fact that she could finish early and walk around the ranch and do her favorite thing, which was being by herself.

There was lots of land on the ranch, more than she'd ever seen, and if you squinted and blocked out the wire fences you could imagine you owned everything all the way to the mountains.

The fence didn't stop small animals from getting through and bugs were all around, including gnats and spiders and sometimes mosquitoes in Grace's room. Even when Ed came and sprayed horrible-smelling stuff, they stuck around. But she supposed the poison did a pretty good job of blocking larger animals like coyotes and the occasional mean-looking stray dog, which she only spotted prowling in the distance before sundown.

Once Ramona came out while she was watching a big male coyote and stood beside her and the two of them watched the creature slink along, slipping in and out of some gray bushes, before disappearing into the big black pointy shadows east by the mountains.

"Know why he's out now, Grace?"

"For food."

"You bet, this is their dinnertime, they got a schedule just like us only they don't need a watch or a clock. Also, nobody serves them, they've got to earn everything that goes into their mouths. It makes them smart."

Grace said, "I know." Edging a few feet away from Ramona's still-working lips, she tried to crawl back into her private thoughts.

Sometimes Grace read books from the living room bookcase, mostly paperbacks about crimes and detectives and people falling in love then breaking up then falling in love again. Most of the new words she came upon she could figure out. Those she couldn't, she looked up in Ramona's big Webster's dictionary. Sometimes she read the dictionary just to read it and discovered totally new words there. There was also TV. She could ask permission to watch but she rarely did because TV was almost as boring as the curriculum packets.

Outside, off to the left side of the big house, was a dry-dirt area with a wooden swing set, a slide, a seesaw, everything set on rubber mats under a huge tree that scattered leaves all the time.

Often Grace swung until Ramona called her in for a meal or something else, imagining she could fly. Occasionally she thought about letting go when she was at the top of her swing, wondering what it would feel like to fly and then crash, but she knew that was stupid so she forced herself to stop those ideas.

Farther back from the play set, behind what used to be the goat corral, gates still in place, was a big rectangular swimming pool that changed color with the heat, clotting with green slime when the temperatures rose no matter how many chemicals Ramona poured into it, muttering and turning grumpy.

Green water meant it was warm enough to swim and one day, when the desert had turned shiny with heat, almost like metal, Grace asked Ramona if she could go in.

"That pea soup? You kidding?"

Grace said, "No."

"Yeah, right. I let you do that, the county could claim I endangered your health."

"There's germs?"

"Well," said Ramona, "probably not, just that gooky stuff, that's called algae, who knows what critters are breeding there."

"Algae's a plant, ma'am."

"So?"

"If it's not poisonous it can't hurt me."

"It could be poisonous."

"The poisonous ones are out in the ocean, they smell bad and they're red."

Ramona stared at her. "You're an expert on algae?"

"It was in two-weeks-ago's packet. One-Celled Organisms."

Ramona stared at her. "Good Lord, child."

"So can I?"

"What?"

"Swim."

"No way, not a chance. Take a look, it's got that skin on top, you can't see under the surface, something happens to you, I'd never know."

Grace walked away.

Ramona called out, "You mad at me? I'm just doing my job, taking care of you."

Grace stopped and turned, knowing she had to keep Ramona happy because this was the best place she'd ever been fostered at. No one bothered her, she could spend so much time alone. She said, "Of course not, Mrs. Stage. I understand."

Ramona squinted at her, finally forced a smile. "Appreciate your understanding, Ms. Blades."

The following day, Ramona caught Grace as she was leaving the house after study-time. "You still want to swim? I did some research and you're right, there's no danger, it's just disgusting so if it doesn't bother you and you stay in the shallow end with me right there . . ."

"It doesn't."

"Make no mistake, Grace, I'll have to watch you like a hawk and you'll have to stay on the surface every single second, I mean every. No deep-sea diving, no head under, not even for a second. Okay?"

"Okay."

Ramona shrugged. "Fine, I don't get why you want to do it but it's your choice. Also, you're going to use an old rough towel with holes in it, no way I'm getting that gook on my good towels."

Grace said, "The gray one?"

"Pardon?"

"The gray towel you keep in the linen closet and never use?"

"Matter of fact, yes," said Ramona. "Gawd, you notice everything, don't you?"

"No."

"What don't you notice?"

"If I don't notice it, I can't know."

Ramona stared at her, toying with her long white hair. "A lawyer," she said. "Things could get interesting around here."

The professor didn't arrive that day, or the next. Or the next twenty.

Ramona said, "Sorry if I got your hopes up, he got called to do more travel."

Grace said, "Okay."

There were few things she cared about. None of them had to do with other people.

One morning, she came down for breakfast and the biggest person Grace had ever seen was sitting next to Ramona at the kitchen table, drinking coffee. An oldish kind of man, younger than Ramona but not young. The fingers he used to hold his coffee mug were so thick and wide they covered the handle completely. Even his hair was big, a high pile of dark-gray waves that stuck out in all directions. When he stood, he blocked out a lot of the room and for a second Grace thought he might hit his head on the ceiling. Then she saw she was wrong, he was shorter than the ceiling. But still huge.

Ramona said, "Rise and shine, Grace, this is Professor Bluestone."

Grace said, "Hello," in her soft, agreeable voice, the one she'd learned to use a long time ago with strangers.

The man said, "Hello, Grace. I'm Malcolm. Sorry for surprising you." He smiled.

Grace looked over at the table. Her usual toast and preserves and rubbery eggs were there, along with a stack of pancakes and store-bought maple syrup in a jar shaped like a bear. Seeing the jar made Grace realize that the huge man kind of looked like a bear, with thick, round features, big soft brown eyes, and long thick arms that swung loosely. Even his clothes were kind of bearish: a baggy, fuzzy brown sweater, super-baggy gray pants, brown shoes worn to tan at the toes.

What was different from a bear were his glasses, round and too small for his wide face, with frames like a turtle's shell. Grace chided herself for the silly thought—that only one thing was different. He wore clothes, he talked, he was human.

But still, kind of like a bear.

Ramona said, "Have some breakfast, young lady."

Malcolm Bluestone returned to his chair, bumping a shoe against a table leg, like the world was too small for him. When Grace sat and reached for the toast and preserves, he was still smiling at her. When she stopped and looked at him, he speared two pancakes with his fork, soaked them with syrup, began eating really fast.

The way a bear would—even the syrup fit, kind of like the honey bears went crazy for when they came out of hibernation.

Lesson Twenty-Eight: Warm-Blooded Mammals and Temperature Adaptation.

For a while, no one talked. Then Malcolm Bluestone pointed to the pancakes. "Anyone else want these?"

Grace shook her head.

Ramona said, "All yours, m'boy."

Which was a funny thing to call an old man. Then Grace realized he was Ramona's dead husband's younger brother, maybe to her he'd always be a kid.

Malcolm Bluestone polished off the pancakes, wiped his lips, poured more coffee.

Ramona stood. "I've got to see about Bobby and that poor little Amber—the one I told you about, Mal, you're the expert but she looks kind of . . . down."

Malcolm Bluestone said, "I'll have a look at her, later."

"Thanks." Ramona left.

Grace nibbled toast she really wasn't hungry for.

Malcolm Bluestone said, "I know Ramona told you about me but if you have questions, I'm happy to answer them."

Grace shook her head.

"No questions, huh?"

"Nope."

"Do you understand why I'm here?"

"You're Steve Stage's brother and a psychologist and you're here to give me tests."

He laughed. "That just about covers it. So you know what a psychologist is."

"A doctor you talk to if something's bothering you," said Grace. "And who gives tests."

Malcolm Bluestone wiped his lips with a napkin. A glossy bit of syrup remained on the skin above his upper lip. "Have you ever met a psychologist?"

"No."

"Are you okay with being tested?"

"Yes."

"You understand why you're being tested."

"Yes."

"Don't want to bug you but could you please tell me what you understand? Just so I can be sure."

Grace sighed and put her toast down.

Malcolm Bluestone said, "I am bugging you. Sorry."

No grown-up had ever apologized to Grace. First it shook her but then it passed through her like air. She said, "The homeschool curriculum packets are easy so Ramona wants you to find out what more I can have to study."

Dr. Bluestone nodded. "That's excellent, Grace. But these tests, they're not like the ones you've had in school. You won't be getting a grade and the questions are structured—they're made up so no one can get all the answers. You okay with that?"

"Yes."

"You don't mind getting some answers wrong?"

"Everyone gets things wrong."

Malcolm Bluestone blinked and righted his glasses. "Well, that's certainly true. Okay, Grace, soon as you're ready, we'll go into the living room and begin. Mrs. Stage promises to keep it quiet for us."

Grace said, "I'm ready."

The furniture had been moved around so that a table that usually stood near a couch was in the center of the room and two folding chairs were positioned opposite each other. On the floor was a briefcase, dark green, with a handle—more like a small suitcase. Gold lettering read **WISC-R.**

Malcolm Bluestone closed the door and said, "Settle where you'd like, Grace," and took the chair facing her. Even sitting, he blocked out a whole bunch of the room.

"Okay," he said. "This test is broken up into sections. On some I'm going to be timing you, using this." Lifting the briefcase with two fingers, as if it were made out of feathers, he drew out a round, silver watch. "This is a stopwatch. On some of the tests I'm going to tell you time's up, don't worry if you haven't finished. I'll let you know beforehand if you're being timed, okay?"

"Okay."

"Okay . . . one more thing: If you're tired or need to go to the bathroom, or need water—which I've brought"—pointing to several bottles in the corner—"be sure to let me know."

"I'm okay."

"I know you are, but should that—never mind, Grace, I have a feeling you know how to take care of yourself."

Some of the test was fun, some was boring. There were questions so easy Grace couldn't believe there was anyone who couldn't answer them, harder questions that she still thought she did okay on. One test was just vocabulary words like in school, another was putting together puzzles. There was math like in the curriculum, she got to tell stories with picture cards, make shapes out of colored plastic blocks.

As he'd promised, Malcolm Bluestone told her when he was going to use the stopwatch. Grace didn't care, there was plenty of time for almost everything and when she didn't get something she knew it was okay because he'd told her it would be like that. Also, she really didn't care.

When he said, "That's it," Grace decided she'd had an okay time. He looked tired and when he offered her water and she said, "No, thank you," he said, "Well, I'm feeling parched," and drained two bottles quickly.

As he finished the second bottle, he put his hand over his mouth to cover a burp but a little croaky noise escaped anyway and Grace had to struggle not to laugh.

He laughed. "'Scuse **me**—any questions?"

"No, sir."

"Nothing at all, huh? Listen, I can score this in a few minutes and give you some feedback—tell you about the things you did especially well on. That interest you?"

"If it helps get me a better curriculum."

"Yeah," he said, "I'll bet you're incredibly bored."

"Sometimes."

"I'll bet nearly all the time." His big bear eyes were aimed at Grace and looked extra eager, like he wanted her to agree with him.

She said, "Yes, sir, most of the time."

"Okay, you can go outside, get some fresh air, and I'll call you in."

Instead of obeying him—because she didn't feel like following any more instructions—Grace went into the kitchen where Bobby sat slumped in his special belted-in chair and Ramona was trying to feed Amber pieces of egg and Amber was shaking her head and whining, "No, no, no."

"What's up, Grace?"

"Can I have some juice, Mrs. Stage?"

"Help yourself."

Bobby made a noise and resumed drinking one of those milk shakes Ramona poured for him into small cups because he wasn't strong enough to hold a big cup.

"That's right," Ramona told him, as if she were talking to a baby, "it is delicious."

Bobby slurped. Amber said, "No, no, no."

Grace poured herself some juice and hung around near the sink and looked out at the desert but really didn't focus on it.

Thinking, as she had a thousand times: **Special needs, she's like the others, gets more money for it.**

Followed by the question that bothered her: **What's my special need?**

Bobby snorted and sputtered and coughed and Ramona rushed over and slapped his back softly until he stopped. Amber started to cry and Ramona said, "One moment, darling."

Grace had wondered for a while about what made Bobby weak and have trouble breathing but knew better than to ask Ramona about something that wasn't her business. Instead, she snuck into his room one afternoon when Ramona was downstairs trying to feed him a snack milk shake and had a look at some of the medicine Ramona was giving him. The words on the labels didn't tell her anything and she already knew about the oxygen tank next to his bed—a bed with side rails, so he wouldn't fall out. But she did notice a piece of paper on the dresser and it had one of those snake symbols doctors used.

The first line read, **County Dependent Medical Status Report: Robert Evan Canova.**

The second line began, **This twelve-year-old Caucasian with multiple congenital anomalies . . .**

Grace heard Ramona coming up the stairs and scooted to her own room. Later that day, she opened the big dictionary and looked up "congenital" and "anomalies" and figured it out: Bobby had been born with problems. That really didn't tell her much but she supposed that was all she'd be able to learn.

Malcolm Bluestone came into the kitchen. "There you are. Ready?"

Ramona looked at him, her eyebrows climbing, like she wanted to be in on the secret.

Dr. Bluestone didn't notice, was looking only at Grace and holding his huge arm out, motioning her back to the living room.

Finishing her juice, she washed and dried the glass and followed him.

He said, "Vitamin C, good for you."

Back at the testing table, he said, "First off, you did extremely well—amazingly well, actually."

He waited. "**Astonishingly** well."

Grace said, "Good."

"Put it this way, Grace, if we were testing a thousand kids, you'd probably get the highest score of anyone."

Again, he waited.

Grace nodded.

"May I ask how you feel about that?"

"Fine."

"Well, you should feel fine. You got an amazing—more than that, your abilities are uniform. That means you did great on everything. Sometimes people do very well on one part but not so well on another part. Nothing wrong with that. But you excelled on **everything**. I hope you feel proud of that."

"Proud" was a word whose definition Grace understood. But it meant nothing to her.

She said, "Sure."

Malcolm's soft brown eyes narrowed. "Let me put this another way: You're almost nine years old but on some of the subtests—on most of them, actually—you knew as much as a fourteen- or a fifteen-year-old. In some cases, even a seventeen-year-old. I mean your vocabulary is fabulous."

He smiled. "I have a tendency to over-explain because most of the children I deal with need that. So I'm going to have to watch myself with you. Like defining 'uniform' when you know exactly what it means."

Without thinking, Grace let the words shoot out. "Having the same form, manner, or degree."

Malcolm smiled. "You read the dictionary."

Grace felt her stomach tighten up. How had he figured her out so easily? Now he'd think she was weird, put that in a county status report.

Or maybe being weird would help her, keep her as a special-needs ward, so Mrs. Stage could keep getting extra money and Grace could stay here.

He said, "That's **fantastic,** Grace, that's a great way to build up vocabulary, learn the structure of language, philology, etymology—where words come from, how they're built. I used to do the same thing myself. Back when I was a bored kid, and let me tell you, that was most of the time because let's face it, for people like us—not that I'm as smart as you—life can get downright tedious if we're forced to go slow. And **that's** what I'm going to help you with. You're a race car, not a bicycle."

Grace felt her stomach loosen.

"I mean that, Grace. You deserve to be considered on your own terms."

A week later he brought her new curriculum materials. A week after that, he said, "How'd you like it?"

"Good."

"Listen, would you mind if I tested you again—just a few questions on the material in the packet. So I can know where we take things."

"Okay."

Ten questions later, he was grinning. "Well, it's obviously time to move on."

Five days later, Ramona brought a box into Grace's room and said, "From the professor, looks like he thinks you're pretty smart."

Drawing out a textbook, she said, "This is college science, young lady. How'd you learn enough to get to this level?"

Grace said, "I read."

Ramona shrugged. "Guess that explains it."

Three boxes later, he showed up again and said, "How's everything going?"

Grace was out by the fence around the green pool, thinking about swimming, not sure if getting all slimy was worth it.

She said, "Fine."

"I'm not going to test you on the curriculum, Grace, not for a while. You tell me you know it, that's good enough."

"I don't know everything."

His laugh was deep and rumbly like it came from deep inside him. "No one does, that would be the worst thing, no?"

"Knowing everything?" That sounded like the best thing.

"Having nothing more to learn, Grace. I mean for people like us, learning is everything."

Almost every time he visited, he said that. **Like us.** Like he and Grace were members of a club. Like he also had special needs.

She said, "Yes, sir."

His look said he knew she was just saying it without meaning it. But he didn't get angry, his eyes got even softer. "Listen, I've got a favor to ask you. Could I test you some more? Not about the curriculum, different types of tests."

"Okay."

"You don't want to know anything about the tests?"

"You don't give shots," said Grace. "You can't hurt me."

His head drew back and he roared with laughter. When he finally settled, he said, "Yes, that's true, these definitely won't hurt. But they're a little different, there's no right or wrong, I'll be showing you pictures, asking you to make up stories. You okay with that?"

"What kind of stories?"

"Anything you want."

That sounded stupid and despite herself, Grace frowned.

Malcolm Bluestone said, "Okay, no problem, let's forget it. Because I can't honestly tell you it'll help you."

Then why waste time?

"It's for my sake, Grace. I'm curious, always trying to understand people, and these tests sometimes help me."

"Someone making up stories?"

"Believe it or not, Grace, yes. But if you don't want to, that's really okay, nothing will change in our—I'll still bring you curriculum materials."

"I'll do it."

"Well," he said, "that's nice of you, but take some time to think about it and next time, let me know."

"I'll do it right now, sir."

"You really don't need to call me sir, Grace. Unless you want me to call you mademoiselle or senorita, or something like that."

Again, a word shot out of Grace's mouth. "Fräulein."

"You know German?"

"It was in the language packet you gave me last week." International Greetings.

"Ah," he said. "Guess I should read the packets myself. Anyway, next time—"

"I can do it now, Professor Bluestone."

"Do—oh, those picture tests. You sure?"

Grace looked at the green pool. Slimier than ever. Once he left, she'd have nothing much to do but start a new packet. "Sure," she said.

. . .

The picture tests were like he'd described, strange. Not photographs, black-and-white drawings of people that she had to make up stories about. Then another one with weird shapes that looked like bats or cats and while Grace talked, Malcolm Bluestone wrote down stuff in a little book.

When that was over, he said, "If you've got energy, we can do something totally different. Tapping and moving along a maze—you might find that fun."

"Okay."

He brought more tests from his big brown station wagon. They weren't fun but they filled in the time and when he drove away, Grace kind of missed being busy.

21

The first time Grace met Shoshana Yaroslav, she watched the woman, four feet eleven, maybe a hundred pounds, looking sweet and innocent and girlish, much younger than her forty years, disable a man named Mac who was twice her size. He was one of Shoshana's intermediate students who'd volunteered for the role of mugger, a former army medic with thick arms, a slab-like build, and the confidence of a guy who could take care of himself.

Shoshana moved so fast it was impossible to process what she'd done. Mac, prone on the mat, caught his breath and grinned and said, "Why the hell do I keep doing this?"

Shoshana said, "Because you are a gentleman."

For the next four months, she taught Grace her philosophy of self-defense and rode Grace mercilessly until the student's responses were borderline reflexive.

Borderline, not absolute, Shoshana was careful to add, because reflexes were "for lower animals, you should never stop thinking."

Black-belted in several martial arts, Shoshana took an approach that was conceptually simple—home in on the enemy's vulnerabilities—but required maddening amounts of practice. And she saw the defensive arts the same way Delaware did: a great workout and a whole lot better than no training at all, but unlikely to stand up against a bad person with a gun or knife or a blackjack.

During Grace's second session, Shoshana looked at Grace's hands. "Do you have strong nails?"

"I think I do."

"Foolish answer, they're too short for you to think anything. Grow them out a bit and see if they hold up. If they do, file them so they're more pointed than usual. Nothing too conspicuous, we don't want anyone calling you Ms. Scissorhands. But do create a tiny bit of blade at the apex. Meanwhile we'll practice with what you've got."

Entering and exiting a side door of the studio, Shoshana returned with a weird-looking wooden board around three feet square and perforated by circular holes. Her other hand held a jar full of brown murky fluid close to her chest. Uncapping the jar released a hideous stench that filled the room: sewer gas overlaid with . . . rotten barbecue?

Grace blinked back revulsion as Shoshana's tiny hand dipped into the jar and fished out something round and glassy and gray that dripped onto the wooden floor.

"Sheep's eye." Flipping the board over, she exposed a series of hinged metal cups backing each hole. Unsnapping one cup, she dropped the sheep's eye in where it nested snugly, then snapped it shut. Repeating the procedure with six additional eyes positioned randomly, she held the board in front of Grace. "Go."

"What do you want me to—"

Grasping the board in one hand, Shoshana managed to reach around with the other and jab. The eyes had seemed out of her visual field but one of them exploded.

"You just failed," she told Grace. "In the time it took to ask a question, your throat would've been cut."

Without warning, Shoshana's hand shot out again, terminating at the spot where Grace's neck joined the hollow above her sternum. A forefinger tickled Grace's Adam's apple. Grace stumbled back but Shoshana pressed forward maintaining the same harassing contact. Grace tried to slap Shoshana's arm away. Now Shoshana was behind Grace, tickling the mastoid process behind Grace's left ear.

Grace wheeled.

Shoshana had stepped out of reach, stood loose-limbed,

hands buried in the pockets of her cargo pants, casual as a tourist.

Grace said, "Okay, I get it."

"That's doubtful, Doctor. Don't say things to make me or anyone else happy."

Grace suppressed a smile. **You may be murderously tough but you don't understand me.**

She lunged for the board. Missed and hit wood and suppressed searing pain in her fingertips and thrust forward again, putting her weight behind the nail-stab.

Shit, the little buggers were hard to hit, and Grace knew immediately that she was way off. Risking another painful collision she checked her blow and feinted to the right. Chose another eye and went for it.

This time her finger impacted a momentary barrier of plastic-like skin that popped. Cold jelly encased the digit to the first knuckle. Ooze flowed over her hand. She pulled free. The room stank worse.

Shoshana Yaroslav propped the board on a table easel. Seemingly indifferent, she destroyed the remaining eyes in less time than Grace had taken for one.

Grace said, "This is useful, let's keep going."

Shoshana said, "Here you don't make the rules. Here you wait and I show you what I use for testicles."

Grace hadn't thought about Shoshana for a while but now, driving away from the cottage in darkness, that little-girl voice sounded in her head.

"If you don't get one thing right at the beginning, you're wasting time. Someone comes for you, get them first."

She drove back to Malibu using a different route: Wilshire to San Vicente to Channel Road to PCH, watching everyone and everything all the way to La Costa Beach, concentrating so hard her head throbbed and that felt great.

Nothing out of the ordinary emerged during this drive

and she spotted no obvious disruption as she sped past her house. That didn't mean someone hadn't managed to pick the lock and get in. If so, they'd learn nothing that could hurt her.

A quick reversal at Trancas Beach, a return to the city, and she was back at the cottage inside seventy minutes. Keeping her distance from the building as she drove and observed.

The sun was peeking through fuzzy gray clouds. Stylish WeHo residents walked stylish dogs and jogged. None of them expressed interest in anything but physical fitness and canine poop and the Chrysler 300—anything square and uncool—was nowhere in sight. But she'd run the car up into a berm so maybe it had sustained enough damage for Mr. Beef to find new wheels.

Interesting game, this: analysis, factoring out variables.

Two more circuits convinced her the coast was clear. She drove to Sunset, turned north on Laurel Canyon, and made it to the Valley by nine a.m.

Breakfast was pancakes and eggs at a coffee shop in Encino. Sometimes she treated herself to the flaps of sugar and starch when she wanted to feel enlarged.

Or, maybe, it dawned on her for the first time, she went for pancakes because the first time she'd met Malcolm that's what he'd been eating.

All at once, she was thinking of colors—green water, red rooms, then Malcolm's brown bearish presence and her eyes burned.

Appetite faded, she left cash on the table and exited.

Checking the coffee shop parking lot, more for practice than out of worry, she drove west on Ventura Boulevard, caught the 101 West at Reseda Boulevard, got off in Calabasas, and checked into a Hilton Garden Inn with a special deal on king-bed rooms.

Fourteen miles from the beach, far enough for comfort.

. . .

Working out in the hotel gym, she showered in her room, dressed in one of two robes hanging in the lav, plugged in her laptop, and connected with Hilton WiFi.

Trying to identify Andrew under his alias was most likely a waste of time but just when you thought you were smart, life could make you feel stupid, so she had to try.

Keywording **andrew toner** turned out to be half an hour of futility as she came up with precisely the useless information Elaine Henke had reported.

Next step: Use **roger,** the name he'd given Grace at the Opus, grouped with **civil engineer** and various Texas cities beginning with San Antonio. That created a list of eighteen names. Eleven came with Facebook or LinkedIn listings and photos that eliminated their owners. An hour later, she'd fished up phone numbers for the remaining seven, on business link sites. Using one of the three prepaid cells, she began calling.

Four men answered their own phones. Three secretaries offered variants of "Hold on, I'll see if Mr. [fill in the blank] is available."

Dead ends.

She paired the name with **homicide, murder,** and **rape.** A staggering number of Rogers had committed serious felonies and it took Grace nearly two hours to eliminate them.

The final iteration was **roger** paired with **brother** and **murderer.** That pulled up a Catholic priest who'd stabbed a nun to death eighteen years ago in Cleveland.

So much for background research. Her best bet was to pursue her pursuers. If they came for her again, it would be at the cottage, probably under cover of darkness. Checking the double-bolt on her door, she slipped on eyeshades and fell promptly asleep. Waking at five p.m., she dressed, exited the Hilton through a rear door that led to the parking lot, and had a look around the immediate neighborhood.

Commercial blocks relieved by industrial parks. A nearby strip mall provided admirable diversity of cuisine and dinner was forgettable pad Thai at a storefront café named Bangkok Benny, chased by iced tea and lots of water.

Returning to her room, she waited until an hour after sunset, retrieved the Jeep from the garage, and repeated the same Malibu-WeHo cycle she'd completed twelve hours ago. Kept doing it, covering the sixty-mile round-trip four times and having to stop for a gas fill-up.

Adding as much variety to her route as possible but no matter what you did you ended up on the coast highway.

She made one more circuit.

No sign of anything irregular.

Not good; this couldn't go on interminably.

22

Then everything changed.

Fifth pass, two fifty-three a.m., and there it was, the familiar blocky bulk of the sedan—indeed a 300, dark gray with blackened windows—parked half a block east of the cottage.

Bent front bumper but otherwise intact.

Using the same vehicle seemed breathtakingly careless.

Or arrogant. If so, all the better.

Grace drove by, regrouped mentally. She'd just driven by the cottage, seen the lights still out, no sign of forcing at either gate. So what was the plan tonight? Break in, rummage for records, and leave? Or lie in wait for Grace.

Or both.

Assuming the worst, Grace circled well east of the cottage and parked two blocks to the Chrysler's rear. Taking what she needed from the Jeep, she got out and stretched. Continued a block on rubber-soled running shoes, concealing herself as best she could in the shadows.

Twenty-three minutes later, a man-sized shape exited the sedan. The door closed. Loudly. No attempt at concealment. Grace was definitely being underestimated but she wouldn't make the same mistake.

She watched as the man walked—swaggered—toward the cottage. A bit taller than average but not huge or particularly wide.

Definitely two of them.

He, too, pressed himself into the shadows.

Grace began the stalk.

. . .

He reached the garage side of her property, looked around briefly, took something out of his pocket, and proceeded to her garden gate. Kneeling, he went to work.

Nothing like the movies, it took a while but finally he was in.

The gate shut silently. Now he was being careful.

Hunter's instincts honed as he neared his goal?

Making sure she wasn't being tailed herself, she padded toward the gate, stopped a few feet short. No sounds from the other side of the cedar fence. He was probably inside—how had he managed to avoid tripping the alarm?

Someone with experience. She stood there, listened, checked up and down the block, finally used her key and cracked the gate an inch. Waited. Spread the wood another inch. Waited again.

Not a peep, not a ruffle of grass.

Definitely inside. She waited for lights to go on, a sound, anything.

Nothing but silence. So maybe he was skulking around in the dark as she had, using a narrow-beam like her Maglite.

She pushed the door wide enough to slip through.

An arm, polyester-sleeved and steel-rigid, shot out from the left and hooked around her neck.

Grace brought her heel down hard on where she guessed an instep would be.

The man trying to drag her back by her neck grunted and paused for an instant. But Grace's rubber-soled shoes lacked the weapon-value of a spiked heel and he said, "Stupid bitch," and Grace felt his other arm leave the small of her back and heard a **snick** and knew he'd be stabbing her.

Reaching up and behind, she clawed her hands and went for his eyes but lacked the reach. Still, the very fact that she'd attacked threw his timing off and he grunted and lost balance and her second claw at his face made contact with flesh.

She dug her nails in deeply, raked down viciously, doing

her best to flay him. Felt dermis and stubble give way, then a warm wet rush.

He cried out in pain and loosened his grip and Grace spun out of reach and they were facing each other in the dark garden.

His features were barely limned by skimpy starlight. Forty or so, angular face, heavy features contorted in pain and rage as his left hand pressed down on the bloody tracks Grace had inflicted on his right cheek.

His right hand held a knife, double-edged, some sort of sling-blade or push-dagger.

"Fucking bitch," he said, and charged her.

The garden—small, concealed from neighborly eyes—must've seemed an ideal kill-spot and he was smiling through his pain as he continued his advance. Moving slowly and steadily.

Grace purposely fulfilled his expectations by mewling, "Don't hurt me, please," and backing away.

That emboldened him and, waving the knife in concentric circles, he prodded Grace toward the rear wall of the garden. Once they reached the wall, no escape, a woman left vulnerable as a rib roast. Confidence loosened his movements.

Grace busted his expectations by charging toward him.

Aiming herself straight at his blade and that confused him the way she hoped it would and he looked down at the weapon as if wondering why it no longer frightened her.

She veered to the right. No knife for her, concealed in her right hand, as it had been from the time she entered the garden, was her lovely little Beretta .22, eleven and a half ounces of lethality.

A gun Shoshana had derided. **"Might as well slap a bad guy with your hand."**

But a petite weapon had its time and place and thinking for yourself was always best.

Her would-be killer wasn't smart enough to imagine.

Never looking down at her hand, he growled and lunged and Grace stepped just clear of the arc of his blade and he ended up slashing air.

Before he could recoup, she thrust forward, pressing the Beretta's stubby barrel against his chest.

Knowing she'd found the spot where his heart resided, she pulled the trigger and danced backward.

His clothing and his body muffled the gunshot but the sharp **pop-slap** was still an assault on early-morning silence and Grace hoped she wouldn't need to fire again.

He stood there. Surprise slackened his face. His arms dropped. The knife fell to the grass.

Still bleeding from the gouges on his cheek, he lurched, stumbled, fell flat on his face.

Grace waited, saw no movement, approached him and stepped hard on his back.

No reaction. Gone, he had to be. She checked for a pulse. Zero. She jostled him hard.

Definitely lights-out.

Standing over him, she appraised the situation. His cheek wound and the bullet hole were smack against her pretty lawn.

She'd have to find a way to clean the grass.

Among other things.

23

One down, one more to go?

Leaving the dead man in her garden, the .22 still pressed to her flank, Grace eased her way out of the gate. Expecting another nasty surprise; this time she'd be ready.

The street was empty.

Again, she walked west—away from the Chrysler—rounded the corner and passed the front of the cottage and was sure no one was lurking there before continuing to the nearest corner where she turned right.

It took a while to reposition herself half a block behind the boxy sedan.

Feeling a visceral sense of purpose, muscular and savage, that she'd never experienced before.

Maybe the gravity of what she'd done—the ending of a human life—would rebound on her but at this moment to hell with the bastard who may have ended Andrew's life.

With his fat friend.

She was alive.

Now I'm more than a murderer's daughter.

She slinked closer to the Chrysler, knew black glass could conceal anything but continued anyway and got right up against the car's rear bumper. Gun in hand, she kicked the rear bumper softly.

No response.

Her second kick was harder. The vehicle remained the stolid inanimate object it was.

Crouching low, she scurried to the front passenger window, pointed the Beretta at the glass. Rapped the window hard with her knuckles.

Silence.

She tried the door. Locked. Same for the driver's side.

If Beefy was in there, he'd have reacted. She retreated and waited anyway. Ten minutes, twenty thirty forty.

The car sat there.

So tonight had been a one-man mission. Maybe Beef had been injured when she'd run him into the berm.

Or he was fine and the two of them simply figured Grace an easy victim.

Invade her space, search her records, and if Mr. Average Size was lucky enough to find her, gut her and slit her throat and dump her in a dingy, demeaning place.

Best-laid plans.

Now he was no-man.

24

Back in the garden, Grace bypassed the corpse and walked to the cottage's rear door. Unlocking and disabling the alarm—he'd never gotten in—she headed for the patient bathroom and retrieved a box of rubber gloves from beneath the sink. Part of the gear used by her once-a-week cleaning woman, Smeralda.

Who, she realized, would be by in three days.

Plenty of time.

Returning outside, she gloved up and shined her Maglite on the corpse. As she'd expected, no exit wound. She prodded his back anyway; not even a bulge. Shifting her beam to the lawn, she searched for the ejected cartridge, finally located it a few feet from the body, nestled in grass.

Pocketing her find, she kneeled by the body, carefully turned it on its back, and illuminated the inert face.

Her initial impression had been on point: forty give or take, unremarkable features leaning toward coarse, two or three days of beard growth, a short, bristly haircut, dark on top, graying at the temples.

The wounds she'd inflicted on his cheek looked deep but were surprisingly pallid and not leaking much blood. She'd figured she'd done more damage. Then she understood: His nonbeating heart had stopped pumping juice to his skin.

His polyester jacket was unremarkable but for the sizable hole above his left breast. Blood rimmed the edges of the shredded fabric, but again, nothing copious.

Like Grace, he wore dark cargo pants, probably for similar reasons. Same for the Nikes on his feet.

Dress for success . . . Mr. Knife meets Dr. Blades . . .

Speaking of which . . . she found the weapon, wiped it down, laid it on the grass, and unzipped his jacket. Underneath he wore a light-colored V-neck T-shirt. No pockets. But the pants offered plenty of storage and Grace found a cellphone, a steel ring hosting a dozen or so delicate-looking lock picks, and a short chain bearing four keys and an alarm trigger with a Chrysler logo.

She took another look at the knife. Nasty little push-blade thing.

She fought off a thought: **This could be him looking down at me.**

Slipping out the garden door again, she scanned the street, found it empty, made her way back to the Chrysler. Beeping the car alarm off, she waited.

Nothing.

Time to have a look.

The interior was spotless but the glove compartment gave up a fat wallet and a folded, legal-sized manila envelope secured by an eyelet and a string. In the trunk, she found three weapons in black nylon cases: a shotgun, a rifle, and a gray-metal handgun, larger and heavier than her Glock.

He'd come with a personal armory but had left all his firepower in the car.

Take a knife to a gunfight . . .

Overconfidence or wanting to avoid undue noise?

Either way, Grace knew she'd been lucky. It took her two trips to get the weapons and the other contents of the car back to her garden, another while to wipe the car down.

Now, seeing the body, she felt nothing but serenity. One day she might wonder what that said about her. Right now, introspection was an enemy; she had three hours until sunrise, needed to use the time wisely.

Yet another silent walk up the street led her to her rented Jeep. Keeping the headlights off, she rolled slowly to her garage. Remote-controlling the door open, she backed into the space vacated by the Aston, sealed herself from view with another click.

A second inspection of the body revealed no additional seepage but when she lifted it at the shoulders, she spied a ten-inch patch of grass where the chest had made contact that was tamped and moist and dark. Above that, a smaller blotch where the cheek wounds had leaked.

Red dew.

Returning to the cottage, she brought back several of the heavy-duty black garbage bags Smeralda favored and a roll of duct tape she'd used years ago, improvising a quick fix of a kitchen sink leak as she waited for the plumber.

Double-bagging Knife's face, she created a makeshift hood that she taped tight. The bags were too small to contain the rest of the body so she cut one into three rectangles and created a triple-ply postmortem plastic bandage that she taped snugly over the chest wound. Two more bags, each lashed tightly at wrist and biceps, served to cover his hands and arms.

She stood and inspected her handiwork. The thing on the ground resembled something out of a horror movie. Snip a couple of eyeholes in the hood and he'd be the crazed killer. As it was, he was the hapless victim, and Grace was fine with that.

Now the hard part. She was strong for her size but his deadweight was substantial. Cutting up another bag, she worked for a long time easing it under the body. Additional tape, quadruple layered, created two loops across his chest and over his knees: handles for gripping the harness she'd fashioned.

As she'd hoped, the plastic served as a lubricant when she began the twenty-foot drag to the garage. But there was slippage as well and the trip was an ordeal. Once she reached the Jeep's rear hatch, she went back and retrieved the weapons and everything else she'd gotten from the Chrysler and placed them on the floor behind the front seat. Lowering the rear seat performed double duty, creating a long bed for storage and concealing the stash from casual inspection.

Getting the body up and in left her panting.

Recovering her breath, she regarded the mummy she'd created with sour pride, checked the rear-deck carpeting for evidence of seepage, found none. But she didn't delude herself that some high-tech DNA swab wouldn't pick up a trace of something.

Returning to the garden, she hosed down the wet spots in the grass, keeping the hose at low pressure to avoid making noise. Finally, the bloodstains had run off completely into the flower beds edging the east wall of the cottage. Using a spade from the garage, she gently tilled the dirt until she was satisfied everything looked normal. A reexamination of the lawn on all fours revealed a few stray specks of dried blood stiffening a few grass tips. Using her Maglite, nail scissors, and a sandwich bag, she snipped and barbered, deposited the trimmings into the bag, which she encased in two other bags, everything sealed. The feather-light package was secreted in her pant pocket. Same for the knife that had nearly killed her, now compressed to a stubby black oblong.

She gave the backyard several more minutes of serious scrutiny, could see no sign of disruption.

The entire encounter with Knife had taken seconds not minutes.

The two of them dancing smoothly, each thinking they were leading.

Back in the garage, she closed the Jeep's hatch, got in the driver's seat, was gone.

Returning to the Valley, this time on Benedict Canyon, she got back on the 101 but exited well short of the Hilton on Calabasas, gliding onto Topanga Canyon Boulevard. To the north was suburbia. South shot straight into a tortuous canyon and that's where she needed to be.

The road that snaked past the junction of Old Topanga and

New Topanga was treacherous if you didn't know where you were going. Grace had driven it hundreds of times at night, for recreation, working the Aston at high speed around S-curves that gave the engine a chance to breathe.

To her left were uninterrupted banks of hillside. The right was the same except when limestone and dirt broke unpredictably, creating thousand-foot dead-drops.

Miscalculate a turn and you were toast.

More than once, Grace, trusting her gut and her memory, had shut her eyes as she raced along the borders of oblivion.

Now she kept them wide open.

During the entire ride, she didn't spot another vehicle but she did notice a few deer standing stock-still, including an elaborately pointed buck who seemed to sneer at her. And as she neared her first destination a smallish canine thing that was either a baby coyote or a fox scampered over the precipice.

Lowering her speed, she searched for a turnoff, found one but bypassed it for another and pulled to the side and U-turned with barely enough room for the maneuver. Doubling back a mile, she parked the Jeep in the narrow strip of dirt running parallel to the blacktop.

That placed her inches from a yawning abyss. Keeping the motor running but the lights doused, she got out, unlatched the Jeep, and eased the plastic-shrouded body down to the dirt. Breathing deeply, she used her sneakered toes and her gloved hands to nudge it closer to the edge.

She'd chosen well; visibility was generous in both directions and the acute slope maximized the chance of a long, unimpeded drop.

She waited to make sure no headlights approached, steeled herself, and pushed the body over. It thumped and rustled, faster and faster, an accelerating drumbeat.

Finally: silence.

If she was lucky her package would remain there a long

time. Or forever. If not, she couldn't see how it could ever be linked to her.

Driving several yards north and reparking, she walked back and flashlit the spot where she'd dumped the body. She hadn't left footprints, the ground was too firm, but faint tire tracks rutted and swelled the dirt and she smoothed them.

Returning to the Jeep she U-turned again, drove south for several miles, stopped and flung the rifle over the side.

Ten minutes later, same treatment for the handgun.

Another five minutes and the blood-tipped grass clippings were history.

Continuing south she came to Topanga's terminus on PCH.

Apparently, her karmic destination.

Maybe at heart, she was just another California beach girl.

She drove fifty miles north to Oxnard, gliding along the blackened agricultural fringes of the gritty harbor town. The knife was flung over chain link onto a strawberry field. Maybe some lucky stoop-laborer would score personal protection.

One of six dumpsters fronting an electronics importer in an industrial park just off Sturgis Road served as the shotgun's new home. The park was deserted and Grace managed to hoist herself high enough to rearrange the container's contents. Tossing cardboard and paper and packing materials like some celluloid salad, she shielded the weapon from easy discovery.

Driving to Camino del Sol led her to Del Norte Boulevard and that got her right to the 101.

She was back in her room at the Hilton at five forty-eight a.m.

25

Fortified by a bottle of water, four caramel caffeine chews, and three sticks of turkey jerky, Grace arrayed the enemy's belongings atop a small desk across from her generous hotel bed.

Wallet, first. Cheap black leather, cracked at the edges, generic, packed chubby.

An up-to-date California driver's license for Beldrim Arthur Benn was stuck in an inner compartment—secreted but hardly hidden. The physical traits and age matched the man she'd shot. Longer hair and a grizzled mustache did nothing to blur the I.D., this was him.

Beldrim. Effete tag for a hit man.

Cut the bitch, Beldrim.

Had he gone by Bell? Drim? Bill?

Grace decided to think of him as Bill.

Bill Benn, man about town.

No longer.

Suddenly, she was seized by anger. When that peaked and flickered out, something else took its place—queasy vulnerability.

The steely resonance of narrowly missed death. The nasty little knife entering her, twisting, ravaging. For no good reason.

She felt cold. Her hands began to shake and a wave of vertigo washed from the top of her head to her now-frigid feet and she had to hold on to the arms of her chair, work at slow-breathing, easing her autonomic nervous system back to equilibrium.

The body initiates, the mind follows . . . here we go, feeling better . . . no, we're not.

Vomiting felt like the right thing to do but Grace suppressed the urge.

It took a while to feel almost normal.

A little improvised mantra repeated six times helped:

Bill Benn, man no longer about town.

Rot in hell.

The address on the license was a P.O.B. in San Francisco.

No credit cards or anything personal in the wallet, cash had given it heft.

Grace counted out nine hundred forty dollars in twenties and fifties, added the bills to her own money stash—victor and spoils and all that—moved the now-thin wallet to the right side of the table.

Next, she turned to Beldrim Benn's cellphone, hopes for enlightenment dimming when she saw it was a cheap disposable, identical brand to the second one she'd bought, with no recent calls registered.

Not a single photo in the digital camera's memory.

Murderous Bill bringing virgin equipment to his assignment. For all Grace knew, the license was phony—a correct image paired with bogus information.

She Googled **beldrim arthur benn,** pulled up a single hit on a seventy-six-year-old man who'd died two years ago in Collinsville, Illinois. Brief obit in the **Collinsville Herald.** Dearly departed Beldrim had been a carpenter. Survivors included a daughter, Mona, and a son, Beldrim A. Junior.

The age fit.

No mention of a wife or a widow. So probably divorced from Junior's mom.

So maybe that is your real name. Or you stole some poor schmuck's I.D.

Adding **junior** to the keywords pulled up two hits, both references to Beldrim Benn Junior's position as director of operations for Alamo Adjustments in Berkeley, California. No indication what the company did.

Something hush-hush?

Alamo, as in remember . . . old grievances?

Then she realized the real monument was housed in San Antonio. Andrew plucking associations from his brain, or had he actually lived there?

She typed in **alamo adjustments,** expecting a website, social networking, a LinkedIn listing, anything.

Nothing.

But logging onto a website that offered pay-per-view access to older phone directories, Grace located a five-year-old address for the company on Center Street in Berkeley. So the company had once existed.

Alamo. Fortress. Good intentions, hopeless cause. Disaster.

Adjustments . . . for what? The only thing that word evoked for Grace was chiropractic and twenty minutes of pursuing that angle proved fruitless.

Back to Benn himself. Going all covert, so something secretive—high-tech—biotech? A toxic threat that Andrew had uncovered and threatened to expose?

Berkeley, the quintessential college town, was crammed with high-tech . . . but Grace couldn't shake the feeling that Andrew had come to her because of an issue with kin. A close relative.

For the time being, she'd stick with that.

Andrew, dead. Probably at Bill's hands. Or those of Bill's partner, the heavy guy who'd tailed her on PCH.

Bill, dead.

One good thing about the bastard traveling light and hush-hush: His weapons were more likely to be unregistered and hard to trace.

Grace inspected the keys on the short chain. Three Schlages in addition to the one that operated the Chrysler. No defining marks.

In the junk pile.

Now the envelope.

. . .

Thin packet. When Grace opened it and shook, a piece of paper dropped out.

Fresh, white sheet, computer-typed. Neatly composed fact sheet on Grace: her name, office address, and phone numbers, professional qualifications, and a grainy black-and-white photo downloaded from the USC psych department faculty face-page.

Seven-year-old headshot, taken right after she'd graduated and was asked to stay on as a lecturer. The youngest person in the history of the department to reach that milestone, Malcolm had informed her.

The three of them—Malcolm, Sophie, her—had been celebrating with an extravagant dinner at Spago in Beverly Hills when he'd made the pronouncement. Sophie smiling in her quiet way, Malcolm downing his third Manhattan on the rocks and beaming.

Grace, nibbling shrimp cocktail and marveling at how she didn't feel any different, enjoyed seeing the two of them like that.

She deserved the job offer but academia held no attraction for her, she'd always been one for reality.

Still, Malcolm and Sophie were happy and that supplied a nice memory . . . don't veer off the track, girl. Grace's jaw clenched and her brain followed suit. A frisson of nausea returned and she got back to basics and examined the headshot Bill had used to I.D. her.

She'd worn her hair down to her butt back then, parted in the middle, naturally straight but for foolish little ruffles at the ends. Ponytailing at the photographer's request "to show us more of your pretty face, Doctor."

Not much difference between the seven-year-old headshot and now; she'd aged well. Providing Bill Benn Junior an accurate likeness. Same for anyone who picked up after him.

Tearing the sheet into strips that she halved twice, she added the resulting confetti to the trash pile. Shaking the envelope a second time produced nothing but she peered inside, anyway. Spotted a small square of paper tucked deep in the bottom fold.

Jostling the envelope failed to dislodge it, so she reached in, curled her fingers and tweezed, extricated a roughly scissored square of newspaper pulp, about an inch and a half wide.

The paper was brown and brittle and as Grace held it, beer-colored flecks dropped onto the table. Laying it down, she had a good look.

Part of a black-and-white photo, obviously cropped from a larger image.

Blue-ink circle around the face of a boy about ten or eleven. Roundish face, handsomely symmetrical, dominated by wide pale eyes. A huge, unruly mane of blond hair sheathed his forehead and hid his eyebrows. Thick, curling strands trailed onto his chest.

A boy swallowed by hair.

He stared straight ahead, but not at the camera. Deep-set, sunken eyes that belonged on an old man had been stretched to their limits by fear.

The result was pitiful. Feral.

Familiar.

Now Grace knew where she'd first seen the man who called himself Atoner.

26

Grace's ninth and tenth birthdays were marked by light but tasteless angel food cake and delicious chocolate mint ice cream served on brightly colored paper plates in the ranch's kitchen.

She knew that Mrs. Stage tried to make a party out of the situation, but each year there were different kids living at the ranch, many too young to understand what was going on, others crying a lot and in no mood to celebrate.

The first time, a week before Grace's ninth, Ramona asked her what flavor cake she preferred.

She said, "Angel food, please," because Ramona always baked angel food and even though it didn't taste like much, Grace knew she could pull it off easily.

"Well, sure, honey, I can do that. How about some special frosting? Chocolate, vanilla? Anything else that tickles your fancy—you tell me piña colada, I'll sure as heck try to find it."

Flavors don't matter. Birthdays don't matter.

Grace said, "Chocolate is good."

Fosters moved in and out of the ranch like cars at a shopping center parking lot. Many were whisked away soon, still scared. When new kids asked Grace questions, she made sure to be helpful; when you had knowledge you were considered bigger than you actually were. She also made sure to feed and change the little kids when there were too many for Ramona to handle at one time and she learned how to hum and coo in a way that calmed babies down.

All that was just the job she'd taken on for herself. There was no point getting to know anyone; the more time she had to herself, the better.

Mostly, she read and walked. The desert turned all sorts of colors when the sun began to fade. Her favorite was a light purple that glowed. The color chart in her science curriculum said it was magenta.

The only constant was Bobby Canova. He couldn't eat cake or ice cream, so during what Mrs. Stage called the "birthday bashes" she propped his chair up against the table and belted him in and fixed one of his nutritional shakes. He'd give one of his hard-to-read smiles and roll his head and make his noises and Mrs. Stage would say, "He loves his parties."

Birthday girl or not, Grace took charge and fed him through a straw. Because the birthday thing was really for Mrs. Stage, not her.

There was another reason she wanted to help, something she'd noticed between her ninth and tenth birthdays: Mrs. Stage was walking and talking slower, standing kind of bent over and also sleeping more. Some mornings, Grace would come down and find the kitchen empty. Get to sit by herself and enjoy the quiet, drinking milk and juice and waiting.

It was as if Ramona had gotten much older, all of a sudden. Grace hoped if she could stop her from wearing out completely, like a rusty machine, the ranch could stay like it was for a while. She began cleaning rooms other than her own, started helping with laundry. Even calling the new pest man, Jorge, when she saw too many big spiders or beetles or white ants.

Ramona said, "Grace, you don't need to be such a worker bee. You're growing up too fast."

But she never stopped Grace from pitching in.

As her eleventh birthday approached, Grace noticed that her work didn't seem to be helping as much; Mrs. Stage was slowing even more and sometimes she placed her hand on her chest as if it hurt to breathe.

That made Grace stop thinking of the ranch as her home and more like just another foster.

One day, she knew, some caseworker would show up and tell her to pack her things.

In the meantime, she'd walk and read and learn as much as she could.

During bashes, Ramona made a big show of bringing the cake to the table, studded with blazing candles, announcing that Grace should stand up while everyone sang her "Happy Birthday" because Grace was the "honoree."

Fosters who were old enough were asked to join in on Ramona's screechy "Happy Birthday" followed by her call for "Many more!" Mostly there were humming and uncomfortable looks around the table, no meaningful supplement to Ramona's tone-deaf delivery.

A few days before Grace's eleventh birthday, Ramona said, "How about lemon frosting instead of chocolate?"

Grace pretended to consider that. "Sure. Thank you."

Opening a drawer, Ramona held up a box of frosting mix she'd already bought. Mediterranean Lemon. "This year, he might be able to make it—Professor Bluestone. That'd be nice, huh?"

"Yes."

"He thinks you're a genius."

Grace nodded.

"He told you he thought you were smart?" said Ramona.

Many times. "Kind of."

"Well . . . I invited him, if he can show up, he will."

He couldn't. Didn't.

Once in a while the caseworker bringing or taking a foster was Wayne Knutsen. When he saw Grace, he'd look away, embarrassed, and Grace wondered why. Then she figured it out: He'd told her he was quitting social services to become a lawyer, hadn't kept his word, and didn't want to be reminded of his failure.

That was the thing about knowing people's secrets: It could make them not like you.

But one evening, after settling in a terrified little black-Asian girl named Saraquina, Wayne headed straight for Grace, who was looking at the desert and pretending not to know he was there.

"Hey, there. Remember me?"

"You brought me."

"There you go," he said, smiling. "Wayne. They tell me you're plowing your way through advanced educational materials. So everything's working out?"

"Yes, sir."

"You get a kick out of hitting the books—out of studying, huh?"

"Yes."

"Well, then," he said, fooling with his ponytail. "Gonna have to start calling you Amazing Grace." His eyes fluttered and he reached out a hand, as if to pat her head, drew it back quickly. "Well, that's great. The fact that you love to study, I mean. I could probably use your help."

"With what?"

Wayne laughed. "Just kidding."

Grace said, "Law school?"

He faced the desert, turned serious, finally shrugged. "You are a sharp one . . . yup, law school, getting through is a challenge. I work all day, go to classes at night, the books aren't interesting like the stuff you're learning."

He sighed. "At your age, I was just like you. Got a kick out of gaining new knowledge. But now? I'm forty-seven, Grace. If I could devote full time to my studies, I could probably do better. But being as it's only part-time, I'm stuck with an unaccredited school. That means not the best school, Grace, so good luck passing the bar—the lawyer's exam."

He kept looking at magenta sand. "It's going to take me a while to finish. If I finish."

"You will," said Grace.

He scratched his nose, turned, and gave Grace a long, thoughtful look. "That's your prediction, huh?"

"Yes."

"Why?"

"It's what you want."

"Hmm. Well, sometimes I'm not sure about that—anyway, continue to amaze us, Ms. Grace. You've sure got the raw material—brains, I mean. That gives you an advantage in this crazy world even though . . ." He shook his head. "Bottom line, you're in good shape, kid."

Grace said nothing.

Wayne said, "That was what we call a compliment."

"Thank you."

"Yeah, well . . . so you really do like it here?"

"Yes."

"She's a good person, Ramona. Can't say no to a kid in need, not many like her. That's why I thought she'd be good for you."

"Thank you."

"I felt you deserved it," he said. "After everything you went through."

No such thing as deserve.

Grace said "Thank you" again.

"Anyway," said Wayne, "I'm glad we could chat . . . listen, here's my card, if you ever need something. Not that you're likely to, Ramona tells me you're pretty darn self-sufficient— know how to take care of yourself."

He kept translating phrases Grace already understood like most grown-ups did. The only one who didn't think she was stupid was Malcolm Bluestone. Except in the beginning, when he also explained too much. But somehow he figured out what Grace understood.

Wayne's pudgy fingers dangled the card. Grace took it and thanked him a fourth time, hoping that would end the conversation and she could go inside and get back to a book on butterflies and moths.

Danaus plexippus. The monarch. Seeing pictures of them swarming a rooftop, a cloud of orange and black, made Grace look up "monarch" in her dictionary.

A sovereign ruler. A king or queen.

Grace couldn't see anything kingy or queeny about the butterflies. She'd have called them pumpkin fliers. Or flame bugs, something like that. Maybe the scientist who named them was feeling like a big shot when he—

Wayne was saying, "No need to thank me, just doing my job."

But he was smiling and looking relaxed.

Make people happy about themselves, they won't bother you.

Grace smiled back. Winking at her, Wayne turned and trudged to his car.

After he drove away, Grace looked at the card.

Wayne J. Knutsen, B.A.
Social Service Coordinator

The first wastebasket she found was in the corner of the living room and that's where the card ended up.

Malcolm Bluestone's appearances were irregular events that Grace looked forward to because he always brought her something interesting: new curriculum materials, books, and best of all, old magazines. Grace found the advertisements the most intriguing features, all those photos and paintings that taught her about the way things used to be.

There were all kinds of magazines. Malcolm was a big reader, too, maybe that's why he understood her.

Réalités seemed to be for people who wanted to live in France and had a lot of money and ate strange things.

House and Garden was about making your house fancy so people would like you.

Popular Mechanics and **Popular Science** showed you how to build things you probably wouldn't use and talked about fantastic things that were supposed to happen but so far hadn't, like flying cars and movies with smells coming out of holes in the wall of the theater.

Once, after reading four copies of **Popular Science** cover to cover, Grace had a night of nice dreams imagining herself flying in a car above the desert.

The Saturday Evening Post had bright, colorful paintings of smiling people with shiny hair, and big families, and birthday and Christmas and Thanksgiving parties so crowded you could barely fit into the room. Turkey, too, there was always a huge roast turkey about to be cut up by a clean-looking man with a big knife. Sometimes a ham, with black things sticking out of it and pineapple slices on top.

The smiling people seemed like space aliens. Grace enjoyed the paintings the same way she liked reading about astronomy.

Time and **Newsweek** wrote about sad, angry, and boring things and gave opinions about books and movies. Grace couldn't see any difference between the two of them and she couldn't understand why anyone would use someone else's opinion rather than their own.

The most interesting magazine was **Psychology Today.** Malcolm began bringing those when Grace turned ten, as if she'd finally earned something. Right away she got interested in experiments you could do with people, things that made them act smart or stupid, hate or like or ignore each other.

She especially enjoyed the ones where people acted differently when they were alone or in groups.

Also, experiments that showed how you could lead people the way you wanted if you made them feel really good or really bad.

Once, after Malcolm hadn't shown up in a long time, he

asked if he could give Grace a few more tests—"nothing time consuming, just more stories about pictures." She said, "Sure," but also waved a copy of **Psychology Today.** "Do you have more of these?"

"I wondered what you'd think. Piqued your interest?"

"Yes."

"Sure, Grace, you can have any back copies I can scare up—you know, I think there might be some in the car."

Grace tagged along as they left the house and walked to his brown Buick station wagon. A woman sat in the front passenger seat, thin-faced with what looked like snow-white hair.

Grace had never thought of Malcolm riding around with anyone.

Then she told herself that was stupid. He was a friendly person, probably had all sorts of friends. A whole world outside the ranch and magazines and psychological tests for fosters.

For some reason, that made Grace's tummy hurt, right under the middle of her rib cage. She looked away from the woman.

The passenger window lowered. A soft, kind of whispery voice said, "Hey, there."

Grace, forced to turn and face the woman, noticed her eyebrows first. Perfectly shaped little half circles. The mouth smiling at her was coated with purple-red lipstick.

Straight white teeth. Pointy chin. A dimple on the left cheek. A really attractive woman; she looked like someone in **Réalités,** wearing haute couture, eating escargots, and drinking Bordeaux in Paris or Cannes or in a grand château in the Loire Valley.

Grace said, "Hi," so softly she barely heard herself. The white-haired woman got out of the station wagon. She was about Malcolm's age and tall—nothing like Malcolm's skyscraper height but still one of the tallest women Grace had ever seen—and thin as a crane. She wore a gray sweater, black pants, and flat silver shoes with gold buckles. Her hair wasn't white; sunlight transformed it to really light blond, kind of gold at the same time it was kind of silver.

What **Réalités** called "ash blond."

Bangs that looked as if they'd been cut with the aid of a ruler reached halfway down a smooth, pale forehead. The eyes beneath the bangs were kind of squinty, widely spaced, with tiny lines at the corners. Deep-blue eyes that settled easily on Grace, and even though the woman was still smiling, Grace felt there was sadness in her.

Malcolm said, "Ms. Grace Blades, this is Professor Sophia Muller. Professor, Grace."

The blond woman held out her hand to Grace. "Ignore all that foofaraw, I'm his wife. Call me Sophie."

Her fingers were long, smooth, cool, with pearly nails that shone like chrome on a car. She looked like a queen in a picture book. Like a **monarch.**

Malcolm was big but he wasn't really monarch-y. More like Little John in Robin Hood. A kindly giant. Not like the one up the beanstalk . . .

Professor Sophia Muller said, "Grace is a pretty name." Wider smile. "For a pretty girl."

Grace felt her face go hot.

Professor Sophia Muller sensed she'd done something wrong because she looked briefly at her husband.

She's his wife, be nice to her.

Grace said, "Thank you for the compliment. Pleased to meet you, Professor Muller."

She's his wife but she doesn't use his name?

No one talked for a moment then Malcolm said, "Oh, yeah, **Psych Today,**" and unlatched the station wagon's rear door, emerging with an armload of magazines.

Professor Sophia Muller said, "So he found a way to unload his collection. Grace, I should pay you for making next spring cleaning easier."

Grace knew she was expected to smile and did.

Malcolm Bluestone said, "I'll bring these to your room."

Grace said, "I can do it."

"Kind of heavy, Grace."

Sophia Muller said, "Let's all do it, three people will make it a snap."

Dividing the magazines, they beelined to the house with Grace leading, Malcolm and Sophie trailing as they curtailed their strides to avoid trampling Grace's heels.

Grace had no idea what they were thinking but she was thinking: **He introduced us. So she didn't know my name before.**

So he never told her about me.

Was that because he didn't talk about fosters?

Or Grace wasn't that important to him?

It was like he'd read her mind because the next time he showed up, a week later, he said, "Enjoying the psych stuff?"

"Yes."

"Sophie really enjoyed meeting you."

Grace lied. "I enjoyed meeting her, too." She had nothing against new people but didn't think much about them.

When she and Malcolm had settled in the living room to complete the second part of the new picture-story test, he said, "You probably figured this out: I never told Sophie about you because of confidentiality—your privacy. Beyond that, I take what we do seriously, it's not a topic for casual conversation. Anyway, it's not about me, you're the star."

"Star of what?" said Grace, even though she had a pretty good idea of what he meant. For some reason, she wanted him to talk more.

"Of what we do together, Grace. My goal is to optimize your education."

Not explaining "optimize." He was the **only** person who treated her like she wasn't stupid.

"I explained—about not discussing you, because I didn't

want you to think you weren't important. On the contrary, you are, and that's precisely why I need to guard your privacy. Even though you have no legal right to confidentiality. Know why not?"

"Because I'm a foster?"

Soft brown eyes drooped sadly. "No, but that's a logical answer. The actual reason is **no** kids under eighteen have a right to confidentiality, even things they tell psychologists. I think that's absurd and terribly wrong, Grace. I think we need to respect children a lot more than we do. So I ignore the rules and keep secrets a hundred percent and don't write things down that kids wouldn't want written down."

His words were tumbling out fast. Dots of pink colored his generous cheeks and one hand was a fist the size of a baseball glove.

Grace said, "Respect your elders but also respect your youngers."

Malcolm stared at her. Broke out laughing. The fist bumped against the tabletop. "That's **brilliant,** Grace. May I borrow it so **I** can sound brilliant?"

"Sure."

"You're exactly right. We need to look at all people as if they're respectable and intelligent. Even infants. There was a psychologist—a famous one named William James, he lived a long time ago, was considered important, anything he said people listened to. He was convinced babies lived in a 'blooming, buzzing confusion.' Like they were insects, like there was no pattern to how they felt or thought or acted. In William James's day, that sounded pretty reasonable. Know why?"

"People didn't know any better."

"Precisely, Grace, and the reason they didn't know any better was because they had no idea how to **measure** what babies were feeling or thinking. Then psychologists got smarter and developed tests and poof!"—he snapped his fingers— "wouldn't you know it, babies got smarter. And that trend continues, Grace. It's what makes psychology exciting, at least to me. We're learning so much all the time. Not just about human infants. Higher animals, too—whales, dolphins, monkeys, even birds—turns out crows are super clever. The smarter we get about understanding them, the smarter they get. So maybe we should start out assuming everyone's smart."

He always liked to talk but even for him this was a lot of words.

Grace said, "Maybe."

Malcolm crossed a tree-trunk leg. "I'm probably being tedious. Anyway, those are the reasons I didn't tell Sophie about you. Precisely **because** you're important."

Grace's tummy began hurting again. The same way it had when Professor Muller told her she was pretty. She covered her mouth with her hand, not wanting something stupid to fall out.

Malcolm said, "Here's a new magazine you might want to take a look at."

Out of his briefcase came a volume with an orange paper cover and no pictures, just words. At the top was the title: **Journal of Consulting and Clinical Psychology.**

"Thank you."

He laughed. "Don't thank me so soon, Grace. See if you like it. This isn't like **Psych Today,** which is for people who haven't studied psychology on a high level. This is for actual psychologists and to be truthful, some of it's rather hard to understand. I don't always understand everything. You may find it the essence of dull."

Grace flipped a page. Lots of words, small letters, a bar graph at the bottom.

He took out the new picture test. "Okay. Let's get to work. And thanks for your continuing help."

"With what?"

"The testing."

"It doesn't bother me."

"I know, Grace. For you tests are mental exercise. But even so, you've helped me. I have a new understanding of ultra-gifted kids in a way I didn't before I met you."

Again, Grace had no idea what to say.

Malcolm ran a finger under the neckband of his turtle-neck sweater. "Hot in here . . . what I'm trying to get across, Grace, is that while you're unique, you have much to teach about how extremely bright children cope with challenges."

The word "challenges" was like a branding iron in one of Steve Stage's western movies, turning the pain in Grace's belly to fire. She moved her hand from her mouth but something she couldn't believe still fell out: "You pity me."

What was worse than the words was the anger in her voice. A bad girl, a demon, talking through her.

Malcolm held up his hands, as if he had no idea what to do with them.

As if he didn't want to be hit.

Grace began to cry. "I'm sorry, Professor Bluestone."

"Sorry for what?"

"For saying that."

"Grace, you can feel or say anything you want."

He handed her a tissue. She snatched it and dried her eyes, disgusted with herself for acting like a demonic baby.

Now everything would change.

More tears trickled out. She slapped them away, pleased that she'd made her face sting.

Malcolm waited awhile before speaking. "I think I get why you're upset. You don't want me to see you as vulnerable. Am I right, Grace?"

She sniffed, dabbed. Nodded.

"Well, I don't see you that way, Grace. Just the opposite, I see you as resilient. So I'm sorry if I wasn't clear."

He waited some more. Grace remained silent, the tissue compressed in her taut hand.

"I came here originally because Ramona told me how smart you were, she was concerned that the regular curriculum was useless. She also gave me your history. Because I asked her, that's what I do, it's part of being thorough. The more I learned about you the more I realized how remarkably you've developed. Nevertheless, I'd be dishonest if I pretended you hadn't faced challenges. We all do. But do I pity you? Absolutely not."

Grace hung her head. She wished this day would end.

"Oh, boy," Malcolm said. "I'm digging myself deeper . . . okay, give me another chance to explain."

Silence.

"May I?"

Nod.

"I like to think of myself as a caring person but pity is **not** part of my repertoire because pity lowers people. However"—he cleared his throat—"I **am** interested in people who deal with tough situations well. How they make sense of their world when things get rough. Because I think psychology needs to be more positive. To learn about strengths as well as weaknesses. Maybe I feel that way because of Sophie, what her parents went through. They endured a terrible experience called the Holocaust—I can't recall if any of the curriculum materials covered that—"

"History, Module Seventeen," said Grace. "World War Two and Its Aftermath. Hitler, Himmler, Nazis, storm troopers, Auschwitz, Bergen-Belsen, Treb . . . linko?"

"Treblinka. Sophie's parents ended up in a camp called Buchenwald. They survived and came to America and were blessed with Sophie and led wonderful lives. When I met them, their joyful approach to life surprised me because when you learn to become a psychologist it's all about problems and weakness and getting to know Sophie's parents taught me I'd missed a lot. Then they died—nothing to do with Buchenwald, they got old and sick and passed. That made me even more intent on understanding people who adjust and adapt well. What I call super survivors."

Grace said, "She uses another name."

"Pardon?"

"You're Bluestone, she's Muller. Is that because she wants to remember her family in a special way?"

Malcolm blinked. "Grace, I am privileged to know you."

Again, the branding iron. Why couldn't she accept nice things?

Grace's eyes shot down to the table, fixed on the orange cover of the **Journal of Consulting and Clinical Psychology**. The articles inside were listed there and the first title she saw was about randomly truncated variable interval reinforcement in a sample of neurologically enhanced hooded rats.

This **was** going to be the essence of dull.

"Yeah, I know," said Malcolm, smiling. "Still, you'll probably get more out of it than my grad students."

Two months after Grace's eleventh-birthday bash, three new fosters arrived at the ranch, in a strange and different way.

The first odd thing was they came at night, when everyone except Ramona and Grace was asleep. Ramona would probably have been sleeping, she'd been going in earlier and earlier, keeping medicine in her apron pocket, muttering about needing to get off her feet. Grace had been studying her intently, trying to figure out when the ranch would close and she'd end up exiled to a place she wouldn't like.

Grace was up because she tended to wake in the middle of the night, feel alert, and read herself back to sleep. That's what she was doing when she heard Ramona descend the stairs.

She went to check, found Ramona at the front door, looking nervous and glancing at the big Hamilton man's watch she always wore, the one Steve Stage had worn when he was alive.

Ramona turned to see Grace. "Got some new ones checking in, Grace. You'd best be heading back to slumber-land."

"I can help."

"No, you go to your room." Speaking more roughly than usual.

Grace obeyed and climbed the stairs. Opening her window, she perched on her bed with a clear view of what was happening down below.

A big dark-green car and a white-and-black police car were parked in front of the house.

Out of the police car stepped two policemen in tan uniforms. Out of the green car stepped a man in a suit with a badge clipped to his breast pocket. All three were big men, with mustaches. They formed a half circle facing Ramona. A conversation Grace couldn't hear lasted for a while, everyone looking serious. Then one of the uniformed policemen opened the rear door of the police car and made a waving motion.

Out came three kids, two boys and a girl.

The smaller boy was about Grace's age, the taller one older—thirteen or fourteen. The girl was the youngest, maybe eight or nine, and she stood in a way that made her seem even smaller than she was.

All three were blond, really light blond, just as light as Sophia Muller. Their hair was like straw in the wind, wild and sticking out all over the place.

Long hair, reaching below their waists, even the boys.

Their clothes looked strange: too-large, loose-fitting black shirts with no collars and baggy, too-long black pants whose bottoms collected on the dirt like accordions.

As if the three of them were members of a club that you needed a uniform for but the uniforms hadn't come out right.

The girl stood close to the younger boy, who was biting his nails and tapping his foot. Those two had round, soft faces and looked almost like twins, if she hadn't been so much younger. He moved his shoulder so it touched hers and she began sucking her thumb. His foot began tapping faster.

The older boy had a longer face. He stood away from them and seemed relaxed, slouching and bending one leg as his eyes moved all over the place. First he stared straight at the house, then past the house and out to the desert, followed by a quick swing toward Ramona.

Then his face tilted upward. Aiming himself directly at Grace. She realized she'd left her light on, was framed like a picture.

The older boy locked in on her eyes and smiled. He was handsome, with a firm jaw and a crooked smile. His look said he and Grace shared a secret. But there was nothing friendly about the smile.

Just the opposite, a hungry smile. Like he was a coyote and she was food.

Grace backed away from the window and drew her curtains.

She thought, but couldn't be sure, that she heard laughter from down below.

The following morning, as usual, Grace was the first to get up and Ramona entered the kitchen as she was pouring herself a second glass of juice.

"Morning, Ms. Blades." Ramona began fiddling with the coffeemaker.

"Who are they?"

Ramona's hands stilled. "I figured you'd be curious. But trust me, Grace, don't be." She kept her back to Grace, as if she and Grace didn't know each other as well as Grace thought they did.

When she'd loaded coffee into the urn, she said, "I'll tell you their names because obviously you need to call them something. But that's it, okay?"

It's not okay at all, it's stupid. "Sure."

"They'll be gone soon, anyway. It's a favor I'm doing for social services because they need a . . ." Head shake. "That's all you need to know, young lady."

Walking to the fridge, Ramona pulled out eggs and butter. Grace said, "Their names . . ."

"What . . . oh, yeah. Okay, the big one is Sam, his brother is Ty, the little sister is Lily. Got that?"

"Yes."

"Sam, Ty, Lily," Ramona repeated. As if Grace needed to memorize a lesson.

Sam. That smile remained in her head, like a bad smell. Ty and Lily had acted like scared babies and she didn't want to spend time with them, either.

Ramona began frying up a clump of her tasteless eggs. The coffeemaker burbled. She looked at her man's watch. "Oops, better check on Bobby."

She went upstairs and returned looking exhausted as she eased Bobby into the kitchen. He was walking on two canes that fit around his elbows, moving slowly, with jerks and starts. In the middle of his trek to the table, he stopped and flashed Grace one of his confusing smiles. Or maybe he wasn't smiling at Grace, just at . . . being there. But it was better than Sam's smile so she smiled back and helped Ramona seat him and strap him in and filled his special cup from one of the cans of nutritional shakes in the fridge.

During Ramona's absence, bumps had begun sounding from above. The three new fosters were awake but they hadn't come down.

Grace fed Bobby his shake. He gurgled and rolled his head, worked hard at sucking up liquid, finally succeeded.

Ramona kept frying. Her reaction to Grace being helpful with Bobby had changed over three years. She'd started out insisting Grace didn't need to work, she was a kid, not a caretaker. When Grace kept up her chores, anyway, Ramona began thanking her.

But that had stopped, too. Nowadays, Ramona said nothing, expecting Grace to be part of the ranch routine.

As she placed a plate of eggs in front of Grace, the bumps from the second floor grew louder and faster and moments later they transformed to the rhythmic **thump-thump-thump** of feet on stairs. Six feet made a lot of noise. To Grace it sounded like stampeding horses in one of Steve Stage's old movies.

Sam appeared first, swaggering into the kitchen as if he'd always lived there. Sharp eyes took in the room, settled on the fry pan. "Thanks so much, ma'am, but I don't eat eggs. None of us do. It's animal matter."

Ty and Lily hid themselves behind him, yawning and rubbing their eyes. Ty was even softer-looking up close, all boy, no man. Sam, on the other hand, had muscles in his arms and the beginnings of facial hair: oily-looking smudges on his chin and above his upper lip.

All three of them had on the same strange black clothing they'd arrived in. Up close, Grace could see the uniforms were hand-sewn, with clumsy, crooked stitching and loose threads, fashioned of a rough fabric that looked more like a bag for potatoes than for clothes.

Another weird thing she noticed now was that Sam wore an earring, a small gold loop that pierced his left lobe.

Grace ignored them and ate but a cold feeling was spreading on the back of her neck. Glancing up from her plate, she saw Sam looking at her. His lips would've been pretty on a girl but on him they looked like . . . a costume.

Grace returned to her plate. He snorted.

Ramona said, "You're vegetarians, huh?"

Sam said, "Most vegetarians eat eggs and milk. We're vegan."

"Be nice if someone told me. So what's your usual breakfast?"

"Greens," said Sam.

"Vegetables?"

"Green vegetables, ma'am. Manna from the earth."

"Wasn't manna birds or something?"

"No, ma'am, that was the miraculous quail visited upon the sinful Hebrews. Manna was a heavenly vegetable."

Ramona grunted. "Greens . . ." She rummaged in the fridge. "I've got lettuce and cucumbers that were supposed to be for dinner but I suppose I can cook something else for dinner. Sit down and I'll wash you a mess of **greens**."

Talking differently than she did to other fosters. Like she didn't want these kids here.

"Where?" said Sam.

"Where what?"

"Where should we sit, ma'am?"

"Where?" said Ramona. "At the table."

"I understand that, ma'am, but where at the table? Please assign us positions."

Ramona put her hands on her hips. Bobby's head rolled. Sam laughed. At Bobby.

Ty and Lily hadn't uttered a word, remained pressed together, same as last night.

Ramona said, "Positions, huh? Okay, you—big brother—sit over there." Pointing to the seat farthest from Bobby. "Then we'll have your little brother sit next to this gentleman, who is Bobby, and you, cutie—Lily—you're between Ty and this young lady, who is Grace. She's very smart and she likes her privacy."

Aiming the statement at Sam. Maybe she'd seen the hunger, too.

Sam grinned. Usually, Grace didn't like being protected, but this morning, she didn't mind it at all.

Sam moved toward her, shifted direction, and followed Ramona's seating instructions. Telling his siblings, "Go."

They obeyed.

Once seated, he flicked his earring. "Privacy is an illusion."

Ramona glared. "Well, then, you go on respecting Ms. Blades's illusion."

"Blades," said Sam, as if he found the name amusing. "Of course, ma'am. We're here to be respectful. And grateful." He snickered. "We're here to be absolutely perfect."

. . .

That day, at ten a.m., Grace experienced a new emotion.

Malcolm Bluestone drove up in his brown station wagon, hauled out what she recognized as testing materials, but when she walked up to him, he said, "Hi, there. I think we'll have some time in the afternoon."

Grace looked at the tests.

"Oh, these," said Malcolm. "I'm going to be spending some time with the new fosters."

Going to be. Not **have to.** That made it **his** decision, he preferred to be with the weirdos in the weird clothes.

Grace turned away.

"Maybe one p.m.?" Malcolm called out. "Love to hear how you liked the anthropology materials."

Grace didn't answer. Her eyes were burning and her chest felt tight.

She'd read about this and now she felt it. Jealousy.

She'd make sure to be somewhere else at one p.m.

Malcolm found her at two thirty. She'd been reading, sitting behind a group of old oak trees on the far side of the green slimy pool, her back feeling the roughness of the bark. For part of the time, Bobby had been nearby. Sitting limply on the pool deck and dangling his feet in the water and laughing, as Ramona clutched his elbow to keep him steady.

Grace's current favorite book was a thick volume on spiders written by a biologist from Oxford University in England. She was concentrating on the wolf spider, with its fangs and its hiding holes from which it killed its food. Wolf spiders also carried their eggs—their babies—on their stomachs. A lot of the killing they did was to stay healthy so they could be good mothers . . .

When Ramona and Bobby left, Grace was reading about the wolf spider's breeding habits and didn't notice.

At two thirty, Grace was thirsty. Figuring Malcolm was gone, she headed back toward the house for some juice. He was just coming out the front door and smiled. "There you are! Got time for anthropology?"

"I'm tired," she said, and went inside.

The following day, he arrived earlier than ever, when everyone was still in the kitchen. Grace was poking rubbery eggs, Bobby was struggling with his nutritional drink, and the new fosters, still in their strange clothing, were eating huge plates of salad.

Sam had given up smiling hungrily at Grace after she kept ignoring him. Now when their eyes met, he yawned and snickered. Ty and Lily continued to have frightened eyes and stick close to each other. Like they were brother and sister but Sam was outside the circle.

If Sam was Grace's brother she'd have kept him outside, too.

When Malcolm entered the kitchen, the room got small.

Sam said, "Again?" with a whine in his voice.

"Only if you're willing," said Malcolm. "But not now, anyway. I need to confer with Grace."

"Confer," said Sam.

"It means—"

Sam laughed. "I know what it means. I just don't get what you'd confer with **her** about."

Malcolm drew himself up even taller. His lips moved, as if he was trying to figure out an answer. Instead, he turned to Grace. "If you've got time, Ms. Blades."

"**Ms.** Blades," said Sam.

Lily let out a small whimpering sound. Sam whipped his head toward her. That silenced the little girl. Ty watched, eyes soft and moist, and Grace felt like telling him everything would be okay. Then she told herself, **That's probably a lie,** and went back to her eggs.

Malcolm said, "Grace?"

"Yes, sir."

"If you've got time . . ."

"Sure," she snapped and marched out of the kitchen.

Sam said, "Someone's got an attitude." He was the only person laughing.

When they were settled in the living room, Malcolm said, "They'll be gone, soon."

Grace said, "Who?"

Malcolm's smile was faint and not at all happy. "Precisely. Okay, the so-called primitive tribes of Borneo and Sumatra. What did you think of their . . ."

For the next hour, Grace listened and commented, told him what she figured he wanted to hear. The jealousy she'd experienced had faded but now she found herself bored with his little speeches, just wanting to be alone.

Still, she cooperated. He'd done lots of nice things for her and she figured she'd find him interesting again.

The next morning, she was up extra early at six, spent some time in bed reading before descending to the kitchen. As she passed the door to the room where the new fosters slept, she heard a young voice whining or crying—a girl, obviously Lily—then a deeper voice shushing her to silence.

She poured herself milk and waited for Ramona. When she was still alone at seven, she began to wonder if Ramona was okay, she'd been looking so tired and seemed to be taking more pills. At seven fifteen, she was considering knocking on Ramona's door. Against the rules, but still . . .

As she contemplated, a terrible noise from the second floor yanked her out of her chair and she shot to her feet.

More crying. But not Lily.

The door to Bobby's room was wide open. Ramona stood at the side of his bed, still in her nightclothes, her mouth sunken looking and different and Grace realized she hadn't put in her teeth. Ramona's feet were bare. Reading glasses dangled from a chain across her flat chest. Moaning and tearing at her hair, she kept staring at Bobby, eyes wild and frightened.

Bobby lay on his back, mouth open wider than ever, his eyes half shut and filmed as if a snail had slithered across them. Shiny stuff streaked his chin. His face was a strange color, gray with green around the edges. Like mossy rock, not human skin.

Ramona moaned and said, "Oh, no," and pointed at Bobby. As if Grace needed direction.

Bobby's pajama top had been ripped open, revealing a sliver of gray skin. No movement from breathing. From anything.

The tube that fed him air at night was on the floor at the side of the bed, still hissing. Lately, Bobby had taken to struggling in his sleep, calling out, making noises that could scare you if you didn't know about him. He'd never dislodged the tube but Ramona worried he might so she'd begun taping the yellowish rubber to his pajama top. Taping it tight, Grace knew, because sometimes she was the one to untape in the morning and that took effort.

The tape was still attached to the tube as it hissed on the floor, a yellowish snake.

Grace stood there. Ramona ran past her, down the stairs. Grace heard the kitchen door slam.

She stayed up there with Bobby for no reason. Looking at him. Looking at death. She'd seen it before but he looked different than the strangers in the red room. No blood, no frenzied twisting of the body, nothing gross, at all.

Just the opposite, really. He looked . . . peaceful.

Except for the weird skin color that seemed to be getting greener and greener.

She went back downstairs, passed the room where the three new fosters slept and heard more shushing.

Then: laughter.

. . .

Ramona wasn't in the house and it took a while to find her but Grace did: outside, standing at the far end of the green pool, still tearing at her hair, pacing back and forth.

Grace approached her slowly. When people got their nerves all excited you never knew what could happen.

When Ramona saw her, she began shaking her head. Violently, as if trying to dislodge something painful that had stuck itself in her brain.

Grace stopped.

Ramona barked, "Go!"

Grace didn't move.

Ramona screamed, "Didn't you hear me? Go inside!"

Grace turned to leave. Before she completed the arc, movement caught her eye and she swiveled quickly.

Just in time to see Ramona's face scrunched up in pain, now **her** color was bad, really pale, and she was clutching her chest and her toothless mouth was an O of pain and fear as she lost balance and stumbled forward.

Eyes rolling back, she fell into the green, murky water.

Grace hurtled toward her.

Ramona was sinking fast but Grace managed to get hold of one of her hands and started pulling. Slime coated both of them and she lost her grip and Ramona began to sink. Throwing herself belly-down on the cement pool deck, Grace regained her hold, added her other hand, yanked hard. Sharp pain cut through her back and her shoulders and her neck.

No matter what, she would **not** let go.

Panting and growling, she managed to pull Ramona up high enough to draw the old woman's face out of the water. The moment she saw Ramona, algae-streaked, mouth wide open, eyes unseeing, just like Bobby's, she knew she was wasting her time, this was her second look at death in one morning. But she held on to Ramona and managed to raise herself to a crouch and draw Ramona a few more inches out of the pool. After that, things got easier because the parts of

Ramona still in the water were floating, her lifeless body co-operating as Grace, still crouching, scuttling awkwardly like a crab, dragged her all the way around the pool to the shallow end where her body floated above the steps and Grace was able to pull her out completely.

Grace stood there, soaked, out of breath. Ramona's death looked worse than Bobby's. Her face was twisted, like she'd died upset about something.

But still not as bad as the red room . . .

Touching Ramona's chest, then making sure by touching Ramona's green-slimed neck, Grace knew for sure.

Gone.

Leaving Ramona on the pool deck, an old, tired dead thing soaking up bright morning desert sun, Grace ran to the house and got on the phone.

The 911 operator asked her to stay on the line. While she was waiting, the three new fosters came down the stairs, this time Ty first, then Lily, Sam backing them up.

Ty's eyes met Grace's. He shook his head and frowned, as if terribly disappointed. Lily knuckled her eyes and cried silently. Sam had no expression on his face.

But when he turned away to look out the kitchen window, with a clear view of Ramona's body, Grace saw the beginnings of a smile curving his too-pretty lips.

An ambulance came first and Grace directed the fire department men to Ramona. Moments later, three police cars arrived, then a green car like the one that had been there when the new fosters arrived. Followed by a blue car and a black car. Four men and two women, all wearing badges, looked at Ramona, talked to the fire department men, finally headed for Grace.

She told them, "There's another dead person, upstairs."

All four fosters were corralled in the kitchen, under the eye of one of the uniformed policewomen, who stood with her arms folded across her chest.

Soon after, the two woman detectives and two male detectives came in and divided up the children. One detective to a kid.

Grace got a small, thin man who introduced himself as Ray but his badge said R. G. Ballance. He took her to the small butler's pantry off the kitchen. He was the oldest of the four detectives, with white hair and wrinkles. Grace's clothes were still damp with spots and shreds of green slime attached.

He pointed to a chair and said, "Sit down, dear," but remained on his feet. When Grace complied, he went on: "Can I get you some water"—checking his notepad—"Grace?"

"No, thank you."

"You're sure?"

"Yes, sir."

"Need a sweater? You know, maybe you should change into dry clothes first."

"I'm okay, sir."

"You're sure?"

"It's drying fast."

"Hmm . . . all right, then, I don't want to ask you to do anything that's hard for you, Grace. But if you could tell me what you saw—if you saw anything—that would be helpful."

Grace told him.

About Bobby in his bed, the air tube on the floor, Ramona standing there, really upset, then fleeing downstairs.

About Grace waiting, wanting to give her time to calm down. Finally looking for her.

Ramona yelling at her to go inside, which wasn't like her, she never yelled.

About Grace starting to obey but then Ramona touched her chest and fell.

When she got to the part about grabbing Ramona's hand and holding on and finally managing to draw her to the shallow end, she told R. G. Ballance a short version.

He said, "Wow, you're to be commended—that means you did something good."

"It didn't work."

"It . . . yeah, I guess so, afraid not. But still, you tried your best. How old are you?"

"Eleven."

"Almost twelve?"

"My birthday was a month ago." **We had angel food cake and chocolate mint ice cream for the third time and there won't be a fourth time.**

"Just eleven," said Ray. "Wow. Well, now, this is a terrible thing for a little girl to see. But you did your best and that's what matters, Grace."

Grace's brain filled with lightning-like starbursts and thunder-like noise. A voice inside shrieked: **Liar liar liar! That's not what matters! Everything will change!**

She said, "Thank you, sir."

"Well," he said, "that probably wraps it up—my guess is Mrs. Stage had a heart attack. Sounds like shock brought it on, seeing that boy in his bed."

"Bobby," said Grace. "Robert Canova."

"Robert Canova . . . what's his story?"

"He was born with problems."

"Looks like it . . ." R. G. Ballance closed his pad. "Okay, you're probably wondering what's going to happen. Obviously, you can't stay here but we'll make sure you're okay, don't you worry."

"Thank you."

"Pleasure, Grace. Is there anything else you feel like telling me?"

Grace thought of three things she could tell him:

1. Bobby's air tube, taped tightly every night, really tight, loose on the floor, hissing like a yellow snake. That made no sense.

2. The look on Ty's face when he came down into the kitchen: sad—more like disappointed. But not surprised. Like he'd expected something bad to happen and that had come true.
3. The smile forming on Sam's lips as he looked out at Ramona's body.

She said, "No, sir, that's everything."

An hour later, the three new fosters had been trundled off in the blue car and Grace was in back of the black car.

At the wheel was one of the woman detectives, brown-haired and freckle-faced. Unlike R. G. Ballance, she didn't introduce herself and as she gunned the engine she chewed gum really fast.

After she'd been driving for a while, she said, "I'm Nancy and I'm a detective, okay? I'm taking you to a place that might seem a little scary. It's called juvenile hall and it's mostly for kids who've gotten into trouble. But there's also a section for kids like you who need to wait until their situation gets clear. Okay?"

"Okay."

"Like I said, it could seem a little—almost like a jail. Okay? But I'll make sure to put you in a safe part. But still, it's not the prettiest situation . . . anyway, before you know it, you'll be out of there. Okay?"

"Okay."

"Really," said Nancy. "Everything's going to work out okay."

27

Sitting in her room at the Hilton Garden Inn, Grace kept looking at the old photo of the blond boy.

Ty.

Andrew.

Atoner.

Viewing the picture made morphing boy to man easy. He'd darkened his hair as Grace just had, and puberty had firmed up his face. But the features remained the same.

Was the reason for the dye job worry that his naturally fair color would trigger Grace's memory? Knowing who she'd been and seeking her out not because of the article?

Even if the article had led him to her, had that triggered recall of the girl living at Stagecoach Ranch?

Who'd been there when the bad things happened.

Then she realized that Malcolm had spent time testing the three sibs so perhaps it **was** him Ty/Andrew had sought. And **that** had led him to Grace.

Either way, it was Grace he'd ended up with. Intending to strip bare old, malevolent secrets.

About the death of Bobby Canova? A vicious brother with a hungry smile?

That seemed scant motive for murder; try proving anything about deaths ruled as natural over two decades ago. So there had to be more.

Grown-up Sam doing grown-up bad things.

As Grace pondered, another terrible possibility intruded: Grace's name **had** triggered Andrew's memory and he'd pulled up her faculty photo.

Known who she was at the Opus lounge.

No, impossible. If he had, no way would he have gone along with . . .

Stop; turn the page, move on.

Find the enemy before he finds you.

Fixing the date of the wild-haired children's arrival at the ranch was simple: two months after Grace's eleventh birthday.

She logged onto the L.A. **Times** archives for that day and plugged in **sam ty lily**. Nothing. Using fourteen additional dates—a week before and after—was no more productive.

Vegans, Sam spouting the Bible, and the homemade clothing suggested a cult or a sect, or at least an odd, isolated upbringing. The trio arriving at night with a two-vehicle police escort—uniforms as well as a detective—suggested serious criminality.

But pairing **cult** and **sect** with the fifteen dates was also a dead end and Grace decided she could keyword forever and miss the crucial cue. Better to examine actual coverage of that period and that meant scrolling laboriously through entire issues of the newspaper.

Fortunately, microfilm was also computer-archived and the **Times** offered free access through 1980, with more recent stories pay-per-view. Grace was about to enter her credit card when she realized she could reach the same destination for free, using her psych department faculty account at the med school library.

Either way, she'd be documenting her search but she couldn't see any way that could be avoided. Or any possibility of linking herself to Beldrim Benn, even assuming his corpse would be found.

She recalled the sound of the body, thumping and rolling into the abyss.

Went the faculty route.

.   .   .

Making her way through months of microfilm was a slow process that produced nothing for hours.

She scrolled back two-thirds of a year before finding it.

Cult Compound in the Desert Offers Up Grisly Clues
Leader, shot by police, may have been a multiple murderer
By Selwyn Rodrigo
Times Staff Writer

Forensic examination of the remains of the Fortress Cult, so called because its leader constructed a walled enclosure of abandoned motor homes and dug out caves at a remote Mojave Desert location, has produced evidence of past killings at the site.

Four months ago, self-appointed "Grand Chieftain" Arundel Roi, born Roald Leroy Arundel, died in a shootout with county sheriffs after reports of child abuse led social service workers to the squalid site that housed what authorities say was a one-man apocalyptic cult based on biblical prophecy, racist "identity religion" and witchcraft.

That visit proved fatal to social worker Bradley Gainsborough, who was shot without warning shortly after entering the encampment. A second investigator, Candace Miller, was also wounded but managed to escape and phone authorities. The pitched battle that ensued saw Arundel Roi perish, along with all three of his common-law wives.

The women, each of whom had a criminal record, were thought to be recruited by Roi, 67, during his time as a prison guard at the Sybil Brand women's jail. All four cultists were found clutching high-powered rifles and, in the case of one woman, a live hand grenade.

Inspection of the grounds revealed a bunker stocked with additional explosives and firearms and another piled high with an assortment of machetes, cleavers and other knives, as well as hate literature and pornography. The appearance of what appeared to be blood, tissue and hair on some of the cutting weapons sparked a coroner's analysis, the results of which have just been released.

Though most of the organic material on the blades remains unidentified, DNA matches to three missing persons have been obtained. The victims were homeless men whose names have not been divulged. All were seen in the company of Arundel Roi or one of his wives at a bar in Saugus. Monetary gain appears to have been the motive, as welfare checks in the names of the deceased were mailed to a post office box rented by Roi.

Further studies will be carried out on soil and other samples at the site, set on a remote pocket of federal parkland rarely encountered by the public due to its inaccessibility and rumors of environmental taint due to a history as a military practice bomb site during the Korean War.

Grace composed a list: **arundel roi, wives, victims, selwyn rodrigo, candace miller.**

She reread the article to see if she'd missed anything. Rodrigo had cited reports of child abuse but made no mention of specific children.

Scrolling back four additional months, she found the original account of the raid. Candace Miller's age was listed as forty-nine, making her seventy-three now. References to the cult's "odd food preferences, survivalist tactics and living off the land" told Grace she was on the right track.

Then the clincher: Roi and his wives had been found wearing "crudely fashioned, homemade black uniforms."

But still no names other than Roi's. Because this was L.A. and it was all about the star.

Same old story, she supposed. Charismatically endowed freak attracts brain-dead followers. Sires children, of course, because megalomaniacs crave self-perpetuation.

The original article also came with a photo: a headshot of Arundel Roi, in his early fifties, back when he'd been Correctional Officer Roald Leroy Arundel.

The guru of the Fortress Cult had probably been decent looking as a young man, with a strong, square jaw, the suggestion of broad shoulders, and neatly pinned ears. But middle age had left him bloated and dissolute, with a loose-skinned face and neck, and heavily pouched, down-slanted eyes that glinted with arrogance.

His hair was trimmed in a white no-nonsense cop buzz. A bushy salt-and-pepper mustache completely obscured his mouth.

The whiskers spread in a way that suggested amusement.

A hungry smile the likes of which Grace had seen before.

She pictured Roi swaggering past the cells of female prisoners, drunk on power and personality disorder and testosterone.

Fox, henhouse.

Several more hours looking for anything she could find on the Fortress Cult exhausted the resources of three wire services and four additional newspapers.

All that energy expended for zero insight; journalism apparently consisted of rephrasing someone else's copy. Though in this case she supposed reporters could be forgiven their thin gruel: The authorities had let out precious little by way of facts.

She searched a year forward. No additional stories on the forensics, not a single word about wives, homeless victims, the impact upon children of being raised on filth and lunacy.

Looking for personal data on the reporter, Selwyn Rodrigo, she found a six-year-old death notice in the **Times**. The reporter had succumbed at age sixty-eight to a "long illness."

The obit outlined Rodrigo's career. Shortly after the Fortress piece, he'd switched to financial and business writing in Washington, D.C., and had stuck with that. A promotion, no doubt, but Grace wondered if Rodrigo had craved escape, switching from bourbon to weak tea.

His survivors were listed as a wife, Maryanne, and a daughter, Ingrid. The former had passed away three years after her husband. No data on Ingrid and no reason to think her father had confided in her.

Turning her attention to the wounded social worker, Candace Miller, she found lots of women with that name but none that matched age-wise.

Now what?

Focus on the kids.

But if information on the cult progeny existed, it would be buried in the inaccessible bowels of social services. She seriously considered tapping Delaware's police connections to see if any other official reports existed, dismissed that quickly: She'd killed a man, the last thing she needed was police scrutiny.

So what to do . . . once upon a time, faced with tough questions, her reflex had been **Ask Malcolm.** At some point—soon after entering adolescence—she'd decided that growing up meant pulling away from Malcolm, sometimes to the point of avoiding him. Still, the knowledge of his presence had been a balm.

Now . . . her nerves were thrumming in all sorts of discordant keys.

Crossing to the mini-bar, she took out a mini-bottle of vodka and considered a mini-drink. Thought better of it and returned the booze to its resting place.

What would Malcolm do?

His voice, in finest low-volume bass register, coated her brain: **When everything's a mess, Grace, it can sometimes help to start at the beginning.**

Grace deep-breathed and relaxed her muscles and concentrated on dredging up long-avoided details about the three children in black. That failed to produce anything new and frustration led to a loose, maddening free association.

Her own life at the ranch.

The night she'd been driven there, her fear as the car hurtled through desolate terrain. Past signs indicating the place where the red room had . . . surrounded her.

So different from previous foster-treks, apathetic drivers showing up unannounced, curt orders to pack her paltry belongings. Dumping her with no explanation and often no introduction.

The worker who'd taken her to the ranch had been different.

Wayne Knutsen. Portly, ponytailed, would-be lawyer. During their final conversation, he'd handed Grace his card. Which she'd promptly tossed. Snotty little kid.

Like Candace Miller he'd be at least seventy. Not a healthy-looking guy at the time so vital old age seemed unlikely.

Not expecting much, she returned to Google.

Surprise, surprise.

Knutsen, DiPrimo, Banks and Levine
A Legal Corporation

Substantial downtown enterprise on South Flower Street, Wayne J. Knutsen the founder and senior partner, presiding over two dozen other attorneys.

A former welfare worker spending his days with "contracts, estates and business litigation"? Could it be?

Grace linked to **KDBL Professional Staff**, found photos and bios of all the lawyers in the firm.

The senior partner was elderly and beyond well fed, completely bald with a tiny white goatee that filmed the first of two and a half chins. He'd posed in navy pinstripes, a snowy pin-collar shirt, and a large-knotted bright-blue tie of gleaming silk.

His smile radiated self-satisfaction. No more rattling compact for Attorney Knutsen, Grace figured him in a big Mercedes.

He'd complained about attending an unaccredited law school but had graduated from UC Hastings, followed up with specialty certificates in tax and real estate law, earned himself numerous seats on bar committees.

If you ever need anything.

Time to test his sincerity.

28

A hotshot attorney would be shielded by layers of assistants so Grace decided to show up in person. Her research in the hotel room had lasted until just after five p.m. and the drive downtown would be wretched but what else did she have to do? She ate a handful of mixed nuts, chewed a stick of beef jerky to pulp, washed the gourmet meal down with a sixteen-ounce bottle of water.

Exiting the room with watchful eyes, she took the stairs to the garage, revved up the Jeep, and was gone. An hour and twenty minutes later she was driving past the gray stone edifice that housed Knutsen, DiPrimo, Banks and Levine and figuring she'd arrived too late, everyone would be gone.

The building was seven stories tall, august and spotless, one of a few older, elegant structures lining one of the more presentable avenues in an inelegant downtown. Parking in a pay lot a block away, she walked, found brass doors open, and rode the elevator up to the sixth floor. Knutsen, DiPrimo, Banks and Levine took up half the square footage; the rest was leased to an accounting firm. Both operations were entered through large, bright, glass-walled waiting rooms that faced each other across a plush-carpeted lobby the color of ripe blueberries.

The woman behind the desk at KDBL (bold brass letters) was young, pretty, alert, and locking her desk.

Grace smiled and said, "Mr. Knutsen, please."

"The office is closed."

"If Mr. Knutsen's in, he'll want to see me. Dr. Grace Blades."

"Doctor," said the receptionist, doubtfully. "He's tied up."

"No problem, I can wait." Grace took a chair, picked

a copy of a thick, crisp glossy titled **Beverly Hills Dream Homes** out of a wall rack, and pretended to be fascinated with vulgar Xanadus. This year, kitchens were the size of ranch houses, forty-seat IMAX theaters the requisite display of wealth.

The receptionist punched an extension, stated Grace's name, and hung up looking astonished. "You'll still need to wait and I'm leaving in five minutes."

Ninety seconds, her phone beeped and she got on, mumbled furtively, frowned. "Come this way."

The office was the predictable corner suite, with two walls of glass offering miles of view to the north and the east. The desk was ten feet of bleached maple semicircle with built-in phone and computer docks. Degrees and other impressive papers were silver-framed and mounted artistically on a rear wall covered with beige grass cloth and capped by shiny bronze crown molding.

Two huge photos, each around two feet square, perched on a matching maple credenza: The nearer showed present-day Wayne Knutsen and another man, younger but not young, maybe sixty or so, slim and gray-haired. The two of them were conspicuously red-nosed, wearing sunglasses and baseball hats, grinning. The other man grasped a fishing rod. A sizable halibut balanced in Wayne Knutsen's pudgy hands.

The second shot was of the same pair, again happy, wearing matching tuxedos and holding hands, standing before a woman wearing ecclesiastical garb and a crucifix necklace. Rice and confetti speckled the carpet below.

No one in the office, then a voice behind Grace said, "Thanks, Sheila, go home, you work too hard."

Studying Grace as he walked behind his desk, Wayne Knutsen, Esq., leaned across the glossy surface and extended a meaty paw. His complexion was florid, his body a collection of loosely assembled, bobbling balloons. But for the tiny chin beard, his face was shaved exquisitely close. Santa Claus after a session of advanced grooming.

If he'd been smiling, Grace might've expected **Ho ho ho.**

He was dead serious and maybe a bit alarmed.

As Grace's hand approached his, she saw a broad platinum band circling his left ring finger. His clasp was brief, warm, dry.

Whatever had tied him up didn't require formality: He wore a bright-yellow polo shirt and seersucker pants, neither of which did a thing for his physique, narrow cuffs barely touching blue suede boat shoes worn sockless. Sunburned bald dome, spotted brown; Grace noticed the baseball hat he'd donned in the fishing photo hanging on the finial of a lamp.

He said, "This takes me back. **Doctor** Grace Blades? I'm not surprised." His stare had intensified but his voice sounded tentative.

Grace said, "I'm not surprised, either."

He blinked. Eased his bulk into a throne-like chair and motioned for Grace to settle in one of three facing chairs.

"Grace Blades . . . this is a **huge** surprise. What kind of doctor are you?"

"Clinical psychologist."

"Ah." Nodding as if that were the only logical choice.

He thinks I've compensated.

"When did you get your Ph.D.?"

"Eight years ago."

Mental calculations caused his eyes to travel horizontally. "You were . . ."

"Twenty-five, almost twenty-six."

"Young." Soft smile. "You still are. Well, congratulations, that's quite an accomplishment. So what brings you here?"

Grace said, "I need to hire you."

"For . . ."

Opening her purse, she removed her wallet. "What's your retainer?"

"Whoa," said Wayne Knutsen. "I can't really tell you that until you let me know what you need."

"Confidentiality, for starts."

"Ah . . . well, money doesn't need to change hands for that, Doctor—may I call you Grace?"

She smiled. "You'd better. I want to pay you."

"Really, it's not necessary. Mere contemplation of hiring a lawyer bestows confidentiality."

"I know that."

His soft belly heaved. "Very well, fork over . . . ten bucks."

"Seriously."

"I am serious, Grace. I'm still trying to process your being here. I must confess when I heard your name I was a bit . . . startled!"

"Sorry for popping in out of the blue but what was startling?"

He clicked his teeth, looked at the ceiling, then back at Grace. "For all I knew you harbored some kind of resentment. For something I might've done a long time ago. Though for the life of me I couldn't imagine what it might be."

Still, he'd welcomed her in. Curiosity trumping worry. Grace grew hopeful.

"On the contrary," she said. "You were the only one worth a damn. That's why I'm here." Peeling off five twenties, she placed them on the desk.

"Interesting version of ten bucks," said Wayne Knutsen. "Funny, I remember math being a strong suit for you. Then again, everything was your strong suit. You were the smartest kid I ever encountered on the job."

"Then let's call this a higher-order calculation."

Wayne Knutsen sighed. "Okay, I'll give the rest to charity. Any preferences?"

"Your call."

"We keep Lhasa apsos—my partner and I—correction, my husband, I'm still getting used to that. So perhaps Lhasa Apso Rescue?"

"Sounds good," said Grace.

"All right, Doctor Grace, you have hired me and your secrets are inviolate. Now, what might they be?"

"First of all, thanks are in order. For caring enough to bring me to Stagecoach Ranch."

His skin went from pink to crimson as he waved that off. But he was clearly pleased. "Just doing my job."

"You did more than that. It made a huge difference, I should've thanked you long ago."

His mouth ticced. "Glad to hear things worked out well. Yes, she was a great woman. How long were you at the ranch?"

Grace said, "Till I was eleven. Ramona died."

"Oh. Sorry—was she ill?"

"Heart condition," said Grace. "She never said anything to the kids but she started looking tired and taking pills and one day she collapsed and fell into the swimming pool."

"My God, that's ghastly," said Wayne Knutsen. "For you as well as her." He shook his head. "How sad. She was an exceptional person."

"She was."

"Poor Ramona," he said. "Had I stayed with the department, I'd have known but I finally left."

"Law school full-time."

"I'd been attending a non-accredited school and it was a waste of time, just a moneymaking scam. But the real reason I left, Grace, is that I'd had enough. Of the entire system, the way kids were treated like property, shuttled back and forth, minimal supervision and certainly no attempt to get to know them in depth. Then there were those cases of abuse, not a rule, an exception, but still . . . I won't get into that."

He rubbed one eye. "I'm not exempting myself from critical judgment, Grace. I was part of it, did far too much by the book. The caseloads they saddled us with made it impossible to work properly. I suppose that's as good an excuse as any."

"Yet you managed to rise above it," said Grace.

He was taken aback. Searched her face for sarcasm. She made sure to let him know she meant it.

He said, "You're being kind but I didn't rise nearly as often as I should have. In your case, it was easy. You **made** it easy. Because you were so darn precocious, I felt there was hope for . . ." He smiled. "I hoped. When I checked one last time with Ramona to see how you were doing—the day before I handed in my walking papers—she said you were fine but shy, keeping to yourself, totally bored with the curriculum. My mind was elsewhere, psychologically I'd quit a long time ago, so I told her there was nothing I could do. Ramona said fine, she'd handle it herself, and hung up. Obviously, she handled it well." Another tremble of lip. "No doubt better than I could've."

Grace said, "It was a job, not a life sentence, Wayne. The way you helped me says you probably helped a lot more kids than you're admitting."

His smile was broad, amused. "I can see you're an excellent therapist, Dr. Blades—gawd, that sounds terrific. **Doctor.** Good for **you**! . . . so what brings you here?"

Grace said, "You gave me your card, said if I needed anything to get in touch."

He flinched. "Did I? You must've caught me in a weak moment. Trust me, by then I was effectively gone. Wondering how I was going to make ends meet. I had to start from scratch, ended up at Hastings, moved north, figuring to do family law. Work for change within the system and all that good stuff, right? By the first semester I felt so free being **away** from the system that I changed my orientation completely and went for the boring stuff."

He laughed. "Boring lucrative amoral stuff. I drive a Jaguar now, Grace. Sometimes I'm cruising along and I laugh at myself."

"I drive an Aston Martin."

"Really." He whistled. "Clinical psychology's been good to you, has it? So what's this about? A patient in a fix?"

"A therapist in a fix."

He sat back and rested his hands on his paunch.

Grace told him only what he needed to know.

Three wild-haired children in homemade black uniforms, a probable child murder by the oldest brother, a second murder by extension.

Two decades later, reappearance by the younger brother, still burdened by terrible secrets and seeking expiation.

Likely dying because of his secrets.

She ended with two components that she hoped would evoke the feelings that had led him to treat her with kindness decades ago.

Her research leading to the Fortress Cult.

The intense personal danger she now found herself in.

No mention of the man in her garden, rolling a body into a ravine, tossing guns, a knife. Living like a fugitive.

Wayne Knutsen listened without interruption, took a moment to contemplate. "Well, Grace, this is quite . . . I don't know what to say, it's almost like something out of a movie."

"Wish it was, Wayne. But it's real, Wayne. And I'm scared."

"I understand . . . twenty-three years ago . . ."

"And a few months."

He looked at her the way a doctor examines a new patient. "We're talking the majority of your life, Grace. A significant slice of mine . . . I'm rambling, this is so unexpected—you really think that older boy killed the sick one—Bobby?"

"I'm sure of it. He had all the early trappings of psychopathy and there's no way that oxygen tube could've come free on its own."

"What if Bobby experienced a seizure and yanked it hard enough—I'm just being lawyerly."

"Bobby could barely walk, let alone muster the strength to rip loose his dressings. Ramona was careful, she taped the tube tight. I know because sometimes I was the one to untape him in the morning."

"She used you as an aide?"

"I insisted on helping, it made me feel strong, in control. And I could tell her own strength was fading."

"I see . . . this is going to be a terrible question, but I'm an attorney, I have to ask." He shifted in his chair. "Given Ramona's fading health, growing attached to this Bobby, is there the remotest possibility that she would have—"

"Euthanized a child?" said Grace. "No way. When she discovered Bobby dead, she was horrified. I'm certain the shock is what finished her off."

"My God," said Wayne Knutsen. "What a nightmare . . . poor Ramona. Poor child—and there was no one else who could've—"

"It was him, Wayne."

"Yes, yes, you'd know. You say his name was Sam? That's not much to go on. How old was he?"

"Thirteen, fourteen, give or take."

"Old enough, I suppose," he said. "What with all the crazy stuff one keeps hearing . . . all right, it's a horrible thing to consider but I defer to your judgment. What happened to you after the ranch closed? Though I'm not sure I want to hear what I suspect." His head shook; his jowls vibrated. One hand swiped clumsily at his eyes.

Grace leaned over and took his hand, comforted him the way she would any patient.

"Actually," she said, "everything worked out fine."

29

Nancy the Detective drove fast to juvenile hall and Grace knew she couldn't wait to get the job over with. Within moments of passing through a series of locked doors, she was gone and Grace was being escorted by a huge black woman who called her "honey," and reassured her she'd be fine.

Saying nice words, but in a tired voice, like she'd swallowed a tape recorder and pressed the **Play** button.

Grace's clothes were taken away and she was given bright-orange pants and a matching shirt. A plastic band with her name misspelled "Blande" was snapped tight around her scrawny wrist. The room she was placed in was tiny and smelled of pee and poop, with crude graffiti all over the walls and bars for one wall. The only window, set high up, was black because it looked out on the night. Furniture was a cot, a dresser, and a metal toilet without a lid.

The big black woman said, "Sorry we got to use a solitary cell for you tonight, honey, but it's for your own good, there's no sense placing you in a dorm, you didn't do nothing to end up here. Not like some of the kids, they're real bad, no need for you to know, just take it as fact, okay?"

"Okay."

"That's why I'm going to have to lock you in, honey. For your own good. Try to get a good night's sleep and in the morning you can ask questions, the morning people gonna answer your morning questions, okay?"

"Okay."

"I mean, honey, you won't be in here long anyway, it's just until your case gets adjudicated. That means fixed up."

I know what it means. Press Stop **on your tape machine.**

"Honey?" the woman repeated.

Grace walked into her jail cell.

The following morning when another black woman came by with breakfast on a tray and said, "Rise and shine, what can I get you, missy?" Grace said, "Books."

"Books . . ." As if Grace had requested moon rocks. "How old are you?"

"Eleven."

"Hmm, see what I can do."

"I read adult books."

The woman frowned. "You talking dirty stuff?"

"No," said Grace. "Grown-up reading material— psychology, biology."

The woman stared at her, skeptical. "You some genius?"

"I'm curious."

"That ain't so good around here, missy."

Six hours later three dog-eared fifth-grade textbooks ended up in her cell. Baby math, baby English, baby science.

This was punishment, Grace decided, for being in the wrong place at the wrong time. She wondered where Sam, Ty, and Lily had ended up. Maybe they were right here in different prison cells. Maybe once Grace was let out, she'd see them. She hoped not.

As it turned out, there was nothing to worry about on that account. For three consecutive days she was never let out, mostly the staff seemed to forget about her. She kept quiet, thinking and sleeping, feeling more and more stupid like her brain was rotting and she was drowning in her own emptiness.

And she'd done nothing wrong. Just like the red room.

Keeping calm wasn't always easy; it required blocking out the cries and screams of prisoners who did make noise.

Sometimes big boys in orange suits, who might as well have been men, walked by loosely supervised by guards who did nothing to stop them from eyeing Grace and rubbing their crotches and saying filthy things. A couple of times, they actually pulled out their penises and stroked them hard while smirking.

The first time, Grace was too surprised to react. The second time, she laughed.

The boy she laughed at was tall and wide, with black fuzz all over his pimpled face. When Grace laughed, he got soft and tucked himself in quickly. His look said if he could rip the bars free, he'd destroy her.

From then on, Grace curled on her bunk, facing away from the scant world beyond.

On the eve of the fourth day, another black woman—the staff seemed comprised totally of such—unlocked the cell and said, "You're out, Miss"—she consulted a clipboard—"Miss Blades. Here's your clothes, get dressed, I'll wait and take you."

"Take me where?"

"Your next destination."

"Where's that, ma'am?"

"They don't tell me, I just do pickup and delivery."

Grace slipped out of the orange uniform, not caring if some filthy-minded boy passed by and saw her in nothing but her underpants. Dressed in the clothes she'd arrived in, she followed the attendant out past the same locked doors that had let her into this hell. Into the small reception room she'd been whisked through.

Malcolm was there.

"My God," he said. "So, so sorry. It took a while to find you."

Grace's belongings dangled from one of his long arms. He held out the other, offering to gather her in, a spontaneous gesture of comfort. Grace didn't like to be touched, never had, and at that moment her aversion dominated common sense.

He's here to rescue me so do everything he wants.

But she didn't want him to hug her, three days in jail had made her even steelier about human contact. She didn't move.

Not smart. Okay. Try.

She took a painful step.

Malcolm dropped his arm.

Now he's mad, why am I being stupid?

Bending, he half whispered, "I'm so sorry, Grace, this never should've happened. I'd like to take you with me, is that okay?"

"Yes."

"Great, I'm parked outside, station wagon's in the shop so I brought Sophie's car, it's just a two-seater but it'll do fine."

Talking fast and nonstop as he walked toward the exit, he held the door open for Grace. As if his own **Play** button had been pushed.

But this was sound Grace wanted to hear.

Sophie's car was an old but gleaming black Thunderbird convertible, upholstered in immaculate white leather.

Grace had seen ads for cars like this in old magazines. Beautiful rich people in their convertibles, racing horses, sitting on impossibly beautiful beaches.

She's rich but he's not? Maybe that's why she keeps her own name. So he'll remember they're separate people, that she has the money.

Malcolm said, "Pretty sporty, no? Sophie's the sporty one," stashed Grace's things in the trunk, held the passenger door open for her, and got in behind the wheel. Even with the seat pushed all the way back he looked cramped, like a grown-up in a kiddie car. He inserted the key in the ignition but didn't start up the engine.

"I'm really regretful, Grace," he said, looking back at the gray bulk of juvenile hall. "This must've been dreadful."

"It was okay."

"Well, you're brave to say that. The problem was I had a devil of a time finding out what happened. Which is outrageous. Ramona is—was—my sister-in-law and as her only surviving relative, any responsibility for her affairs is totally mine. I miss her deeply . . . I was never informed about anything, Grace, showed up at the ranch, found it empty, began calling the authorities, got stonewalled. Finally, a supervisor at the sheriff's told me what happened. After the shock wore off, I said, 'What about the kids?' That's when he told me about Bobby. Once **that** shock wore off, I pressed him on the other children and he said he didn't know. Even though, turns out it was his people who brought you here, the idiots. It's unconscionable, Grace, stupid bureaucrats treating you like a felon."

Grace shuddered, not sure why. She wished he'd just drive.

He said, "Poor thing," and reached out an arm again to offer comfort, checked himself immediately. Turning the key brought the car to roaring life. Malcolm began driving out of the parking lot. Slowly, like speed frightened him. Being timid seemed wrong for this car. Maybe Sophie treated it properly.

When he reached the exit to the street, Grace said, "Where are we going?"

He braked, slapped his own forehead. "Of course, how would you know? Sorry, again, I plead temporary attention deficit due to . . . I'm taking you to my house. Our house, mine and Sophie's. If you approve, I shouldn't assume anything. Though to be honest, Grace, there's no better alternative right now—"

"I approve," said Grace. "Please drive fast."

She expected a long trip, figuring the ugly area where juvenile hall sat would be far from a house nice enough for Malcolm and **wealthy** Sophie Muller.

She was half right: The house was huge and beautiful and so were its neighbors, with wide green lawns, old trees, bright flowers. But it didn't take that long to get there, Malcolm driving on a street called Sixth that passed through a lot of grayness and shabbiness.

He pulled into the driveway, said, "Voilà."

The house was two stories tall with a high pointy roof covered with what looked like gray sheets of rock. The front was brick with dark beams crossing it in a bunch of places. Grace recognized the style from her reading: Tudor, named after a family of English kings. She had no idea people lived in them in America.

"To give you your bearings," said Malcolm, "this neighborhood is called Hancock Park, and the street is June Street. It's more for bankers and lawyers and doctors than professors but this is where Sophie's parents lived. They were among the first Jews allowed to buy—not that you need to hear about that, sorry."

A beat. "Sophie and I are Jewish, you know."

"I know."

"Oh," he said. "Our names tipped you off?"

"The Holocaust."

"Ah . . . smart thinking. Anyway, we're not at all religious, so it's not like you're going to have to learn rituals and prayers, that kind of thing."

Rituals and prayers sounded interesting to Grace. Among the materials Malcolm had given her were articles on all kinds of religious customs.

"Anyway," he said, squeezing himself out of the Thunderbird and retrieving Grace's things. By the time he circled to open the passenger door Grace was already out.

His key unlocked a heavy wooden door with a brass knocker shaped like a lion. Grace followed him into an empty room with black-and-white-checked marble floors that seemed to have no purpose other than sitting in front of a much larger room. That space was full of old-looking fat sofas and chairs with lots of pillows, dark wood tables with curved legs, fancy-looking dark wood bookshelves stuffed with books. More books sat on the floor. In one corner stood a clock even taller than Malcolm. On the left side, a carved wooden staircase with wide steps led upstairs. A blue-and-red-and-white rug ran down the center.

The back wall of the big room was a bunch of glass doors that offered a view of a garden.

Not the acreage of the ranch, this property was smaller but not small, with a swimming pool that was bright blue and clear, trees with low-hanging branches, beds of red and pink and white flowers, and the greenest grass Grace had ever seen. She was breathless.

Professor Sophia Muller appeared, as if magically, wearing a dark-blue sweater unbuttoned over a top of the same color, tan slacks, and flat brown shoes. Her ash-blond hair was tied in a bun. Eyeglasses dangled from a chain around her neck.

She smiled and held out her hand to Grace. Doing both a little shyly, as if she wasn't used to visitors.

This time Grace did the right thing and offered her own hand.

Sophia Muller said, "It's so nice to have you, Grace."

She took Grace's things from Malcolm, told him the station wagon was fixed; if he wanted he could call a cab and catch the dealer before closing.

He said, "You sure?"

"Yes, darling. I need the T-Bird tomorrow."

Malcolm nodded and walked through the big room, turned through a right-hand doorway and was gone.

Sophia said, "Come, your room is ready."

Up the stairs they went.

"Voilà," said Sophie.

The word was obviously a family saying. Grace resolved to find a dictionary as soon as she could.

The room Sophia had taken her to was the size of three rooms at the ranch, with windows on two walls that looked down on the beautiful garden.

But it wasn't fancy, just the opposite. The bed was grown-up-sized but covered with a plain white cover, the walls were tan, looked old, had no pictures or decorations. The floors were bare wood. No furniture at all.

"Everything happened quickly, no time to furnish properly," said Sophia. Unlike Malcolm, she explained but didn't apologize. Maybe because she was the rich one?

"I like it," said Grace.

"You're being gracious but we both know this is a work in progress, so bear with me, Grace. You and I will go shopping soon enough, we'll set it up so it's appropriate for a young woman of your age and intelligence."

Grace said nothing.

Sophia said, "That sound okay?"

"Yes."

"Meanwhile, you must be hungry, I'm sure that hellhole served you swill. So come down to the kitchen, we'll find you some decent food."

Grace followed Sophia down the stairs. Sophia moved quickly, not bothering to check if Grace was okay.

She figures I'm fine. This is a new kind of person.

And thus began the good part of Grace Blades's life.

30

Grace's summary of that time to Wayne Knutsen, Esq., was brief and matter-of-fact.

He said, "Thank God for people like that," and Grace thought he sounded a bit rueful, as if he'd missed out on something.

Taking advantage, she said, "Anyway, I need your help."

He said, "Hmm. Okay, my police contacts aren't half bad."

"I'd prefer not," said Grace. "The police won't take me seriously."

"Why wouldn't they?"

"It's old news and pure supposition, not a shred of evidence."

Wayne labored to his feet, took a few steps, returned to the throne behind his desk. Businesslike now. "You're right. Objectively, there isn't much to go on, what would I tell the chief—" Color spread from his chin to his forehead. Continued on to his bald pate, turning him into a well-dressed tomato. "Forgive the pretentiousness, he and I have attended some of the same fund-raisers. In fact, that's why I'm dressed like this. Hotsy-totsy golf day at a pardon-the-expression country club. But no more name-dropping, I promise."

"It's names that I need, Wayne. **Their** real names—Sam, Ty, Lily. So I can find out what happened to them."

He gave her a long, searching look.

"Know thy enemy, Wayne. I can't live like this, wondering if he's lurking around every corner."

He tented his fingers. "All this because you believe he killed his brother."

"His brother a few days ago and Bobby Canova twenty-three years ago. And who knows how many others in between."

And almost me.

"Why would there be others?"

"Because someone malignant that young isn't going to devote his life to good deeds."

Wayne didn't answer.

Grace said, "I've never been more certain of anything."

"That handicapped boy—"

"Bobby Canova. His death record will be listed as accidental. But Sam pulled out that air tube, there's no other way it could've happened. I saw him that morning, Wayne. He was proud of himself. Smiling with contentment. The same smile he wore when he saw Ramona's body. He made **sure** I saw him. Wanting me to know that he was taking credit for her death, as well."

Wayne winced.

A soft man, a caring man. Grace worked with that. "He enjoyed it. That kind of appetite doesn't just disappear, Wayne. I'm certain he's done others."

"So calculated at that age . . ."

"My point exactly, Wayne. We're talking A-plus psychopathy. I need you to help me find him."

"And when you do?"

"Once I gather enough facts, you can talk to the police chief or any other big-shot contacts. Until then, without sufficient facts, I'll only be putting myself in the crosshairs."

Wayne thought for a while, rational, deliberative, the way a good lawyer should be. He pulled a pen out of a desk drawer. Gold-plated, a Montblanc that had to cost four figures. "And how, exactly, am I supposed to find out this little monster's real name?"

"I don't know," said Grace. "But you're all I've got."

Actually, she had plenty of suggestions. **You were part of the damn system so work it, turn those years into something positive.**

But the old joke was true:

How many shrinks does it take to change a lightbulb?
Only one but the bulb has to want to change.

Better he should come to the conclusion himself.

Still, on the off chance he didn't, Grace would do her damnedest to lead him there.

The throne swiveled. Wayne leaned back and half reclined. Crossed his ankles. Rolled the pen between chubby fingers.

"Twenty-three years ago," he said. "Social service records were as confidential then as they are now."

"Officially," said Grace. "We both know how that works."

He didn't answer.

"Officially," she said, "foster homes were loving places straight out of G-rated sitcoms, run by caring, compassionate guardian angels. Officially, endings were happy."

His head lowered. Studying the leather top of his desk.

"Besides, Wayne, there's no such thing as privacy in the Internet age."

Several more moments of silent contemplation followed. "All right, no promises, Grace, I'll see what I can dig up. I suppose it's the least I can do by way of expiation."

He had nothing to make up for. But let him think he did.

He walked her to the door, asked her if she needed anything else.

"Names will be a good start."

"In the unlikely event I actually come up with something, where can I reach you?"

She'd come prepared with the number of one of the disposable cells on a small, pink Post-it.

He glanced at it. "Your office?"

"My office is closed until future notice."

His face fell. "This really is serious."

"I wouldn't be here otherwise, Wayne."

"Yes, yes, of course . . . all right, I'll do my best. Either way, you'll hear from me in—say two, three days. By then I should know if it's possible."

"Thank you, Wayne." Grace kissed his cheek.

He touched the spot, reverently. "Thank **you**. For becoming the person you are."

Watchful, ever watchful, Grace left the office building, retrieved the Jeep, and drove back to the Valley, pleased with congested traffic that gave her time to think.

By the time she reached her room at the Hilton, she was tired and hungry. Plenty of jerky remained in her provision stash and the dry salami hadn't been touched. But hazarding a real meal seemed low-risk so she took the stairs down, checked out the lobby, continued to the hotel restaurant.

Seated at a corner table with a wide view of the entire room, she ordered soup, salad, a ten-ounce rib eye, medium rare, and iced tea.

The waitress said, "We're pouring passion fruit tonight."

"Passion is fine."

Decent-enough grub but the generic room was thinly populated. Mostly business types, trios and quartets, pretending to talk to one another but really focused on phones and tablets and personal agendas.

One solo: a thin-haired and slightly puffy but strangely handsome, fortyish man in a dark-blue shirt and gray slacks reading the **Times** and drinking a beer in a nearby booth. Handsome enough to draw forth extra-helpful smiles from the waitress. He reacted politely before returning to the sports pages.

Between Grace's soup and salad, her eyes met his. Brief smiles were exchanged. Friendly but mildly conspiratorial?

Grace knew that look.

Perfect setting, a hotel that catered to out-of-towners.

Not tonight, dear.

Moments later, Grace's suppositions were shaken by the

appearance of a cute blonde wearing a big diamond on her left ring finger.

Kisses and smiles all around. Hubby finished his beer and the couple left, her hand tapping his butt a couple of times.

Was she slipping? No, he'd definitely given her the eye. Blondie had no idea what lay ahead of her.

Grace ate her steak too quickly to taste much, went back to her room and double-bolted the door.

She fell asleep almost immediately, with barely enough time for self-instruction:

Tonight: no dreams.

Successfully blank and reasonably refreshed, she awoke at six a.m., ready to work.

No message from Wayne, no surprise. Way too early for him to try to worm his way into social service records. Assuming he wouldn't change his mind.

A bleeding heart, Ramona had called him, and Grace hoped his cardiac muscles remained mushy. But he might balk at wading into a mess. Or simply change his mind. So Grace had to consider reneging a possibility.

With or without him, she'd keep going.

The way it always had been, always would be.

Using another prepaid phone, she checked her service for messages.

Three new possible patients. They'd have to wait until Dr. Blades got her house in order. But the cry for help from a former patient, a woman named Leona who'd lost an arm five years ago after being set ablaze by a lunatic boyfriend, required immediate attention.

She reached the woman at home in San Diego. The crisis was an attack flashback, the first in three years, and you didn't need to be a master therapist to figure out why: Leona had met a new man and allowed herself to hope, only to experience him drunk and verbally aggressive.

"I thought, Dr. Blades, that he was going to attack me. He claims he'd never do it but I don't know."

You sure as hell don't.

Grace said, "You did the right thing by calling."

"Really? I'm a little . . . ashamed. I didn't want to bother you. Make you think I was falling apart."

"Just the opposite, Leona. Asking for help is a sign of strength."

"Oh. Okay. Yes, I know you've told me that but until now I didn't need help."

Things change, honey.

"True," said Grace. "Now you do and I'm here for you and you acted accordingly. That's flexibility, Leona. That's why you've adjusted so well and will continue to do so. How about starting at the beginning . . ."

You *did* need to be a master therapist to take care of a crisis long-distance while sitting in a generic hotel room, worried about your own survival.

Grace spent eighty minutes on the phone and Leona hung up sounding reasonably mended. Well enough not to ask for a face-to-face. Grace would've despised having to put her off.

Free of professional responsibility for the moment, she took a long hot bath, toweled off, and subjected her clothes to the sniff test. No stale aroma, she'd never been an odoriferous girl. At least another day of use.

She found what she was looking for on the Internet, packed everything up, and settled her hotel bill. Gassing the Jeep at a nearby filling station, she checked the oil and tires and used a squeegee to clean the windows.

At the nearest Staples she headed for the self-service machines. The neck-tattooed stoner behind the counter didn't look up when she paid cash.

Back in the Jeep, she removed five cards from a neat stack of fifty and placed them in her purse. The rest she stashed in the glove compartment.

The stiff, polished beige paper she'd selected had a nice feel to it. Bold embossed lettering implied confidence.

M. S. Bluestone-Muller
Commercial and Industrial Security
Risk Assessment

In the lower left corner of the card was a random P.O.B. that claimed to be situated in Fresno. In the lower right, Grace had listed a phone number that connected to a seldom-answered landline in a basement psych lab at Harvard. An extension phone grad students had stashed in a drawer years ago so they could ignore it and sleep off hangovers.

Starting up the Jeep, she tuned the satellite radio to light classical and caught the beginning of the fourth Bach cello suite, Yo-Yo Ma at his best.

Nothing like being in the company of genius on a road trip.

31

The three hundred and eighty miles between L.A. and Berkeley could be covered in one adrenalized day. But between having to stick to speed limits and bathroom and food breaks, Grace figured she wouldn't arrive until late afternoon or early evening.

Too late to learn anything about Alamo Adjustments.

There was also the fatigue factor to consider: A pumped-up sympathetic nervous system would mask her body's natural tendency to slow down. She wouldn't be at her best.

So a two-day trip it would be, taking the inland route and spending the night near the halfway mark—Fresno or its environs. Up early tomorrow, she'd arrive at the university town well before noon, have plenty of time to find her bearings.

She drove to a 7-Eleven, stocked up on more snacks, and sat in the parking lot reviewing the mental ledger she'd already gone over twice after deciding to take the trip.

If Mr. Beef was still looking for her—quite likely—being away from her home and her office would make her vulnerable to break-ins.

On the other hand, there was nothing in either location that could benefit the enemy and stuff was replaceable.

She wasn't.

Then there was the matter of payoff: Merely checking out a neighborhood where a defunct business once sat could very well prove futile. Worse, she'd come up empty on Alamo Adjustments and if the enemy lived nearby, risk giving herself away.

The enemy; time to put a face on her quarry.

She imagined him: a tall, glib, probably still attractive man of thirty-seven or thirty-eight. A charmer with secrets worth killing for and, if he wasn't as smart as he thought he was, possibly a criminal record.

If he **was** smart, he'd coasted for over two decades, maybe living a respectable life but definitely wreaking havoc on the sly.

If he'd attained public respectability, his secrets were well worth killing for.

Grace had passed through Santa Barbara, was nearing Solvang, still with no word from Wayne. He'd said to give him two or three days but she figured that was just a hedge and her faith in his follow-through diminished with each freeway exit. Because let's face it, it was a simple matter of calling the right person. Either he could or he couldn't, would or wouldn't.

She turned up the music, checked the tripometer. Two hundred ninety miles to go at sixty-five per. Her foot itched to exert more force on the gas but she'd already spotted three highway patrol cars. Still, she was feeling energized, chipper, maybe she would pull off a one-day trek. Find an appropriately bland business hotel in the good part of Oakland that bordered Berkeley, spend a quiet night, be up early to hunt.

As she neared Lompoc, Wayne called.

Grace said, "You found something."

"Of a fashion."

"I'm listening."

"Hey," he said, suddenly jocular. "'S great to hear from my favorite niece . . . meetings all day? Tsk, I sympathize, dear . . . sure, that would be great, let me write it down . . . the Red Heifer . . . Santa Monica . . . six-ish work for you?"

Surprised by someone entering his office? Fast on the uptake; Grace was glad she had him on her side.

The ride back was two and a half hours, minimum, longer if rush-hour traffic got ugly. But even with that, plenty of squeeze room.

She said, "See you soon, Uncle Wayne."

He hung up without laughing.

The restaurant was old-school: commodious vaulted dining room, green-flocked wallpaper, dim lighting, olive leather booths, noise-damping faux-Persian carpeting. The art was a mix of Flemish still-life prints, goofy cartoons about wine, and a huge butcher's chart to the left of the bar that segmented a pitifully oblivious steer into steaks, chops, and roasts.

Grace arrived ten minutes early but Wayne was already there, half his rotund form visible, the rest hidden by the shadows of a remote corner booth. Despite brisk dinner business, the banquette next to his was unoccupied. A martini in which three toothpicked olives floated looked untouched. He nibbled on bread, barely acknowledged Grace as she slid in beside him.

Today he was dressed to impress, in a soft-shouldered tan suit, a pale-orange shirt, and the same aggressive blue tie as in his official headshot. He remained stoic but took Grace's hand and gave it a brief squeeze.

"Uncle," she said. "Thanks for taking the time."

He smiled weakly. "Family is family."

A white-jacketed waiter came over. "Still no food, Mr. Knutsen?"

"Nope, just drinks, Xavier." Turning to Grace: "Katie?"

Grace said, "A Coke, Uncle Wayne."

"Coming up," said the waiter. Wayne pressed a bill into his hand. The waiter's eyes rounded. "You already gave me, sir."

"Consider it a bonus, Xavier."

"Thank you so much." He scurried off.

Grace said, "Bonus for the empty booth next door?"

Wayne stared at her, sighed, turned away and pretended to study a framed drawing of a dead rabbit dangling amid fruit, flowers, and herbs.

Grace's soda arrived, borne by a racewalking Xavier. She sipped. Wayne didn't touch his martini. She waited as he worked his way through the entire basket of bread. Munching and flicking crumbs from his sleeve, he muttered, "Last thing I need, carbs."

Xavier jogged over with a fresh basket, filled water glasses, asked if everything was okay.

"Perfect," said Wayne.

When they were alone again, Grace said, "You're a regular."

"I try to get here when I'm on the Westside. I live in San Marino."

He'd driven cross-town in serious traffic, intent on keeping this away from his home base. But he **was** comfortable enough to show her to the waiter. So this was a place he used for pleasure, not business.

Grace said, "Well, I appreciate your taking the time—"

"But of course, you're my client." He reached for his martini, took a long swallow, ate one of the olives. Chewing more than was necessary, he looked around the room, sat inert for another half a minute, reached into an inner suit pocket and drew out an envelope.

Small packet, something that might be used to mail back an RSVP. Grace concealed her disappointment. She'd hoped for a meaty packet of confidential documents.

Wayne dropped his hand and handed her the envelope under the table. The damn thing was light enough to be empty.

A hundred-thirty-mile backtrack for . . . ?

He said, "Put it away, you can examine it later."

"Of course. That was quick. Impressive, thanks."

"I wish I could attribute it to my virtue but quite the opposite."

Puzzled, Grace studied him.

He said, "I acquired it through lack of virtue, dear. More than that, sin. Of the deadly variety."

Grace scrolled through the classic septet.

"Greed," she said.

Wayne rubbed his thumb and forefinger together. "You always were quick, Dr. Blades. Yes, the old filth and lucre. Speaking of iniquity, I couldn't find anything on those Fortress nuts. Including court records."

Grace said, "There was no prosecution because everyone died in the shoot-out."

He fished out another olive. "And you know that because . . ."

She realized she didn't know. One of Sophia's old jokes came to mind: **Assume means make an ass out of u and me.**

Grace frowned.

Wayne said, "I raise the issue because one maniac leader and three acolytes doesn't make for much of a cult."

She shrugged, still warding off shame at her muddled thinking.

Wayne said, "On the other hand, perhaps it was a mini-cult."

The two of them laughed. Hard to say who was straining harder for levity.

Grace drank soda. Wayne finished his martini and waved for another. After Xavier delivered it, she said, "If there were others, why weren't they arrested? Why wasn't anyone else mentioned in the article?"

"Why, indeed, Grace, so you're probably right. What surprised me, though, was the utter lack of coverage after the shoot-out. Generally, the press loves that kind of thing—psychological autopsies and such." Another finger rub.

Grace said, "Someone had the clout to keep it quiet?"

"The possibility comes to mind."

Grace thought about that. "Makes sense—maybe to get a family member off the hook. But not Roi, he was a prison guard, no connection. So one or more of the women."

"My thoughts exactly," said Wayne. "And my mind conjured a rich, stupid girl probably with drug issues. I see it all the time, working with wills and trusts."

Another long swallow. "The implication, of course, is dire, Grace."

"More rocks to turn over."

He turned and stared. "Rocks that don't want to be turned over."

Grace shrugged. "On the **other** other hand, perhaps there were only four of them and that made them puny media-fodder in the post-Manson-and-Jim-Jones age."

"Anything's possible," said Wayne. "The hell of it is we simply don't know, do we, dear?"

Grace didn't answer.

He returned to his drink, stirring, staring into a tiny crystalline universe. "You step back into my life and I'm more anxious than I've been in a long time."

"I'm sorry—"

"Not your fault, it is what it is—sorry, I shouldn't have said that."

Grace touched his hand. "Wayne, I deeply appreciate everything you're doing but there's no need for concern. All I need is information."

He laughed. "There you go, I feel **so** much better knowing you're off tilting at who-knows-what."

Grace said, "My contacting you proves I'll be okay."

He frowned. "What do you mean?"

"Not only am I self-protective, I know how to ask for help."

He scowled, drank. "I suppose I appreciate it."

"Appreciate what?"

"Your coming to me. Because Lord knows I could've done a helluva lot more back when you were a kid."

"Wayne, of all the people—"

He waved her off. "What did I really do for you other than delegate responsibility?"

"Ramona was—"

"The best alternative, granted. But as soon as I punted to her, I washed my hands. Of you, of everyone, of the entire system. Sure, I can rationalize it as burnout, but what does that say about my character?"

"I think your character is beyond—"

"When Ramona called to tell me she thought your IQ was through the roof, I kissed her off, darling. How did I know she'd take care of it optimally? How would it have hurt me to spend some time researching curricula? And please don't tell me everything worked out fine. The issue isn't outcome, Grace, it's process."

Grace exerted gentle pressure on his hand. His skin seemed to ping, as if electrified. "Please, Wayne, do not excoriate yourself. You and Ramona were the only people in the system who made a difference. A significant difference."

"Whatever . . . so what did I sell out for? Another system equally amoral—worse than amoral, Grace. Venal, I'm an extremely well-paid attack dog." He finished the second martini. Smiled. "Of course I do get to wear Brioni."

Xavier started from across the room. Wayne shooed him away. "Grace, please reconsider this quest of yours. There has to be a better way."

Grace squeezed his fingers. "I'm no martyr, Wayne, but there's really no choice, we both know that knowledge is power."

Dropping her hand into her purse, she ran a fingertip against the small envelope.

The resulting sound—doll's nails on a toy chalkboard—caused Wayne to jump. He pulled his hand away from Grace's. "Look at it after I leave, Grace. And please, not here."

"Absolutely, Wayne. And I swear, you'll never be connected to this."

"Well . . . ," he said. Instead of finishing the sentence he slid clumsily out of the booth. "Pressing social event in Pasadena at eight and I'm sure you'd rather be . . . doing what it is you plan to do, rather than jawing uselessly with an old fart."

Removing several bills from a gold clasp, he placed them gently on the table and was gone.

Grace got to the restaurant parking lot in time to see him tooling away in a silver Jaguar sedan. The valet counted out what looked like a generous tip.

She drove two blocks south, parked on a quiet residential block, slit the tiny envelope open with a fingernail.

Inside was a flimsy square of paper folded in half. The kind of cheap stock you'd find on a memo pad headed **From the Desk of** . . . if the person with the desk was low on the corporate totem pole. He'd probably lifted it from a gofer's cubicle.

She unfolded and read three typed lines.

Samael Coyote Roi
Typhon Dagon Roi
Lilith Lamia Roi

Something on the flip side, as well:

Lilith: to Howell and Ruthann McCoy, Bell Gardens, Ca.
Typhon: to Theodore and Jane Van Cortlandt,
Santa Monica, Ca.
Samael: to Roger and Agnes Wetter, Oakland, Ca.

No dates for any of the adoptions. For all Wayne's filth and lucre, a nervous leaker had been unwilling to hand over hard copy.

But Wayne had listed the three names twice. On the outer page, more likely to be seen first, **just** the names. First and middle.

He wanted Grace to **focus** on the names.

She reread them. Weird-sounding monikers, she'd check them out. But what snagged her attention was a change in sequence. On the outer page, the list went oldest to youngest, but when listing the adoptions, Wayne had reversed the sequence.

Because that was the actual chronological order? Non-threatening, silent, querulous little "Lily" finding a permanent home first?

Mild-mannered, quiet Typhon lucking out next.

Leaving firstborn Samael, despite belief in his own charisma, to wait. Maybe in the hellhole Grace had experienced . . .

The real surprise, Grace supposed, was that he'd been adopted at all, given his age. Most adoptive parents craved warm and cuddly, not postpubescent and strong-willed.

So maybe interesting people, Roger and Agnes Wetter.

Of Oakland, California.

Right next to Berkeley.

She drove to an Internet café a few blocks west. Figuring out the theme behind the names was a couple of clicks away.

Samael, Hebrew for "God's venom," was a favored tag for seriously dark-minded Satanists. **Coyote**—who knew?—evoked an American Indian devil.

Typhon: a Greek devil. **Dagon,** a Philistine sea demon.

Lilith, according to myth, had been Adam's first wife, a lusty, disobedient wench who'd been eliminated in favor of compliant, fruit-loving Eve. Despite being adopted as an icon in some feminist circles, she was also part of the satanic pantheon.

Last but not least, **Lamia.** A night-prowling Greek devil who preyed on children.

Charming.

So crazy, power-mad Arundel Roi had embraced the dark side. So what else was new?

There had to be more . . . maybe emphasizing the names

was Wayne's way of letting her know not to waste her time, they'd been changed.

Or he was seriously freaked out and still trying to deter her.

If so, sorry, Uncle.

She got on the 405 South and drove to an Enterprise rental lot in Redondo Beach, where she exchanged the Jeep for a Ford Escape (how appropriate). The story she'd prepared—preferring something smaller—remained an unspoken lie. The clerk never asked, challenged by paperwork and eager to get back to texting.

Redondo was a pretty beach town but too low-rise and open, the vacation feel all wrong. Heading east to its utilitarian neighbor, Torrance, she booked herself into a Courtyard by Marriott, ended up with a room that was close to a Xerox of her digs at the Hilton Garden.

The comfort of familiarity. Grace had guided countless patients in that direction.

But setting up her laptop and connecting to blessed business-hotel WiFi, she warned herself not to get too familiar with anything.

For someone like her, no point to it. Nothing lasted.

32

G race began by searching **roger agnes wetter.**
Instant hit: 1993 **San Francisco Examiner** follow-up coverage of the 1989 Loma Prieta earthquake.

That 6.9 temblor had battered cities from San Francisco to Santa Cruz, taking down homes, commercial buildings, freeways, a serious chunk of the Oakland Bay Bridge. Sixty-three fatalities, nearly four thousand serious injuries, over ten thousand people left homeless, loss of power for millions.

Six billion dollars' worth of nightmare for policyholders, an actuarial disaster for the insurance companies who'd promised to take care of them.

Four years later many claims had been paid but often after prolonged delays and manipulative legal wrangles. The article described cases that remained unsettled. Often the culprits were fly-by-night insurers declaring bankruptcy rather than paying out claims. In other cases still-functioning companies continued to stall.

Stalemates approaching half a decade have been achieved using rotating freelance adjustors who lose paperwork compiled by their predecessors, impose new demands and promulgate needlessly complicated and misleading forms to be filled out under unreasonable deadlines. These fly-by-nights also make a habit of missing appointments or claiming policyholders failed to show up in person at inspections, falsely stating that absenteeism voids policies. Even when paperwork manages to work its way through the bureaucratic morass, damage is often grossly underestimated. In some instances, psychological pressure to settle at low levels of compensation is accomplished with cajoling and threats.

"They told me," said one struggling octogenarian who'd lost her home and insisted on remaining anonymous, "that if I didn't take six hundred dollars for the whole kit and kaboodle, they'd sue me and I'd end up losing my Social Security."

One firm whose name keeps coming up as a player in some of the poorest and hardest-hit Bay Area communities is Alamo Adjustments of Berkeley. Alamo's representatives, whom many policyholders describe as "just kids," have submitted the highest rate of claim denials, nearly 80 percent. Similar allegations against Alamo when it was based in San Antonio, Texas, have surfaced. Alamo's president, Roger F. Wetter, didn't respond to inquiries.

Samael, last of the Roi orphans to be adopted. Until a perfect-storm encounter with a seasoned psychopath wanting to be a dad.

Had the adoption been more about training an acolyte than nurturing an orphan? Roger Wetter, adept at using young thugs, figuring Mr. Venom of God would be the perfect addition to his family?

Roger and Son . . .

Roger. The name Andrew had claimed when chatting with "Helen" in the Opus lounge.

Grace and Andrew had both hidden behind alter egos but for Grace the choice had been casual, plucking the name of the woman she'd most recently spoken to. Had he dug deeper, becoming "Roger" that night because Roger had been on his mind?

Because the brother he'd known as Samael, the monster he feared, was now Roger **Junior**?

She typed away and found a seven-year-old obituary in the L.A. **Daily News** for Roger and Agnes Wetter, of Encino.

The couple, described as "elderly," had vanished during a boating trip off Catalina Island, their forty-foot catamaran found drifting and unoccupied. Divers had failed to find the bodies.

No mention of vicious business practices, only that Wetter was a "freelance investor," his wife a "homemaker and docent."

So Alamo had nothing to do with the Fortress Cult, it was simply a recycle of a company started in San Antonio. The city Andrew had claimed as home because it, too, was on his mind?

Probing the past because he'd learned of sins in the present. Not just those of the brother he'd once known as Samael, but of an entire family criminal enterprise?

After being taken in by separate families, had the brothers somehow resumed contact? From Berkeley to Encino. Right over the hill from Andrew's adopted home in Santa Monica. For all Grace knew, they'd run into each other at a football game. So many other opportunities—for all she knew they didn't have to resume, had maintained contact all those years.

Grace reread the Wetters' obit. One year prior to the accident at sea, Alamo Adjustments was still operating in Berkeley. With Beldrim Benn Junior running security. An outfit like that would need muscle and Grace had no problem imagining a much younger Benn scaring away poor, old, disenfranchised policyholders.

But shortly after, the family had moved. Motivated by too much scandal to sit on? Or, as Senior's "freelance investor" status implied, had he simply retired to enjoy the fruits of sin?

Nice house, nice boat, wife a docent, all the signposts of the leisurely good life.

An adult son the couple had raised since adolescence?

Sole heir?

. . .

Most California counties were happy to give up their coroner's records if you ponied up a fee, filled out forms, and were willing to wait weeks, even months. Several online services obliged cheaper and quicker and within seconds Grace had summaries of the deaths of Roger Wetter, seventy-five, and Agnes Wetter, seventy-two.

Cause of Death: Unknown but suspected drowning. Manner of Death: Accidental.

Nearest Kin: Roger Wetter Junior. Center Street, Berkeley. The same address as Alamo's business headquarters.

Samael had, indeed, morphed to Junior. Seven years ago, he'd have been thirty or so. Had he decided to cash in early? Had Andrew found out and, still guilty—**A. Toner**—over his failure to report Bobby Canova's murder and who-knew-what-else, wrestled with exposing his brother's parricides?

Approaching thirty himself, he'd needed encouragement to do the right thing because he was conflicted, trying to deal with evil kinship.

Turning to the great Internet oracle for wisdom, he'd happened upon Malcolm's research on survival and guilt, learned Malcolm was deceased but noted Grace's frequent co-authorship at the tail end of Malcolm's career. Switched his sights to her and came upon the solo article that clinched it.

But again, Grace was forced to wonder: Had he somehow suspected Grace was the subject as well as the author? No one else had. Then again, no one else knew about the girl living at Stagecoach Ranch the night Bobby Canova died.

She scoured her memory—had they even talked once as kids? She didn't think so. Had Ramona introduced her beyond "Grace"?

Stop. Reload.

The facts were what mattered: Andrew had found his way

to her, everything had gone to hell, and he'd died terribly within hours of leaving her office.

Googling his adopted parents, the Van Cortlandts, stopped her short.

Six-year-old obituary in the L.A. **Times.**

Dr. Theodore Van Cortlandt, retired endodontist, seventy-nine, and Jane Burger Van Cortlandt, retired hygienist, seventy-five, had perished six years ago during a hike in the Santa Monica Mountains, the victims of a calamitous fall due to a freak rockslide.

Hurriedly, Grace logged back onto the death-report service.

Cause: Blunt trauma. Mode: Accidental.

Sole heir, a son: Andrew Michael Van Cortlandt. Living at the same Tenth Street address. An engineer.

He'd used his adopted first name. Artlessness or arrogance?

The similarities between the deaths fought Grace's image of Andrew as moral combatant and gave way to a far uglier scenario.

Two pairs of elderly affluent parents, a couple of sizable inheritances.

Big bro sets the example, little bro follows a year later?

Back to their devil roots as Samael Coyote and Typhon Dagon?

But if Andrew had been involved in murdering his parents, why show up at Grace's office?

Atoner.

He'd come for the same reasons most conspirators spill: racked with guilt, worried about his own skin, or both.

Or worried—no, terrified—because a new threat had arisen from his brother?

And if Roger Wetter Junior, a multiple murderer, had found out his weakling sib was planning to blab to a therapist, he'd be sure to act decisively.

By coming to Grace, Andrew had pasted a target on her back.

She forced herself to reel back the night she preferred to forget, reviewing the details of their time together in the Opus lounge. His story had been a mix of truth and lies.

Not Roger, but yes, an engineer.

Not from San Antonio. But, yes, in L.A. on business. But nothing to do with his work. His was the business of self-preservation.

Thinking herself the director, not an actor, Grace had bought every word.

Had he been that good? Or had she slipped too deep into her own screenplay? All those wonderful lies spun for countless men she'd lured into hunger for her.

She began crying. No sense trying to stop it.

When the tears dried up, she sat in her hotel room emitting dry-eyed growls that tapered to pathetic mewling. Hating her weakness, she slapped herself across the face twice and grew silent. A quickly gulped mini-bottle of vodka from her hotel mini-bar left her parched and hot and jumpy. She drained two bottles of water, deep-breathed for a long time, was finally able to return to her laptop.

More work to do. **Three** children of Arundel Roi had showed up that night at Stagecoach Ranch.

33

Even before her fingers touched the keyboard, Grace had a good notion of what she'd learn about Howell and Ruthann McCoy of Bell Gardens.

Older couple victimized by a fake accident. Seven or fewer years ago, if some twisted reverse birth-order game was at play.

The prime scion of the Fortress Cult rewarding the people who'd taken in him and his siblings with slaughter for monetary gain.

But as the web kicked back an immediate response, Sophie Muller's cool, erudite voice sounded in Grace's head.

Ass u me.

Not seven years ago, ten.

Not California.

This obituary showed up in the **Enid** (Oklahoma) **News & Eagle.**

Family Perishes in Waukomis Home Fire

The bodies of three people, all believed to be members of a Waukomis family, were discovered this morning in the burned-out wreckage of a house on Reede Road. Preliminary examination indicates that the male and two females who perished were Howell McCoy, 48, his wife, Ruthann, 47, and their only child, a daughter, Samantha, 21. The possible use of an accelerant has led Waukomis PD to call in arson investigators from Enid.

All three victims were found in bed with no signs of a struggle. According to Waukomis investigators, the McCoys

and their daughter were deaf, leading to the possibility
that they slept through a break-in. The house's location, on
a four-acre lot in a secluded section of town, would shield
criminal activity from casual view. A missing five-year-old
Ford pickup points to robbery as a possible motive.

The McCoys moved to Oklahoma four years ago
from California, settling on a property owned for three
generations by Ruthann McCoy's family. Neighbors report
them as pleasant but loners, possibly due to their hearing
impairment, with few social ties to the community. Neither
the parents nor the daughter were employed and county
records indicate that all three residents received disability
benefits.

"This is terrifying," said a neighbor. "Nothing like this
happens here, we never even bother locking our doors."

A follow-up article two weeks later confirmed the arson,
with gasoline as the accelerant. The pickup was located a
week after the fire, over six hundred miles away, near Rocky
Mountain National Park in Colorado.

Grace pulled up a map. From Waukomis to the park was a
fairly straight westward trip, consistent with eventual return
to California.

Samael—or, and Grace had to face it, possibly Samael
and Typhon—setting out on a road trip for their first family
slaughter?

County benefit checks put the lie to an inheritance motive. Why travel thousands of miles to immolate a shy, inoffensive **poor** family?

Three deaf people sleeping through a nighttime break-in.

Grace hadn't picked up on Lily's hearing impairment. She
hadn't paid much attention to the Roi kids, period.

Looking back, the little girl hadn't uttered a word. But
neither had Ty. The same went for lots of new arrivals at the
ranch, children numbed by the foster process or stunned by
unfamiliar surroundings.

Lily, hearing-impaired. Ty, choosing not to speak? Both driven to mute submission by their older brother?

The same subservience that had led them to keep silent about Bobby Canova?

A remorseless murderer by early adolescence, Samael/Roger had two decades to hone his craft. For whatever reason, Typhon/Andrew had finally decided to do something about it and had ended up stabbed to death.

She searched the Center Street address that Roger Wetter Junior had listed as his home. The building was the subject of a brief squib in a local paper, due to be revamped for a mixture of commercial and government uses funded in great part by federal grants.

An image search revealed a blocky, six-story structure that looked like an old factory. Nothing residential about it. One of those loft situations? Or had Roger simply lied and his home was somewhere else?

She ran another search on him, came up empty.

But **andrew van cortlandt engineer** pulled up five hits, all to Asian bridge and dam projects contracted to Schultz-McKiffen, an international construction firm. In each case, Andrew's name came up as a side detail: He'd been part of a working team of nearly a hundred staffers, one of fourteen structural engineers.

No personal details, no photos. Schultz-McKiffen's headquarters were in Washington, D.C., with satellite offices in London, Düsseldorf, and Singapore. One hit cited Andrew's attendance at a meeting in Germany.

Officially living with his parents but a world traveler.

Grace endured more recall of every moment she'd spent with him. She had trouble recasting the earnest, troubled young man as a cold-blooded murderer, even working under the tutelage of his psychopath brother.

But anyone could be fooled and the facts told her not to trust her instincts: His sister had been burned alive a decade ago but he'd been allowed to live until days ago, suggesting some sort of favored status in his brother's mind. The kind of privilege that came from co-conspiracy.

Using the Tenth Street address of the Van Cortlandts, she tried several real estate sites, found what she was looking for at the third.

The property had been sold for $2.7 million to a family trust representing the interests of William and Bridget Chung. William's name popped up as president of an Internet start-up company in Venice.

Selling the homestead two years after his parents' death, Andrew had cashed in big-time.

No reason for the Chungs to know anything about his motives for selling but maybe they—or someone in the neighborhood—would recall something Grace could use.

Tomorrow: Berkeley. Today: Keep it local.

Torrance to Santa Monica was a half-hour hop under ideal conditions. Nothing about L.A. was ideal anymore and it took Grace an hour and eighteen minutes to reach the two-story sage-green Craftsman where Andrew Van Cortlandt had spent his privileged adolescence.

Attractive, well-maintained structure, with a full-width front porch, a neat square lawn flanked by a pair of mature magnolias, precise beds of flowers rimming the grass. Generous but proportional to the narrow lot and dwarfed by the newer look-at-me Spanish and Mediterranean stucco heaps that replaced several older structures.

A silver Volvo station with a **Save the Bay** bumper sticker sat in the driveway. Grace parked six houses south and turned off her engine. Eight minutes later a slim, ponytailed, thirty-ish blonde wearing a shoulder-baring blue cashmere sweater over white skinny jeans teetered on three-inch heels as she toted an almond-eyed, doll-like infant and a diaper bag into the Volvo.

The woman-likely-to-be-Bridget-Chung spent a considerable amount of time offering Tenth Street a view of her enchanting glutes as she settled the baby into a rear restraint-seat. Far too little attention was paid to cross-traffic as she backed out of the driveway at full speed.

The Volvo narrowly missed colliding with a white Lexus barreling from the north. Horn honks were followed by window-glass-muted outrage from the older woman behind the wheel of the Lexus.

No reaction from Lithe Mom Bridget. As she drove away, her hand and eyes were fixed on her phone.

Smiling and texting.

Grace remained in her Escape for ten additional minutes. Several more cars drove by, all luxury models. A two-minute lull broke when a slim, middle-aged woman who could've been Bridget Chung's mother stepped out of the neighboring Spanish—one of the older, original houses, a smallish one-story—and began watering potted plants near her front door.

Grace got out, walked to the green Craftsman, and studied its façade.

The woman stopped watering. "May I help you?"

Squinting, tight-lipped. One of those Neighborhood Watch stares.

All the better.

Grace smiled and approached her.

The woman remained wary, hands tight around the handle of her watering can. Her lips moved as she read the fake business card Grace held out.

"Commercial and Industrial Security. Like alarm systems?"

"We consult to individuals and corporations contemplating real-estate transactions."

"Consult about what?"

"Residential patterns, upkeep, environmental and civic issues that might come up."

"Come up when?"

"In the event of a transaction." Grace cocked a head at the Craftsman.

"They're selling? To a company?"

"That I can't say, ma'am. I get a list of addresses, come out and record the data."

"Well, you need to know that this is a first-class neighborhood."

"No doubt about that, Ms. . . ."

"**Mrs.** Dena Kroft." She glanced at the green house. "If it was up to me, they'd be out tomorrow."

"Problem neighbors?"

"Loud," said Dena Kroft. "Parties all the time, yelling around the pool, what sounds like heavy drinking. He's some kind of computer nerd, Asian, more money than God. She's an airhead."

Loathing was fertile grounds for rapport. Grace said, "That's obvious from her driving. Just as I got here, she zoomed out of her driveway, nearly T-boned another car. With her baby inside."

"Exactly," said Dena Kroft. She handed the card back. "We've been on the block for thirty-two years. It was a perfect neighborhood until the N.R.'s started moving in."

"N.R.'s?"

"Nouveau riches," said Dena Kroft. "Asian, Persian, or they can be anything, whatever. They tear down lovely houses, get variances through their connections, and build monstrosities on every inch of lot. If you want all interior space and no greenery, why not just get a condo?"

"Indeed," said Grace.

"Before **them,** the block was mostly doctors, top-notch people on the staff at Saint John's. My husband's a radiologist there. Peter Kroft."

As if Grace was supposed to recognize the name. "Great hospital."

"Best in the city," said Dena Kroft. "I was hoping **he'd** keep the house. The son of the people who lived here."

"He's a doctor?"

"Some kind of engineer." Kroft leaned in, lowered her

voice. "Adopted, but you'd never know. They actually got him into Harvard-Westlake." Peering at Grace. "Did you go to Buckley? You look like a girl in my daughter's class."

"No, ma'am, sorry. You'd never know he was adopted because—"

"It's like going to the pound and picking out a mutt, you never know what you're going to end up with. But Teddy and Jane were fortunate with Andy. A very well-behaved boy, quiet, no shenanigans."

Grace said, "Sounds like the perfect neighbor."

"The perfect neighbors would be a quiet **family**," said Kroft. "But certainly, a quiet young man would be better than the likes of **them**. It's a lovely house, though a bit dark. I must admit I'm a bit peeved that Andy wasn't more sentimental. He was never here, anyway. Ended up selling."

"Maybe he thought it was too much house for one person."

"One adapts," said Dena Kroft. "But he was away all the time. In the Orient, that's where he spends a lot of time. He was there when Teddy and Jane had their accident—they fell off a mountain hiking. They were always hiking, big physical fitness buffs, you know."

"Must've been hard on him," said Grace. "Being away."

"Andy? I'm sure. He showed up two days later. I remember him being dropped off by a cab, carrying his bags, looking terrible, just crestfallen. I suppose he can't be faulted for not wanting to be tied down with the property but I sure wish he'd done his civic duty and sold to somebody decent. So tell me the truth, young lady. You're one of those credit checkers, right?" She hooked a thumb at the green house. "They're in trouble, all that computer money is smoke and mirrors and they're going to lose the place."

Grace smiled. "You never know, Mrs. Kroft."

Dena Kroft laughed. "What goes around comes around."

34

Before returning to Torrance, Grace had dinner at a quiet place in Huntington Beach, was back in her room by nine p.m.

Figuring Andrew's age was the same as hers, give or take, she searched for records of his high school days at Harvard-Westlake. The prep school was protective of its alumni, offering nothing, and an online search company required too much personal info to justify learning about his extracurricular activities.

One impressive fact: He'd gotten into an exclusive Ivy League feeder after spending his childhood in a squalid desert cult. And witnessing bloodshed.

You and me both, Andy.

Curious if his academic success had continued, Grace paired his name with each of the Ivies. Wondering if the two of them could've actually been at Harvard together.

But nothing from the hallowed halls of Cambridge. Same for New Haven, Princeton, Philadelphia . . .

Then she thought **engineer** and tried MIT and Caltech. Zero.

No big deal, there were plenty of other top schools to choose, beginning locally: USC, where Malcolm taught and Grace had earned her doctorate. The Pomona colleges, UCLA. If none of those panned out, the other UCs—**Berkeley.**

The most venerable University of California campus dominated the city where Andrew's brother had lived and learned the dark side of the insurance business.

The only business, it occurred to Grace, that thrived on **not** providing service. Talk about a psychopath's dream.

Had the brothers' reunion begun with a chance meeting on Telegraph or University Avenue?

Pairing **andrew van cortlandt** with **berkeley** and every other UC campus produced the same negative results. Most students spent their undergrad years without attracting attention so this entire approach could be a waste of time.

She made one more stab, anyway: Stanford. And wouldn't you know.

Seven years ago, Andrew Van Cortlandt, age twenty-seven, had won an engineering department award for a doctoral thesis exploring the structural damage wreaked upon the Oakland Bay Bridge by the Loma Prieta quake.

Samael helps his father torment disaster victims, Typhon seeks scientific enlightenment.

Palo Alto, the town Stanford ate for breakfast, was less than fifty miles from Berkeley. The schools were rivals, academically and athletically. Stanford had been founded by a rich man irate over his son's rejection from Berkeley.

That made an encounter between the brothers, planned or otherwise, damn feasible.

Grace imagined it: Two damaged souls separated during adolescence bump into each other as young men. Easy recognition. Auld lang syne.

The two of them have a couple of beers, decide to rekindle their relationship. But the passage of time has done nothing to alter the original dynamic: glib, dominant Samael; quiet, submissive Typhon.

Had Mr. Venom drawn his little brother over to the dark side? Convinced him to collaborate on a hideous plan?

Time to get rid of the fools who adopted us, score some serious bucks.

A problem: no fit with the murder of the McCoy family, ten years ago. So maybe Roger had done that one alone. For fun, thrills, some kind of sick, dark joke. Same reason he'd snuffed out Bobby Canova.

Or: a rehearsal for what was to come.

Or: Roger had located his baby sister first, tried to get **her** to return to the fold, but she'd refused. Maybe even threatened to go public on Bobby.

Bad move, Lily.

The taste of murder still sweet on his tongue, he reunites with Andrew a few years later and hatches a plan.

Maybe even a barter: **I kill yours, you kill mine.**

How convenient that would be: a pair of outwardly unrelated staged accidents, the sole heirs equipped with perfect alibis, should suspicion arise. But it hadn't; the deaths had been convincing enough to fool two coroners.

If Dena Kroft was correct, Andrew had been in Asia the day his parents tumbled off a cliff. For all Grace knew, Roger Wetter Junior had been surfing in Maui when his parents were dumped in the ocean.

Neat, clean, sewed up tight.

Accidents were the ultimate loss of predictability and control. The Reaper swinging his scythe unmindful of personal agenda or best intention. Grace was no stranger to instability. Every morning she reminded herself anything could happen anywhere anytime to anyone. Despite that, she felt her chest tighten and her head filled with thoughts and images she'd believed long vanished.

Turning off the lights of her cookie-cutter hotel room, she crawled into bed and drew the covers completely over her. Sucking her thumb, she gave herself the command for dreamlessness.

This time her will failed her and she did nothing **but** dream, REM waves offering up the adventures of a woman who looked exactly like Grace but wore black tights and a cape and was able to perform miracles of time, space, and matter.

She awoke feeling great. Less so when she realized she was still an earthling.

. . .

Out of the Marriott by nine fifteen a.m., she stashed her dirty clothes in a hotel dumpster and drove to the Redondo Beach wig salon she'd spotted on the way to the hotel. The cheerful, curvy women who operated the pink-and-lace shop giggled approvingly when Grace informed them she needed a new look for her boyfriend. When she added that money was no object, they became her new best friends.

She wanted to come across high-tax-bracket because a quick survey of the goods displayed on pink Styrofoam stands was disappointing. Nearly all of them, even selections approaching four figures, looked stiff and unconvincing.

The exception was a collection of five wigs exhibited in a tall, locked Lucite case behind the register. Even up close, these could've fooled her.

Within moments, "Hi, I'm Trudy" and "Hi, I'm Cindy" were schooling her in the composition of the "absolute best hair masterpiece available."

European-cuticle human hair preselected for natural silki-ness and processed in tiny batches at an exclusive French "atelier." Hand-tied lace top, meticulously wefted back, and hypoallergenic tabs located at crucial "slick-spots," a natural hairline that only resulted from "long years of experience and major talent, basically a hair Rembrandt."

Grace tried on two wigs from the case and bought them both, a honey-blond layered thing that reached three inches beneath her shoulders and an artfully streaked brunette flip half a foot shorter. Each listed for twenty-five hundred dol-lars but she bargained Cindy and Trudy down to thirty-eight hundred for the pair. Pretending to scan the store again, she pointed to an electric-blue pageboy near the entrance.

"You don't want that, it's a cheapie," said Trudy.

"Tacky, just for fun," said Cindy. "We keep it like for teen-agers, parties, you know."

Grace winked. "Todd can get tacky. How much?"

"Aha!" Cindy giggled and checked. "Sixty-three."

"Can you throw it in?"

The women looked at each other. "Sure."

As Grace left, boxes in tow, Cindy called out, "Todd's a super-lucky guy."

Trudy said, "You can take photos but trust me, don't post them, ha ha ha."

Next stop was a small optician's store where Grace confounded the owner by asking for frames set with clear glass.

He said, "I've only got three or four. We use them as demos."

"I'll take them."

"They're no good for anything."

"It's for a movie."

"Which one?"

Grace smiled and drew a finger across her lips.

The man smiled back. "Ah, okay." The cash Grace forked over kicked up his glee. He said, "Anytime, I'd love doing movies."

Eleven a.m., a beautiful California morning.

Grace was embarking later than she'd planned, but still with ample time to reach her destination and catch some quality sleep tonight, dreamless or otherwise.

During breakfast, she'd changed her mind about taking the inland route, opting for the coast highway in order to avoid the blahs. As she cruised into Malibu and reached La Costa, she allowed herself a quick glance at her house, resisting the urge to go in and stand on her deck, listen to the ocean, scrub gull shit off the railing.

One day, she'd be back. Lulled by the tides, riding waves of solitude.

An hour and a half into her second attempt north, she was hyper-alert, nibbling jerky as she passed Santa Barbara. A few scorched spots remained on the eastern hillsides, scars from a fire the previous spring that had ravaged a couple thousand acres before the winds cooperated. Nothing insidious behind the blaze; a perfectly legal campfire had gotten out of hand.

Unlike the gasoline-fueled blaze that had destroyed the McCoys.

The deaths of the McCoys were beyond evil. Take away the profit motive and why bother?

If Samael/Roger had been acting out a family-cleansing fantasy, why kill Lily but leave Andrew alive?

Then she remembered: He hadn't.

Still, the time-lapse puzzled. Ten years between Lily and Andrew. Sister first—had she been a priority?

Grace recalled how closely the tremulous little girl had stuck to the boy she knew as Typhon. The brother who'd been gentle with her.

Unlike Sam, who'd held himself apart from both his younger sibs.

Lack of attachment: another psychopathic quality.

All three kids had grown up suckling on a curdled brew of megalomania and isolation. Yet only one of them had evinced obvious cruelty at the ranch.

Just the opposite, in the case of Typhon. Grace had seen him treat Lily with . . . tenderness. And everything she'd learned about the man Typhon grew into—what she'd observed firsthand—worked against his being a cold-blooded murderer.

Yet his adoptive parents had also met an unusual end.

She drove a few more miles before realizing an interesting irony: The sons of Arundel Roi had waited longer to be adopted than their cute little sister, but once they'd been taken in, they'd scored the kind of affluent dream placements social services rarely produced, growing up as rich boys.

Lily, on the other hand, had remained working-class, at best.

That brought her back to the boys' adoptions: Why had the Van Cortlandts and the Wetters, prosperous enough to go the private route, dealt with social services at all?

People like that didn't have to settle for teenage boys hauling serious baggage.

Grace knew nothing about the Van Cortlandts but what she'd learned about Roger Wetter Senior said he had as much use for altruism as a snake had for lace panties.

A man who made his living cheating poor people suddenly proffering the milk of human kindness to an orphan? No way.

On the other hand, a man like Wetter Senior **might** be swayed by a concrete incentive, as in cold hard cash. And that fit with Wayne's musings about the Fortress Cult avoiding extended press coverage due to a high-level connection.

Had one of Roi's three co-wives been a rich girl—the prodigal daughter of a family with the clout to play human chess on a tournament level?

A couple of grandsons sired by a lunatic and mothered by a reprobate slut? Shucks, nothing money couldn't take care of.

It would've taken serious money to lure grubbers like Roger and Agnes Wetter into parenthood. As for the Van Cortlandts . . . who knew?

To a crooked businessman like Roger Wetter, the deal would've been enticing: serious money for short-term stewardship because Roger né Samael was due to reach majority in a few years.

Andrew né Typhon shortly after.

But neither of the boys had cut the cord at eighteen, Roger listing the Alamo address as his own and probably working Daddy's insurance scams.

Andrew, bright, obedient, outwardly pliable, taking well to the life of a Santa Monica preppie. Perhaps Ted and Jane had grown to love him. Or establish a reasonable facsimile. Grace imagined the Van Cortlandts feasting on parental pride when their boy secured admission to Harvard-Westlake, then to a still-unidentified first-rate college, then to grad school at Stanford.

The research award at twenty-seven. A doctorate in engineering.

But once financially independent, Andrew had decided
to work on the other side of the world; you couldn't move
much farther from hearth and home.

So perhaps his affection for his new parents hadn't run
deep.

Get what you want from them, move on.

Years later: Collaborate to have them tossed over a cliff?

Grace shifted back to Roger Wetter Junior. No evidence,
so far, of academic accomplishment on his part. But no need
to get A's in the Wetter household. Other qualities were
prized higher.

The very qualities Venom Boy possessed in spades before
he met the Wetters.

Senior takes Junior into the family business, tutors him in
the fine points. Then Senior announces his retirement, he
and Mom move to L.A.—pulling the rug out from under
Junior?

Now you're on your own, son.

Soon after, Mom and Dad experience the cold blue kiss of
the ocean.

Head swimming, Grace pulled off at the next exit.

Sad little intersection housing two gas stations, an Arby's,
and a Pizza Hut. Nothing with WiFi. She drove farther east,
spotted an even shabbier commercial block featuring mostly
boarded-up storefronts but also a Wild Bill's Motor Hotel
decked out with a poorly painted sign of said lawman on a
bucking bronco and smaller placards claiming satellite TV,
massage beds, and Internet hookup.

She paid cash for a forty-three-dollar room, scrawled
something illegible in the register, ignored the oh-sure smirk
of the moron behind the desk.

Parking in front of the unit, she took her bag and her laptop to a room reeking of Lysol and hard-boiled eggs. Opening the drapes on a flyspecked window in order to keep the

Escape in view, she sat on a mattress that felt stuffed with mixed nuts, tried to log on, failed, repeated, failed again.

On her fourth attempt, the Data Monster announced itself with an insipid chorus of beeps.

roger agnes wetter theodore jane van cortlandt rewarded her with three immediate hits.

Correction: one hit, reiterated twice.

Both couples had lent their names to the steering committee of a political fund-raiser. Big bash, nearly fifteen years ago, the Biltmore Hotel, downtown, championing the reelection of State Senator Selene McKinney. Old news cached on the site of the party-planning outfit that had set it up.

McKinney served the affluent Westside, including the Van Cortlandts' upscale slice of Santa Monica. Her district didn't include the Wetters' abode in Encino but back then, the couple had lived in Northern California so there had to be more than constituency at play.

You didn't need to be a constituent to benefit from a politician's good graces.

Grace googled McKinney and got a Wikipedia bio. The legislator known as Ms. Moderate had won that election but eighteen months later, she was dead, victim of a heart attack.

Born to big money, McKinney's decades of public service had earned her seniority and the plum positions that went along with it. At the time of her death she'd long chaired the Senate Standing Committee on Insurance. Which put her in charge of "indemnity, surety, and warranty agreements."

A woman well worth supporting, if you were Roger Wetter Senior. She'd also served on the dental health licensing committee, which might have put her in contact with Dr. Van Cortlandt.

Grace continued to search, switching between her keyboard and eyeballing the rented SUV through the window. One time, she had to step out of the room, as two boys, fifteen or so, began slinking around, walking expensive tenspeed bikes up to the Escape and eyeing the rear hatch.

Cheap motel, low-rent district, but these two were well dressed, well fed, nicely tended. Couple of rich kids biking down from one of the horsey estates that rose above the tree line to the east?

A quick stare-down from Grace caused them to hightail. Softies. Grace returned to her laptop, pairing **selene mckinney** with **roger wetter, alice wetter, alamo adjustments, insurance scam.** When that brought up nothing, she plugged in a stream of additional bad deeds: **bribery, extortion, con, deception, fraud.**

Still, nothing.

She phoned Wayne Knutsen.

His voicemail message was curt, almost dismissive, you'd never associate it with the man who'd come through for her twice.

"It's me. Did Selene McKinney have a daughter?"

She'd packed up when movement outside her room's window caught her eye. The pair of adolescent reprobates had returned and one boy was leaning insolently against the SUV's right-side headlight.

As if he owned the damn thing.

Grace flung her door open, strode to the driver's door, tossed in her belongings, started up, revved hard, and peeled out in reverse, knocking the kid off balance and causing him to cry out.

She drove off the motel lot, glancing at her rearview mirror. The kid had remained on his feet but looked shaken, mouth agape, holding his hands up as if questioning the gods.

Unwilling to believe anyone could **do** that.

Shocked that not everyone **cared** about him.

Get used to reality, you spoiled little bastard.

35

Twelve-year-old Grace lived with two strangers in a big, beautiful house in Hancock Park.

Nice while it lasted. It wouldn't, of course, she understood reality. A few years in one place, a few in another, you never knew what the next day would bring.

But she had to admit being taken in by Malcolm and Sophie was by far her best turn of luck. And she was determined to learn as much as she could until they got tired of her.

Apart from the house being big and beautiful and always smelling clean and fresh, apart from the room they let her use as her bedroom being huge and comforting and now, furnished graciously, Malcolm and Sophie were nicer than anyone she'd ever met.

They made it easy for Grace to hold on to herself and not be swallowed up by what they preferred. Maybe that was because Malcolm was a psychologist, an expert on kids. Even though he'd never had any.

Or maybe it was more than that; after a month or so, Grace couldn't help thinking he and Sophie seemed to really care about her comfort, nutrition, and general state of happiness. But they never pretended they were her parents, never asked to be called Mom and Dad. Grace wasn't sure how she'd feel if they had. She'd never called anyone Mom or Dad.

She thought about it and decided to go along with whatever they wanted that didn't actually hurt her.

Anything to stay in this heaven.

. . .

A few months later, she was still calling them Malcolm and Sophie, and Sophie had taken to routinely calling her "dear." Malcolm usually never called her anything except once in a while, Grace. Mostly he just talked to her without a label. As if there was always a conversation going on between them and no one needed to get formal.

Grace began to think of them as a pair of new friends. Or maybe "acquaintances"—she liked that word—it sounded exotic and French. Same for "compatriots." "Associates," too, though that was more official than exotic.

So now, she had **acquaintances** who were much older and smarter and had a lot to teach her. And rich, as well.

One day, Malcolm asked if she'd ever thought about going to school.

It made her afraid and a bit angry, as if he'd finally had enough and was thinking about sending her somewhere and when she said, "Never," some of that anger came out in her voice. She had to hold on to her hands so they didn't shake.

Malcolm just nodded, and rubbed his big chin the way he did when he was thinking about something puzzling. "Makes sense, be hard to find a peer group for you—for anyone as brilliant as you. Okay, fine, we'll continue with home study. I must confess, I like it myself—finding material for you is a serious challenge. Just wanted to make sure you weren't getting lonely."

I'm my own best friend. I don't know what lonely is.

She said, "I'm ready for the next lesson."

Grace's nearly thirteen years on the planet had told her trust didn't mean much, except for trusting herself. But the funny thing was, Malcolm and Sophie seemed to trust **her.** Never forcing food on her that she didn't like, never telling her when to go to bed or when to get up. Though to be honest, they didn't have to, Grace rose before they did and read in bed, and when she was tired she told them so and returned to her room to read herself to sleep. After she first moved in, Sophie asked if she wanted to be tucked in.

Ramona had only asked the one time, after that she'd just done it, and Sophie asking probably meant she didn't want to do it but was being polite.

So rather than make Sophie put out a special effort, Grace said, "No, thank you, I'm fine." And she was. Enjoying the quiet of the magnificent room they were letting her stay in. Though once in a while, she wouldn't have minded a tuck-in.

Sophie said, "As you wish, dear," and Grace put herself to bed.

As far as she could tell, being a professor was easy; Malcolm would drive to the university but not really early, and sometimes he'd come home when it was still light outside. Some days, he never left at all, working in his wood-paneled study, reading and writing.

Grace thought: **I'd like this job.**

Sophie was a professor, too, but she never went to work, just puttered around the house, cooking for herself and Grace, supervising Adelina, the nice but not-speaking-English cleaning woman who came in twice a week and worked hard and silently.

Sophie also went on shopping "excursions," which could mean anything from buying groceries to coming home with boxes and bags of clothing for herself and for Grace.

She was probably doing **some** kind of work because she had her own study—a small room off her and Malcolm's bedroom with no paneling, just a desk and a computer. Other than pictures of flowers on white walls, nothing fancy. When she did go in there, she kept the door open but she'd remain at the desk for hours, reading and writing, usually with classical music playing softly in the background. When mail came to her it was addressed Prof. Sophia Muller or Sophia Muller, Ph.D.

Reading and writing was what Grace was already doing, what kind of deal was this professor stuff? Grace started to think she should **really** learn to be one.

Three months after Grace's arrival, Sophie cleared up the mystery. "You probably wonder why I'm here all the time."

Grace shrugged.

"Next year, I'll be back on campus like Malcolm—teaching, supervising grad students. But this year I'm on something called a sabbatical, it's kind of a racket for professors, once we get tenure—once the university figures it wants to keep us around—we get a year off every seven years."

"Like Sabbath," said Grace.

"Pardon?"

"Work six days, rest on the seventh."

Sophie smiled. "Yes, exactly, that's the concept. Not that I'm supposed to be loafing, the understanding is I'm to do independent research. This is my second sabbatical. During the first, Malcolm and I traipsed around Europe and I churned out papers that no one read. But I'm older now, prefer to basically be a homebody and get paid for it. You won't tell on me, will you, dear?"

Laughing.

Grace crossed her heart. "It's a secret . . . you do read and write."

"I'm writing a book. Allegedly."

"What on?"

"Nothing that's going to hit the bestseller lists, dear. How's this for a catchy title: **Patterns of Group Interaction and Employment Fluctuation in Emerging Adult Women.**"

Grace thought that sounded like a foreign language, she'd never pick up a book like that. She said, "It's pretty long."

"Way too long. Maybe I should call it something like **Chicks and Gigs.**"

Grace's turn to laugh.

Sophie said, "The title's the least of my concerns. It's excruciating for me, dear, I'm not a natural writer like Malcolm—so what would you like for dinner?"

Malcolm kept bringing Grace harder and harder lessons. When she hit pre-calculus she needed some help and he was able to explain things clearly and she thought, **His students are lucky.**

Most of the other stuff was easy, floating into her brain like iron to a magnet.

Life at the big beautiful house was mostly quiet and peaceful, everyone reading, writing, eating, sleeping. Malcolm and Sophie never had guests over, nor did they go out and leave Grace alone. Once in a while a thin white-haired man in a suit would stop by and sit at the kitchen table with them, going over paperwork.

"Our lawyer," Malcolm explained. "His name is Ransom Gardener. The only things he grows are fees."

Every so often, Gardener showed up with a younger man named Mike Leiber. Unlike the lawyer, who always wore a suit and looked serious, Leiber had long stringy hair and a beard, arrived in jeans and untucked shirts, and never said much. But when he spoke at the kitchen table, everyone listened to him.

Malcolm and Sophie never explained who he was but after his visits they were a strange combination of seriousness and relaxation. As if they'd just taken a hard exam and had done well.

Twice a month or so, Malcolm and Sophie took Grace to nice restaurants and Grace wore clothes Sophie bought for her that she'd never have chosen.

She stretched to try new foods when Malcolm and Sophie offered them to her. Even if something looked unappealing, she didn't complain, just the opposite, she smiled and said, "Yes, please. Thank you."

Same for the clothes. They came wrapped in tissue paper and bore the labels of stores that sounded expensive, some with French names, and she could tell Sophie had taken a lot of time finding them.

Grace thought of them as costumes. Dressing up for the part of Good Girl. She began to wonder when the play would end but got bad stomachaches when she thought too much about that. Chasing those thoughts out of her brain, she concentrated on the good things happening right now. Sometimes concentration gave her a headache.

As part of fitting in and being easy to live with, she began brushing her hair a lot, until it shined like Sophie's and one day Sophie gave her a brush from England that she informed Grace was made from "boar bristles" and guess what, it made Grace's hair even shinier so she resolved to pay special attention to what Sophie said.

Being clean and smelling good was important as well, so she showered every morning and sometimes a second time before she went to bed. Flossed her teeth and brushed twice a day, the way she'd seen Sophie do. When a few hairs sprouted in her armpits and she detected faint odor coming from them, she looked in her medicine cabinet and found a brand-new container of roll-on deodorant and began to use it regularly.

Somehow, someone—no doubt, Sophie—had known what to do.

Shortly after she began living with them, they brought her to a woman pediatrician who examined her and gave her shots and pronounced her "fit as an Amati."

Same for an extremely old dentist who cleaned her teeth and told her she was doing "an excellent job with your oral hygiene, most kids don't."

When her shoes grew tight, Sophie took her to a store on

a street called Larchmont where the salesman treated her like a grown-up and asked her what style she preferred.

She said, "Anything."

"That's a switch, usually kids are demanding." This remark aimed more at Sophie than Grace.

Sophie said, "She's an easy girl," and hearing that, Grace filled with warm, sweet feelings. She'd passed her **own** test.

When the three of them were together, she made sure to look into their eyes when they spoke, pretended to be interested in what they talked about when she wasn't. Mostly she **was** interested. In their discussions of history and economics, of how people behaved alone and in groups. Usually they began including Grace in the conversation, but soon they were talking past her, allowing her to just listen, and she didn't mind that one bit.

They talked about art and music. About how bad certain governments were—Nazism, communism, Malcolm pronouncing that any kind of "collectivism is simply a way to control others." They discussed what kinds of societies produced what kinds of artists and musicians and scientists and how there wasn't enough "synthesis between art and science."

Every discussion sent Grace running to her dictionary and she figured she was learning more just being with them than from the homeschool curriculum.

When they asked her opinion, if she had one she offered it briefly and quietly. When she had no idea, she said so and more than once Malcolm nodded approvingly, saying, "If only my students knew enough to admit that."

Sophie: "If only everyone did. Starting with pundits."

Another word filed for future investigation.

Malcolm: "Pundits are nitwits, for the most part."

Sophie: "Any self-designated expert is by nature fraudulent, Mal, no?" To Grace: "That applies even to this guy and myself. Just because we have fancy professorial titles doesn't mean we know any more than anyone else."

Malcolm: "Anyone including you, Grace."

Grace shook her head. "Maybe I know more about being twelve but you know more about almost everything else."

Laughter from across the dinner table.

Sophie: "Don't be so sure, dear."

Malcolm, chortling: "Looks like we fooled her." He leaned over, as if to tousle Grace's hair. Stopped himself. He never touched her. Grace was thirteen and in all the time she'd been living here, physical contact between her and Malcom had been limited to accidental brush-bys.

Sophie occasionally touched her hand, but not much else. Fine with Grace.

Now Sophie put down her silver salad fork and said, "Honestly, dear, don't sell yourself short, you know more than you think you do. Yes, experience is important. But you can gain that. All the experience in the world won't help an idiot."

"Amen," said Malcolm, and he speared another lamb chop.

Sophie had served up a platter of chops along with tossed salad, thick fried potatoes, which Grace found delicious, and brussels sprouts, which smelled and tasted to her like something dying.

Sophie: "Don't eat the sprouts. I've cooked them poorly, they're bitter."

Malcolm: "I think they're fine."

Sophie: "Darling, you think canned sardines are gourmet fare."

"Hmmph."

Grace ate another yummy piece of potato.

Especially with Sophie, Grace was careful not to overdo the good-manners stuff because Sophie was good at spotting fakes. Like with antiques in the magazines she subscribed to. Sometimes she'd look at a picture of furniture or a vase or a sculpture and nod approvingly. Other times, she'd say, "Who do they think they're kidding? If this is Tang dynasty I'm Charlie Chaplin."

In general, Grace was polite but normal about it. Following a rule she'd set for herself a long time ago.

If people like you, maybe they won't hurt you.

Sometimes, mostly at night, alone in her big, soft, sweet-smelling bed, snuggling under a down comforter, sucking her thumb, Grace thought about Ramona.

The slimy-green pool.

That inevitably connected to Bobby in his bed, air tube hissing.

Terrible Sam. His brother and sister, scared as squirrels fleeing a hawk.

When those thoughts invaded Grace's brain, she worked hard to throw them out—to **evict** them, a word from her vocabulary lesson that she liked because it sounded hard, mean, and final. Finally, she figured out that the best way of clearing her brain was to think of something nice.

A delicious dinner.

Recalling Malcolm saying she was brilliant.

Sophie's smile.

Being **here.**

Two months after her thirteenth birthday—an event celebrated at the fanciest restaurant Grace had ever seen, in a hotel called the Bel-Air—she discovered something other than sucking her thumb that helped her feel peaceful: touching herself between her legs, where hairs were sprouting like grass. Feeling dizzy and nervous, at first, but afterward warm and soft in a way she'd never experienced.

And she could do it by herself!

Combine all those things and bad thoughts didn't have a chance.

Soon, she stopped remembering anything that had happened before she lived on June Street.

.   .   .

Sophie could cook very well but, as she reminded Grace more than once, she didn't like it.

"Then why do you do it?"

"Someone has to, dear, and Lord knows Malcolm's a disaster in the kitchen."

"I can learn."

Swiveling from the big six-burner Wolf range, Sophie looked at Grace, sitting at the kitchen table, reading a book on the birds of North America. "You'd learn to cook?"

"If you want me to."

"You're offering to relieve me of culinary duties?"

"Uh-huh."

Sophie's eyes got a little wet. She put down her pot holder and came over to Grace, cupped Grace's chin and bent, and for a moment Grace was worried Sophie was going to kiss her. No one had ever kissed her, not once.

Maybe Sophie could tell Grace was worried, because she just chucked Grace's chin and said, "That is a gracious offer, my dear Ms. Blades. One day I may take you up on it, but please don't ever feel you need to take care of us. We're here to take care of you."

It was the first time since Grace had moved in that someone had touched her nicely on purpose.

"Okay?" said Sophie.

"Okay."

"Then it's settled. We will cast off the shackles of domesticity tonight and the eminent but selectively inept Professor Bluestone will take us both out to dinner. Somewhere pricey and chichi. Sound good?"

"Sounds superb." Another great word.

"Superb it is, dear. I'm thinking French because no one understands haute cuisine like the French."

"Haute couture, as well," said Grace.

"You know about haute couture?"

"From your magazines."

"Do you know what "haute" means?"

"Fancy."

"Strictly speaking it means 'high.' The French are all about dividing their world into highs and lows. With them, there aren't just restaurants, there are cafés, bistros, brasseries, and so on."

"Which one are we going to tonight?"

"Oh, definitely a restaurant. Malcolm must treat us like the haute gals we are."

That evening, at a place called Chez Antoine, Grace had a complicated time. Wearing a stiff dress that scratched her, she was a little frightened of the dark, nearly silent room filled with fast-walking black-suited waiters who looked as if they were ready to find fault.

She said yes to everything, enjoyed the meat and the potatoes and some of the green vegetables. But she felt her stomach heave when one of the grumpy waiters brought out little iron skillets of—could it be, yes it was—oh, God, **snails**! As if that wasn't enough, another waiter brought plates of little bony things that looked like baby chicken legs and Grace thought how mean to kill tiny chicks but then Malcolm explained they were the sautéed limbs of **frogs**!

She tried not to watch as Malcolm and Sophie stuck tiny forks into the snail shells, pulled out gross clumpy lumps covered with parsley, chewed and smiled and swallowed. Tried not to listen as the frog legs crunched under the weight of Malcolm's heavy jaws.

Look listen learn, look listen learn.

When Malcolm held out a frog leg to Grace and said, "Don't feel obligated but you might surprise yourself and like it," Grace sucked in her breath and took the smallest nibble and found the taste not great but okay.

Pretend it really is a baby chicken. No, not that, too gross. How about an adult chicken that just didn't grow because it was sick or something.

A chicken with a problem in the pituitary gland. She'd learned about that in her biology lesson two weeks ago.

"Thank you, Malcolm."

"Glad you like it."

I like everything about this dream.

By age fourteen and a half, Grace had begun to think of herself as belonging in the big beautiful house. Dangerous feeling, but she couldn't help it, she'd been here longer than anywhere else.

Except that place in the beginning but that didn't count.

Sometimes she even let herself imagine she belonged to Sophie and Malcolm. But not owned in that crazy way she'd read about in the poems she studied. This was something more . . . civilized.

Three months ago, she'd taken a huge chance and allowed her fingertips to brush Sophie's hand when they were shopping at Saks, in Beverly Hills. Lingering long enough for Sophie to maybe understand.

Sophie squeezed Grace's hand gently and took hold of it and the two of them walked that way for a few moments until Grace grew twitchy and Sophie let go.

Later, when they were finishing a light lunch in the Saks tearoom, Sophie was the one to initiate: running her long, delicate fingers along the side of Grace's cheek.

Smiling, as if she was proud.

They'd come to buy bras for Grace.

Sophie remained outside the dressing room, but not before offering advice: "Make sure it fits perfectly, dear. It will mean all the difference between proper support and backaches when you're my age."

Grace understood; Sophie's bosoms were large for a woman so slim. Grace's own breasts were little more than bumps, though her nipples had doubled in size.

She said, "Makes sense. Thanks for taking me, Sophie."

"Who else, dear? We girls have to stick together."

. . .

By fifteen, Grace had small, soft tufts of blond armpit hair and a reddish-blond triangle of pubic hair that she explored with her fingers to get herself in the mood before she masturbated each night. Downy nearly white hairs on her legs were close to invisible but Sophie showed her how to shave them anyway, without nicking herself.

"Use a fresh disposable razor every time and put this on first." Handing Grace a glass bottle filled with golden lotion, the label lettered in French cursive. "It's got aloe in it, that's a spiky plant that looks pretty unimpressive but is impressively multitalented."

Grace knew about aloe, about all sorts of botanical specimens. Her lessons were all college-level or above now, and Malcolm informed her that her vocabulary was that of "a doctoral candidate at a damn good university, remarkable, really." Everything floated easily into her brain except math, but if she worked hard enough she could get that, too.

And that was her world: the three of them, Ransom Gardener every so often, occasionally Mike Leiber.

Mostly, her studies.

Once, in the beginning, Malcolm and Sophie had asked her if she wanted to meet other children. Grace decided to be honest and said, "I'd prefer not," and when they asked again, months later, and got the same answer, the subject never came up again.

Then . . .

It was a Sunday. Grace was fifteen and two months.

Malcolm raked leaves in the backyard and Sophie read a stack of magazines under the giant quince tree at the rear of the garden. Grace was off by herself, stretched out on a lounge chair near the rose beds, reading Coleman's text on abnormal psychology and trying to fit people she'd known into various diagnostic categories.

Suddenly Malcolm stopped raking and Sophie stopped

reading and the two of them looked at each other and came over to Grace.

A couple of giants converging on her.

"Dear," said Sophie, "do you have a minute?"

Grace's stomach—her entire gastrointestinal tract, she'd learned anatomy and could visualize the organs—began quivering. She said, "Of course." Amazed at how calm she sounded.

Or maybe she didn't because Malcolm and Sophie looked uncomfortable and when grown-ups looked that way it was a bad sign.

A **precursor.**

"Let's go inside," said Sophie, and that clinched it. Something terrible **was** going to happen. Grace was surprised, but at the same time she wasn't because you never knew when life would turn disappointing.

Sophie took Grace's hand and found it clammy with sweat but she held on and led Grace into the house, ending in the kitchen. Explaining, "I'm in the mood for lemonade," but not coming close to convincing.

Malcolm, trailing behind and still looking uncomfortable— that horrible **concerned** look—said, "Lemonade and ginger cookies. To hell with the avoirdupois."

Sophie set the lemonade and three kinds of cookies on the kitchen table. Malcolm ate two cookies immediately. Sophie looked at him and raised an eyebrow and held the plate out to Grace.

"No, thank you." Now Grace's voice was quivering stronger than her intestines.

Sophie said, "Something wrong, dear?"

"No."

Malcolm said, "You've got a sensitive antenna, Grace." Addressing her by name; this had to be **really** bad.

They were kicking her out. What had she done? Where were they sending her?

She burst into tears.

Sophie and Malcolm leaned forward, each of them taking a hand.

"Sweetheart, what's wrong?" said Sophie.

Grace was helpless against the torrent of water pouring from her eyes. She felt out of control. Like the psychotics she'd read about in Malcolm's psychology books.

"Grace?" said Sophie, stroking her hand. "There's nothing to be upset about. Really—"

Then the water stopped pouring out and words took their place, as if someone had turned Grace upside down and shaken the speech out of her. "I don't want to leave!"

Sophie's deep-blue eyes were huge behind her glasses. "To leave? Of course not—oh, my God, you thought—Mal, look what we've done, she's terrified."

And then Professor Malcolm Bluestone, who'd never touched her, walked behind her and placed one huge, padded hand on her cheek, the other lightly on her shoulder, and kissed the top of her head.

Another man might've spoken softly and gently. Malcolm boomed with authority. "You are not leaving, Ms. Grace Blades. You are ensconced here for as long as you choose to be. Which from our perspective is forever."

Grace cried some more until she'd emptied herself of tears and had to gasp to regain her breath. Feeling relieved but now worse than stupid—idiotic.

She vowed never to lose herself that way again. No matter what.

Sophie inhaled deeply. "I reiterate what Malcolm said: You're here, period. But there will be a change and you need to know about it. My sabbatical—my extremely extended sabbatical, as you know I cadged another eighteen months out of the rotters by forgoing salary—has come to an end. Do you understand what that means?"

Grace said, "You have to go to work."

"Four days a week, dear. The rotters have loaded me up

with classes, allegedly because of budget cuts, tenure be damned." Sophie's smile was wry. "The fact that my alleged book hasn't materialized hasn't helped my position."

Malcolm said, "You'll finish when you're ready, darling, they just need to—"

Sophie waved him quiet. "So sweet and psychologically supportive, Mal, but let's all be honest: I've idled and now the piper must be paid." She turned back to Grace. "Malcolm's sabbatical doesn't come around for another three years. That means both of us will be going to work."

Grace said nothing.

"You understand?" said Sophie.

"No."

"You can't be here by yourself."

"Why not?"

Sophie sighed. "We should've prepared you. Be that as it may, reality is upon us and we must cope. Why can't you remain unattended? Because if something happened—a fire, God forbid, or a break-in—and we'd left you alone it would be calamitous, dear. Even if you weren't hurt, we'd lose our guardianship and possibly face charges of neglect."

"That's inane," said Grace. "And insane."

"Maybe so, dear, but the fact is, you're too young to be by yourself all day and we need to find you a school. We must work together to obtain the best fit available."

Grace looked at Malcolm. He nodded.

She said, "Isn't there a school on your campus? The one where your students do research on kids?"

Malcolm said, "That is for children with learning problems. You are quite the contrary, you're a learning superstar. We've done our research and narrowed down the possibilities, but you need to weigh in."

Grace said, "Thank you, I appreciate the effort but nothing will fit."

"How can you be sure, dear?" said Sophie.

"The thought of school is repulsive."

Malcolm smiled. "Repulsive, repugnant, repellent, and quite possibly regressive. But, unfortunately, necessary."

"There's really no choice, dear," said Sophie. "We're hoping this process doesn't turn out more difficult than it needs to be. That you might actually find the experience rewarding."

"Or at least interesting," said Malcolm.

Grace said nothing.

"It might only be for a year or so," said Malcolm.

"Might?" said Grace.

"Given your present academic level you'd easily qualify for college at sixteen. In fact, on a purely intellectual level, you could handle college right now. But we don't believe sending you straight from homeschooling to university at fifteen is a great idea and I'm sure you concur."

Grace thought about that. Realized she'd never been to USC with either of them. But she had seen pictures of colleges. Read about college life in books and magazines. Photos that showed students who looked like adults, relaxing on the grass, huge buildings in the background.

As inviting as an alien planet . . .

Malcolm said, "Do you? Concur?"

Grace nodded.

"Good, then. Onward."

Sophie said, "A year or so spent in high school could serve as an excellent preparatory experience for college."

"Prep school," said Grace.

"Literally and figuratively, dear."

"Holden Caulfield hated it."

Sophie and Malcolm both smiled.

Malcolm said, "Yes, he did, but admit it, Caulfield was basically a snide, spoiled twit. The arrival of the Messiah would leave him unimpressed."

Despite herself, Grace laughed.

"You, on the other hand," he went on, "are a young woman of substance. Surely one year, give or take, spent in the company of other highly gifted adolescents won't trip you up."

Grace said, "A school for the gifted?"

"Would you prefer a clutch of morons?"

"Mal," said Sophie. To Grace: "We've narrowed it down to two."

They brought out brochures.

The Brophy School was a forty-minute drive to Sherman Oaks in the Valley and featured an emphasis upon "high-level academics combined with personal growth." High school only, student body of one hundred twenty.

Malcolm said, "It's a little bit lax, standards-wise, but still serious."

Grace said, "Personal growth?" She snickered.

"Rather touchy-feely, yes."

"What about the other one?"

"The Merganfield School," he said. "From seventh through twelve but small classes, the student body maxes out at seventy."

"Smaller classes and **extremely** rigorous," said Sophie.

Grace said, "No personal growth, huh?"

Malcolm smiled. "I asked Dr. Merganfield about that, as a matter of fact. He said growth comes from achievement. He's a bit of a martinet."

Sophie said, "It's somewhat authoritarian, dear."

Malcolm said, "Lots of structure."

Grace said, "Where is it?"

Sophie said, "Not far from here, actually. One of those big mansions, near Windsor Square."

Grace said, "Is it expensive?"

Silence.

Sophie said, "No need for you to worry about that."

"I can pay you back," said Grace. "One day, when I'm successful."

Malcolm reached for a cookie, changed his mind. Sophie sniffed and wiped at her eyes.

"Dear girl," she said, "we have no doubt you'll be success-ful. That, in itself, will be our payment."

Malcolm said, "Not that we need recompense."

Grace said, "I hope it's not too expensive."

"Not at all," said Malcolm, blinking the way he did when he tried to hide something from her.

Grace said, "Sounds like Merganfield's the optimal choice."

"You're sure?" said Sophie. "It really is a no-nonsense place, dear. Maybe you should visit both of them." She broke out into laughter. "How foolish of me. Touchy-feely isn't your thing. If you approve of a place, you'll thrive."

"First, visit," said Malcolm.

"Sure," said Grace. This hadn't turned out so bad. Taking a cookie, she reached into her vocabulary vault. "Guess now I'll have to be pro-social."

Two days later, she took the Merganfield admissions test in the mahogany-paneled reception room of the cream-colored building that served as the school's main building, the only other structure a triple garage converted to a no-frills gym.

Sophie had called the place a mansion. To Grace, it felt like a palace: three stories on Irving Street, easily double the size of Malcolm and Sophie's Tudor. The house sat centered on a vast, park-like lot surrounded by black iron fencing. Trees were huge but most looked neglected. Lawns, hedges, and shrubs appeared shabby.

The style was one Grace recognized from her readings on architecture: Mediterranean mixed with a bit of Palladian. To the north were the enormous homes of Windsor Square, to the south the office buildings on Wilshire.

The exam duplicated many of the IQ tests Malcolm had administered to Grace and with the exception of some of the math, the achievement components were only challenging at the uppermost levels.

"Same old story," Malcolm had warned her. "Impossible to get everything right."

No matter how long they knew each other, Grace decided, he'd never stop being a psychologist.

The letter of acceptance arrived a week later. The owner-headmaster, Dr. Ernest K. Merganfield, was a short, slight man with little personal warmth but, somehow, an aura of reassurance. He wore a short-sleeved white shirt, plaid slacks, and rubber-soled blue cotton shoes, and Grace came to learn that was his daily uniform.

He had two doctorates: a Ph.D. in history from Yale and an Ed.D. from Harvard. The teachers were all Ph.D.'s, mostly retired college professors, with the exception of Dr. Mendez, the biology instructor, who was an elderly retired medical pathologist. Upper-class students—sophomores, juniors, and seniors—took their classes on the top floor, with some rooms offering nice views. Grace's score on the exam qualified her to be a fifteen-year-old senior, but when she arrived to join her classmates she found she wasn't the youngest in the class, not even close.

Sitting next to her was a twelve-year-old math prodigy named Dmitri, and behind her were fourteen-year-old twins from Nigeria, children of a diplomat, who spoke six languages fluently.

No one exhibited any curiosity about her entry in the middle of the school year and soon Grace learned why: Her brand-new peers were, for the most part, shy, introverted, and obsessed with scholastic achievement. Of the eleven students in her class, seven were girls, four quite pretty, but none with any fashion sense.

Then again, without Sophie, Grace figured she'd have been clueless about clothes, makeup, nickless shaving. How to walk and talk. How to hold a fish fork.

Merganfield students had biological parents who probably

didn't care much about anything but their getting into a top college. The twins had already been guaranteed admission to Columbia in two years.

The lack of maintenance Grace had noticed in the garden extended to the interior. Bathrooms were old and balky and papered with warnings not to flush anything but toilet paper and "scant amounts of that."

Of the four boys in her class, one was obese with a stammer, two were shy to the point of muteness, and one, the oldest pupil in the senior class, was a tall, rangy, good-looking seventeen-year-old named Sean Miller, gifted in math and physics. He had dark curly hair, hazel eyes, nice features marred by virulent acne.

Also shy, that seemed to be the Merganfield way. But definitely interested in Grace, she could tell because every time she looked up from her notebook, she caught him averting his eyes. Just to confirm her hypothesis, she sidled up against him at the end of rhetoric class and smiled.

He colored crimson around his zits and lurched away, as if hiding something.

Definitely hiding something. The front of his khaki pants had tented.

This could be interesting.

Three weeks after arriving at Merganfield, having earned nearly straight A's on every test and certain that she was considered "fully integrated," she encountered Sean Miller as he left the garage/gym that hardly anyone used because P.E. was optional (though Dr. Merganfield did espouse "Grecian ideals of integrating mental and physical mastery").

Not a chance encounter. Grace had observed Sean and he was predictable as a well-tuned clock, lifting weights and running on a treadmill every Wednesday after class. Grace had finally convinced Malcolm and Sophie to let her walk the mile and a half home, promising to keep to Sixth Street, with its busy traffic and easy visibility. Tonight, both of them would be coming home late due to meetings. Sophie had pre-cooked a tuna noodle casserole for Grace to microwave.

She wasn't hungry for pasta and canned fish.

Sean Miller learned that quickly enough.

Soon, they were doing it every Wednesday, outside behind the gym, and Grace had shoplifted enough condoms from a local pharmacy to keep everything nice and safe.

The first time Sean attempted to talk to her afterward, she quieted him with a finger over his lips and he never tried that again.

36

It was one p.m. when Grace drove away from Wild Bill's, leaving the two punks gaping. If her energy held up, she could make the trip in six or seven hours. If she started feeling less than optimal, she'd stop in Monterey.

For the first fifty miles, she tried to empty her head by listening to music.

Unsuccessful; her brain pinged rudely through Bach and doo-wop and alternative rock and jazz, a heckler at a lecture.

Random noise clarified to a yammering voice reminding her.

She'd killed a man.

How did she feel about that?

She didn't know.

Rationalization was obvious: bad guy, obvious self-defense. But still, it was odd. The fact that she'd actually ended a life.

The permanence.

The sound of her victim's corpse bumping down the canyon grew to a drumbeat.

Her **victim.**

Not an everyday event, dispatching another human being. She knew from her training that soldiers had trouble getting used to it.

So how did **she** feel about it?

She **really** didn't know.

Focus.

All right then, the old affective system, first. Mood-wise, she'd have to describe herself as calm, settled. Basically okay.

What did that say about her?

Murderer's daughter, prisoner of genetics? Keeping up a family tradition? Could she have adapted more smoothly

than most to the military? To something expressly homi-
cidal, say, sniping?

She'd worked with former snipers, had a decent idea about
what that entailed.

Sitting there, suppressing your breathing, focusing on the
target, reducing organic matter to a kill-spot.

Could she do that?

Probably. Whatever it took to survive. She'd always been
driven to survive. Which was why she was still around.

A bit of luck didn't hurt, either. Fate, karma, divine will,
choose your delusion.

Be nice to have religious faith, to believe in life fitting together like a gorgeous puzzle. And looking back at her own
life, Grace could see how an otherwise rational person could
tease out a pattern that really didn't exist.

Hard-luck orphan with a Ph.D. and a house on the beach.
Pretty damn miraculous when you thought about it, call
Hollywood!

To Grace, it just felt like her life.

Still, it would be nice to have faith in something. To believe she was destined to be around.

Meanwhile, survival meant you took care of business, so
that settled it, she was fine, had done what was necessary.

As she repeated that mantra, keeping her foot steady on
the gas pedal, Beldrim Benn's face faded in her head until it
was little more than an airy sketch.

She kept going and it thinned to random lines.

A dot.

Erased.

So why did her eyes ache? The sound . . . **bump bump
bump** . . . No, the **Escape** was bucking and swaying and she
realized she'd allowed herself to speed up—edging close to
ninety—taxing its suspension.

She quickly slowed down. Checked the rearview and saw
nothing but asphalt.

She'd be fine.

Twenty miles later, Benn's stubbly visage had crept back into her consciousness and nothing she did could get rid of it.

She stopped fighting and just went with it, allowing herself to wonder.

Did he have a wife? Kids? Were his parents alive? What about hobbies? Something other than knifing people?

Switching to the right lane, she reduced her speed further. Annoyingly, though, her pulse had quickened, she could feel the thrum in her neck, at her wrists, her ankles, all those pressure points thumping like a steel band. And now her aching eyes were wet . . .

The Escape had settled at fifty-five. Time to work on slowing her own engine.

Reaching for the beef jerky, she chewed two sticks to pulp. Worked her jaws like a maniac and finally scoured her brain free of memory.

She was coasting smoothly when the disposable she'd used to call Wayne beeped.

She said, "Uncle."

"I'm happy to be your uncle, but no need for subterfuge, I'm alone."

"Me, too. What's up?"

"Got your message about Selene McKinney. Talk about a blast from the past. It took some time to figure out who to call but I think I may have something."

Grace said, "She had a child." **A girl, tell me a girl.**

Wayne said, "Apparently, quite a while back, a girl lived in Selene's house but no one ever confirmed she was Selene's daughter. In fact the assumption was that she was a niece or some kind of ward because Selene never introduced her as a daughter and more important, Selene had never been known to date a man. Or a woman. Her sex was politics."

"Single woman lives with a child who isn't hers?"

"It wasn't that uncommon back then, Grace. Families were closer-knit, people took in relatives all the time."

"How long ago are we talking about?"

"Shortly after Selene was first elected, which would make it at least forty years."

"How old was the girl?"

"My source recalls her as six or seven, but she won't swear to it, she honestly can't remember the details. Whatever the arrangement was with Selene, it was brief. The girl was seen at the house for a couple of years, then she wasn't."

Grace calculated mentally. Forty-six or so, today, meant a woman in her early twenties at the time of the Fortress Cult showdown, no problem having three kids.

So lovely when things came together. "Does your source have any theories about what happened to her?"

"She claimed she'd never thought about it and I believe her. Let's just say curiosity isn't her strong suit. When I pressed her, she said young ladies of a certain age often got sent to boarding school but that was just a guess. Bear in mind that Selene was born into huge money, politics was her avocation. We're talking social circles neither of us have experienced firsthand, Grace, but I know a few things about the mega-rich because my father was a chauffeur for a banking clan in Brentwood. All the children were sent away to 'develop.' It wasn't out of the ordinary. Dad used to joke that if he had the money, he'd do the same to my brothers and me so he could enjoy his life. Would you care to tell me why you're interested in Selene McKinney years after her death?"

"At this point, everything's conjecture."

"I'm okay with conjecture, Grace."

Grace tried to sort out her answer. Wayne didn't wait. "All right, then, do you have a moment to listen to **my** conjecture? You're thinking the girl could be the mother of those cult children, one of the lunatics who died in the showdown." A beat. "How am I doing, Dr. Blades?"

"Very well."

"What led you there, Grace?"

"The only link I can find between the boys' adoptive parents is Selene."

"What link is that?"

"Both couples attended her reelection fund-raiser."

"The boys but not the girl."

"From the sequence you gave me I'm assuming the girl was adopted first."

"That's correct."

"You couldn't obtain exact dates—"

"It was all I could do to produce what I did."

"Right," said Grace. "Highly appreciated. Anyway, Lily was adopted by a working-class family but the boys ended up in affluent homes. I figured they might've knocked around the system for a while, being high-risk adoptees, but now you've brought up the boarding school theory, perhaps they got farmed out that way. Either way, the time came when they needed homes and Selene cashed in IOUs."

"All that," said Wayne, "because of a fund-raiser?"

"Conjecture," Grace reminded him, "but the time line fits. And think about it: How often do high-risk male fosters end up on Easy Street?"

The same went for high-risk female fosters. Sophie's face flew into Grace's head, then Malcolm's. Both smiling, encouraging. **Proud.**

Wayne said, "You okay?"

"I'm fine."

"It sounded like you gasped and then you didn't reply when I said something."

Not good, girl. "Sorry, got the sniffles, Wayne. Anyway, that's my working theory but I'm a ways from proving it. You've been a peach, thanks again."

Wayne sighed. "I hope I've actually helped you."

"Of course you have."

"I wish I could be as certain as you, Grace."

"You're worried about me. I appreciate that but don't be."

"Easy for you to say, Grace. I'm more than worried, I'm frightened. Especially if you are right. What you've told me about the older one—Samael—has really sunk in, I can't stop thinking about poor Ramona, that crippled boy. Top that off with someone who'd do that to his own **brother**? You're the psychologist, you know the kind of pathology that implies."

"I do, Wayne. That's why I'm careful."

"With all due respect, you may not be the best judge of your own precautions, Grace—now, don't be angry at what I'm going to say but I need to say it. No doubt the notion of running away from anything offends your sensibilities. But sometimes avoidance **is** a good strategy."

And she hadn't even told him about the parricides.

The Escape bucked again; she'd edged back up to eighty. **Focus, focus.** She slowed.

"I agree, Wayne. I have nothing against any strategy, per se."

"But . . ."

"I need to collect data so I can make intelligent decisions."

Wayne sighed.

"I promise to be careful," she said.

Wayne said, "Oh, boy." His voice caught. "Oh, Grace, the things that revisit us. Is there ever an end to them?"

On the verge of tears.

Think of him as a patient.

She said, "You're a wonderful person. You saved me and I'd never abuse your trust by placing myself in danger."

Beyond that, my friend, I adore myself. Hence a dead man bump-bumping into a ravine.

Wayne said, "All I did was what I was supposed to. Take care, Grace."

Click.

Grace placed the phone on the passenger seat, reached

for a water bottle, and settled in. Moments later, she caught color and movement in the rearview mirror.

Flashing blue and red lights.

Brief squirt of siren. Black-and-white riding her tail.

She pulled onto the shoulder of the highway.

37

The cop car was an aggressive little supercharged Mustang, the cop it discharged, a highway patrolman no older than Grace and probably younger. Medium height, solidly built, approaching with the usual swagger.

The suspicious cop-squint that verged on paranoia.

As he reached her driver's window, she compiled more visual data: Hispanic, dark hair gelled, nice golden complexion but for a diagonal scar across the bridge of his nose. A badge that read **M. Lopez.**

By the time he arrived, Grace had fine-tuned the optimal smile: minimal, slightly intimidated but not antsy.

M. Lopez's eyes were blocked by mirrored shades. His mouth was small, almost prissy. "License, registration, insurance."

Grace obliged. "This is a rental, would you like my personal insurance?"

Instead of answering, he inspected the license. "Malibu. You're a ways from home."

"Road trip," she said.

"All by yourself, ma'am?"

"Meeting friends in Carmel."

"Nice place."

"I'm looking forward to it."

"Hmm . . . you know why I stopped you."

"Sorry, I don't."

"I spotted you talking on a cellphone. Followed you and watched you continue the conversation for a prolonged period of time."

Not prolonged enough to spot me hauling at eighty per.

And swerving. He'd watched her for only a few moments—the tail end of her conversation—but that was enough.

Grace said, "Oh. Yes, I was, Officer. **Darn.** I asked the rental agency for hands-off, they didn't have it."

"That doesn't excuse you, ma'am. What you did was extremely dangerous," said M. Lopez. He leaned in closer. "Driver distraction is one of the most frequent causes of fatal accidents."

"I know, I feel like a total idiot. My only excuse was that it was a patient emergency."

"You're a doctor?"

"Psychologist."

He studied her. "You can prove that."

Grace showed him her state license.

M. Lopez said, "Well . . . it's still dangerous, Doctor. Don't imagine your patient would appreciate having her therapist smashed to bits."

Her. Assuming women talked to women.

Grace allowed her smile to widen. "No, that wouldn't be helpful for her."

Her attempt at wit fell flat; M. Lopez just stared at her. Grace pretended his eyes were warming up behind the shades and that helped her maintain her cool.

She said, "Collision therapy, that would be a first."

His lips twitched. Fighting not to smile back. He lost the battle, permitted himself a partial grin.

They always lost.

As he began to feel more friendly, the rest of his body agreed, posture relaxing. Removing his shades, he revealed big, soft brown eyes. "Patient emergency, huh? Like what?"

"I can't tell you that, Officer. Strict confidentiality."

That seemed to please him. With cops, you were always passing tests. With anyone.

M. Lopez said, "You won't say even if it means you get a citation?"

"Even so," said Grace. "Guilty as charged, I'll take my medicine."

M. Lopez's little mouth screwed up like a pig's tail. The radio on his belt squawked. He picked up and listened and barked, "Ten-four." To Grace: "Gotta run, Doctor. Big crash back a few miles. Ambulances and all. Maybe due to driver distraction. Someone else's disaster is your lucky day."

"Thank you, Officer."

M. Lopez waved her papers before returning them. "But let's not count on any more luck, okay? No more cellphone, even with a patient emergency. You exit in a safe place and commence, okay, ma'am?"

"I promise."

"Good." Needing the last word; Grace let him have it.

Returning to his hot rod, he revved and swooped onto the highway at an outrageously excessive speed, lights rotating, siren on full-alarm.

Completing the fifteen-second drag race to the nearest exit before vanishing in a Doppler cloud of noise.

Grace let out breath slowly, said, "You've still got it working, girl," and drove off.

Or maybe her charm had nothing to do with it and M. Lopez had it right: Someone else's misfortune was her lucky break.

If she didn't think it amoral and futile she'd have prayed for more of the same.

38

Merganfield School allowed students to learn at their own pace. In most cases, the pressured darlings who'd lived their entire lives being told they were geniuses pushed themselves at warp speed. No one pressured Grace but she discovered that her rate of learning was as quick as her most neurotic classmates.

Midway through the year, she'd completed much of the Merganfield "great books" curriculum with straight A's but tried to keep her progress from Malcolm and Sophie.

Because once they knew college was the optimal choice there'd be another sit-down.

But by the time she was nearing the end of her first year at the school, her perspective had changed. Approaching sixteen, she found herself craving even more solitude. Tolerating Sophie and Malcolm's conversation, appreciating them, they were clearly wondrous and wonderful people. But secretly, she found herself wishing they'd leave her alone for long stretches.

This, she supposed, is adolescence. Though it felt like more of being herself.

The psychology books she borrowed from Malcolm's shelves said "emerging adulthood" was all about establishing "autonomy" and a "sense of self." One out of two wasn't bad; she'd never totally depended on anyone but sense of self remained a mystery. Mostly she lived hour by hour, trying to do things she enjoyed. Including those stolen moments with the always-grateful and somewhat clearer-skinned Sean Miller. (Did Grace deserve credit for reducing his zits? She'd heard that was an old wives' tale, but you never knew.)

Whatever the reason, he was looking better, and she was pleased with her growing sexual skills; Sean was like modeling clay.

She was also viewing leaving for college as a not-tragic possibility. Though another option was staying at home and attending USC, where Malcolm and Sophie taught.

Commuting with them to campus . . . no, that didn't feel right.

In any event, there was no sense pushing the issue and when summer came around and she had the possibility of attending summer school at Merganfield, she said sure.

Every one of her classmates was also there. Even the Nigerian twins, who'd heard from Princeton after their Columbia acceptance and were New Jersey–bound, felt impelled to study all summer.

The session went smoothly, go-with-the-flow working for Grace until a morning in mid-June, when Sophie puttered with uncharacteristic nervousness at the Wolf range and Malcolm cleared his throat.

This time they faced her across a table groaning with bagels and Sophie's aquavit-cured gravlax.

This time she was ready.

Malcolm began with a little speech about Grace's amazing scholastic accomplishments, singling out her thirty-page paper on the pre-czarist rulers of Russia, her over-the-moon grades, SAT scores that put her in the top tenth of a percentile, nationally.

Grace didn't argue but she was far less impressed by her own achievements. Everyone at Merganfield got A's because why should the "highly gifted" perform other than at an "exemplary level"? And among the psychometrics Malcolm had been administering to her for years were various versions of the SAT. Grace had caught on, long ago, to what the test's designers were after, the predictable vocabulary words, the math problems that allegedly tested abstract thinking.

By now, she could pencil the dots in her sleep. So when Malcolm paused to chew on a poppy seed bagel, she said, "I know. We need to talk about next year. Don't worry, I'm fine with the change."

Malcolm, mouth full, chewed faster.

Sophie placed a hand on her left bosom and smiled. "We're that transparent, dear?"

"You care about me. I appreciate it. I've matured and I'm okay with change."

Sophie blinked. "Yes, well—that's a relief. But you know, it could be a huge change—much more so than Merganfield."

"I'm ready," said Grace. "Have been for a while. The only problem is the money. I can't keep mooching off you, there has to be a plan for tuition repayment."

Malcolm swallowed. "Don't be silly, you're not mooching."

"Absolutely not," said Sophie.

Grace fingered the hem of her cashmere top and smiled. "How would you describe it?"

The kitchen clock ticked. Generally Sophie was the first to break long silences. This time Malcolm said, "I consider your education—we consider it—an investment. Someone of your caliber has the potential to accomplish Lord knows what."

Sophie said, "It's also an investment in **our** well-being. We care about you, Grace. We want to be secure in the knowledge that you're self-actualizing—oh, scratch that—we're so pleased you're growing up . . ." Her new smile was fragile.

Malcolm said, "All right, then, we're all on board, no more chatter about repayment. However, a core issue remains—"

Sophie broke in: "Please don't take this wrong, dear, but our relationship—not the emotional aspect, the legal aspect—is ambiguous."

Grace's gut lurched and filled with acid. She was almost certain what they were getting at. She hoped she was. But with people—even good people—you never knew.

Plus, she'd read enough of **Bulfinch's Mythology** to know happy endings were for babies.

So if she was misreading, no sense embarrassing herself, making it awkward for everyone. She put on her best calm smile.

Malcolm said, "What would you say to formalization?"

Sophie said, "He means adoption, dear. If you so choose, we'd like you to become a legal member of our family, Grace."

The same gut that had constricted now blossomed and filled with honeyed warmth. As if a gentle light—a soft, soothing night-light—had been implanted inside Grace.

She had been right! This was the stuff of which dreams were made, she felt like whooping and cheering but her jaw had locked and all she could produce was a weak, "If that's what you want."

Oh, how stupid!

"It is," said Sophie. "But the key is what you want, Grace."

Grace forced out the words. "Yes. Of course. It's what I want. Yes. Thank you. Yes."

"Thank **you**, Grace. It's been a wonderful experience having you here." Sophie got up and hugged her and kissed the top of her head. In an instant, Malcolm was also standing behind her and Grace felt his massive hand rest lightly upon her shoulder before withdrawing.

Grace knew her body was stiff, knew she should be reacting differently—appropriately—but something stopped her. As if a barrier, a neurological levee—what did the physiology book call it?—a **septum** had been inserted between her brain and her mouth.

She said, "It's been great for me, too." Then, finally: "You're wonderful people."

Sophie said, "That's so sweet," and kissed Grace's hair, again.

Malcolm said, "Here, here. I want some of that cake left over from last night."

. . .

Despite the way that morning had begun, the topic of college and its financing slipped away and Grace wondered if Malcolm and Sophie felt she wasn't mature enough.

A few days later, at dinner, Sophie announced that Ransom Gardener, the lawyer, would be stopping by at nine.

Grace said, "The hippie, too?"

Sophie and Malcolm laughed and Sophie said, "Good old Mike? No, not tonight."

Good; Leiber never noticed Grace, anyway. Recently, he'd been arriving with a BlackBerry and rarely taking his eyes off the screen.

Mr. Gardener, on the other hand, always took the time to greet Grace and smile at her. Grace wondered if Mike Leiber was his ward, someone with a disability that the attorney took care of. Someone whose biological parents were unfit. Or uncaring, they just felt like ditching a weirdo.

Did lawyers do that? Grace supposed they did anything that paid well.

Gardener arrived right on time, wearing a black three-piece suit and a thick gold silk tie and carrying two large briefcases. More like suitcases, really.

"Evening, Grace."

"Hi, Mr. Gardener."

He hefted the cases. "This is what we lawyers do, make simple things complicated."

Sophie led everyone to the big table in the dining room, where she'd set out store-bought cookies and bottled water. Malcolm appeared, as if on cue, and everyone sat.

Ransom Gardener was the first to speak, pulling a sheaf of papers from one of the cases. "Congratulations, Grace. I've got the paperwork for your adoption. You're a minor but someone of your age and brains needs to know what they're involved in. So, please."

He slid the papers to Grace. She said, "I'm sure it's fine."

"I'd read it if I were you," said Malcolm. "For all you know, you're signing away your books and your clothing to Hare Krishna."

Ransom Gardener chuckled. Sophie smiled and Grace did as well. Everyone on edge, eager to fake levity.

Grace took the papers. Small print, big words; this was going to be a drag.

Sophie said, "Yes, dear, it's a chore, but learning to be meticulous with documents is a useful skill."

"Punishment for success," said Malcolm. "Unless you're an attorney."

"Now, now," said Ransom Gardener. "Unfortunately, you're right, Mal."

"Now and always, Ran." Malcolm ate a cookie, then another, brushed crumbs from his sweater vest.

Grace read. The documents were even worse than she'd expected, repetitive, verbose, dull, devoid of humanity. All of it boiling down, by the final page, to the fact that Malcolm Albert Bluestone and Sophia Rebecca Muller (heretofore to be referred to as "the Applicants") wanted to adopt Grace Blades (heretofore to be referred to as "Said Minor").

Stating the obvious while murdering the English language. Grace knew she'd never be a lawyer.

She finished and said, "Clear as a bell. Thank you for taking the time, Mr. Gardener."

Gardener gave a start. "Well, that's a first. Someone appreciating me."

Malcolm said, "Feeling emotionally needy, are we, Ran?"

Gardener chuckled again and lightly cuffed Malcolm's shoulder. Their interplay suggested a personal relationship. Gardener had white hair and sunken cheeks, as if his teeth had receded, and Grace had always thought of him as an old man. But seeing him next to Malcolm made her realize they were around the same age, could be longtime friends.

Or perhaps not, and she'd just witnessed banter between two gregarious men. She'd never seen them socialize, only the meetings that she assumed were about business, the privileges and obligations of wealthy people.

Then again, Malcolm and Sophie never socialized with anyone. Ever.

Something else that made living with them ideal.

Gardener said, "Well, you're very welcome, young lady. And as I said, you're a minor, which unfortunately gives you little by way of rights. But I have drafted a brief document that I'd like you to sign, if you agree. It's not binding but I felt you deserved it because of your high intelligence."

A single page slid across the table.

The same obtuse legalese. This one said Grace knew what was going on and consented to being Malcolm and Grace's adopted daughter.

She signed it, using her best penmanship. Thinking: **This is the most important document of my life, make it elegant. Memorable, the way John Hancock had.**

My declaration of wonderful dependence.

Nothing really changed, no pressure to start calling them Mom and Dad, no further mention of the new legal status. On the one hand, Grace liked that. On the other, it was a bit of a letdown.

What had she expected? Glass slippers and a pumpkin coach?

On weekdays, breakfast was generally a do-your-own-thing affair. Everyone rising at different times, Malcolm not much of a breakfast eater, period. Sophie tried to sit down with Grace as she nibbled cereal and bolted down orange juice squeezed from trees out in the garden, before Grace walked to Merganfield, but often her schedule on campus made that impossible.

Several mornings after signing the adoption documents, Grace came down and found a formal breakfast set up. Starched linen draped over the table, soft-boiled in porcelain egg cups, neatly arrayed chunks of French cheeses on the good china, triangles of whole wheat toast lined precisely in a silver rack.

Coffee **and** tea, no room for error.

Malcolm and Sophie were already seated. Another production? Oh, boy. Grace knew the thought was brutally ungrateful but sometimes all she wanted was to be left with her thoughts and fantasies.

This morning, it was more a matter of fatigue; she hadn't slept much, alternating between flights of glee and pangs of anxiety. Wondering obsessively: What did her new status really mean? Would they at some point want to be called Mom and Dad, were they just waiting for the right psychological moment?

Mom and Dad.

Mother and Father.

Mater and Pater.

Your Lordships . . . was she now officially a Bullocks Wilshire and Saks Fifth Avenue princess? Had she ever been anything else since arriving on June Street?

Would some prince appear now that she qualified socially?

Would he remain a prince or turn into a frog when she kissed him . . . worse, a toad.

A lizard.

A serpent.

What did all this **mean**?

The most terrifying question of all: **Is this a dream?**

No, it couldn't be. Because she was wide awake, lying on her back in a big, luxuriant bed in a big, luxuriant room, a place they said was hers but was it really?

Was she anything more than an honored guest?

Did it matter?

Now, at the breakfast table, Grace rubbed her eyes and sat down, watching soft-boiled egg shimmy as her hand bumped the cup.

Sophie said, "Tough night?"

As if she understood.

Maybe she did. Maybe Malcolm did, too. He was a psychologist, trained to read emotions, though, to tell the truth, sometimes he seemed oblivious to the world around him; Sophie was the perceptive one. The one who shopped with her. Started off selecting her clothing, then gradually eased out of the process, allowing Grace to make her own decisions.

Sophie made her medical and dental and hairdresser appointments. Sophie had found her the dentist, the pediatrician. Now a gynecologist, a pretty young woman named Beth Levine, who examined Grace gently and offered her the option of birth-control pills.

It was Sophie she smiled at now. "I'm okay. This looks yummy."

She ate a bit of egg, a nibble of toast, drank most of a cup of coffee, then stopped and smiled at both of them. Letting them know she was patient with whatever they had in mind.

But hopefully, not another bunch of emotion, please no more of that. Yes, her fortune had turned golden, but at some point it was like overeating: You paid with heartburn and sleepless nights.

Malcolm said, "We're feeling great about everything."

"I am, too. Thank you."

"Your being happy is all the thanks we need, Grace. We should be thanking you—" He laughed. "Oh, hell, talk about maudlin—hey, let's everyone go round the table and hold hands and sing 'Kumbaya' and thank everyone else, we'll have a group encounter Thank-a-Thon."

Grace laughed with him.

Sophie said, "If you don't mind, we do need to talk about college. The way I see it, there are two options: Stay another full year at Merganfield, which would be a holding pattern, but that's okay should you choose it, you're way ahead of the game. Or you could apply for spring acceptance at a college and if you got in, spend only half a year at Merganfield. You'd still be barely sixteen when you started so if that sounds daunting, I—we understand. We just don't want you getting bored."

"I could get a job."

"A job?" said Malcolm. "Let me tell you something, work's highly overestimated."

Chuckling and turning to Sophie for appreciation. She was dead serious, fixed on Grace. "What kind of job?"

"I haven't really thought about it, I'm just offering it as a possibility."

"Would you prefer to have some time to consider that, dear? Though, frankly, I'm not sure what you could do other than work at a fast-food joint. Not because you're unqualified. It's simply the way things are set up in this society."

"Flipping burgers, hmm," said Grace. Flashes of restaurant leftovers in a double-wide caused her to sway. "Maybe not. What's that spring acceptance like?"

"It's tough to pull off, dear. And it can be difficult socially, because you'd be stepping into an environment where everyone else has had months to get acquainted."

As if I'm going to socialize any more than you do. Than I do.

Grace said, "Why's it tough to pull off?"

"Colleges and universities are the most procedure-bound institutions around and they revolve around fall acceptances. Exceptions are made but they're few and far between."

Grace said, "There must be empty slots due to people who drop out."

"There are," said Malcolm, "but they're mostly filled with transfers from other universities."

Sophie said, "Still, as I said, exceptions are made. For people such as yourself." She licked her lips. "I'm going to level with you, dear: We've taken the liberty of inquiring and though it's not a certainty, it is a possibility. There's a problem, though."

"What's that?"

"Your choices would be limited. There are only two places

where Malcolm and I have received positive responses: USC and Harvard."

"Where you work and where you went to school," said Grace.

"Go Crimson," said Malcolm, as if nothing mattered less than attending Harvard. But he read everything Harvard mailed him and wrote occasional checks to various endowments.

Sophie said, "Well, technically, I went to Radcliffe, women weren't accepted at Harvard, back then, but yes, those are places where we have personal relationships. Princeton might be a possibility but they and Stanford refuse to commit to a level where I'd be comfortable taking the risk. Meaning if we turned down USC and Harvard, we might be left with nothing."

"USC and Harvard," said Grace. "There are worse choices to make."

"You need to understand," said Malcolm. "If you endured the full year at Merganfield and applied for the fall, you'd likely get in everywhere. The Ivies, Stanford, anywhere you choose. Hell, anyplace stupid enough **not** to take you doesn't **deserve** you."

Sophie said, "So you're narrowing your options, considerably."

I live in a narrow world. Boundaries keep me safe.

Grace said, "I understand. But trust me, this is great, I'm fine with it. Which do you think I should choose?"

Sophie said, "We can't make that decision, dear. It's really up to you."

"All right, then. How about some parameters?" Using a word she'd learned from one of Malcolm's statistic books. Great word, she used it at Merganfield whenever she could. Even with Sean Miller. **Time for some new—ahem—parameters.**

"USC," said Malcolm, "is a fine, fine institution. Harvard is . . . Harvard."

He seemed to be struggling. Grace wanted to save him. "Could I apply to both?"

"Sorry, no, they're both insisting acceptance means commitment."

"I bear all the risk."

"Welcome to the world of higher education, Grace."

Sophie said, "Let's back up a bit. Give you **parameters.** We're talking apples and oranges, on more than an academic level. In one case, you'd stay in L.A., would have the option of dorming in or continuing to live here. In the other you'd be clear across the country and learning to deal with some extremely cold weather." She smiled. "Though I suppose the opportunity of some nice warm winter clothing isn't half bad. Think shearling, dear."

Grace smiled back. "Would I get the same education?"

Malcolm said, "You'd get an excellent education at both places. Anywhere, really, the crucial ingredient is the student, not the college. There are plenty of smart kids at USC but it's more . . . heterogeneous. And while there are stupid people at Harvard, you'd be more likely to meet blocs of individuals closer to your level."

Who cares?

"There's also," said Sophie, "and I shudder to say this, the matter of prestige. A Harvard degree is given a lot of weight by employers and such."

"Far more than deserved," said Malcolm. "Didn't know a blessed thing when I graduated. Didn't prevent consulting firms from wanting to hire me."

"You remained there for your Ph.D.," said Grace.

"I did. I'd planned to go to Chicago or Oxford but I met a gorgeous girl from Radcliffe who was also pursuing her Ph.D. at Harvard." He shrugged. "The rest is domestic history."

Sophie said, "Romantic twist, he tells everyone that story. The truth is, he'd decided well before meeting me."

"I dispute that."

"Darling, you know we've been through this. When we moved and I cleaned out the apartment, I saw the correspondence between you and Professor Fiacre."

"Letters of inquiry," said Malcolm, "are not letters of intent."

Sophie waved him silent. Their fingers touched. Talking about their student days, however briefly, had brought a flush to their cheeks.

Maybe Harvard was an interesting place.

Grace said, "How would you feel about my staying in L.A.?"

"Of course, we'd be fine with it," said Sophie. "Whichever you choose."

"The same goes for Boston?"

A beat.

Sophie said, "Absolutely. We could visit you."

"Give us a chance to revisit old haunts," said Malcolm.

Grace waited.

Sophie understood the silence. "Would we be insulted if you left? Think you ungrateful? Absolutely not. At your age it's normal to want to attain autonomy."

"Develop a sense of yourself," said Malcolm. "Not that you don't have one, of course. But . . . it's a growth process. Your self-image at twenty-five won't be the same as it is at sixteen."

"Sixteen," said Sophie. "I must confess, I keep thinking about that. Not only would you be stepping into an already established social scene, you'd be younger than almost everyone."

"But she'd also be a helluva lot smarter," said Malcolm.

"What would I need to do to apply?" said Grace. "In either place."

Malcolm said, "Fill out a form, send your transcripts and your SAT, sit for an interview with an alumnus."

That sounded pitifully simple. Grace said, "There's still the matter of money."

"The old moochery thing? Don't give it a thought."

Grace didn't reply.

Sophie said, "Why don't we cross that bridge when we come to it?"

"All right," said Grace. "I appreciate your setting up contingencies in both places. Could I have a couple of days to think?"

"I'd expect no less than careful contemplation from you," said Malcolm.

Grace finished her soft-boiled egg.

She'd let the time pass. Ask for a third day in order to appear **contemplative**.

But she'd already made up her mind.

39

Grace stopped in Monterey, finding a casual fish restaurant where, surrounded by families and older couples, she fueled up on grilled salmon, steak fries, and a pot of serious coffee. Thirty-five minutes later, she was back on the road.

Refreshed, purposeful, spotting no cops, she sped.

She pulled into Berkeley just before nine p.m., encountering clear, starlit skies and plenty of street life. A welcome sense of familiarity took hold, though she hadn't been here in years. But back in her twenties, she had flown up fairly frequently, delivering papers, co-authored with Malcolm, at oh-so-earnest symposia.

He had no professional need to do any of that but indulged in occasional scholarly gregariousness. Grace's purpose had been hanging out with him. She recalled the inevitable after-parties with a smile. Standing on the sidelines, glass of white wine in hand, as Malcolm regaled a generally sour lot of academicians with anecdotes plucked from a life lived well.

He'd been so different from them, a redwood among dry weeds.

In her free time, Grace had explored the university town, always finding it an interesting study in pretense. Berkeley was blessed with gorgeous, rolling topography, bordered by hills where trees and shrubs thrived with little care, graced with stunning views of ocean and bay and bridge, everything centered on the vast emerald spread of a venerable campus.

High-end restaurants abounded—Shattuck Avenue's sobriquet was the Gourmet Ghetto. And neighborhoods like Berkeley Hills and Claremont sported grand old houses dating from an age when Northern California was the financial hub of the state. Despite all that, the city seemed to cultivate shabbiness, like one of those old-money dowagers pretending they hadn't lucked into a life of privilege.

Being overrun with students and hippie-anarchist-nihilist alums who refused to leave didn't help. Nor did a political climate that thrived on class envy and political correctness and welcomed the homeless without elevating them.

Where Berkeley's unique ethos really hit you was when you got behind the wheel. Five minutes after rolling into town, Grace had to brake suddenly to avoid pulverizing a pedestrian who leaped off the sidewalk into nocturnal traffic.

A kid, probably a sophomore, long hair streaming above his chiseled spoiled-brat face as he grinned and flipped her off and continued sprinting straight into the next lane of autos. More sudden stops, more one-fingered salutes.

Two blocks later, two girls did the same thing.

I walk, therefore I am virtuous and own the streets and fuck you gas guzzlers!

In Berkeley, even basic locomotion was a political statement.

Grace continued to explore from behind the wheel. Even more street life on the main drags of Telegraph and University. She veered into quieter nocturnal territory, cruising toward the building on Center Street where Roger Wetter Senior and his adopted son had established their headquarters years ago.

Too dark to make out details from across the street. The six-story structure faced a flat, sparse park ringed with trees but scruffy at the center. Beyond the grass stood the dark bulk of Berkeley High.

Seeing the school reminded Grace of Roger Wetter Senior's enlistment of young thugs to intimidate elderly earthquake victims. Had he found his troops right here?

Something else struck her: Knife-wielding Mr. Benn

would've been a young man back then. The likelihood he'd been part of the scam seemed stronger.

As she idled, a figure skulking through the park caught her eye. Stooped, emaciated man, lurching drunkenly, holding something in a paper bag. She drove on, hung a U, parked close to the building.

Six flat stories of characterless night-gray stucco. Ragged black holes in place of doors and windows, the roof mostly gone, rafters tilting upward like splintered chicken bones.

Blocking entry was a chain-link fence. Behind the diamond-shaped holes of the barrier Grace made out an earthmoving machine.

A white placard on the fence was too far to be legible. Movement to her left made her turn quickly. The lurching guy was getting closer. She prepared to leave but he headed up the block, stumbling drunkenly.

Grace hopped out of her SUV and examined the sign. Demolition notice, some sort of government-funded project.

If Alamo Adjustments still existed, she'd have to look elsewhere to find it.

Or maybe she wouldn't. Because it was Mr. Venom she really wanted and if he still owned the structure and dropped by to oversee the government-funded transformation of his property . . .

Shuffling sounds behind her. Hand in her bag, she rotated carefully.

The lurching figure from the park was back, approaching her, hand out.

Old, bent-over guy reeking of booze. She gave him a buck and he said, "Bless you," and moved on.

She continued driving around, taking her time as she searched for appropriate lodging, was intrigued by a drab-looking place smack in the middle of the University Avenue bustle. Arching green neon letters crowned the entry.

OLD   HOTEL

No accommodation of the youth culture? Then she edged closer to the sign and saw the out-of-commission **S**.

The Olds Hotel occupied a mixed-use building with storefronts at street level and rooms above. A black-painted arrow directing the weary traveler to the top of a grimy flight of concrete stairs.

Grace circled the block. The Olds offered an outdoor parking lot in back, mostly empty now and guarded by a flimsy wooden yardarm. Entry was simple: Push a button and drive through. Exit required a token from the management.

Grace returned to the front of the hotel and examined the businesses below. Two stores to the left, a vintage-clothing store might be of use. Not so the cut-rate hair salon next door.

To the right of the hotel entrance was perfection: a photocopy/self-print outlet advertising discounts for theses and dissertations. More to the point: The place was open twenty-four hours a day.

Grace parked illegally and zipped in. Ignored by a student-aged boy engrossed in **Game of Thrones,** she printed herself a new batch of business cards on cheaper paper than those proffered by M. S. Bluestone-Muller, Security Consultant.

S. M. Muller, Ed.D.
Educational Consultant

claimed a Boston number that would lead to a long-defunct pay phone in the lobby of the main branch of the Cambridge public library. Back in her student days, Grace had used the booth to phone a boy at Emerson, a would-be theater director whom she'd met in a dive bar. He'd swallowed her story about being an L.A.-based aspiring actress and she'd slept with him three times, barely remembered his face. But the booth's phone number remained etched in her memory. Funny the things you held on to.

Returning to the Escape, she drove around to the rear of the Olds Hotel and toted her suitcase up the hotel's rear staircase, also concrete and every bit as grungy.

At the top was a musty-smelling lime-green hallway lined with doors painted to match and carpeted in wrinkled khaki-colored polyester.

At the front of the building was a glassed-in reception desk. The clerk was no older than a sophomore, Indian or Pakistani or Bengali, and like his compadre down in the photocopy shop, he couldn't have cared less about Grace's arrival, choosing instead to continue texting manically.

When Grace informed him, plaintively, that her wallet had been stolen along with her credit cards, would he please accept her business card for I.D. and cash as payment, his thumbs barely faltered as he muttered, "Uh-huh."

"What's the rate for a room?"

Click click click click. "Fifty a night, five extra for cleanup service. We only have some a floor up."

"Fine, and no need for cleanup," said Grace, forking over two hundred dollars.

The kid ignored the fresh new card. "What's your name?"

"Sarah Muller."

"Write it down, okay?" Sliding the log book toward her.

She scrawled, he handed her a key attached to a minia-ture white-plastic milk bottle. "You want orange juice in the morning? We don't serve breakfast but I can tell them to leave you juice but it's not fresh or anything, just bottled."

"Also not necessary. Any coffee?"

The kid aimed world-weary eyes at the front steps while continuing to click away. "Peets, Local 123, Café Yesterday, Guerrilla Café. Want me to keep going?"

"Thanks," said Grace. "May I assume you've got WiFi?"

"Down here it's okay," said the kid. "Up where you'll be

it sometimes sucks." His fingers moved faster. He paused to read a return text. Laughed weirdly.

Grace inspected the milk bottle for a room number: 420.

The kid said, "It's just Forty-Two, I don't know why they add a zero."

"Top floor?"

"There's only this and one more." He typed some more. Said, "Clown," then "Loser," then "Asshole."

The room was surprisingly large, smelling of Lysol and stale pizza, with a pair of twin beds covered in garish floral spreads separated by a particleboard nightstand. A Gideon Bible with most of the pages gone filled the stand's drawer. Two beds but only one pillow, on the right-hand mattress, lumpy as a skin rash, tossed haphazardly.

The walls were stippled green plaster. Floral drapes that matched the bedspreads failed to close completely over a cracked, yellow window shade. Despite that, no annoying light or noise. The window faced the parking lot, shielding Grace from the din on University.

One dresser, of the same flimsy fake wood. Dead silverfish in the top drawer, the others were clean and lined with butcher paper.

The bathroom was cramped, tiled in cracked white hexagons splotched with gray and yellow and rust. A skimpy white towel was embroidered **OH**. The tub would accommodate a toddler. The shower sputtered brown until it finally diluted to a clear trickle. The lidless toilet hissed.

Perfect.

Grace went to sleep.

She was up at seven thirty the following morning, feeling amazingly refreshed. Trying her laptop, she found the WiFi deficient as advertised. Enduring a lukewarm shower, she dressed in jeans, rubber-soled low-heeled boots, and a charcoal-colored cotton sweater, leaving her wigs in her luggage. Stuffing her little Beretta and its ammo into the center of her suitcase, she swathed both in layers of clothes.

Far from burglar-proof but a lowlife would have to be looking.

The Glock and the laptop ended up at the bottom of her bag.

Time for nourishment.

Nippy morning, University was already filled with foot traffic.

One thing about college kids and self-styled rebels: They loved to eat. The choice of cuisines was staggering and Grace finally settled for a Parma ham, Bermuda onion, and Anaheim chili omelet, thick slabs of sourdough bread imported from across the Bay in San Francisco, a glass of fresh-squeezed mandarin juice replete with pulp and seeds, and decent coffee at a café that claimed to be local, organic, sustainable, and opposed to any form of military activity.

Sustained gastronomically, she checked out the used-clothing store near her hotel, found a navy peacoat that didn't smell too bad for thirty bucks. Shifting to a bin of hats, she found the odor test tougher to pass but finally came up with an oversized, soft wool gray ski cap that had bypassed mold and must. Her nose did pick up the faintest nuance of hairspray, and she hoped her predecessor had been a stylish, meticulous girl. Inspecting the interior nap for nits or anything else remotely disturbing, she found nothing untoward and bargained the cashier down to five bucks.

The cap slipped over her head, totally concealing her cropped hair. Devoid of makeup and newly clad, she was Berkeley Anonymous.

Leaving the Escape in the hotel lot, she picked up the Examiner from a street stand and walked to Center Street. In daylight, the park across from the condemned building wasn't half bad, the grass greener than she'd expected, the trees at the periphery huge and lush and decently shaped. In the background, kids streamed near the high school, making predictable adolescent noises.

No activity behind the chain-link fence. Grace took a close look at the construction notice. The building had been condemned and permits had been granted for a project titled Municipal Green WorkSpace. Lots of official stamps, city, county, and state. Handwritten additions in blue marker listed the contractor as DRL-Earthmove. Date of completion was eighteen months in the future but given the lack of progress that seemed fanciful.

Modifications included "seismic retrofitting." Like a too-easy punch line, the irony was unsatisfying.

Grace crossed the street to the park. Only three benches in the entire acreage: a pair under the trees now occupied by snoozing homeless men, and one, unused, with a slightly oblique view of the building site.

She sat down, hid behind the newspaper, took occasional, unfruitful peeks.

Nearly an hour passed and she was about to leave, fixing to return later in the afternoon, when a voice behind her said, "Help a friend?"

She turned slowly. The man hovering behind the bench was dressed shabbily and his skin bore the rare-steak glaze that typified life on the street.

His hand was out, no subtlety there. But not the lurcher who'd scored her dollar last night, returning for an encore.

This guy was much shorter, maybe five three or four, and slightly hunchbacked with cottony white chin whiskers, equally skimpy muttonchops, and a milky left eye.

Grace gave him a buck.

He looked at the bill. "Thank you profoundly, daughter, but that won't even purchase coffee in this foodie burg."

Grace tried to stare him down. He smiled, did a little jig. Winked with his good eye. Surprisingly acute eye, the color of a clear Malibu sky. On closer inspection, she saw that his frayed, baggy outfit had once been high-quality: gray herringbone jacket, brown Shetland sweater vest, white-on-white shirt, droopy olive twill pants, cuffs dragging in the dirt. Even this close, no booze reek.

And his nails were clean.

He stopped dancing. "Not sufficiently impressive? Care for a tango?" Bending low, he dipped an imaginary partner and, despite herself, Grace smiled. He was the first person to entertain her since . . . in a long time.

She gave him a ten.

He said, "Indeed! For that, I'll fetch both of us coffee!"

"I'm fine, treat yourself."

He took a deep bow. "Thank you, daughter."

Grace watched him scurry off and decided to stick it out on the bench for a while. As if the old tramp had revved up her endurance.

After another thirty-five minutes with nothing to show for her patience, she was folding up her paper and making sure her Glock hadn't shifted awkwardly in her bag when Little Mr. One-Eye returned and thrust something at her.

Fresh-baked croissant, the aroma was wonderful. Set neatly on waxed paper in a small cardboard box. A bakery called Chez something.

She said, "Thanks but I'm really not hungry."

"Tsk," said One-Eye. "Save it for later."

"It's okay, enjoy." She began to rise.

The bent old man said, "Why are you studying that hellhole?"

"What hellhole?"

He pointed to the condemned building. "The boondoggle, the scama-rama, the suck-on-the-public-teat extravaganza. You've been watching it since you got here. Or am I mistaken?"

"It's a con, huh?"

"May I?" He pointed to the bench.

Grace shrugged.

"Not much of a welcome," said the little man, "but beggars-choosers-and-such." He plopped down as far from her as possible, got to work on the croissant, nibbling daintily and constantly brushing away crumbs.

A fastidious bum. His shoes were battered wingtips, resoled countless times.

When he finished eating, he said, "What was your major? You did go to college?"

"I did."

"Here?"

"No."

"What did you study?"

Why bother lying? "Psychology."

"Then you know about the Hebbian synapse, Friedrich August von Hayek."

Grace shook her head.

"Kids today." One-Eye laughed. "If I told you I studied economics with Hayek, you wouldn't believe me so I won't waste my breath."

"Why wouldn't I believe you?"

"Well, I did, daughter," he said, grinning. Intent on a monologue. "Had no problem with the man's accent—Friedrich the Great. Though others did. Try to disprove that fact of nature, daughter, and you'll come out on the losing end, I'm telling you nothing but truth. You may be cagey about your alleged education but I have nothing to hide. I took courses in a swirl of eclecticism down in La La Land, the sixties, before Leary and Laing made madness socially acceptable."

He tapped his own head. "Born too early, by then they were talking to me in here, forcing me to ignore them. I eschewed food and water for stretches, I went without female companionship for a century, I traversed campus wearing paper bags on my feet and avoiding the **I Ching**. Despite a closet full of haberdashery and an Anglican mother. Nevertheless, I learned my social science."

He waited. Grace said nothing. "Oh, bosh," he finally said. "**Ook**-la. Palm trees and pedagogy?"

Grace stared.

One-Eye exhaled in frustration. "Ookla? Numero Two campus? Predicated on **this** place being Uno."

It took a moment for Grace to decode that. "UCLA."

"Finally! **Sí, sí,** the wilds of Westwood, back before the hippies and the libertines took over. Before everyone talked about social justice but no one did anything about it. More like so-**called** justice. Or should I say So**Cal** justice and we all know about the morality of manipulative movie moguls."

A withered hand gestured toward the construction site. "Case in point. Green. Ha. So is snot."

"You don't approve."

"It's not up to me to approve, daughter, the die is cast."

"For the project."

He shifted closer to her, brushed away nonexistent crumbs. "It's perfidy grounded in hypocrisy, mendacity, and two-facedness. The prior owner of that rather homely pile of mud was a villain who had the good graces to die but also the poor judgment to sire a second-generation villain who trumpets social justice and greases the palms of **forward**-leaning politicians. Same old story, no? Caligula, Putin, Aaron Burr, name any petty alderman of Chicago at random."

"Politics corrupts—"

"Think about it, daughter: You inherit a decrepit pile of bricks, what should you do with it . . . hmm, shall I ponder—I know, let's sell it to the city at an inflated price then propose a snot-green project to build cubicles for yet more bureaucrats and manage to insinuate ourself as the builder."

Now Grace was on full alert. "One-stop shopping, huh? Doesn't look as if much has been done."

He frowned. "Was a time a man could find refuge in there."

"In the building?"

Three hard nods. "Was a time."

So the place had served as a squat. Grace said, "When did that stop?"

"When the family tradition recommenced."

"What tradition?"

"Have you not been paying attention?"

Grace shot him a helpless look.

He said, "All right, I'll slow down and enunciate—where did you say you went to college?"

Grace said, "Boston U."

"Not Harvard-grade, eh? All right, you're too young to remember this but once upon a time an unpleasant shifting of tectonic plates wrought devastation upon the land upon which we now sit. Bridges crumbled, a baseball game was interrupted, and if that's not spitting in the eyes of all that is patriotic and sacred, I don't know what is—"

"The Loma Prieta quake."

The old man's single functional eye widened. "A student of history. At BU, no less."

Grace said, "It's not exactly ancient history."

"Daughter, nowadays anything prior to five minutes ago is ancient. Including the messages transferred into here by the powers that be." Tapping his forehead again.

He stood, smoothed his trousers, sat back down. "So . . . the plates shifted and the dishes shattered. Heh heh! Then the second disaster ensued, villains profiteering as they always do when collectivism and the collective unconscious collude to triumph over the will of man and by man I mean both sexes so please no whinnying about sexism, daughter."

Grace looked at the construction site. "The people involved with that profiteered from the quake?"

"Insurance," he said. "Essentially, a game of chance with infrequent payoffs. But even in Vegas machines pay off occasionally."

"They didn't."

He crooked a thumb in the direction of the high school. "The young are essentially unsocialized savages, correct?

Lords, flies, et cetera, if anyone should qualify for capital punishment it's fourteen-year-olds. But one villain easily sniffs out another and those Fly Lords were entrusted with the task of pressuring the common folk not to pursue recompense."

"The guy in charge of that project hired students to intimidate—"

"They might as well have worn suicide vests. These were terrorists, nothing more, nothing less, and they enabled the villain to buy up distressed properties for an off-key song and sell them back to the you-know-who."

"The government," said Grace.

"Agency A, Agency B, Agency Zeta—**that** one implanted an iridium electrode right here and attempted to convert me to Islam." He tapped his right temple. "Fortunately, I caught on and managed to deactivate it."

He yawned, dropped his head, began snoring.

Grace said, "Nice talking to you."

She was a few yards away when he said, "Anytime."

40

O kay, so now she had a confirming source.

Psychotic to be sure, but with enough occasional lucidity—and premorbid intelligence—to take seriously.

She found a moderately busy Internet café farther up on Center Street, brought a latte and a bagel she had no intention of eating to a corner booth. One sip later, sitting among students and those pretending to be students, she'd logged onto the wide wide world of random knowledge.

Municipal green workspace pulled up a dozen hits, mostly government documents composed in agency doublespeak. After wading through a few choice sections, Grace got the gist: The construction project had moved quickly through numerous city and state committees and subcommittees, received approval a little over a year ago, with the contract awarded on the basis of "specialized bidding contingency" to DRL-Earthmove, Inc., of Berkeley, California.

From what Grace could tell, "specialized bidding" meant there'd been no competition at all, with DRL judged to possess unique qualifications: "eco-sensitivity," "foreknowledge of site history and ethos," and "emphatic local emphasis, including employment of Berkeley residents with set-asides for inner-city applicants from Oakland and other nearby economically disadvantaged neighborhoods."

Grace hoped to see Roger Wetter Junior's name surface in the documents but DRL's CEO and sole proprietor was one Dion R. Larue. Disappointed, she Googled and pulled up three hits, all squibs from fund-raisers Larue had attended.

The recipients of the developer's generosity included a local food collective called the Nourishment Conspiracy;

the Trust Trust, an Oakland gang-rehab program; and UC Berkeley's experimental film festival of four years ago, the theme being Liberation: National and Personal.

The Nourishment folk had thanked their donors with a vegan banquet and provided photos on their Facebook page.

Grace scrolled through shot after shot of glowing, smiling countenances.

And there he was.

Tall, handsome, well-built man in his thirties, wearing a black-and-gold silk brocade tunic over black jeans. Shoulder-length blond hair was parted in the middle and worn loose, Anglo-Jesus style. A gray-blond stubble beard was film-star correct.

Dion Larue's stance was relaxed as he held a glass of something orange in one hand and draped his free arm over the lean, bare shoulders of a brunette in her late twenties. Not a stunner but attractive. Dramatic cheekbones, as if an ice cream scoop had been taken to her face.

Azha Larue, wife of the boss. Exotic name but nothing but Celtic in her features.

Her smile seemed forced. His was high-wattage.

But the emotion of the moment was irrelevant; his eyes told the story. Piercing yet strangely dead. Eyes Grace had seen before.

As she continued to study the photo, years peeled away and reality slithered out. Twenty-three years had passed since Samael Roi the teenage Venom Prince had showed up at Ramona's ranch with his sibs and murdered a crippled boy, indirectly caused Ramona's death, and shattered Grace's status quo.

Dressed in black, then as now.

The bastard had changed his name. Wanting to rid himself of his adopted father's local baggage? If so, it had worked, if you didn't factor in the overreaching memory and loose associations of Little Mr. One-Eye.

From Roger to Dion . . . ?

As if a switch had been flipped, Grace's brain decoded, scrambling and reassembling letters as if they were game tiles.

Dion R. Larue.

Arundel Roi.

Perfect anagram.

Forget the man who'd made him wealthy, he was out to honor his birth father's identity. Prioritizing bloodline over everything that had happened since the shoot-out at the Fortress Cult.

This was more than a psychopath ridding himself of an uncomfortable history.

This was an attempt at reincarnation.

Now the murders of three sets of parents made strange, cruel sense: Samael Roi reconstructing a childhood spent with a madman and his concubines. Out with the old, in with the new.

Specialized bidding, indeed.

An elderly schizophrenic might recall the bad old days of crumbling bridges and splintering soil, the Wetter family's exploitation of the helpless, but no one else in this city that prided itself on human rights seemed to know or care.

No surprise, Grace supposed, in the Age of Endless Chances and Reinvention.

An uncomfortable truth settled in Grace's gut: **I've also benefited from that.**

Staring at Dion Larue's smug smile, she couldn't help but think of him as her playmate, perched on the other end of a cosmic seesaw.

The two of them, perfect rivals.

She hadn't chosen to do battle. But now . . .

Drinking her second refill of coffee—add that to her breakfast caffeine and her heart was thumping and racing—she shifted her analysis to Andrew né Typhon Roi. Surer than ever that she'd been right about the reason he'd sought help.

Needing to sort out his own lineage of evil.

But the question remained: Had he **committed** evil?

True, Palo Alto being near Berkeley easily accounted for a chance meeting between the brothers. Or did she have that backward and had the sons of Arundel Roi reunited long ago, both agreeing to settle in the Bay Area?

Samael honing his psychopathic skills.

Typhon, brighter, outwardly moral, working on building a professional career.

An alliance set well before the slaying of their adopted families? The thought repelled Grace but she needed to face it: The man she'd known as Andrew may have committed outrages and finally found the guilt too much to live with.

Including the death of his sister, because she'd been judged too bonded to the McCoys to be integrated into the new clan his brother envisioned.

Did Typhon/Andrew's survival years after Lilith's demise mean he'd been a co-conspirator? Or simply a silent witness his brother had trusted to maintain silence?

Either way, he'd died because of what he knew and Grace supposed it didn't much matter. Still . . . it was time to learn more about the pleasant, pliable man she'd met in a hotel lobby. But first, she needed to educate herself about his sole surviving sibling.

Snapping a bite out of her bagel, she searched for anything related to the new corporation Dion Larue had created. She found no other DRL-Earthmove projects in Berkeley but seven years previous the company had snagged a similar government-funded contract near Gallup, New Mexico, converting a block of derelict shops to an "environmentally friendly" industrial park aimed at enriching "local culture."

Larue's partner for that one had been one Munir "Tex" Khaled, a dealer in Indian art. Googling that name brought up a homicide case: Khaled had been found shot to death in the desert near the Mexican border. That location had obvious implications and rumors of a drug connection had endured.

As far as Grace could tell, the crime remained unsolved. Nor could she find any evidence of the Gallup project ever breaking ground.

That despite a golden-spade groundbreaking ceremony attended by hard-hatted politicians. By a hard-hatted Tex Khaled, as well. The former art dealer was a small, dark-haired man in his sixties wearing a brown shirt tucked into daddy jeans secured by an enormous tooled-silver belt buckle and a string tie fastened by an equally oversized chunk of turquoise. Next to him stood a younger, jubilant Dion Larue, also protectively helmeted and wearing a blousy white buccaneer's shirt that exposed a deep V of smooth tan thorax.

But clothing wasn't what caught Grace's attention, or even the likelihood that Tex Khaled had posed happily with his murderer. She'd fixed on a figure standing behind Larue, slightly to the right.

Early thirties, slightly taller than average, coarse features. Not the shaved-head Beldrim Arthur Benn she'd encountered in her garden. The long-haired, shaggy-mustached visage from Benn's driver's license.

Despite the smiles of nearly everyone else in the shot, Benn appeared watchful, even grim. **Nearly** everyone else because of one other exception: a man positioned next to Benn and around the same age and height as Benn but twice as wide.

A bullet-headed rhino with sparse fair hair, a face the shape of a pie tin, squinty eyes, and tiny, close-set ears.

Mr. Beef. Central-casting thug. Maybe that's why Benn, less obtrusive physically, had been sent to West Hollywood to take care of Grace. Leaving Rhino to dispatch Andrew.

She wondered if the heavy man was still in L.A.—maybe tossing her office—or back here with the boss.

The disposable cell she'd used to call Wayne chirped. His private number. She switched it off and continued to search for info on DRL-Earthmove.

Nothing. Time to switch gears and veer into territory she knew well.

The engineering section of the inter-university peer-review-journal website coughed up three articles authored by Andrew Van Cortlandt during the year of his postdoctoral fellowship at Stanford. All were math-laden treatises exploring the structural properties of conductor metals under various electrochemical and thermal conditions.

All had been co-authored with Amy Chan, Ph.D., of Caltech.

Backgrounding Chan revealed that she'd served her postdoc at Stanford the same year as Andrew before taking a lectureship in Pasadena. But that position had lasted only two years and now she was an assistant professor of engineering right here at UC Berkeley.

The department's website offered up a headshot of a pleasant-looking woman who could've passed as a high school senior, with a small-boned face surrounded by long black hair trimmed into straightedge bangs. Amy Chan had continued to delve into the world of structural integrity and had received high marks for teaching from undergrads.

Grace knew reading too much into a face—into anything—was foolish. But Chan's portrait projected diffidence by way of soft eyes and a bashful smile.

Time to take a risk. She phoned Chan's office extension. If she got a bad feeling, she could hang up and ditch the phone.

A woman with a whispery, slightly tremulous voice picked up.

"Is this Professor Chan?"

A beat. "I'm Amy." Chan **sounded** like a high school senior.

Grace said, "My name is Sarah Muller, I'm an ed-psych consultant from L.A. who was friends with Andrew Van Cortlandt."

"Was?" said Amy Chan. "You're no longer friends? Or . . . ?"

"It's complicated, Professor Chan, and I know this sounds strange, but I'm worried about Andrew and if you could find the time, I'd appreciate talking to you."

"Worried about what?"

Grace waited a second. "I'm concerned for his safety."

"Something has happened to Andrew? Oh, no." Words of dismay delivered in an even tone. The tremulousness was gone and Grace's guard went up but she persisted. "What exactly are you saying?"

"Could we meet to discuss it, Professor?"

"You can't tell me now?"

"The last time I saw Andrew he seemed troubled. Nervous. He refused to say why and I haven't heard from him since. He'd mentioned his work with you, so I—Professor, I'd prefer not to get into any more over the phone, but if meeting's a hassle, I understand—"

"No," said Amy Chan. "Not a hassle." The vibrato had returned. "I just finished office hours, have a few other things to do. I suppose I could use a breather."

"Anywhere you'd like, then."

"How about up near Lawrence Hall—the science museum? Not inside the building, the front area."

Grace knew the spot. She'd been to Lawrence during one of her trips with Malcolm, found the museum full of kids. The site was up in the hills, above campus. The open area Chan had requested offered gorgeous views of the Golden Gate Bridge and the skyline of San Francisco that caused people to linger.

Safe place to meet a stranger. Careful woman but that would work to Grace's benefit, as well.

She said, "Sure. When?"

Amy Chan said, "How about two p.m.?"

Before Grace could agree, the line went dead.

. . .

She returned to the Olds Hotel, encountered the conspicuous aroma of marijuana in the dim hallway. Several steps later, a door to one of the rooms opened and a couple in their forties staggered out. Bumping against each other, they headed her way, the man lean and black, the woman white and heavy. Grace took her time approaching them, one hand in her purse.

When she was a few feet away, the man gave a courtly bow and said, "**S'il vous plaît.**" The woman giggled, "I second that," and stepped aside to allow Grace to pass.

Once inside her room, Grace changed into her notion of educational consultant duds: off-white blouse, gray slacks, beige nylon cardigan, brown flats. Off went the stocking cap. On went the brunette hairpiece, which she combed and fluffed to look fuller. The wig cooperated beautifully; paying for real hair had been a good idea.

Next step: true-blue contact lenses that would make her eyes memorable, even behind the nonprescription glasses.

Checking the disposable cell Wayne had just called her on she found no message. Deciding the phone had outlived its usefulness, she lifted a corner of the bed, placed it under a stout metal leg, and sat down hard. The gizmo was a cheapie but tougher than Grace had figured and it took four attempts, using all of her weight, to crack it. But once the initial wound had been inflicted, subsequent stomps reduced the phone to shards, and she finished by disemboweling the little oblong. Removing the three remaining sticks of turkey jerky from their resealable packet, she collected every visible bit of plastic and poured the ruins of the phone inside the bag. She wasn't really hungry but neither was she stuffed, so she ate the jerky, extricated the second disposable from her luggage, and returned Wayne's call.

No answer, no voice mail. Deleting any record of the call, she checked her watch. Over two hours until the meeting with Amy Chan. It had been a while since she'd run or done any serious exercise. Time for a brisk walk?

But when she stepped out onto University, the thought of immersing herself in the rhythm of a university town—the youthfulness, the bumper-sticker philosophy, the calculated rebellion—was suddenly more than she could bear.

Returning to her room, she set the alarm on her watch and lay faceup on the sagging bed.

Nothing like solitude for nurturing the soul.

41

After a week at Harvard, Grace understood the place. Basically, it was Merganfield on steroids. Though, to be clear, the precious little highly gifties at Merganfield were more uniformly smart than the Harvard student body.

From what she'd observed, there were two ways her fellow students dealt with their good fortune at being accepted into the exemplar of Elite American Education. The first was to be honestly obnoxious, dropping the H-word into every conversation, wearing crimson wherever you went. The second was to pretend to be coy. ("I go to school in Boston.") Either approach spoke of smugness and self-congratulation and Grace had actually passed a group of freshmen and heard a girl say, "Let's face it, we're going to run the world. So how about we do it compassionately?"

She decided to adopt a third tack in order to optimize her time in Cambridge: Stick to herself and get out as quickly as possible.

That meant declaring a major early—easy, she'd already decided on psychology because nothing else seemed remotely interesting and Malcolm was a happy man—then getting requirements out of the way by taking on a far heavier load than recommended.

Extra credits could be accumulated easily by filling free time with the Mickey Mouse courses known as "guts." So-called serious classes turned out to be no big deal, either. The cliché about Harvard turned out to be true: The toughest part was getting in.

But while grades and exams were no issue, the way the university fashioned its social structure was. During your first year, you got assigned to a freshman dorm. After that, it got complicated.

Grace's dorm was a building called Hurlbut Hall overlooking Crimson Quad, where she lucked into a sizable single room with a tottering old desk, a nice view of lawn, trees, and ivied brick, and a defunct fireplace. Someone had taped the outline of a cop-show corpse to the scarred oak floor and Grace left it in place. Someone else had taken the time to glue hundreds of pennies onto the wall of the corridor just outside her door. What the intended message was, she never learned, but every so often coins went missing.

Malcolm and Sophie flew out with her for orientation and remained for a couple of days to settle her in. When they saw her room, they looked at each other and nodded approvingly.

Grace said, "Good."

Malcolm said, "Hurlbut? Great. Now you've got plenty of time to build your group."

Grace said, "What group is that?"

"For your sophomore year you move to a house with a suite of other students."

"What's the difference between a dorm and a house?"

"Well . . . not much, I suppose. But your house will remain with you for three years, the goal is for you to feel proprietary. My house was Lowell."

"You had a group?"

"Indeed, I did. Including Ransom Gardener. Not only do we continue to do business together, we remain chums. That's the benefit of the system, Grace. One acquires enduring relationships."

"Did Mike Leiber go here, too?"

The question surprised Malcolm. "No, Michael's an MIT grad, but for our purposes, he's self-taught."

So you didn't need all that social nonsense. Grace said nothing, distracting herself with the taped body outline.

Clean job, maybe a science major. She'd enjoy living with the geometry.

Sophie said, "It needn't be difficult, dear. Over a year's time you create a group of friends and move in together."

"What if I prefer to remain alone?"

Another long look passed between them.

"Hmm," said Malcolm. "It's usually not done that way."

"I can't stay in this room next year?"

"Dorms are only for freshmen, Grace."

"That's kind of rigid."

"Tradition, Grace." Malcolm frowned and Grace realized she'd made him uncomfortable. As she considered her next response, Sophie said, "You know, Mal, I think there are some single rooms in Pforzheimer."

Grace said, "What's that?"

"Another house, dear."

Malcolm said, "You'll be fine, Grace, no rush, give it time."

But he looked more nervous than Grace had ever seen him and even Sophie didn't seem too calm. They'd been more restless than usual during the flight from L.A., fidgeting, talking, and drinking more than usual. Neither the taxi ride from Logan airport nor setting foot on campus had settled them down.

Grace realized their anxiety could be a problem if they felt they needed to stick around and overprotect her. As much as she appreciated them, the whole point of this was beginning a new phase in her life.

She smiled and hugged both of them and said, "Well, I'm sure it'll work out. This is amazing. I **love** it, thank you **so** much."

Malcolm said, "In terms of—I'm sure you'll own the place soon. But if there's ever an issue you feel you need help with—"

"You bet," said Grace. She spread her arms and smiled and touched her mattress. "Meanwhile, this is **perfect**."

She hugged both of them, doing it for their sake but also feeling something rising from deep inside her. They owed her nothing but had chosen to change her life. These were wonderful people. Angels, if angels had actually existed.

She would make them proud.

She told them so and Malcolm blushed and Sophie's eyes moistened and she said, "You always do, Grace."

Malcolm dared a squeeze of her hand. Sophie touched her face briefly.

Grace embraced them once more and flashed the most confident smile she could muster.

Inside, she was thinking: **Pforzheimer.**

That night they had dinner at Legal Seafood where everyone ate too much and Malcolm drank too much and ended up offering multiple toasts to Grace's "extraordinary achievements." The following morning, when she saw them off in front of the Inn at Harvard, they looked uncertain and Grace added more reassurances, careful to look nonchalant even though her own tension had grown during her first night in Hurlbut. Sleep had been a challenge, woken as she was by whoops and stomping feet in the corridor well into the morning hours. The best and brightest acting like any other group of adolescents.

The taxi back to Logan finally arrived and Grace waved goodbye at its rear window until the vehicle slipped out of sight on Massachusetts Avenue.

Malcolm and Sophie had changed their minds about flying straight back to L.A., opting instead for a quick trip to New York for some "museum overload."

Boston had no shortage of great museums and Grace knew they'd decided to stay close until they were sure she really was okay.

Another sixteen-year-old might've been peeved by that.

Grace enjoyed being cared for.

. . .

Early into a straight-A+ first semester, Grace had figured out that, like the L.A. County social service bureaucracy, Harvard prided itself on accommodating "special needs." She spoke to a resident dorm advisor and lied about needing solitude in order to deal with "an inborn sensory sensitivity to light and sound" and bagged a single at Pforzheimer for the following year.

"It won't be much by way of square footage," said the advisor, an ectomorphic grad student in literature named Pavel. "Not much more than a closet, really."

"No problem," said Grace. "A closet will help with my hang-ups."

Pavel squinted. "Pardon—oh, heh, good one. Yes, yes, good. Heh."

With that out of the way, Grace was free to continue acing every course and by the end of her sophomore year, she'd begun to kiss up to specific psych profs in order to lay the groundwork for nabbing a research job in her junior year. Though Malcolm and Sophie had introduced her to alcohol in an optimal way—allowing her to taste fine wines, avoiding power struggles—she'd decided early on to avoid any mind-altering substances and stuck to that.

Not boozing or doping wasn't easy in a libertine environment if you lacked spine or got too social. In addition to the expected overindulgence in weed, Grace had observed plenty of coke sniffing and hallucinogenic dabbling. Even some heroin use, mostly by self-tortured theater students.

But the big drug at Harvard was alcohol. On many a Friday afternoon, beer trucks pulled up to the eating clubs that were Harvard's version of fraternities, and unloaded cases of cheap brew. The college had no official Greek life but it was only a matter of nomenclature. Like much at Harvard, entry to the clubs was by invitation only and males dominated. Of course, girls were needed for the parties and feminism blew out the door when beer and fun beckoned and more than once Grace had been beckoned by a drunk preppie as she walked past a club.

As her college career progressed, she watched lithe vixens grow beer bellies and the reek of vomit in dorms and houses was **eau de Monday.**

Grace found herself a different form of recreation: hunting appropriate males with whom she could have pleasurable, unemotional sex.

"Appropriate" meant no jocks or elitists, nor anyone too gregarious because none of those could be trusted to keep their mouth shut. The same went for letch professors and horny grad students, anyone who might conceivably be able to wield power over her. The final group she eliminated were the blue-collar townies who trolled for Ivy League pussy in the bars that littered Cambridge. Too much potential for class envy.

That left a select group of targets, shy boys, loners, like herself, but no schizoids whose avoidance of others was rooted in deep, crazed hostility. One Unabomber was enough.

Over the three and a half years Grace spent at Harvard, she slept with twenty-three young men from Harvard, Tufts, BU, BC, and Emerson. Pleasant lads lacking self-confidence and experience who were thrilled to have Grace educate them.

She had her own definition of "special needs."

In the process of grooming and snagging, she learned about herself as well—what bored her, what turned her on quickest. How it needed to be more than the thrill and release of orgasm; she had to take control. What one slightly built but energetic lad studying the history of American film had termed "you like doing the director's cut."

When he'd said it, Grace had been riding him and she stopped and panic tightened his face. "Uh . . . sorry . . ."

"Is that a problem, Brendan?"

"No, no, no, no, no—"

She winked, offered the merest pelvic twitch. "You're sure I'm not being too bossy?"

"No, no, no, I **love** it. **Please don't stop.**"

"Okay, just as long as we're in agreement." Laughing, she planted his hands on her breasts, showed him how to softly twist her nipples, and resumed rocking and rolling. Beginning slowly for her own benefit, then picking up speed. Brendan came seconds later. Stayed hard until she finished and came a second time.

"Excellent," she told him, figuring he'd be good for another couple of romps. Five times with anyone was her max, more often she broke it off after one or two. No sense getting them too attached. Plus she bored easily.

She was up-front about breaking things off but refused to explain. For the most part, flattery and her best blow job took care of any transitional issues.

As Grace neared her twentieth birthday, she'd amassed enough credits to graduate a semester early and had produced a sixty-seven-page honors paper on cognitive processing that earned her a departmental distinction and a summa on her diploma. One of her psych profs, a gentle, thoughtful woman named Carol Berk who'd spent her professional life studying minuscule correlates of family structure, guided her to join the psych honor society, Psi Chi, nominated her successfully for Phi Beta Kappa, and suggested Grace remain at Harvard for grad school.

Grace thanked her and lied. "I really appreciate the vote of confidence, Professor Berk, maybe I will."

But she'd had it with cold weather and self-importance and the tendency to politicize everything from breakfast cereal to reading material. She'd also lost patience with having to explain why she preferred not to attend social gatherings. Had overheard one too many of her alleged peers refer to her as "different" or "weird" or "asocial" or "autistic."

On top of all that, she was beginning to tire of the shy boys, had found herself working harder to come.

But none of that really mattered.

She'd known all along what her next step would be.

As her junior year drew to a close, she phoned Malcolm and told him she'd be coming home for the summer. He and Sophie had seen her a month before, the second of their twice-yearly visits, and she'd hadn't mentioned anything about returning.

He said, "No summer school this time?"

"No need, I'm finished."

"Finished with your research?"

"With nearly everything. I'll be graduating a semester early."

"You're kidding."

"Nope," she said. "Done, kaput. I'd like to talk to you about doing some research in L.A., and about grad school."

"So you've definitely decided?"

"I have."

A beat. "That's terrific, Grace. Clinical or cognitive?"

"Clinical and I want to do it at SC."

"I see . . ."

"Is that a problem, Malcolm?"

"Of course not, Grace. Not in terms of your qualifications, that is. With everything you've accomplished and the kind of GRE score you're bound to get, any school will be happy to have you."

"Including SC?"

Another pause. "Yes, of course, the department would certainly be pleased."

"Interesting grammar," she said.

"Pardon?"

"Not they **will** be, Malcolm. They **would** be. It's conditional on something?"

"Well . . . Grace, do I need to spell it out?"

"If it's something other than the obvious," she said. "E.g., you and me, nepotism blah blah blah."

"I'm afraid that's it, Grace."

"Are you saying your presence **will** disqualify me?"

"I'd hope not." He laughed. "There I go with more conditional . . . I must admit, you've surprised me with this, Grace."

"Why?"

"Pardon?"

"Why the surprise?" she said. "There's no one whose work I admire more than yours."

"Well," he said. "That—that's extremely gracious . . . you're saying not only do you want to study at SC, you're planning to be **my** student?"

"If it's possible."

"Hmm," he said. "I have to say, it's not the kind of thing that comes up in departmental meetings."

Grace laughed. "Paradigm shift. You always say that they can be useful."

He laughed back. "So I do, Grace. So I do."

She wasn't sure what he had to go through, but a month later, she had her answer. Formally, she'd be required to apply like everyone else. But Malcolm's tenure and status and "other factors" made her acceptance inevitable.

Grace had a notion of what other factors meant: He wasn't her biological father. So, officially, no nepotism.

That, she confessed, did tighten her chest a bit and make her eyes hurt.

But on balance, everything was working out just as she'd planned.

42

Grace's catnap lasted the perfect twenty minutes. Reinserting the bright-blue contacts and re-donning the fluffed-up brunette wig, she washed her face, brushed her teeth, dabbed on extra deodorant, and reassured herself that she was Sarah Muller, Educational Consultant, with expertise in psychometric testing.

All that, and two guns in her oversized bag.

Leaving the hotel via the back door, she drove down Center Street, again passing the construction site. Still no activity and her psychotic pal was nowhere in sight. But a few high school kids were loitering in the park, for the most part tough-looking boys. Maybe they'd driven away the homeless men.

She drove to Lawrence Hall, arriving seventy minutes prior to her appointment with Amy Chan. That gave her time to find an ideal parking spot near the entrance to the lot across the street from the museum. Perfect for making a quick exit, plenty of time to scope out the front plaza.

The day was gorgeous and clear, cool air wafting gently under a stunning sky that matched her contacts. Off to the west, the Golden Gate Bridge was a flash of rust-colored brilliance. San Francisco Bay was a roiling pewter broth, chop whipped up by wind, frigid water frothing like freshly beaten meringue. Tugs and tourist boats and a few fishing craft rocked and rolled. On one of her visits, Grace had toured Alcatraz, wondered what it would be like to bunk down in a cell if you knew you could get out.

The plaza was spotless and nearly empty, just a couple of young shapely women who could be moms or au pairs,

standing by as ebullient toddlers ran and jumped and ca-
vorted across the open space.

Grace knew she'd never have children but, from a distance, she found kids pleasing and agreeable, not yet fucked
up by life. In grad school, opportunities had come up to
learn child therapy and she'd been required to spend three
weeks observing at a preschool but had never opted to go beyond that. What she'd learned was that kids, even toddlers,
were damn good at solving their own problems if so-called
grown-ups didn't intervene and impose their will.

She proceeded to the center of the plaza, was nearly butted
by one of the little boys, a stocky mini-elf with a mane of
long red hair, racing blindly and whooping with joy.

She smiled and sidestepped and one of the young women
yelled, "Cheyenne!" The boy sped on, unheedingly.

Grace murmured, "Good for you, kiddo."

Reversing direction, she exited the plaza, crossed the street,
took a lovely walk up a pathway that snaked into the green
hills of Berkeley.

She returned at one fifty-five. Professor Amy Chan was already there, wearing an outfit not unlike Grace's: blouse,
sweater, slacks, all in a monotone of navy blue.

Chan sat on a bench that faced the Bay, head down, engrossed in a book. Grace made sure to approach in a way
that wouldn't startle her, pacing a wide conspicuous arc that
would give Chan plenty of time to take Grace in.

Despite that, Chan didn't glance up until Grace was ten
yards away. Her face was unreadable.

Grace gave a friendly little wave and Chan waved back
and put down her book. Hardcover novel called **The Genius.** Something Chan could relate to?

Chan slipped the volume into her purse and stood. Her
tote was a macramé thing even larger than Grace's. Wouldn't
it be hilarious if she was also packing?

"Hi, I'm Sarah. Thanks so much for meeting with me."

"Amy." The two of them shook hands. Chan's grip was gentle and soft. Five six or so, she was slim and leggy, long hair drawn back in a ponytail. No makeup, no perfume. Patting the bench, she waited for Grace to settle then positioned herself to Grace's right.

The spot she'd chosen offered both of them a glorious view of the Bay. It also made avoiding eye contact easy as both of them stared straight ahead.

Amy Chan said, "You're in education, Sarah?"

"Used to teach, now I consult to private schools—anxious kids and highly anxious parents."

"Know what you mean," said Chan. Grace's sidelong glance caught a split-second wince on Chan's face. Hints of a childhood not devoid of pressure? Grace resisted the temptation to continue interpreting; Amy Chan's issues were no concern of hers unless they involved Andrew Van Cortlandt.

Figuring a physical scientist wouldn't appreciate dilly-dallying, Grace got right to it. "As I mentioned over the phone, I'm concerned about Andrew."

Amy Chan didn't respond. Her hands rested on her knees but her fingers curled upward, as if repelled by the touch of her own trousers. "You found my name on some of Andrew's articles?"

"I did. In fact, I couldn't find anyone else Andrew published with."

"For you to seek me out, Andrew must be important to you."

"I admire him."

"Understandable," said Amy Chan. She turned sharply. "Please be frank: Do you suspect he's in danger? Or worse?"

"I don't know," Grace lied. "But there's a good chance of it. As I said, he's been looking extremely tense—I'd even say frightened and for the past few weeks I haven't been able to reach him. I had to travel up here, anyway, so when your name came up . . ."

"Andrew and I haven't been in touch for a while," said Chan. "We were just friends. In grad school." She blinked four times. One of her hands had balled into a fist. "Any hint what's been on his mind?"

Grace exhaled. "I tried to find out but that seemed to bother him. He did drop one thing: It related to his family. Which I don't know much about, until that point I'd thought he didn't have much in the way of family, being adopted, no sibs."

"His family," said Chan. "That's it?"

"He wouldn't go into details, Dr. Chan. The truth is, though I like Andrew a lot, I realize now that I never knew much about him. He was kind of, I don't know—secretive?"

"Reticent," said Chan.

"Yes, exactly."

"How long have you known him, Sarah?"

"A year or so. You go back longer so I thought you might know more."

"Actually, I haven't talked to Andrew in a couple of years," said Chan. "Slightly longer—maybe two and a half years when he was in San Francisco on business and phoned me and we had dinner."

Chan craned and looked straight at Grace. "Were you and Andrew an . . ." She smiled. "The only phrase that comes to mind is 'an item.' As stilted as that sounds. And if that's being too nosy, forgive me."

Grace smiled back. "No, we weren't, Dr. Cha—"

"Amy's fine."

"We weren't an item, Amy. Just friends, as well. Just like you."

Chan said, "Interesting, no?"

"What is?" said Grace.

"Two women who admired him but no romance. Are we sensing a pattern here?"

Grace pretended to ponder. "I guess so."

"Did you ever wonder about Andrew?"

"About what in particular?"

"His sexuality in particular, Sarah."

"You thought he might be gay?" **Think again, girl.**

"At some point that's exactly what I wondered," said Amy Chan. "Because I'd never known him to have a romantic relationship with a woman . . . I'm not saying he never did, just that I never saw it." A beat. "He certainly didn't come on to me. Which, I must confess, was a bit of a self-esteem assault, initially. Not that I'd fixed on him as a mate, I've had boyfriends and currently I'm engaged."

"Congratulations."

"Yes, I'm quite happy . . . anyway, Andrew was intelligent, considerate, attentive, and courteous. Just about the perfect man, no? We spent lots of time together in the lab as well as working on our publications. But there wasn't an ounce of chemistry and not once did he try to take it further."

"I understand totally," said Grace. "I guess I've had the same experience with him."

"Where'd you meet him, Sarah?"

Grace thought: **Keep your lies close to the truth. Less stretch means having to remember less.**

She said, "I hate to admit it, but in a bar. Not a dive, a nice place, the lounge of a hotel in L.A., both of us were traveling on business. I thought he was attractive right from the get-go and he was easy to talk to. We ended up having dinner but that's where it ended, it was as if he needed to rush away. A couple of days later we ran into each other again and did some touring. He told me he grew up in L.A. It was nice having someone who knew the city show me around."

Faint pink spots dotted Amy Chan's delicate jawline. "And after that you met other times?"

"Just a few. When our travels coincided . . . I believe it was four times over the next year. I welcomed it as a nice friendship. Travel can be so lonely, port in a storm and all that."

"That's how I feel about conventions, Sarah. So he never took it to the next level."

"Never."

Amy Chan seemed pleased by that. Not as detached as she'd claimed?

Grace said, "I guess I'd gotten used to it, Andrew's thing was friendship. I guess in a way I found it comforting—pleasant company, no pressure. Still, I found myself caring about him and when he started to act differently—the last couple of times I saw him—it troubled me. Then he stopped responding to emails and I found myself wondering."

"Something related to his family."

"He had told me he was adopted, so I wondered if it had something to do with that—one of those roots things, gone wrong, I've seen it in a couple of my students. I know he was close to his adoptive parents, he told me he was devastated by their deaths. Maybe with them gone, he'd decided to search."

Grace shook her head. "This is probably silly, I'm getting involved where I shouldn't."

Chan sat silently. Then: "I wish I could tell you your concerns are unfounded. But the last time I saw Andrew, something did happen that I found curious."

She turned back toward the stormy water. "We went to dinner. I chose the restaurant, a place called Café Lotus, it's since closed down. I'm a vegetarian and though Andrew wasn't, he was fine with that, of course. You know how agreeable he is."

Grace nodded. "So easygoing." **If only you knew, Amy.**

"But not lacking a backbone." Chan blinked. "Anyway, we were having a perfectly nice time, catching up." She smiled. "To be honest, mostly I talked and Andrew listened, he's always been a good listener. Anyway . . . all of a sudden, another party was seated at a table near us—right across from us—and Andrew looked their way and his demeanor changed totally. As if a mood switch had been flicked. He seemed to have trouble concentrating and he stopped eating. He was also flushed, even though he hadn't been drinking—

the place was alcohol-free. I asked if anything was wrong—
was he allergic to something? He said no, he was fine and
tried to pretend he was okay. But he wasn't, Sarah. He
looked . . . stricken. Kept sneaking glances at the people
across from us. So obviously I looked over at whoever it was
who'd freaked him out and he pretended they hadn't and
we tried to continue as if everything was okay. They looked
perfectly normal. A man and a woman. Then I saw that the
man was sneaking looks at Andrew as well, and now Andrew
was avoiding eye contact and getting even jumpier. Then all
of a sudden, the man got up and came over and smiled at
Andrew but he didn't call him Andrew, he called him Thai,
which I thought was weird, because obviously Andrew's not
Asian. Then I thought: Andrew works mostly in Asia, maybe
he'd acquired some kind of nickname. In any event, Andrew didn't correct him, he just said, 'Excuse me,' and got up
himself and he and this guy moved to a corner near the exit
door and had a brief but what looked to be a pretty intense
conversation. Meanwhile, I'm staring and so is the woman
with the other guy—she's just as surprised. Then the other
guy claps Andrew on the shoulder and gives him a business
card and Andrew returns and makes out like nothing's happened. But after that, he was **really** distracted. We'd planned
to catch a movie on campus after dinner and all of a sudden
he's apologizing profusely, saying he's wiped out, sorry for
being a downer, he really needs to sleep because he's leaving
early in the morning."

Amy Chan shrugged. "That's the last time I saw him,
Sarah. I figured it was some kind of unpleasant issue, maybe
something in Asia. Not my business, so I forgot about it."

"What did this other guy look like?"

"Nothing scary—kind of good-looking, actually. Long
blond hair, beard, around Andrew's age. Well dressed but
in kind of a rich hippie mode, kind of über-Berkeley. And
unlike Andrew, the contact between them didn't seem to
bother him. Just the opposite, he seemed super mellow."

The noise level had suddenly risen on the plaza. More young women with kids.

Amy Chan said, "That's it, Sarah. I guess all we can do is wait and hope for the best."

"Guess so," said Grace. "Thanks for taking the time, Amy. Meanwhile I've got some anxiety-prone middle schoolers to deal with in Atherton."

Chan smiled. "A few more years and they'll be my concern."

43

Grace drove away from the museum and cruised downhill until she reached the upper edge of campus. Backing into a **Staff Only** parking space at the rear of what looked like a physical plant, she deep-breathed and tried to settle down.

Amy Chan likely viewed their conversation as unproductive but Grace had learned plenty. A chance meeting between brothers had, indeed, uncorked a whole bunch of darkness eventually leading to Andrew's demise.

Had his reaction to spotting the piece-of-work now known as Dion Larue been surprise after a long absence? Or dread after repelling Larue's attempts to reestablish contact?

Grace had unearthed Andrew's Stanford link easily enough. No reason Big Brother couldn't have done the same.

The emotions Chan described were telling: Andrew shaken, Venom Boy enjoying the experience.

Getting in a dig by addressing Andrew by his cult name.

Thai. Not quite, Amy. **Hello, Ty.** A bit of naughtiness, that.

Two years ago was well past the murders of the McCoys, the Wetters, and the Van Cortlandts. And while Andrew's shock at seeing his brother didn't eliminate the possibility that years before he'd collaborated in the killings, Grace was shifting to his being innocent. Because nothing about him implied cruelty and the man Chan had described meshed with her own impressions.

Meaning Big Brother had engaged in solo slaughter, which fit perfectly with the already high-level teenage psychopath she'd witnessed at the ranch. With the bullying scamster Mr. One-Eye had described.

If that wasn't enough, the anagram said it all. Arundel Roi comes to life as Dion Larue.

She pictured whoever he'd been ten years ago driving to Oklahoma, torching poor little Lily and her family, dumping their truck and returning, sated, to California.

Though the same question persisted: Why eliminate his sister but allow his brother to survive?

Maybe because Lilith was deaf and deemed defective while Ty had earned a Stanford Ph.D. and was seen as potentially useful.

Structural engineer, big projects in Asia. Dion Larue fancied himself a developer but he was small-time—scamming the city of Berkeley in order to rehab a dump. Perhaps he'd seen Andrew as a ticket to bigger and better.

Andrew turning him down could've caused all sorts of untoward reactions.

Which brought her back to Larue's murder of the Van Cortlandts. Why would he think that would've curried favor with Andrew?

Because like all psychopaths he was grandiose, and convinced of his own personal magnetism, assumed worship on the part of others.

You know all that money you got to inherit young, bro? Guess who did that for you.

Samael/Dion would've appreciated that kind of "favor," but Ty/Andrew had been sickened and horrified. Traumatized sufficiently to seek professional help.

And that had turned him into a huge liability.

Turned Grace into collateral damage.

She realized she'd been concentrating hard enough to lose contact with her surroundings and looked around. Still no trolls, ogres, or hulking thugs. But an unmistakable chill of threat was tracing up and down her spine.

Act, don't react.

She got out of there, fast.

. . .

Returning to city center, she drove along Telegraph, found metered parking, and scored an out-of-the-way table at a different Internet café. A sign warned that the toll for logging on was food, not just a beverage, so she bought an iced tea and a mozzarella and allegedly heirloom tomato panini, left the sandwich swaddled in its oil-spotted, recycled paper wrapping.

She began by assuming Beldrim Benn's age to be the same as Roger Wetter Junior's, or close to it, and a fellow student at Berkeley High. Calculating the year of Benn's high school graduation, she plugged in his name and keywords and waited as the café's overtaxed bandwidth finally kicked in.

Nothing from the school itself, but the rarely accessed personal website (**You Are Visitor 0032**) of an optician in Stowe, Vermont, popped up. The star of that obscure show was now a paunchy and slope-shouldered fellow named Avery Sloat, who adored his family and his golden retriever and his LensMaster franchise but whose most treasured moments seemed to be his years on Berkeley High's Yellow Jackets varsity wrestling team.

As proof of that, Sloat had posted a low-resolution group photo of said grapplers in their red-and-gold athletic togs, circling his own image in white just in case you missed it.

Grace tried to enlarge the shot but couldn't, made do with getting close to the screen and matching faces with the small-print roster at the bottom.

Roger Wetter Junior had not been on the team. No surprise, she supposed. A pretty boy like him wouldn't risk injury nor would he be interested in a fair fight. But there was B. A. Benn, second row to the right, a surly-looking, pimply, shaggy-haired middleweight.

Above Benn, in the top row, there was only space for five boys because each was massive; the heavyweight division, bursting out of their XXXXL jerseys.

Any one of whom was large enough to be the bastard she'd run off the road.

Andrew's likely killer.

She studied the photo. One meat-mountain was Samoan, another black, the remaining three, white kids. One of whom was the younger manifestation of the man who'd stood behind Dion Larue in the New Mexico photo.

Hands vibrating, she stilled an index finger and found the name in the roster.

W. T. Sporn.

Uncommon surname, a stroke of good luck. She typed away.

Unlike Beldrim Benn, Walter Travis Sporn's criminal history, though relatively petty, had attracted the attention of local papers in San Mateo and Redwood City. No infractions for the past fifteen years, but before then, a nice lucid pattern. No way Sporn's clean record since then meant he'd reformed. More likely, he'd gotten better at avoiding responsibility. From ages eighteen through twenty-two, Sporn had been busted three times for drunk and disorderly, twice for battery, once for assault. From what Grace could glean from the short, dispassionate Crime Blotter accounts, everything stemmed from bust-ups at bars. No follow-up on how Sporn's cases had been disposed but Grace doubted he'd served much serious jail time; in a world teeming with violence, bashing a few faces was no big deal.

Maybe he'd evaded arrest by submitting to the leadership of a far brighter villain.

Any self-congratulation at I.D.'ing Sporn faded as she realized she was no closer to finding him or Larue.

Time to try Wayne again, hopefully he'd learned something and wasn't just being protective. But still no answer or message at his private line. Finishing her tea, she took her sandwich with her and handed it to an emaciated homeless woman who was astonished by the unsolicited generosity.

Back in the Escape, she gave Center Street another try,

made half a dozen uneventful passes, timed over an hour to avoid being conspicuous, and saw nothing.

Time to regroup.

Then she saw him.

Big man working his way out of a black Prius parked illegally in front of the site. Pulling to the curb, Grace watched as Walter Sporn waddled to the padlock that secured the chain-link, let himself in, relocked.

Smoking a cigar and wearing a black mock-turtle over black sweatpants and black sneakers.

He had to be well over three hundred pounds. But not a roly-poly pushover; a substratum of muscle underlay the fat and, despite the rocking gait imposed by tree-trunk thighs, he moved quickly and confidently.

So confident he wasn't bothering to check out his surroundings when he emerged a few minutes later, returned to the black Prius, and drove away.

Gliding right past Grace.

Why would he be vigilant? For years—decades—he and his buddies had gotten away with everything.

Grace let a pickup truck with a Berkeley city emblem pass before pulling out.

The truck gave her perfect cover. Evasive driving, huh, Walter?

Time for a little motorcade.

44

Walter Sporn, a poor fit for the Prius, drove south of campus and turned onto Claremont Boulevard, continuing into a neighborhood of large, gracious Craftsman, Tudor, and Mediterranean houses on tree-dimmed streets that evoked Grace's years in Hancock Park.

This was the Claremont district, one of the college town's most affluent enclaves and home to generations of old money, brand-new Silicon Valley profits, professors with trust funds. Grace knew the area well; a couple of times Malcolm had booked rooms at the Claremont Hotel, a giant century-old masterpiece of architectural excess tricked out with overlapping triangular segments and a landmark tower and set on twenty or so acres atop a hill that offered spectacular views. During their stays, Grace and Malcolm had breakfasted in the dining room. Memories of that time had slipped from her consciousness—as a rule, the past held no attraction for her—but now she recalled Malcolm's seemingly endless appetite for pancakes and scholarly discussion and smiled.

Far cry from her current digs at the Olds. One adapted.

With the truck still between her and Sporn, she swerved slightly, just in time to catch Sporn turning onto a street called Avalina. A sign said **No Exit.**

Parking, she jogged to the corner and peered up the block. Short block, full view all the way to the end of the cul-de-sac. She watched as the Prius turned right into a driveway, counted houses to pinpoint the location, returned to the Escape and waited.

When Sporn hadn't reappeared in an hour, she hazarded a stroll.

The houses lining Avalina perched atop sharply sloping

lawns, many partially blocked by mature vegetation. The property Sporn had entered was nearly at the street's terminus.

Gigantic Tudor, slate-roofed and multigabled, weathered brick face nearly blocked from view by unruly ten-foot hedges, three massive redwoods and two nearly-as-large cedars. And, incongruously, a thatch of spike-leaved palms. Tiny bluish-white flowers speckled the hedges, which had been trained into an arch that stretched over the cobbled-and-dirt drive. The Prius was parked behind its twin.

Two black cars. Black clothes for Sporn, same as the children of Arundel Roi the night they'd showed up at the ranch.

Grace continued to the end of the street, reversed direction and crossed the street, and pretended not to take another look at the brick mansion. Not a single glint of window glass behind the veil of green but that didn't mean much.

Memorizing the house's address, she forced herself to walk away slowly.

Back in her room, she tried the Olds's WiFi again, found it no more useful than before. But her disposable cell worked just fine and she tried Wayne, yet again.

This time he picked up. "Where are you?"

"NoCal."

"Lovely region. May I hope against hope that you've decided to settle for sightseeing?"

Grace laughed. "What's up, Uncle?"

"Oh, well," he said. "At least you're okay."

"I'm great."

"Does that mean you've accomplished whatever it was you set out to do and are on your way back home?"

"Making progress."

Silence.

Grace said, "Really, I'm fine."

"So you say . . . you will take care of yourself." A command, not a request.

Grace said, "Of course."

"If you don't make a solemn pledge to that effect right now, I won't tell you what I learned."

"I pledge allegiance to the flag of Wayne—"

"I'm serious, Grace."

"I promise. Everything's fine, really. What did you learn?"

Wayne cleared his throat. "Let me preface this by reminding you that I can't vouch for the factuality of what I'm about to tell you. But my source has never let me down."

Sounding every bit the lawyer.

"I'll bear that in mind, Wayne."

"Okay . . . as you might expect, this has to do with the late Ms. McKinney. Who, as we discussed, does not appear to have ever indulged in a romantic or sexual relationship with anyone or anything at any time."

Grace waited.

"However," said Wayne. "And this is a big however, Grace, my source—a new one, one can't keep going to the same well—claims that at some point in middle age, Selene began to regret not having a family." A beat. "It's a common thing . . . she tried to solve her problem by adopting."

"Tried? Someone with her clout was turned down?"

"Oh, she was allowed, all right," said Wayne. "Scored herself a white girl—not a baby, perhaps she had no stomach for poopy diapers—a lass of around eight or nine. A name beginning with a Y—Yalta, Yetta, something like that."

Grace heard him sigh.

"Here's the painful part. The poor thing was with Selene for a couple of years, enjoying the life Selene was able to provide until Selene realized she wasn't cut out for motherhood, after all, and solved **that** problem by giving the girl back."

"Shit."

"Indeed," said Wayne.

"Who'd she give her to?"

"Unknown, Grace, but presumably to whatever agency or shyster colleague of mine found her the poor thing in the first place. Can you imagine the hurt? Rejected twice?

Good Lord. No surprise that led to the poor thing developing problems."

"What kind of problems?"

"The kind that end up with a young woman being incarcerated, Grace."

"Sybil Brand," said Grace. "Where she met Roi."

"That's where girls who acted out criminally went in those days, Grace. It keeps getting worse. Somewhere along the line, she had two children of her own."

"Only two?"

"Yes, I wondered about that," said Wayne, "but that's all my source is aware of. Here's the story and it goes back twenty-five years ago, Selene throwing herself a party for the Christmas season—she was always fêting herself—big garden affair at her home, the right people on the guest list, rented topiary and all that. My source is a right person and this is what she—what was observed: At some point during the bash, there was an attempt by my source to use the powder room but it was occupied and an alternative was sought. What presented itself was a lav in the utility wing, off the kitchen, and as my source did her thing and was walking out, she heard a commotion."

Another throat clear. "A bit of peeking and eavesdropping ensued. Selene was in the kitchen, full regalia, smoking like a chimney and having words with a young woman dressed in black. Not chic black, shabby duds. My source couldn't hear what was being said but the hostility was obvious. And flanking the young woman were two boys clad the same way, not tykes—not small boys, ten, eleven. Both sat silently, looking 'stricken' as their mother and Selene went at each other. Finally, Selene picked up her phone and summoned security staff but before the guards could arrive, the young woman yanked the boys away and ran out through the back door. Upon which Selene muttered something to the effect of 'good riddance to bad rubbish.'"

"Not very grandmotherly," said Grace.

"Not very human," said Wayne, with sudden fury in his voice. "You're the one with the Ph.D., Grace. Tell me: Why doesn't evolution select against human monsters?"

A host of answers flooded Grace's head. Including: **Where else would we get our politicians?**

She said, "Good question. Twenty-five years ago is about one year before the shoot-out at the Fortress Cult."

"Exactly, Grace, exactly. Perhaps Yalta, whatever her name was, realized something bad was brewing and came to Selene for help. What she received was anything but."

"And soon after, everyone at the compound perished except for three kids."

"Yes, three. So where was the daughter that day? I don't know, Grace, but my source is certain: two boys, only."

"Maybe Lily wasn't Yalta's, Wayne. The account said Roi had three wives. That could be why she wasn't adopted by a wealthy family. Selene had nothing to do with her."

It could also explain why she hadn't been spared. Half sibs didn't count.

Wayne said, "You could be right. In any event, we have motivation for Selene finding homes for the boys. Not guilt over turning them away, anyone who acted the way she did is far too callous for remorse, no?"

"Agreed," said Grace.

"On the other hand, having the boys at the mercy of the system raised the risk of Selene's rejection coming to light. So she called in markers from people who owed her. A pair of couples who were childless and would accept older children with baggage."

"Especially if the offer was sweetened with some cash."

"Hmm," said Wayne. "Selene certainly wasn't lacking funds. Yes, that makes perfect sense—now, what does all this mean for you, Grace?"

"I'm not sure."

"Do you really need to pursue this further?"

Grace didn't answer.

Wayne said, "You say you'll be careful with such confidence. I wish I could be sure you weren't humoring me."

"I'm not," she assured the kind, moral man who'd done so much for her.

Lying without a trace of regret.

Third Internet café, this one a casual Vietnamese eatery around the corner from the Olds. What netted her access to the electronic universe was a bowl of pho that she actually had an appetite for.

She spooned the broth into her mouth, enjoying the bite of hot peppers not quite tempered by coconut milk. Pork, shrimp; glassy rice noodles that slid down her gullet.

Everything crystallizing. She could **feel** it.

She plugged in the address of the big brick house on Avalina and pulled up a City of Berkeley Landmarks Preservation Commission staff report, dated three years earlier.

> Structural Alteration Permit Application
> (LM#5600000231) for rehabilitation of City
> Landmark, The Krauss House; including in-kind
> replacement of (historic and non-historic) window
> sashes and (non-historic) doors on the main house
> and replacement of (non-historic) drainage gutters,
> composite/slate/shingle roof and skylight on the
> carriage house addition. Prepared by . . .

Five city employees claimed authorship of that golden prose. Next came small-print paragraphs of something called a CEQA determination that had deemed the proposed project

> categorically exempt pursuant to Section 15331
> (Historical Restoration Rehabilitation) of the CEQA
> guidelines.

> Property Owner: DRL-Earthmove.

Paging through the rest of the document, Grace put together the house's history. Built in 1917 for a metals dealer named Innes Skelton, it had served as a private residence until 1945, when an art history professor and collector of Asian ceramics named Ignatz Krauss purchased it for use as a private museum.

From what Grace could tell, Krauss had set up one of those arrangements with the university in which he got tax write-offs for his collection and could enjoy them at will but would bequeath the collection and the building to UC Berkeley upon his death.

Krauss had passed away in 1967 and the pottery was auctioned off shortly after. The structure remained in the university's possession for eight more years, designated as housing for distinguished visiting faculty, after which it was swapped to the city of Berkeley for a commercial building downtown that the university wished to use for administrative facilities.

What the city did with the place was unclear, but four years ago it had sold the property to DRL after buying the building on Center Street from Larue for four million dollars. The only stipulation: "timely application for landmark preservation" of the house on Avalina.

The following year, Dion Larue had apparently complied, filing the necessary papers and pledging to do exactly what the city dictated.

Playing good boy?

When Grace saw how much he'd paid, she understood why.

Eight hundred grand. She was no expert on Berkeley real estate but that had to be way below market. Looking up sales of other houses on the block, she quickly confirmed her suspicion. Comps ranged from $1.6 to $3.2 million.

Venom Boy had scored a coup. Especially when you figured in four million for the dump on Center, which had to be top-market, and scoring a no-bid contract to demolish and remodel for government offices.

Backroom dealing was the milk of politics but Dion Larue appeared to own a herd of dairy cows.

Multiple murderer acquiring the patina of an eco-conscious, diversity-minded, local-renewable businessman.

Riding the crest of new-age politics through a combination of slickness and connections.

She finished her pho, returned to the Olds, and redigested the terrible story Wayne had unearthed: a child rejected twice. Three times—arriving at Selene McKinney's, sons in tow, seeking shelter only to be turned away.

Twenty-five years ago, Ty had been nine, Sam, eleven. More than old enough to know what had happened.

Sitting by their mother in the kitchen, docile and silent. Not long after, she and her co-wives and the devil who'd ruled them were dead, leaving three children to the mercies of the system.

Tragic; could you blame a boy for going bad?

You sure could.

Turning the tale over and over, Grace found herself growing steely. She knew all about rejection and loss, deep wounds of the soul that required psychic excavation and cauterization, the acid wash of self-examination.

Life could be a horror.

No excuse.

45

Twenty-one-year-old Grace lived in a studio apartment on Formosa Avenue in L.A.'s Wilshire district.

She'd raised the issue of independence three weeks after returning to L.A. from Harvard. Grad school would begin in a month and she wanted as much settled as possible.

She waited for the right time to bring up the topic with Malcolm and Sophie; at the end of a pleasant, quiet Sunday brunch at home, expecting surprise, maybe barely concealed hurt feelings, even gentle debate.

She'd prepared her tactful rebuttals, drawing upon her own flood of gratitude and their desire, of course, to do what was best for her.

Malcolm and Sophie showed not a trace of surprise. Nodding in unison, they assured her they'd pay rent for anything reasonable.

Three and a half years in Boston and they haven't missed me?

Or, to put a benign slant on it, like so many older couples, perhaps they, too, craved a bit of freedom.

Still—idiotically—Grace felt a bit . . . empty at the lack of debate. Then she saw that Sophie's beautiful blue eyes had grown damp and that Malcolm was avoiding looking at her and his jaw was knotted.

Leaning across the kitchen table, she touched both their hands. "I'll probably be here all the time, anyway. Mooching food, schlepping laundry, not to mention all the contact you and I will have day-to-day, Malcolm."

"True," he said, fidgeting.

Sophie said, "Any laundry you schlep will be welcome.

Though you should probably look for a building with on-site machines. For your own convenience."

"Get a place with top-notch facilities," said Malcolm. "That's of the utmost."

Sophie said, "And of course you'll need a car." She laughed. "No new clothes, though. Your current wardrobe is far too elegant for your future peers."

Malcolm said, "Oh, the students aren't that bad, Soph."

"Oh, they're dreary," said Sophie, laughing again, a smidge too loudly. Using the moment to sneak a swipe at her eyes. "I refer to my department as well as yours, Mal. No matter what their circumstances, our young scholars pride themselves upon coming across as starving martyrs." She turned to Grace. "So, alas, no cashmere, dear. The Tenth Commandment, and all that."

Grace said, "You bet."

No one spoke. Grace found herself fidgeting and now Sophie was engaging her with a solemn stare and Grace realized she'd been talking about more than attire.

Thou Shalt Not Covet. Reminding Grace she'd be entering grad school laden with baggage.

Of all the schools, Professor Bluestone had to bring her here?

Adopted or not, she's still his family, it's corrupt.

Her acceptance means someone else fully qualified was rejected. If she's as smart as they say, she could've gotten in at plenty of other places, why hog a space here?

On top of that wouldn't some distance be healthy for both of them?

On top of that, **they say she'll be working directly** with him. **Talk about lack of boundaries.**

Now Malcolm was also regarding her oh-so-gravely.

The same unspoken warning from both of them: Be smart and keep a low profile.

Sage advice, to be sure. Grace had figured it out a long time ago.

. . .

Resentment was understandable. Clinical psych programs at accredited universities were limited to students for whom grant funding was available, leading to tiny classes—USC accepted five first-years out of a hundred as many applications.

The program was rigorous and laid out clearly: three years of coursework in assessment, psychotherapy, research design, statistics, cognitive science, plus a minor concentration in a nonclinical field of psychology.

In addition, students assisted faculty with research and saw patients under supervision in the department's campus clinic, leading to six twelve-hour days each week, sometimes more. Off-site externships for which SC students competed with applicants from all over the country were mandatory, as well. By the fourth year, a faculty doctoral committee needed to be in place, comprehensive exams passed, research proposals approved.

Then came the crucial final chapter, the step that could end in disaster: conceptualizing and conducting significant, original research and writing it up as a dissertation. Only once that was under way were candidates allowed to apply for a full-time internship at a facility approved by the American Psychological Association.

Grace figured she could do it all quicker, without much sweat.

Her plan of attack was simple, replicating her experiences at Harvard: be polite and pleasant to everyone but avoid emotional entanglements of any kind. Especially now; entering under a cloud, she couldn't let interpersonal crap get to her.

But her classmates, all women, three with Ivy League B.A.'s, turned out to be a pleasant bunch, exhibiting not a trace of resentment. So either she'd earned their acceptance quickly or everyone had worried for nothing.

Faculty were another matter, a definite chill wafted toward

her from some quarters. No problem; compliance and subtle flattery went a long way with academicians.

She didn't lack for a social life, what with casual lunches with her classmates during which she listened a lot and said little, and the customary Sunday brunches with Sophie and Malcolm, plus dinners out at white-tablecloth eateries twice a month.

Toss in the occasional off-campus lunch with Sophie, sometimes followed by shopping trips for "appropriately casual garments," and her plate was full.

Her relationship with Malcolm changed, as their contact increasingly centered on research and personal chitchat eroded. That ended up suiting both of them. She'd never seen Malcolm so animated.

Solo jaunts to campus movies and museums—LACMA was walking distance from her apartment—supplied all the extracurricular culture she needed.

Of course, sex played a role during those years, as she stuck with the familiar but lowered the frequency because it took less to satisfy her. Pulling out the cashmere and the silk, heels, and all the other good stuff, she had no problem snagging well-dressed attractive men in upscale cocktail lounges and hotels.

Many of her targets turned out to be traveling from other cities, which was optimal. Others were escaping marriages gone stale or simply tired of domestic obligation.

To Grace they were all temporary playmates, and for the most part, everyone walked away happy.

With drama neatly sidestepped, she was free to ace every course and treat twice as many patients as anyone else at the campus clinic. The same went for research projects, and by the end of her second year, she'd co-published three articles with Malcolm on resilience and three of her own on the aftereffects of trauma, one of which saw light in the **Journal of Consulting and Clinical Psychology**.

Simultaneously, she was analyzing the best places to extern, with an eye toward making contacts where she might want to intern. The choice quickly became obvious: the Veterans Administration hospital in Westwood, for all the problems with the system, one of the premier training facilities in adult psychology.

More important, a V.A. placement would give her experience in the treatment of terrible things. Because neurotic angst—dilettantes and sluggards trying "to figure it out" or pay for friendship—bored and annoyed her.

She craved the red meat of real psychotherapy.

After a year as a student therapist, she'd gotten to know everyone who mattered at the V.A., was perceived as the best and the brightest, her internship application a formality.

Four years after enrolling in grad school, she had her Ph.D., presented to her personally by Malcolm, Harvard-robed and beaming, at the doctoral ceremony in Town and Gown Hall. She'd also been accepted for a postdoctoral fellowship at the same V.A. If it ain't broken don't fix it.

By age twenty-seven, she was still living frugally in her single on Formosa and investing ten percent of her stipend in a conservative stock fund. After passing national and state licensing exams, she was asked to stay on at the V.A. as clinical faculty, an invitation she gladly accepted. The position was exactly what she craved: continuing education about people whose lives had been blown to bits, sometimes literally.

The V.A. had changed since Malcolm's grad school days, when the typical patient was often cruelly libeled as an elderly chronic alcoholic for whom little could be done.

GOMERs, snotty medical residents called them. **G**et **O**ut of **M**y **E**mergency **R**oom.

The V.A. that Grace encountered was a high-intensity facility where the evils of war manifested by the hour. Beautiful young American men and women, maimed and mutilated in hot, sandy places by fanatics and ingrates they thought they'd been sent to liberate. The physical wounds were profound. The emotional aftereffects could be as bad or worse.

The patients Grace saw struggled to adjust to missing body parts, permanent brain damage, blindness, deafness, paralysis. Phantom limb pain was an issue, as were depression, rage disorders, suicidal risk, drug addiction.

Which wasn't to say every vet was damaged goods—a libel that raised Grace's ire because she respected those who'd served at such a high level. Nor was post-traumatic stress disorder the default. That was a bum rap created by craven Hollywood types exploiting the misery of others for the sake of a screenplay. But even when the damage was subtle, it could impact daily living at a profound level.

Grace never presumed that her own childhood was even a close match for what her patients were going through. But she knew it gave her an edge.

Right from the start, she felt **at home** with them.

They sensed it, too, and soon, following her pattern, she was treating twice, then three times as many patients as anyone else at the hospital.

More important, she was getting results, with patients and families increasingly requesting her as their therapist. The V.A. staff took notice, happy to have someone carry the elephant's load.

That didn't stop some of her colleagues from viewing her as a spooky workaholic who cropped up on the wards at all hours, seemingly immune to fatigue. Was she, they wondered, bipolar? One of those adult ADHD types?

And why didn't she ever hang out with anyone?

But the smart ones kept their mouths shut, enjoying how much easier she made their lives.

One night-shift RN began calling her "the Victim Whisperer." A fellow postdoc, himself a Vietnam vet who'd gone back to school in middle age, led a support group for paraplegics with her, expecting to teach "the young cute chick" all about suffering.

Soon he was terming her "Healer of the Haunted."

That one, Grace liked.

One evening, leaving the hospital and walking to the used BMW 3 that Sophie and Malcolm had "picked up for a song," she spotted a middle-aged woman waving at her.

Stout, blond, nicely dressed. Working hard at pasting a smile on her face.

"Dr. Blades? Sorry, do you have a second?"

"What can I do for you?"

"I'm sorry to bother you—you probably don't remember me, you're treating my nephew?"

Confidentiality precluded an answer, even if Grace had known who the woman was talking about.

"Oh, of course, sorry," the woman said. "My nephew is Bradley Dunham."

Sweet boy, originally from Stockton, frontal lobe damage that had scrambled his emotional life. But still gentle, so much so that Grace wondered what led him to the marines. On their sixth session, he'd told her.

I graduated high school and there was nothing else I could think of.

Grace smiled at his aunt and the woman apologized again. "This isn't about Brad. It's about my own son, Eli. I'm Janet."

Finally something Grace could respond to. "Is Eli a patient here, as well?"

"Oh, no, he's not a vet, Dr. Blades. Anything but. He's . . . for two years he's had what I guess you people would call issues? Intense fears? Anxiety disorders? Also compulsive behavior that's getting worse and worse, to the point where— not that I can blame him, Doctor, sometimes I'm a basket case, myself. Because of what happened."

The woman sniffed back tears.

Grace said, "What happened?"

And that changed everything.

. . .

Eli's parents, both CPAs, had been victims of a home invasion that left Eli's father stabbed to death and his mother severely beaten. Eli had come home to find the massacre, called 911, and ended up as a prime suspect subjected to days of intense, borderline-abusive grilling by the police. The cops' suspicion continued until three gang members attempting a similar break-in were identified as the savages in question.

By then, the damage was done: Eli, always a "sensitive boy," had retreated to mute isolation in his room, adopting a growing array of odd tics and habits: pacing and retracing, curtain-pulling, hand-scouring with harsh powdered soap, skin-picking, near-constant eyeblinks.

For twenty-two months, attempts at treatment by a psychiatrist, then a psychologist, had brought no success; neither doctor was willing to make house calls and Eli's attendance at their offices deteriorated from spotty to never as his condition worsened.

Janet said, "I'm at my wit's end. I know what you've done for Brad. He says everyone talks about you. Money's no object, I promise you that, Dr. Blades. If you could see your way to at least meeting Eli."

"In your home."

"He refuses to go out."

"But he is open to a therapist coming to him."

"You'd do that?" said Janet. Her face fell. "Honestly, I don't know, Doctor, I'm grasping at straws."

"You haven't discussed this with Eli."

"Eli won't let me discuss anything with him, Doctor, he's made himself a prisoner. I leave food in the hallway and he waits till I'm gone to retrieve it. But even if it doesn't work out, I'll be happy to pay you for your time. Including your driving time. With money up front, cash if you so desire—"

"We'll work out the details," said Grace. "Where do you live?"

. . .

Four months later, Eli, quirky since childhood and never destined for gregariousness or a conventional life, was able to leave his home, stop torturing his skin, and abandon his other tics. A month after that he was holding down a home job as a billing clerk for an online vintage clothing site.

Two months later, shambling through a nearby park, he met a girl as shy as he. Soon after, the two of them were having ice cream together a couple of times a week. That hadn't lasted but Eli now saw himself as "datable" and was girding himself to try online sites.

"I know that can be a risk, but it's a start!" exclaimed Janet. "You've done miracles for him, Dr. Blades."

"Appreciate your saying that," Grace told her. "But Eli's done all the hard work."

Three weeks after terminating with Eli, her second private referral came in. A woman Janet had met in a crime victims' group.

No need for house calls on this one but Grace had no office for private patients. She asked her immediate supervisor about the ethics of using her V.A. office after hours. Knowing he did the same thing himself, to the tune of doubling his income.

He said, "Well, it's . . . we're in a gray area." Lowering his voice: "If you don't overdo it and your regular work gets done . . ."

By the end of her first year as an attending psychologist, Grace had amassed a private patient load that forced her to make a change: reducing her hours at the V.A. to fifteen a week and giving up all benefits. She rented an office in a medical building on Wilshire near Fairfax, walking distance from her apartment.

Her income doubled, then trebled, then doubled again. Her patients got better.

Free enterprise. It fit her beautifully.

. . .

Shortly after her twenty-seventh birthday, during one of the Hancock Park brunches with Malcolm and Sophie, which she'd continued to attend without fail, Malcolm chewed and finally swallowed a chunk of bagel layered with glistening gravlax and asked if she'd be interested in teaching part-time at USC.

That threw her; she figured the university was happy to be rid of her and the boundary issues she'd raised. On top of that, her relationship with the people she'd come to view as her parents had evolved in an interesting manner.

She and Sophie were sharing more purely social girlie stuff but distance had interposed itself between her and Malcolm.

Perhaps some of that resulted from a young woman and an old man having little in common. But Grace wondered if part of it stemmed from Malcolm's disappointment at her decision to bypass academia for private practice.

If so, he disguised any chagrin with compliments that could be taken as double-edged:

You were such a brilliant researcher. But of course the core of our discipline is helping others.

Grace thought: **Blame yourself. It might've started out as a project for you, 'Enry 'Iggins. But your kindness and humanity took over and molded the hell out of me.**

When Malcolm looked wistful, Grace made a point of kissing his cheek and smelling his bay rum aftershave. It had taken a long time to manage snippets of physical affection for both him and Sophie but she'd worked on it and now she felt comfortable.

She told herself she loved them but didn't spend much time figuring out what that meant.

The key, after all, wasn't words. It was how she treated them and that she knew she'd aced, making sure she was unfailingly cheerful, courteous, agreeable.

Sixteen years had passed since Malcolm had plucked her from juvenile hall and in all that time, nary a cross word had ever been exchanged, and how many families could make that boast.

When Malcolm offered her the teaching position that Sunday morning, she smiled and kept her voice even and squeezed his now liver-spotted hand. "I'm flattered. Undergrad?"

"No, graduate classes only. Clinical One, maybe some neuropsych testing if you've stayed current with that."

"I have," she said. "Wow."

"Of course I think you're overqualified, if it was up to me the offer would've come the moment you got your license. But you know . . . anyway, the idea originated with the rest of the clinical faculty, I'm simply the designated messenger."

He ate more bagel and cured salmon. "You may meet up with other alums. There's a new attempt to exploit the abilities and the experience of our more gifted students." He blushed. "Also, there are fiscal issues."

Grace chuckled. "They think I'll work cheap?"

Sophie said, "Cheaper than a full-time tenure-track person."

Malcolm said, "Yes, yes, but that's really not it, in terms of you, specifically. You're their first pick. You've acquired a reputation."

"For . . ."

"Effectiveness."

"Hmm," said Grace. "What exactly would this entail?"

Malcolm's big shoulders dropped. Relieved. "I was hoping you'd say that."

By twenty-eight, Grace was making a serious six-figure income in private practice and enjoying her one day on campus as a clinical assistant professor of psychology.

The secondhand BMW functioned smoothly, her single on Formosa continued to suit her, and her stock fund was growing safely and steadily.

Cocktail lounge trysts continued around L.A. and extended abroad, as she began treating herself to high-end, bi-yearly vacations. She toured European and Asian cities, returned home with selected bits of couture and erotic memories that fueled her solitary hours.

Life was coasting along just fine. Grace figured she could do this for a while.

Fool that she was.

Shortly before her twenty-ninth birthday, she was yanked out of sleep by pounding on her front door.

Forcing herself alert, she threw on sweats, selected a butcher knife from the block in the kitchen, and approached the noise warily.

"Grace!" hissed a voice on the other side. Someone stage-whispering. Trying not to wake the neighbors?

Someone who knew her name . . .

Keeping the knife ready, she unlatched the door an inch but kept the chain-lock in place.

Ransom Gardener stood in the hallway, looking ancient and unkempt, white hair flying, eyes red and raw, lips trembling.

Grace let him in.

He hugged her fiercely and broke down in sobs.

When he finally pulled away, Grace said, "Which one of them?"

Gardener howled: "Dear God, both, Grace, both of them! Sophie's . . . T-Bird."

Grace's mouth dropped open. She stumbled back as Gardener stood in her living room and his body was racked with heaving moans.

She felt frozen. Enveloped by a hard shell—an insect's chitin.

Visualizing the small black convertible speeding somewhere.

Exploding into bits.

She tried to speak. Her larynx and lips and tongue had apparently fled her body. She was certain that her trachea had departed as well because it didn't feel as if she was breathing but somehow she was . . . existing.

Respiring through her pores?

Ransom Gardener continued to sway and sob. Grace felt herself grow dizzy and gripped the wall for support. She managed to totter into her kitchen, groped wildly for a chair. Sat.

Now Gardener had followed her in, why had he done that, she wanted him **gone.**

He said, "Fucking drunk driver. He was killed, too. Fuck him to hell."

Suddenly, Grace wanted to ask where, when, how, but nothing south of her brain was working. And even that— the electrical jelly in her head—felt wrong. Fuzzy, soggy . . . impaired.

Now she was one of her patients.

For what seemed like forever, Gardener hugged himself and cried as Grace sat there, inert, plagued by insight:

Empathy was the biggest lie of all.

46

Needing to turn herself cold, cruel, collected, Grace lay on the sagging bed in the Olds Hotel and dredged up just enough pain and rage and sorrow to light the spark.

Primed, she drove out of Berkeley, south to Emeryville. At an independent sporting goods store she paid cash for beach sandals, insect repellent, black rubber-soled walking shoes, a black ski mask with eyeholes. The mask and shoes were the relevant purchases, the others an attempt to bury them within a larger context.

Returning to the hotel, she dined on jerky and trail mix, drank water, peed, drank some more, drained her bladder again, then did some stretching and push-ups and took a nap.

No need to set an alarm. She wouldn't be going out until after dark.

By seven p.m. she was up, energized, alert. Thirty-eight minutes later, she'd parked the Escape three blocks from the house on Avalina and was walking. The new shoes squeaked, so she turned in the opposite direction and worked them silent.

Cool night, which made the jacket with the four pockets visually and functionally appropriate. Her wigs were back at the Olds. Her clipped hair felt tight and right under the knit cap she'd bought at the surplus store.

Green contact lenses this time. Like a cat.

She began prowling.

No sounds issued from the big homes atop their slopes. Most were dark and that made sense, if what Grace had observed in L.A. held true here: the larger the mansion the less likely it was to be used full-time, rich folk traveling or enjoying satellite homes.

Malcolm and Sophie had lived in one big house and had rarely ventured far. They'd reminisced about foreign travel but hadn't used their passports since taking in Grace.

A case of been-there-done-that? Or wanting to be there for her?

Grace's eyes began to ache and she scolded herself; distraction was the enemy. As the big brick house neared, she slowed her pace.

When she got there, she took a position slightly past the hedge that arched over the driveway. The house was lit scantily, haphazardly, randomly placed low-voltage bulbs creating a crazy quilt of illumination and black patches.

Only one window in the mansion was backlit: top floor, right of center. Someone home or a security play. No other obvious signs of self-protection—alarm sign, camera, trespassing warnings, motion detectors.

Confident fellow, Dion Larue.

Only one black Prius in the driveway tonight. Same license plate as Walter Sporn's ride. Did Sporn live here? That fit a cult situation. If so, Larue was deviating from his daddy; Arundel Roi had limited his acolytes to women and the children he sired with them. Then again, this was the age of equal rights . . . or maybe Grace was getting overimaginative and Sporn was nothing more than in-house security during the boss's absence.

Or a babysitter; talk about a gruesome contingency.

Did Larue and his wife even have kids?

God, I hope not.

The fact that Grace had no idea—knew so little about Larue—drove home how much needed to be accomplished.

She walked to the dead end, receded into the shelter afforded by an unlit berm, and studied the street from a new perspective. Convinced she hadn't been spotted, she returned to the Escape, locked the doors, and waited.

Forty-eight minutes later her patience was rewarded when another black Prius rounded the corner. As it neared the big brick house, Grace got out and jogged after it.

She arrived just in time to see the second vehicle pull in behind Sporn's.

Head- and taillights died. A man got out at the driver's side. The inconsistent lighting made gleaning details difficult, the figure flickering in and out of her visual field in strobe-flash fragments.

Like watching a light show; with each freeze-frame, data accumulated.

Tall.

Long-haired.

And there was the beard, fuller and longer than the stubble he'd sported in the fund-raiser photo, Grace could see an outer rim of hair haloed by freckles of light.

Flowing garments—a knee-length tunic. Over what appeared to be tights.

Slim legs. Slim overall build. Head held high—and there was his profile again, the beard-tip aiming forward like a lance ready for battle.

He began walking toward the house, his carriage suggesting nothing but confidence.

No doubt about it, this was him, and Grace watched as he strode up the long drive toward his front door.

When he was halfway there, the Prius's passenger door swung open and a woman got out. Nearly as tall as Larue. A dress hanging just below her knees.

But less confidence here—stooped posture, rounded back.

Grace prayed for her to illuminate herself and finally she did, showing her profile.

Unmistakable flash of uncannily sculpted cheekbone.

The wife, what was her name . . .

Azha.

She began trailing Larue's approach to the house, shoes

crunching on gravel. Dion Larue didn't turn or acknowledge her, just the opposite, he picked up his pace.

The woman followed at a widening distance, as if that was her custom.

Was well away from the door when Larue closed it.

Locking her out? Tense night for the golden couple?

Azha Larue continued trudging, as if being shut out of her own home was business as usual, and when she reached the door, she opened it with a mere twist of her hand.

Larue had left it unlocked. Delivering some sort of message? Or simply asserting his authority by making her go through the effort?

Whatever the motive, the few moments Grace had just observed reeked of arrogance and hostility on Larue's part.

Subservience on Azha's, which could prove relevant.

Grace copied down the plate number of the second Prius then crept forward and dared a look inside the vehicle using whatever ambient light was available. As luck would have it, a bulb wired to a tree shone directly onto the front seat.

As luck would have it, nothing but seats and dashboard.

Retreating to the shadows, Grace watched the brick house for another quarter hour, spent an additional hour in her SUV, making sure no one came and went, finally returned to her hotel.

No more sleep. Calculation.

47

Malcolm and Sophie's funeral was held a week after their deaths, at the Laguna beachfront home of Ransom Gardener. Lovely day on the rim of the Pacific, cobalt skies encroached upon by silky silver clouds floating in from the north.

Laguna was sixty miles south of L.A. Grace realized that each time Gardener had visited, he'd driven over an hour. Dedicated lawyer.

The things you think of.

The things you avoid.

Malcolm and Sophie had left clear instructions for cremation and Gardener had taken care of that. Grace stood, in a white dress, barefoot on the sand as he walked toward her toting dual silver urns. He'd asked if she wanted to toss. She'd shaken her head and that had seemed to please him.

Depositing human ashes into the Pacific undoubtedly violated state, county, and municipal codes. Gardener said "Fuck it" and the dust flew.

He'd been swearing a lot since that terrible night in Grace's apartment, revealing a whole other side to the temperate lawyer she'd known for years.

Since then, under the guise of comforting her, he'd been imposing himself upon her daily, arriving with food she had no interest in eating, then plopping down on her living room couch and reminiscing nonstop. What else was left when you felt empty? Grace didn't join in but that didn't make a difference; Gardener couldn't stop sharing.

Many of his stories began the same way: his first day at Harvard, a cosseted Upper East Side Manhattan preppie and Groton grad, projecting a veneer of confidence but feeling anything but. Floundering, scared, but all that resolved soon after meeting Malcolm—"the best thing that happened to me during my entire time at Cambridge"—who knew a huge, hulking Jewish guy from Brooklyn would end up a lifelong friend?

"More than a friend, Grace. Words fail me, perhaps there **are** no words for it, he was . . ." For the hundredth time, tears beaded at the tops of Gardener's sunken cheeks and lost the battle with gravity.

"Here's the thing, Grace, not only was he mentally and physically impressive, he could be relied upon to use both those endowments sparingly. With discretion. With taste. But when you needed him, he was damn there, Grace. Drunken townies thinking they could kick the stuffing out of us, they learned their lesson fast."

The image of Malcolm duking it out in a Somerset dive would've amused Grace, if she'd been capable of feeling anything.

She let Gardener prattle on, pretending to listen.

Professional training coming in handy.

Since learning of the catastrophe, she'd retreated into an insensate fog, as if locked in a sterile glass bubble where her eyes worked mechanically but couldn't process and her ears were unplugged speakers. When she took a step, she knew she was moving, but she felt as if someone else was pushing the buttons.

Her brain was flat and blank as unused paper.

It was all she could do to sit and stand and walk.

She figured she was faking normal pretty well because no one at the funeral seemed to be regarding her with over-the-top pity.

The guests were faculty and students, Gardener and his wife, a plump woman named Muriel, and the ever-silent Mike Leiber, dressed like a bum and lurking at the rear with that odd, spacey look on his now-gray-bearded face. A brief touching speech by Gardener, who choked up at every other sentence, was followed by overly long bullshit orations delivered by professors from Malcolm's and Sophie's departments.

Then: cheese and crackers and bland white wine on the beach as the waves lapped and the sky finally turned charcoal.

As everyone left, one thing struck home: Grace was the only family present. She knew neither Malcolm nor Sophie had living relatives but until then had never thought much about it. Standing alone, watching what remained of them settle to silt on the water, only to be washed away, she realized how alone they'd been before taking her in.

Did that explain it?

Could any act of nobility—or evil—ever be explained fully?

No, there had to be more, she was being pathologically analytic because damn it to hell she felt ready to explode.

Malcolm and Sophie deserved better than dime-store analysis.

Malcolm and Sophie had loved her.

The day after the funeral, she was alone in her apartment and finally able to cry. She did little but cry for a week and when Gardener showed twice during that time, she ignored his knock. For the next two weeks, she stopped taking his calls. Same for calls from patients and referral sources. Leaving a "family emergency" message on her voicemail. Good time for the Haunted to think about someone other than themselves.

On the morning of the fifteenth day after It Happened, Gardener showed up again and Grace supposed she could tolerate him. She cracked the door. Mike Leiber was with him and suddenly Grace didn't feel like letting either of them in.

"Yes, Ransom?"

"You all right, dear? Haven't heard from you."

"I'm coping."

"Yes . . . we're all struggling to cope—may we chat for a moment?"

Grace hesitated.

"It's important," said Gardener.

Grace didn't reply and Gardener edged closer. "I promise not to get all soppy, Grace. Sorry if I took advantage of your tolerance."

Behind him, Mike Leiber stared into space. Grace wanted to hit him.

Gardener said, "Please, Grace? It's for your sake. Matters that absolutely need to be dealt with." Sounding like a lawyer again. Mike Leiber's eyes remained flat as pond pebbles.

Gardener put his hands together, as if in prayer.

Grace undid the chain.

She led both men to her kitchen where Gardener placed a large crocodile-hide briefcase on the table and drew out a pile of documents. Leiber seated himself facing Grace but turned away immediately and busied himself with her refrigerator door. A host of diagnoses sprang into Grace's mind. She blocked them. Who cared?

As Gardener arranged his papers, he wrinkled his nose. The room smelled of stale grease. She'd survived on forgotten food foraged from her cupboards and fried things she often burned—crap she'd normally shun. She hadn't aired the kitchen out. Hadn't showered for two days.

Gardener said, "Okay," and squared the edges of the two-inch stack he'd created. "As you may have suspected, you're Malcolm and Sophie's sole heir."

"I didn't suspect. I haven't thought about it at all."

"Yes . . . of course—I'm so sorry, Grace, this is . . . but in any event, things need to be dealt with and here we are. You are the sole heir. Thus, you need to be apprised of your new situation."

"Okay. Apprise me."

Mike Leiber said, "It's more than okay."

Grace shot him a sharp look. He was already back studying the white expanse of fridge.

"Well, yes," Ransom Gardener said. "What Michael is saying, Grace, is that Sophie and Malcolm were extremely wealthy, you are the beneficiary of a combination of Sophie's own inheritance and years of prudent investing undertaken since Sophie and Malcolm's marriage." He glanced at Leiber.

Leiber shrugged.

"Michael here is somewhat of a financial mastermind."

"Load of crap," said Leiber. "Buy low, sell high, avoid stupidity."

"You're being overly modest, Mike."

Leiber crossed his arms over his chest and got that blank look in his eyes again. Suddenly, he sprang up, "Gotta go. Catch some foreign exchanges."

"I drove," said Gardener. "How will you get back to the office?"

"Bus," said Leiber. To Grace: "Sorry you had to learn this way. Hope you don't fuck it up."

When he was gone, Gardener said, "As you've obviously noted, Michael's an unusual individual. His years at MIT were rough. Malcolm helped him."

Grace sat there.

"Then again," said Gardener, "you're probably not surprised by that—by anything I could tell you about Malcolm or Sophie . . . so . . . here are the details."

For all his initial babbling, Gardener was able to transition to pure lawyerly efficiency, communicating the facts with admirable clarity.

The house on June Street was worth between three and a half and four million dollars. The stock fund Malcolm and Sophie had set up for Grace within months of adopting her had grown to five hundred seventy-five thousand dollars.

"The fund is all yours, now, but some of the proceeds from selling the house, should you choose to sell it, will go to taxes. If we use every arrow in our quiver, my estimate is you'll end up with four mil, give or take."

Grace said, "Fine, I'll pay you to do the paperwork."

"I've already begun, dear. I'm already the executor, no additional fees projected."

"Don't executors bill by the hour?"

"No set rules, Grace."

"I don't need a handout—"

"That's not what this is, Grace, it's basic decency, I can't tell you what they meant to me."

Worried he'd lapse into more nostalgia, Grace said, "Thank you." She'd buy him a gift, something extravagant. In his house, the day of the funeral, she'd noticed a collection of art deco glass. His wife stroking a vase as she walked by.

Gardener made no attempt to move.

Grace said, "Anything else?"

Gardener gave a sad smile. "As they say on those commercials for cheap knives, 'But wait, there's more.' "

Grace closed her eyes. Her nerves were frayed raw, it was all she could do not to shove him out of her kitchen.

"So," said Gardener, "there's the four million. Which by itself is a nice boon for someone as young as you, the potential for growth is enormous. But." He gave a flourish. "There's also a bit more money that Malcolm and Sophie had invested for themselves. Mike's done a wonderful job with those funds, too. And before him, his father did the same thing—Art Leiber was one of the premier money managers on the eastern seaboard. Another chum of Malcolm and mine from Lowell. Wonderful man, he passed years ago, bladder cancer. There were questions about Mike's ability to handle things but he's proven himself quite nicely."

Here we go again.

Gardener must've sensed her impatience because he drew himself up. "What you're about to see, Grace, illustrates the power of compound interest. Buying solid investment products and not touching them."

He breathed in. Plucked three sheets of paper from the pile and slid them across the table.

Columns of stocks, bonds, funds, things Grace knew nothing about. Small-print letters and numbers, everything blurring.

She looked away. "Okay, thanks."

"Grace!" said Ransom Gardener with alarm in his voice. "Have you seen it?"

"Seen what?"

He snatched up the bottom sheet, reversed it so Grace could read, and jabbed a spot near the bottom.

Grand Total.
Twenty-eight million, six hundred fifty thousand dollars.

Plus forty-nine cents.

"That," said Gardener, "is **after** taxes, Grace. You're a very wealthy woman."

Grace had read all those lottery-winner stories, people resolving life wouldn't change. But of course it always did, pretending otherwise was idiocy. No sense ignoring her new circumstances; the key was to make sure she remained in control.

She phoned Mike Leiber and told him she'd be withdrawing some money but wanted him to continue managing the bulk of her fortune as before.

He said, "If you have to spend, use the income, not the principal."

"What income is that?"

"Don't you read? You've got munis—tax-free bonds. The interest is over six hundred K every year. That enough for shoes and manicures, right?"

"More than enough. So we'll continue as before?"

"Why not? You don't care if I don't do the dog and pony, right?"

"Pardon?"

"For most clients I have to visit twice a year with charts and crap and show what a good job I'm doing. Malcolm and Sophie knew it was a waste of everyone's time. But Gardener insisted."

"No need, Mike."

"Also," said Leiber, "I'm telling you this at the outset: Some years you'll do better, some worse, anyone who tells you different is an asshole con man."

"Makes sense, Mike."

"You can call if you have questions but your questions are unlikely to be uninformed. Better to read the monthly statements, everything's spelled out. If you want more, I'll recommend reading a book on basic investing, Benjamin Graham's the best."

"I'll bear that in mind, Mike."

"Good. Oh, yeah, I'll send you some checks so you can withdraw whatever you want."

"Thanks, Mike."

"Whatever."

Over the next year, Grace sold the house on June Street, consigning the more valuable antiques and objets d'art with a dealer in Pasadena and storing Malcolm and Sophie's papers in a warehouse that specialized in document safety. One day, she might read them.

Using the proceeds from the house, she avoided capital gains tax with a 1031 exchange: snagging the house on La Costa Beach for a good price because it was tiny and unsuitable for more than one person and the Coastal Commission was balking at issuing building permits. Additional cash was spent on a cottage in West Hollywood that she converted to her new office.

The day after closing on both properties, she drove to a

dealership in Beverly Hills, traded in the BMW, and bought the Aston Martin, black and barely used. The previous owner had discovered he was too large to fit comfortably in the cockpit. The Toyota station wagon, also barely used, was parked in a corner of the lot. It turned out to be owned by the salesman. She shocked him by making an offer, ended up bundling it into the deal as a practical fallback.

She'd known she wanted a sports car, had even considered a vintage T-Bird but decided that would be literal and stupid and trite.

The first month she owned the Aston, she put on two thousand miles. The combination of excessive speed and recklessness felt strangely redemptive.

Maybe one day she'd stop imagining the night they'd been taken from her.

She'd learned nothing about the accident. By choice. Had refrained from talking to Gardener or the highway patrol, requesting records, any sort of clarification.

She didn't even know if the drunken waste of space who'd destroyed so much was male or female.

Despite everything she told her patients about open communication, she craved the balm of ignorance. She supposed that could change.

Meanwhile, she'd drive.

48

The morning after catching her first glimpse of Venom Boy as an adult, Grace set out for the Claremont district.

By seven a.m., she was sitting under a giant umbrella-shaped tree and studying the scant traffic traveling to and from Avalina Street. The tree, a species she couldn't identify, was the largest of an old-growth copse that rimmed a patch of lawn claiming to be Monkey Island Park.

No simians in sight, no water, no island. Nothing at all but a third of an acre of grass surrounded by stout trunks and overarching branches heavy with chlorophyll.

Arriving here would be a giant letdown for a kid with visions of chimps in his head. Maybe that's why the place was empty.

Making it perfect for Grace.

No contact lenses today; her eyes were concealed by sunglasses. She'd hazarded the blond wig, but combed it straight and free of creative waves and flips and gathered a foot of ponytail through the slip-hole of her unmarked black baseball cap. Warm morning so no jacket, just jeans and a tan cotton crewneck, athletic socks and lightweight sneakers. Everything else she needed was in her oversized bag.

She'd picked up a **Daily Californian** near her hotel, opened it, and pretended to care about campus life. A few people walked near the park but no one entered.

At eight forty-five a.m., Walter Sporn emerged from Avalina in a black Prius and headed north.

At nine thirty-two, Dion Larue did the same. Larue drove too fast for Grace to catch many details but in the daylight, his hair and beard flashed golden, with an almost metallic glint.

As if he'd gilded himself, a self-styled graven image.

Grace remembered a technique she'd learned about when consigning Malcolm and Sophie's decorative objects: ormolu, a process where gold paint or leaf was applied to a baser metal like iron or bronze.

Basically, trying to make something more than what it was.

She closed her eyes and processed what she'd just seen. As Walter Sporn zipped by, he'd been frowning. Dion Larue's handsome face had the same upward tilt of nose and jaw that she'd observed last night as he left his wife out in the dark.

Overweening arrogance and why not? No one had told him no for a very long time.

Grace readied herself for another look at the big brick house.

But give it more time, just to be sure. No reason to rush.

Twenty-two minutes later, two female pedestrians rounded the corner of Avalina and headed straight for her.

Both blond, the taller one pushing a baby stroller. As they got closer, the baby's round, white disk of face came into view. Also fair-haired.

Grace's wig made it an Aryan morning at Monkey Island Park.

The newcomers didn't alter their trajectory but did stop well short of Grace, settling near the center of the lawn. The taller woman faced the stroller and began unstrapping the baby, as Grace watched, yards away, shielded by her sunglasses and her newspaper. She'd already registered a guess as to the stroller pusher's identity and a turn of face confirmed it.

Subservient Azha, her hair a bit limp, center-parted, and held in place by a leather band that was pure hippie redux. She had on a black cotton shift cut slightly higher than the dress Grace had seen last night, this one just meeting her knees. On her feet were flat sandals. No jewelry, no watch.

In the daylight, her face was handsome, just short of pretty. But those cheekbones.

Grace visualized Dion Larue out to reshape his world, wielding one of those gauges favored by sculptors and carving away at his wife. Azha sitting immobile and mute throughout the process, wracked by exquisite agony, as the psychopath who dominated her scooped and contoured and bloodied her down to the bone.

Nice metaphor and all that but Grace stopped indulging herself, no time for fanciful bullshit.

For all she knew, the woman was one of those jellyfish who enjoyed having doors shut in their faces.

She raised her paper an inch higher, watched Azha remove a blanket from the back of the stroller and spread it on the grass. When satisfied with its smoothness, she removed the baby from the stroller, held it up to the sun and beamed.

Tiny little thing, well shy of a year, chubby legs kicking in glee. Dressed in a white onesie, thank God for no black. Lowering the baby and pressing it to her bosom, Azha folded herself carefully and settled on the blanket, crossing her legs in some sort of yoga pose.

Hugging the baby for a moment, she plopped it down next to her. The tyke bobbled and swayed and fought to remain upright, finally succumbed to gravity and began falling backward only to be saved by the flat of Azha's hand on its back.

That level of balance suggested five, maybe six months old.

Smiling, Azha kept her hand in place, allowing the child to pretend it was sitting of its own accord. That lesson in false confidence worked: The baby laughed. Azha laughed back, said something and kissed the baby's nose.

All this was happening too far out of earshot to make out content but the melodious quality of Azha's voice floated across Monkey Island Park.

The baby reached for her and she allowed it to grip her finger, began rocking it gently in a new game of balance.

All the while, the shorter woman had stood by in silence.

As if realizing it, Azha turned and looked up at her and pointed to the grass.

Moving woodenly, the shorter woman sat.

She was about the same age as Azha, thicker-built and plain-faced. Her hair was tied in dual pigtails far too child-ish for her and her black dress appeared to be of the same light cotton as Azha's but cut fuller, almost haphazardly, as if the tailor's attention span had wandered by the time he'd gotten around to her.

At this distance, her features came across small and flat in a doughy face, her eyes squinty. She was positioned on the other side of the baby but paid no attention to it. Instead, she stared off into the distance. Vacantly, it seemed to Grace. Mike Leiber's soulmate?

Second by second, her body sagged lower until she was hunched, limbs settling flaccidly. Grace continued spying as the woman's mouth dropped open and remained that way. Azha played with the baby but her companion seemed cut off from the fun. Indeed, from all of her surroundings. Grace began to wonder if she was subnormal intellectually.

Or perhaps, like so many others attracted to cults, she was damaged goods—brain damage due to dope, some other psychoneurological insult.

Whatever the reason, she continued sitting like a lump and it went on that way for a while, neither Azha Larue nor the baby paying her any mind. Then Azha turned and took hold of the other woman's chin delicately and guided her face so that they faced each other.

Manipulating her, the way you would a toy. The shorter woman complied as if made of soft plastic, maintaining eye contact but not responding after Azha said something to her. But when Azha handed her the baby, she accepted it and Azha lay down flat on her back and placed her left arm over her eyes.

Naptime for Mommy.

Whatever the other woman's deficits, Azha trusted her with her child. And she did know how to hold it properly, nestling it close to her, supporting the supple neck.

The baby was at ease with her, as well. Relaxed, smiling, laughing again when the short woman chucked it under its chin.

A gesture not unlike Azha's toward her.

Azha was dozing now, chest rising and falling rhythmically as her companion did a fine job of babysitting. The infant never wavered from good cheer; lucky kid, blessed with a good temperament.

How long would that last?

Suddenly, the shorter woman placed the baby belly-up on the grass. Again, no fuss from Model Tot, as it gazed upward. Now the woman had altered her own position and was hovering above the baby. Looking directly down at it.

Azha Larue's chest rose and fell at a slower pace. Her companion watched her for a few seconds then returned her attention to the baby.

Waving her hands at the infant—some sort of pantomime show, or just weird movement by a weird woman—no, there was purpose to this, the baby knew it, was rapt as fingers flew.

Rapid movements taking shape. Communicating.

The baby continued to pay attention as the hands above it shaped air, pointed, circled.

Comprehending. As pre-verbal babies often did when trained in American Sign Language.

49

Could it be?

Of course it could.

Lilith had been eight or nine when Grace first saw her, putting her at nearly thirty now—the age of the shorter woman.

Nothing at odds with the smaller woman's appearance either: a fair-haired deaf-mute girl grown to a fair-haired deaf-mute woman.

Not mentally dull, just cut off from Azha Larue because Azha didn't know—or didn't care to know—sign language. Manipulating Lily's face and speaking directly at her.

Read my lips.

Azha had also ignored Lily completely until the moment she needed her—**Watch the baby so I can catch some Z's.** Not the approach you took with a friend, this was more master–servant.

Like any cult, Dion Larue's family embraced a strict line of command: Guru at the top, followed by the guru-ess, then the worker bees.

Lily with her deafness and her passivity was the perfect serf. What must be crippling passivity in light of Larue's murder of her parents.

Had Larue found another woman of approximately the same age and size to substitute as a sacrifice? A hitchhiker or a street girl he'd picked up during the drive from California to Oklahoma? Burning the house down because how better to obliterate physical evidence?

Maybe one day, she'd look into it . . .

First guesses are often right on, maybe because they spring

from a deep, intelligent place in the unconscious, and Grace realized hers had been freakishly acute.

Venom Boy, wanting to relive the glory days of his father's insanity, moving steadily toward that goal for a decade. Slaughtering the McCoys as they slept silently in their little Oklahoma house but taking Sister Lilith with him first.

Confident she'd offer no resistance. And if she did, he had ways of handling it, witness Brother Typhon.

Amy Chan perceived the meeting in the restaurant as a chance encounter but perhaps it had been anything but. Big Brother watching his brother for a while. Learning he was in town and stalking him from behind the wheel of his Prius.

Watching as Amy and Andrew entered the vegan joint— maybe a place he frequented himself, if he continued to eschew animal products. Announcing to Azha, still and silent in the passenger seat, that he was treating her to dinner out.

No argument from her. About anything. Ever.

The "spontaneous" encounter had spelled the beginning of the end for Andrew.

Your basic spider-fly scenario.

Because Andrew hadn't reacted well, none of that Lily-passivity.

On the contrary, he was repulsed.

Idiot Typhon had turned moral.

Thinking about it, Grace was surprised to feel herself shuddering. Flipping a page of the **Californian,** she scanned a paragraph of self-righteous student journalism. Something about micro-triggers of pre-post-traumatic "discomfort" due to a long list of isms . . .

Cries from the lawn snapped her out of that.

There he was.

Gilded and straight-backed, handsome face uglied by rage.

Grace watched, unable to act, as Dion Larue raised his foot and kicked the sandaled sole of a now-awake and wide-eyed Azha. Azha sat up looking panicked and Larue turned his wrath on Lily, now holding the baby. Stabbing an accusing finger at her. Snarling something.

He began fluttering his own hands as he berated her—a mocking parody of sign language.

The baby, easygoing until now, wrinkled its face and turned scarlet and wailed. Larue ripped it out of Lily's hands hard enough to whip its tiny head forward, then back. Too much of that and school would be a challenge when the kid grew up.

The baby cried louder. Larue looked at it as if it were an insect.

Contemplating something terrible? Would Grace be forced to act? What a disaster.

She got ready to spring from behind her arboreal shield. Thankfully, Larue thrust the baby into the shaking hands of its mother. Began attacking her verbally, waving a fist as if it were a cudgel.

Too distant to make out words but imagined lines of dialogue sailed through Grace's brain like subtitles.

You fell asleep? Gave it to her?

Your job, not hers.

She was signing at it, you idiot. Since when do we allow that?

Azha hung her head. Larue clapped his hands on his hips, raised himself taller, and glared down at both women.

The baby cried louder.

Larue advanced on it with a fist and Azha placed a hand over its mouth.

Larue stood there, yet another Crown Prince of an entitled generation.

Azha Larue managed to roll her child close to her breasts while extending both hands toward him, her head bowed lower.

Forgive me, for I have sinned.

Larue watched his wife demean herself then barked something harsh and turned back to Lily and kicked her hard on a bare shin. Azha winced in empathy. Lily didn't respond.

Larue's face began darkening. He rocked on his heels, fingers drumming his hips.

His kicking foot raised higher.

How much could Grace allow? But again, she was saved from action as Lily began aping Azha's penitent gestures.

Going through the motions, Grace thought, but not feeling it.

Larue agreed; he kicked her harder.

Lily bent nearly double, face in the grass, and that seemed to be the proper response because Larue turned his back on all of them and pranced across Monkey Island Park, creepily effete.

Heading in the opposite direction from where Grace sat and now she spotted the faint gleam of sunlight on black automotive paint, peeking through foliage in random triangles and rectangles.

His Prius parked at the periphery. She hadn't seen him drive up.

She needed to be more careful.

50

Grace watched for two more days, was rewarded with a pattern.

Both mornings, Walter Sporn and Dion Larue continued the same approximate routine: separate Priuses driving north from Avalina, Sporn first. The first morning, only ten minutes separated their departures and Grace followed Larue, unsurprised to see him head to the construction site on Center and park illegally behind Sporn.

Sporn waited for the boss before getting out and unbolting the padlock on the chain link. Both of them passed through and then, as before, Sporn relocked. Walking around the right side of the gutted structure, the two men didn't show themselves until twenty-four minutes later. During that time a Berkeley parking nazi gave tickets to a couple of other cars but let the Priuses be.

The prince was connected.

Larue emerged first, jaunty as always, walking ahead of Sporn who carried a cheap-looking briefcase. They separated, Larue heading back in the direction of Avalina, Sporn east. Grace made a quick decision and followed Sporn.

He didn't drive far, just a few blocks into a neighborhood of shabby apartments. Idling by the curb, he got on his phone. Moments later, a kid who might've been a student or just one of those campus hangers-on appeared from a three-story blue stucco dump with a sign out front advertising weekly, monthly, and yearly rates.

Early twenties, Caucasian, with dreadlocks ranging from bronze to black, the new arrival wore red skater shorts, a baggy green **Free Palestine** T-shirt, and sockless black high-tops. Nervous dude, looking both ways three times before crossing a street devoid of traffic. Scratching himself, jumpy eyes darting randomly.

Grace, half a block up, watched as Sporn handed Dreadlocks the briefcase. Words were exchanged. Dread slipped something into Sporn's meaty palm.

Well, well, alternative financing for Larue's wheels and deals. The long-delayed construction site a perfect place to stash controlled substances. Or weapons. Or both.

Not only had Larue boondoggled the geniuses who ran the city with the sale of the property and subsequent contract to rebuild, he'd snagged himself free storage.

Having his minion do a dope deal in full daylight. Talk about confidence.

Sporn drove away, leaving Dread to pick at his face, bounce on his toes, and scratch his scalp as he held the briefcase the way Azha and Lily had held the baby. Finally, he ran across the street and back into the blue building.

Tweaker by habit, dealer by necessity. Maybe some of the meth would reach his clients.

The second morning, Grace remained parked in the Escape with an oblique view of Avalina as the Priuses did their thing, this time fifteen minutes apart.

From what she'd seen so far, no one else lived in the big brick house—Larue's cult still in its formative stages?—but she couldn't be sure.

If she hadn't observed the scene at Monkey Island Park, she'd never have learned about the women and the baby, so theoretically, Larue could have a harem stashed in there. But a full day of observation convinced her it was probably just him, Sporn, Azha, and Lily.

And the poor little kid.

The men came and went but since Larue's tantrum in the park, the women hadn't shown themselves.

Grace found herself thinking about the baby more than she could afford. How quickly Larue's presence had transformed it from cheerful to terrified. What lay in store for . . . no sense speculating, there was work to be done.

That night, she watched the house while on foot. Same minimal illumination from the top-floor window.

No movement at all from Sporn but Larue drove away just before ten p.m. and Grace followed with her headlights off until he hit Claremont Boulevard, where she could interpose a couple of vehicles between them.

Larue continued toward the Claremont Hotel and crossed the border between Berkeley and Oakland. Sailing through the initially stylish streets of the other Bay city, he kept going until the symptoms of a neighborhood gone bad grew flagrant: busted streetlamps, trash on the sidewalks, neon blink of all-night liquor stores, check-cashing outlets, bail bonders, pawnshops. The few pedestrians in sight were obvious night-crawlers, including plodding women in halters, shorts not much more than belts, and five-inch heels.

Larue stopped just shy of all that, pulling to the curb on a block of now-dark thrift shops. The Prius's lights blinked and switched off and one of the streetwalkers headed its way. Younger than the others, petite and shapely, she wore white lace that could've been underwear and hot-pink patent-leather shoes. Despite her youth, her gait was stiff and painful. Maybe the shoes but Grace suspected there was more: She'd lived too quickly, turned her bones brittle and old.

The hooker arrived at the Prius's passenger door. No conversation, she just got in. She remained inside for just short of ten minutes, tottered out wiping her mouth with her bare arm.

Larue swung a quick U and drove off before she had a chance to leave.

Once parked in front of his big brick house, Larue bypassed the front door and walked around the left side of the massive, darkened structure.

Grace waited until all was still and silent and shadowed his path. The front drive widened as it girded the house—cracked asphalt now broad enough for a car and a half, leading to a generous backyard that appeared overwhelmed by foliage. The rear of the house, as dark as the front, first impression would've been no one home.

But weak light fluttered and flickered through the heavy branches of conifers and sycamores and unruly shrubs.

Coming from the rear of the property. A second structure back there.

Larue's permit application to redo the Krauss House flashed in Grace's head.

. . . **replacement of drainage gutters** blah blah blah **on the carriage house addition.**

A building once used to house vehicles would explain the width of the drive but now access was completely blocked by vegetation.

Still, that light . . . Grace froze as, above her, a window began cranking open on the house's second story.

New sound: a man scolding a woman.

He goes out and gets head from a hooker, comes home and finds fault with her?

Another sound: the sharp report of skin on skin. Then: male laughter. Followed by a protracted, theatrical yawn.

I'm so bored with you.

Crank crank; the window opened wider.

His nibs liked fresh air.

Grace, still motionless, holding her breath, wondered why lights had been left on in the carriage house when Larue, en famille, was ensconced in the manse.

Nothing happened for a long time.

Then: snoring through the open window.

She got the hell out of there.

51

The following night, she was prepared.

Black cotton tee, black stretch jeans, black silent walking shoes, the jacket with ample storage.

In one upper pocket, Grace placed latex gloves purchased at a pharmacy on Telegraph, in another the eyeholed black ski mask. The lower pockets were already doing their bit.

Driving through silent Berkeley streets, she parked four blocks away. That distance came with a risk: Getting away would be prolonged. But keeping her SUV out of view from immediate neighbors tipped the balance.

Receding into the shadows when she could, she proceeded toward Avalina, encountering no one, not even a stray cat, and continued to the end of the cul-de-sac where she waited and watched.

Both Priuses in the drive. The same window lit, the same low-voltage hodgepodge.

When nothing happened for half an hour, she put on the mask and the gloves and entered the property. Stopping again to assess, then continuing. Repeating the process.

Just as before, getting around to the back of the house was simple. The window Larue had cranked remained shut.

The same light blinked from the rear. Provided just enough illumination for her to make out vestiges of former grandeur.

Tamped-down dirt remained where lawns had once flourished, vacant flower beds were sectioned into hexagons and circles by fractured brick edging, arms of boxwood lacked entire chunks, dead trees turned to thatch gave way to bullying by thriving competitors—mostly cedars whose branches dragged in the dirt.

She pushed forward, maintaining the same walk, stop, turn, watch routine. Slow going but no need to rush. Finally she got close enough to the carriage house to see that the branches stretching diagonally across its front were flimsy, allowing a filtered view of the overall structure.

The size of a double garage, the building sported a too-heavy slate roof and a girdle of brick running along its lower half. The top section was leaded-glass panes. More of a conservatory than a coach house. The interior fit horticultural usage, too: rows of ceramic pots long emptied of plants lined sagging wooden shelves. Shards and fragments littered a buckling cement floor.

Most of the windowpanes were flyspecked, pigeon-streaked, or just filmy from poor maintenance. But those of the door had been cleaned and it was through them that Grace saw it.

Lily lying on her stomach, stretched out on a green-painted potting table, facing the door.

Shapeless black dress pushed above her waist. Both hands dangling over the table rim.

Her lips were turned down but the rest of her face remained expressionless.

Looming from behind, Walter Sporn pumped himself in and out of her.

From the angle of entry, clearly not vaginal sex. Sporn wore a black T-shirt but was otherwise naked, his skin the consistency and color of cold tallow, pants and shoes and socks gathered in a heap in a corner.

The light Grace had seen issued from a six-bulb fixture missing three bulbs.

Eyes squeezed shut, piggy face contorted in what looked like rage, Sporn thrust. The table rocked. Lily's face remained still as that of an inflatable sex toy.

Sporn began smacking Lily's ass hard enough to turn it magenta, switched to grabbing her hair and yanking her head upward. Every movement was harsh, rapid, punishing. Nothing altered the frown on Lily's lips, the blankness everywhere else.

Resigned.

As Grace thought through her next move, Sporn released Lily's hair and shoved her head hard, causing it to flop on the table. The enormous hand he'd freed reached around and ringed Lily's throat and now something changed in her listless eyes.

Wider, brighter. The incandescence of fear.

Then again: nothing.

Surrender.

Grace sucked in breath and reached into her right-hand lower jacket pocket just as Sporn's other hand began flailing Lily's butt hard enough for the sound to filter through glass.

She pushed the door, felt it give, sprang forward, her silent entry aided by Sporn's still-clenched eyelids and his raspy laughter as he smacked and throttled Lily.

Lily saw Grace. Her eyes widened. Her mouth formed an oval of surprise.

A willing participant? God, Grace hoped not.

No. The poor thing was nodding at her. Encouraging her. That reverted to terror as Sporn's paw tightened around her neck. Her tongue flopped. Her lips swelled and her eyes rolled backward.

Grace ran forward, Glock in hand. Sporn, still lost in sadistic ecstasy, didn't notice. Then Grace's toe kicked something on the floor—a piece of terra-cotta that began rattling on the cement, insistent as a snare drum.

Sporn's eyes opened. Rage reddened his irises. His lips drew back in a snarl.

Not just a swine, a wild boar, feral and crafty.

Gleeful fury as he saw that his assailant was female and wispy. The leer of a wrestling favorite entering the ring, prepared to demolish.

He let go of Lily and rushed at Grace, lips curling higher,

revealing nasty-looking peg teeth. Below the hem of his T-shirt, a jelly-filled sack of belly flopped up and down. Tree-trunk thighs, on the other hand, were firm. His penis, shiny with lube and ruddy at the tip, was shrinking comically above shrunken steroid balls.

Shooting him in the groin was tempting but no sense substituting symbolism for common sense.

Grace stepped back as if afraid of his attack, waited until Sporn was well away from the table where Lily remained prone and inert, then aimed three bullets at his open mouth.

Two found their mark, the third shattered the space between Sporn's nose and upper lip. Surprised—abashed—his eyes widened and he kept coming at her, a felled redwood.

Then he stopped. Stared at Grace's black-masked face. Said, "Huh," and now it was his eyes that were rolling back. His knees buckled and he fell to the ground and he toppled over, face-first.

Blood leaked onto the ground as he twitched a few times before growing still.

Just for good measure, Grace shot him a fourth time in the back of the head. Straight trajectory to the medulla oblongata, where a bullet was certain to snuff out basic respiration. Who knew her grad school neuropsych would come in so handy?

She turned to Lily, who still hadn't moved.

Had she, indeed, been a willing partner in a long-standing B-and-D game rather than a victim? Grace didn't want to have to deal with an unplanned foe.

Holding the Glock at her side, she approached the table but stood well back as she tried to engage Lily's eyes.

Lily did nothing. Then she mouthed something.

Thank you.

Grace nodded and pointed at Lily's pushed-up dress. Lily, suddenly embarrassed, rolled onto her side and moved her shoulders, trying to raise her arms to pull it down.

A mere shrug resulted. Arms refusing to cooperate.

Paralyzed? Had Sporn's abuse of her neck injured her cervical spine?

But then Lily's right hand quivered and she was able to shake it. Then the left. Awakening after going numb from the pressure.

She began covering herself but not before Grace took notice of buttocks splotched raw and littered with tiny bleeding crescents—nail marks. Similar marks were scabbed. Where the skin hadn't been clawed it was black-and-blue.

Blood oozed from some of the fresher wounds and a separate trail of crimson ran from between the cheek crack down the left thigh.

Lily tried to lift herself, couldn't. Grace prepared to help her.

Lily's face changed.

Animated by horror as her lips worked and her eyes blinked faster than Grace thought possible.

Lily arched her neck. Pointed.

A warning.

Something behind Grace.

Too late.

52

Dual points of impact ignited sparks of agony.

At the small of her back and the nape of her neck, the latter from an attempt to yank at her ski mask from behind. She twisted out of the way but went down hard, scraping her face and her knees and her elbows on the harsh, cold floor of the conservatory. The Glock flew from her hands, thick plastic thudding to the right side of the green table where Lily now sat up, hands to her mouth, whimpering.

Dion Larue's attire told Grace she hadn't screwed up, just an unlucky break.

Black silk robe with red quilted shawl lapels, loosely belted over a naked body.

Butting Grace with that level of force had splayed the robe's flaps. Larue's body was hard, tan, defined, a whole different species from Sporn. Up close, she made out the details of his face. The murderous boy who'd showed up at the ranch, taking so much from her so quickly.

Harder, craggier, but just as handsome. No mistaking the eyes, cold but active. Assessing nonstop.

Despite some consternation when he glanced at Sporn's whale-corpse, no lagging of confidence as he smiled wolfishly.

The look on his face an essay on the calculus of violence. The same determinedly destructive expression hunters got when they locked in.

Grace forced herself not to look at the Glock but tried to recall how far away it had landed. Still in reach if she lunged skillfully? Doubtful. Was it worth a try, anyway?

Dion Larue snorted. A low wet sound issued from between his lips and he clawed his hands and advanced on Grace, snickering, pectorals flexing, genitals swinging.

No penile shrinkage for him; this body came alive with the expectation of blood.

"A chick," he said. "Are you fucking nuts?"

He laughed—more like a cackle, unbecoming for a stud. One of the clawed hands rolled into a fist and now Grace noticed something gripped by the other. Small tube, red, the word **Love** barely visible.

His own personal container of lube; the boss had come to join the party.

Now he was going to have a different kind of fun.

A bare foot kicked out viciously, just as it had at his wife's foot at Monkey Island Park. But harder, much harder, and when he made contact with Grace's ribs and pain seared her, she knew he'd broken something.

Rolling to her right she went for the Glock.

Larue had anticipated the move, kicked the weapon away, bent and tried to catch Grace again with a pointed foot—a martial arts thing, she vaguely remembered Shoshana showing her something like it.

She scurried backward, avoided the blow. Dion Larue grunted and bent low and moved toward her faster but instead of making contact, he feinted to one side, then another.

Came up holding the Glock.

"Stupid cunt. Who the fuck are you?"

Erection in full bloom.

Grace said, "Shouldn't you finish Walter off first?"

Nothing profound, nothing clever, but it threw him, he'd assumed Sporn to be dead, Sporn **was** dead so what the fuck was this dumb cunt—and now Larue was realizing he'd been had and he roared and attacked.

But the split second it had taken for his thoughts to reassemble had been enough for Grace to reach into another bottom pocket of her jacket, not the easiest move, she was right-handed and this was the left pocket, definitely a disadvantage but you worked with what you had because there was no choice and what she had in her nondominant hand was her lovely little Beretta, which she transferred to her right hand and aimed upward.

Dion Larue snarled, "Fucking bitch."

Same exact thing Beldrim Benn had said in her backyard.

So unoriginal, these psychopaths.

Grace emptied the gun into him. The erection went first, the rest didn't really matter.

Unlike Sporn, he died silently, immediately, landing on his side then tipping onto his back.

No doubt about this one. His hard bronze body was a sieve.

Collecting every shell, Grace approached Lily, now sitting atop the potting table, shivering.

Placing a finger softly on Lily's lips, Grace focused Lily's head the way Azha had.

Made sure Lily was looking squarely at her, Grace cocked an eyebrow. Enunciated clearly.

"You'll keep this between us?"

Deaf and mute and brutalized beyond imagination, Lily spoke. Projecting a single word as clearly as a hearing person.

"Yes."

Choosing to believe her because what choice did she have, Grace left the way she'd come.

53

EAST BAY MESSENGER

Your Alternative Berkeley-Oakland Weekly
March 14, 2015
Double Murder Linked to Meth
by Fatima Card, Messenger Staff Writer

The fatal shootings, ten days ago, of two men in the posh Claremont district have been linked to a business dispute among methamphetamine traffickers, according to Berkeley PD sources. While withholding the bulk of the details, the cops are letting on that an anonymous tip led them to discover that both victims were "active participants" in the speed biz and that the murders bore the hallmarks of professional executions, possibly by Mexican gangs.

The homicides, to which there were no witnesses, went down in the guest house of a mansion on Avalina Street, a turf where violence is rare, taking the lives of the house's registered owner, Dion Larue, 38, a building contractor whose outfit DRL-Earthmove, Inc., is rumored to have profited from hand-in-glove relationships with several politicos, including at least three Berkeley city council members. The second victim, Walter Sporn, also 38, worked for Larue as an on-site building supervisor and had been observed entering and exiting one of Larue's current projects, an eco-rehab on Center Street, where a "significant" cache of meth was found.

None of our glorious elected officials have chosen to comment.

What a shock.

54

G race hangs from a wire.

Half a mile below her, the jungle floor is green and dense and welcoming and if she strains a bit to one side she can spot slivers of ocean above the trees.

It is ninety-two degrees and humid; she could be forgiven a bit of sweat.

But she's dry as dust.

This isn't the tourist-friendly zip-lining she tried a couple of years ago in Puerto Vallarta and found wanting, with its half a dozen stations hovering over maybe two hundred feet of drop, tourists holding an ergonomic omega-shaped bar as smiling guides shout encouragement in English while maintaining full control over the mechanism as arrival at each new tree is heralded by praise and ice-cold lemonade.

This is a hardcore Costa Rican zip-lining, where the local surfers claim the sport originated. A meant-to-be-bowel-churning "canopy experience" buried in the lushness of that beautiful little country's Pacific coast.

The setup is anything but casual and touristy: twenty wooden platforms nailed to some of the rain forest's tallest trees, some of the planks warping and showing their age, some even cracked and revealing an eyeful of infinity.

Getting to many of the stations requires serious hikes on dirt ribbons barely wide enough for a fashion model or bounces on rope bridges that appear designed to fail.

That many segments means over two consecutive hours on the wire, if no one runs into significant difficulties.

The nerve center of the operation is a shack set deep enough in the forest that GPS cannot locate it. Tiny, gorgeous poisonous tree frogs scamper fearlessly, their jewel-like bodies hued coral red and lime green and royal blue, all of the above pied with ink-black spots so perfectly round they look fake.

The staff consists of half a dozen drowsy surfers of various ethnicities, all of whom are resentful about having to work for money. Empty bottles of tequila, vodka, and mescal abound in the "office." The comprehensive medical history consists of a single question. "Are you okay?"

No one in Grace's group, even those who've approached the day with obvious anxiety, admits to not being okay. There are four people besides her: two young guys—a bit overly boisterous, which probably means they're jumpy— and a married couple in their fifties who've failed to reach consensus about what they are about to do.

She: (smiling) Isn't this going to be fun?

He: (scowling) Depends on your definition.

Training consists of showing everyone the thick leather gloves they'll need to wear as they position both arms awkwardly behind their heads cupping the wire but not touching it. The only way to slow down or brake is to grip the wire and without gloves, that would sever a hand as if it were lunch meat.

It's all a matter of pressure, explains the surfer-in-charge, an African with heavy eyelids and a beautiful British accent.

Too "delicate" and you'll mess up your wrists and keep going anyway.

Too "clamping" and you'll come to a halt prematurely and get stuck dangling half a mile up with no one able to reach you. Should that occur, the only remedy is self-help: reversing the position of your hands, which will spin you in the opposite direction and leave you with your back to your destination.

Then: laboriously, hand over hand, moving blindly, you will haul yourself to safety and hope for the best. Should you grow fatigued?

The African winks and shrugs.

. . .

Grace hangs back and waits until the other four have begun, then approaches another surfer, a Latino with stoned glazed eyes.

"I want to do it alone."

"Senorita—"

"How much?"

"We don't do that?"

Grace repeats the questions. The surfer's brows knit. He consults two other surfers, cites an outrageous price.

Grace laughs and names her price.

The surfers react with feigned outrage.

Ninety seconds later, an agreement is reached.

She waits until the message comes down the line: The group has completed ten stations, slowed a bit by several instances of "self-help."

The African says, "Okay," and he and Grace set out.

Everything goes smoothly until on her final ride, heading toward the twentieth station where tequila and champagne await, she grips the wire hard midway through her hurtle.

She dangles.

Doesn't move.

Silence wafts through the jungle. Then: birdcalls. Then a distant prop plane.

Finally, the African behind her yells, "What?"

Grace doesn't answer.

His voice rises. So does that of the blond surfer, probably a Scandinavian, waiting for her at the other end.

She dangles.

Both men are shouting.

Grace hears the word "crazy."

She laughs.

Now the Swede or whatever he is stands near the lip of the twentieth platform and points at her beseechingly.

"Change the hands."

Grace kicks her legs ever so slightly. The wire hums. She moves back and forth, kicking some more, like a kid on a swing. Playing the wire, setting off a musical note.

The surfers scream.

The music blocks out everything.

She thinks of red rooms, many red rooms, a scarlet labyrinth.

A small black convertible speeding up a road that turns red.

Looking up, she examines the clasps that hold her to the harness that connects to the wire.

How easy it would be . . .

The African screams.

The Swede screams.

Only when remnants of reality have been blotted out does Grace act.

Closing her eyes, she shifts hands.

Rotates.

What if she did unbuckle a clip?

What would falling that far and that fast feel like?

Would anyone care?

No matter, she would.

Smiling, every muscle functioning precisely the way it was intended, she pulls herself to safety.

ABOUT THE AUTHOR

JONATHAN KELLERMAN is the #1 **New York Times** bestselling author of more than three dozen bestselling crime novels, including the Alex Delaware series, **The Butcher's Theater, Billy Straight, The Conspiracy Club, Twisted,** and **True Detectives.** With his wife, bestselling novelist Faye Kellerman, he co-authored **Double Homicide** and **Capital Crimes.** With his son, bestselling novelist Jesse Kellerman, he co-authored the first book of a new series, **The Golem of Hollywood.** He is also the author of two children's books and numerous nonfiction works, including **Savage Spawn: Reflections on Violent Children** and **With Strings Attached: The Art and Beauty of Vintage Guitars.** He has won the Goldwyn, Edgar, and Anthony awards and has been nominated for a Shamus Award. Jonathan and Faye Kellerman live in California, New Mexico, and New York.

jonathankellerman.com
Facebook.com/JonathanKellerman